Ash and Echoes

August Li

DSP PUBLICATIONS

Published by
DSP PUBLICATIONS

5032 Capital Circle SW, Suite 2, PMB# 279, Tallahassee, FL 32305-7886 USA
http://www.dsppublications.com/

Ash and Echoes
© 2014 August Li.

Cover Art
© 2012 Anne Cain.
annecain.art@gmail.com
Cover Design
© 2012 Mara McKennen.
Cover content is for illustrative purposes only and any person depicted on the cover is a model.

ISBN: 978-1-63216-608-1
Digital ISBN: 978-1-63216-609-8
Library of Congress Control Number: 2014947596
Second Edition December 2014
First edition published by Dreamspinner Press, June 2012

Printed in the United States of America
∞
This paper meets the requirements of
ANSI/NISO Z39.48-1992 (Permanence of Paper).

Ash and Echoes is lovingly dedicated to my two dear friends, Julian Maxwell (Max) and Autumn Leigh Schemery. Your feedback, support, and encouragement have been—and I hope will continue to be—invaluable to me. Thanks for both inspiration and advice. I'm lucky to know you and grateful to have you in my life.

Also for Rosepetal, wherever you are….

—Gus, June 2012

Glossary

Abode of Shades—The realm of the Cast-Down, the unworthy dead, and all those rejected by the goddesses.

Bairn—The second highest title of nobility in Selindria, after "valen."

Cast-Down—A term used to refer to those gods and goddesses disowned by The Thirteen because of their wickedness. Most pious Selindrians will not speak of them. In some rare cases, a person can be referred to as Cast-Down.

Emiri—An ethnic group, or possibly a completely different race of people, who arrived in Selindria about 150 years ago. Their name is derived from "*Emir*," the word for the sea in their language. Emiri have no formal homeland and are expert mariners. Their culture and values are quite different from that of Selindrians, and this leads to many misunderstandings.

Eru—The Emiri word for "wind."

Espero—A large and wealthy island nation to the southeast of Selindria, best known for the high population of mages and the arcane university there.

Estrella Lake—A huge freshwater lake in the northernmost corner of Selindria. Aside from providing most of the nation's water, it has a religious significance, is surrounded by shrines and temples, and is often visited by those on spiritual pilgrimages.

Everdale—A fertile valenny near the center of Selindria, which provides most of the kingdom's food. Sister province to Merryvale.

Eyrle—The third highest title of nobility in Selindria, after "bairn."

Fane—A legendary mage-emperor who ruled over a period of unimaginable peace and prosperity eons ago. Eventually he demanded his people worship him instead of the goddesses, and the ensuing war destroyed the known world. No one knows if Fane ever actually existed, but his story is told as a cautionary tale and given as the reason mages are forbidden to rule.

Gaeltheon—A powerful nation to the east of Selindria, across the Kanda River, almost equal in size and wealth.

Kanda River—An enormous river separating Gaeltheon and Selindria. The Kanda is fed by Estrella Lake and considered holy by association.

Lapir Mountains—A huge, impassable mountain range marking the eastern border of Gaeltheon. No one has crossed them in centuries, and what lies on the other side is a subject of speculation.

Lockhaven—An ancient valenny, ruled by the L'Estrella family for as long as anyone can remember. Because it houses the sacred Estrella Lake, Lockhaven is highly respected throughout Selindria.

Meritage—The oldest and largest city in Selindria. Meritage is a port along the Kanda River, and while it is held by the Selindrian monarch, the territory around it is unstable and ruled by barbarians and warlords.

Merryvale—A fertile plain, sister province to Everdale.

Mir—An Emiri ship's captain.

Muri-ku—A very potent Emiri beverage made from fermented sea plants.

Narxium—A tree producing a fatally poisonous sap. It grows only in the Forest of Elwyd.

Order of the Crimson Scythe—A legendary and unstoppable cult of assassins. Thalil is their patron. While many people doubt the existence of the Crimson Scythe, their symbol, the red crescent, is still the most feared icon in the land. The Crimson Scythe are considered almost supernatural. When they have marked someone for death, that person has no chance of escape.

Selindria—The most powerful kingdom in the known world.

Starmont—The highest peak in Selindria, marking the northern edge of Estrella Lake. In the past, many Selindrians believed the goddesses resided atop Starmont, but that belief has been abandoned by all but the most superstitious.

Syrai—The Emiri word for "friend," used to express a wide variety of relationships from casual acquaintance to intimate partner.

Tam—The lowest title of nobility in Selindria as well as a common expression of respect, similar to "sir."

Thalil—A very powerful Cast-Down god associated with seduction, subterfuge, murder, and deceit. He is the patron god of assassins, particularly the Order of the Crimson Scythe. Thalil, usually portrayed as a beautiful youth, is also associated with male beauty and homoerotic love. The Thirteen Goddesses forbid his name from being spoken, and his worship is punishable by death. Thalil is known by many epithets, some of which are: He Who Stands Just Out of Sight, The One You See at the Last, The Whisper Heard Too Late, The Dark One, and The Invisible Blade.

The Thirteen, or The Thirteen Goddesses—The main and most important deities of Selindria and Gaeltheon. They have many sons and daughters, both benevolent and Cast-Down. They are sometimes referred to as the sisters. Each goddess presides over a month, or moon, of the year.

Valen—The highest title of nobility in Selindria, second only to the royal family. Valens rule large holds of land known as valennies.

THE GODDESSES AND MONTHS

Both Selindria and Gaeltheon observe a thirteen-month lunar calendar. Each month, or moon, is presided over by one of The Thirteen Goddesses.

Fayelle, ruler of the first month—A virgin goddess of purity. While compassionate, she is a very demanding goddess who expects perfection from her devotees.

Sarmine, ruler of the second month—The goddess of romantic love and marriage. Most weddings take place during Sarmine's Moon.

Mother Goddess, ruler of the third month—The only goddess without a name, she is the matron of all living things. Her month is a time of devotion and celebration. The Mother Goddess is said to love all her creations, even the Cast-Down.

Myint, ruler of the fourth month—The goddess of warfare, battle, weaponsmiths, armorers, and martial arts. She is the patron goddess of all knights.

Diarana, ruler of the fifth month—The goddess of travel and transition. She is the patron of children coming of age. Certain worshippers of Diarana maintain that the goddess loves and protects men and women who favor the clothing of the opposite gender. This belief is not widely accepted.

Vestrafori, ruler of the sixth month—The goddess of truth and justice, protector of the blind and mute. Vestrafori's priestesses conduct all legal proceedings in Selindria and Gaeltheon, and their verdicts are absolute.

Laud, ruler of the seventh month—A mysterious goddess associated with fate, the passage of time, and abstract concepts. Her devotees live hermitic lives of deprivation and contemplation.

Jelsyn, ruler of the eighth month—The goddess of artisans and merchants. She adores handmade items, particularly woven cloth. Jelsyn is also said to protect the poor.

Berris, ruler of the ninth month—The goddess of farming, plenty, and the harvest. Her festival is one of the most joyous occasions of the year.

Ix, ruler of the tenth month—The goddess of the wilds and protector of forests and animals. Ix is well known to favor those who follow instinct over reason. Ix is also associated with the moon.

Strella, ruler of the eleventh month—The goddess of the sun, stars, and weather, Strella is also a liaison between humans and the goddesses. She carries prayers to the goddesses and guides the worthy dead to their rest.

Illira, ruler of the twelfth month—The goddess of music, poetry, history, and communication. She is the patron of all storytellers and scholars.

Pherara, ruler of the thirteenth month—The goddess of magic and arcane scholarship, and patron goddess of Espero. Most people feel Pherara values only her mages and turns her back on those without the gift. She is not widely worshipped outside Espero.

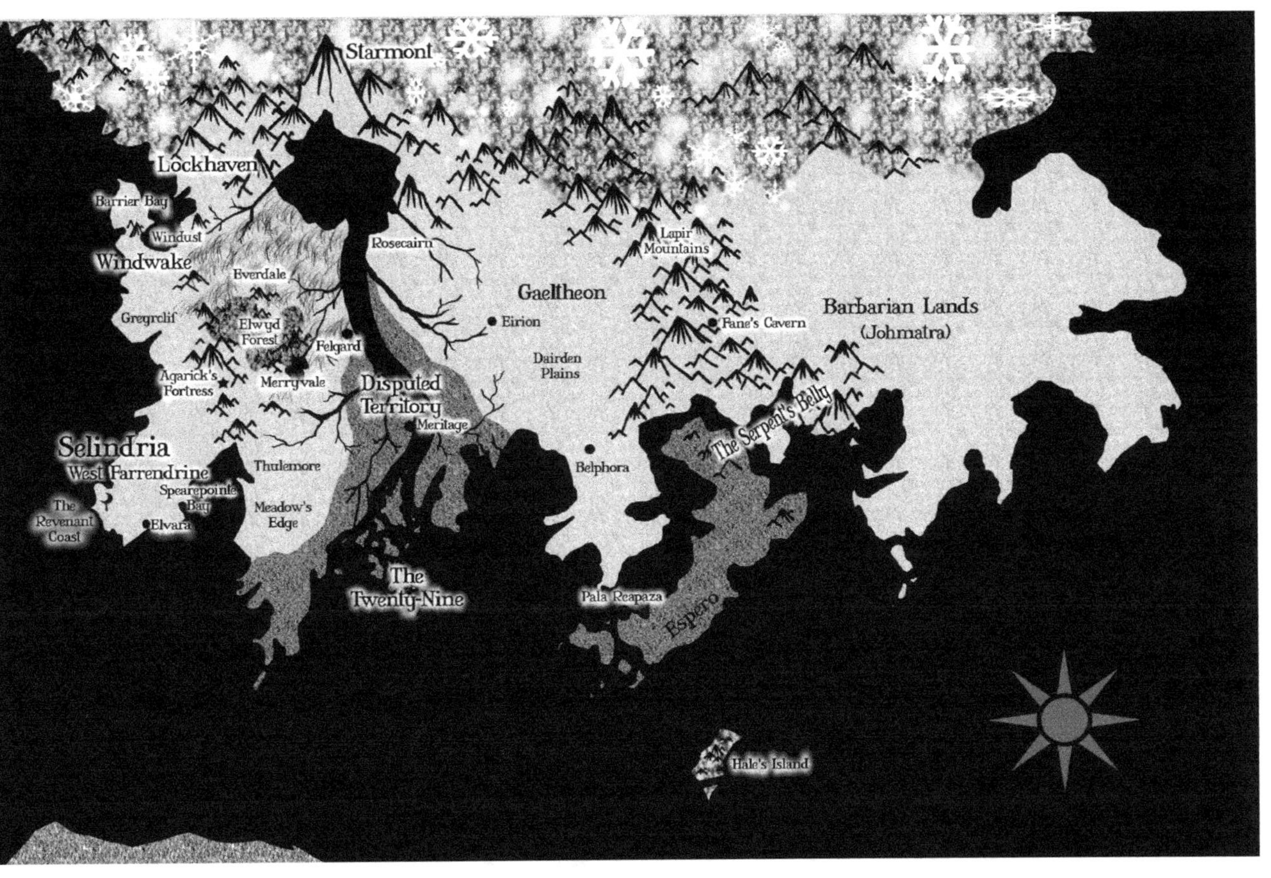

Starmont
Lockhaven
Former Bay
Windust
Windwake
Gregcliff
Elwyd Forest
Agarick's Fortress
Merryvale
Frögard
Rosecairn
Eirion
Gaeltheon
Lapir Mountains
Pane's Cavern
Barbarian Lands
(Johmatra)
Dairden Plains
Disputed Territory
Meritage
Selindria
West Farrendrine
The Revenant Coast
Spearpoint Bay
Elvara
Thulamore
Meadow's Edge
The Twenty-Nine
Belphora
The Serpent's Belly
Pala Reapaza
Esparto
Hale's Island

Chapter
One

The seventh day of Strella's Moon

YARROW ADORED his anonymity. Anonymity softened the world, the invisibility giving him a feeling of safety and freedom. It might be illusion, but illusion had its place sometimes. Unfortunately, the others of the world loved the trivial trappings of status, the power that stemmed from being a little more important than those beneath them, the idea that they mattered somehow beyond their frivolous stations. They had no idea of their place in the grand scheme of things, beyond their paltry power struggles and hollow victories. Yarrow hated being bothered with trifling problems and things beneath him, which, in his opinion, included almost everything. He hated pettiness, though the rest of the world seemed to embrace it. All the more reason to retreat from society and its pretense, it seemed to Yarrow. He despised the powers trying to force him back into the irrelevant and transient maneuverings of the privileged. He resented returning to this castle at all.

Do we have to be here? The voice circled Yarrow's thoughts in the dark, and for a moment he sank underwater, into blackness. A silken voice slid against his bare skin, sharp tines brushing over his goose-bumped flesh, no less frightening because the voice and its source lived within him. *I'm hungry, beloved—and bored.*

Give it time.

Yarrow wore garments neither too shabby nor too fine: a shirt and trousers, once black, now faded to slate, dull ebony leather pauldrons, boots and bracers, a few belts, and a dark, hooded cloak. His clothing allowed him to pass through the castle gate without being mistaken for a servant and ordered off on a trivial errand, and without being marked as a courtier and fawned over, another barrier he'd constructed between him and the mundane foolishness others so valued. Among the dozens of scurrying workers, merchants, horse-drawn carts, foot soldiers, and knights on horseback, Yarrow entered the courtyard without attention. He knew that would change if he threw back his cowl and revealed his anything-but-anonymous visage beneath. Since he didn't want to be bothered, he kept his eyes on the wet, gray stone, fouled with mud, straw, and horse dung as he made his way around the great castle toward the stables and carriage houses at the back.

Smoke from the smithies, the kitchens, and the many small fires, around which infantrymen huddled for warmth, rose into and blended with the smudged, charcoal sky. The stink of the fumes, combined with the odor of animals and unwashed men, burned the lining of Yarrow's nose. He'd become unused to human civilization and the crowding and stench towed in its wake. As he walked between the outer wall and the citadel, he felt a familiar shiver up his spine. It nudged at the base of his skull, gently at first, then insistently. Yarrow let his mental barriers lower, and tendrils of the other awareness filled his head.

What is it now? he asked the presence that shared his body. He already felt irritated by the cold, the wet, the stink, and the trifling chore for which he'd been summoned. It had been many years since he'd felt welcome or comfortable at this fortress, and its towers and turrets, looming over him and throwing thick shadows across the yard, conjured confusing recollections and set him on edge. He found himself in no mood for further annoyances.

What a hassle, Yarrow. It's dull and it smells.

Yes, I know, and I don't like it any more than you do, but I've received a royal summons, and even I can't ignore that.

Let me wear the body, the other voice suggested hungrily. *I'll show this king of yours we aren't to be commanded.*

You'll stem your thirst for blood immediately, Yarrow ordered. The other's rapacious lust had already started to spread to the young man and influence his decisions and desires. Yarrow caught himself mopping his lips with his tongue, a little excited to show the king the power heating his veins. He squelched it with reluctance. *You'll keep quiet whilst I speak to the king. I don't want to be distracted. With any luck, I can get us out of this fool's errand, though I can't make any promises.*

Might I wear the flesh later?

It's not the *flesh, it's* my *flesh, and you'd do well to remember that,* Yarrow chastised, his temper flaring. *Now, be quiet.*

A chill, light rain began to fall as Yarrow turned the corner and entered the expansive space in front of the stables. Six fancy passenger carriages and an equal number of carts stood in a line facing the back gate. Several dozen foot soldiers and half a dozen knights waited beside them. Two guards wearing cobalt and white tabards with the great bear on its hind legs, the royal livery, over their mail suits crossed their halberds in front of Yarrow when he attempted to approach the procession. The other presence grew offended and prepared to retaliate, but Yarrow soothed it.

To the guards he said, "I am Yarroway L'Estrella, of the Valenny of Lockhaven. I'm expected."

"Forgive us, tam," said one of the men, rain running in rivulets from his chain mail hood and down his face. "We didn't know it was you."

They stepped apart to allow Yarrow passage. Yarrow curtly nodded his gratitude, even as his lips curled at the title of tam. It was little more than a common expression of respect. Yarrow felt much worthier than his older brother of being valen, though he had no real desire to rule Lockhaven. Still, he felt like the king ought to lay the title at his feet, just to give him the pleasure of turning it down.

Let me wear the body and then—

No, Yarrow warned. *Hush. The king is coming.*

A quartet of atonal horns sounded as the monarch approached, flanked at each shoulder by three guards in shining silver plate. King Agarick, a middle-aged man with brown hair and a beard streaked with silver at the corners of his mouth, wore a harrow-wolf's fur cloak atop his own armor. A young page tried desperately to shield his sovereign from the rain with an oilcloth umbrella, though Agarick stood at least a foot and a half taller than the shivering boy. Fat, gray droplets ricocheted off his broad shoulders and the slimy stone, outlining the men, horses, and carriages in chill mist.

"His Majesty Agarick, High King of all Selindria," announced one of the trumpeters.

Everyone present, aside from Yarrow, dropped to one knee and bowed his head. Yarrow stood looking at their stooped shoulders, the frigid rain running uncomfortably beneath his collar and down his spine. He pushed his sopping fringe out of his eyes and met the dark gaze of the monarch. "Uncle," he said with an almost imperceptible dip of his head.

A collective gasp of shock rose from the kneeling soldiers, courtiers, administrators, and servants. Yarrow regarded his fingernails. He knew Agarick wouldn't honor his affront by acknowledging it, and his guess proved right.

"Nephew," the king said, feigning a belly laugh and holding his arms open. "How good to see you again after all these years."

The men on their knees in the wet offal began to rise and whisper anxiously to one another. Yarrow added to their astonishment when he hesitated to embrace his uncle. Agarick strode confidently toward him, unwilling to be made a fool of a second time. He squeezed Yarrow's small body in his powerful arms, brusquely and without affection, making Yarrow flinch and almost gag. Panic rose in him for the few seconds he stood trapped in the thick, unyielding arms. The king smelled of sweat despite the chill, horses, dogs, and ale. "Good of you to come, Yarroway."

The young man, half the size of the king, wriggled away and stepped back. "I hardly had a choice, Uncle." Yarrow saw Agarick's jaw twitch in irritation and fought not to smile.

After another false laugh the king said, "You make it sound as though I dragged you here in chains."

"Practically. I have my own pursuits to attend to, tam. It is the greatest inconvenience to be called here for this silly task."

"How dare you," Agarick snarled, lunging at Yarrow, who stepped to the side and swept off his hood.

The king hesitated at the sight of Yarrow's jagged, messy layers of snow white hair and ice blue eyes. Some Emiri paint curled from Yarrow's hairline to the center of his right brow and spiraled out beneath his eye in three intricate, swirling lines that loosely resembled long lashes. More elaborate dark blue lines rose from his collar and twined up the side of his neck before disappearing into the hair behind his ear. Those in attendance inhaled in unison. Yarrow lifted his chin, reveling in his intimidating appearance. Not so long ago, he'd hated the way he looked. Now, when he needed to, he used his aspect as another way to keep others at a distance.

The king stammered. "I, nephew, I have not seen you since your foreign pilgrimages and the exotic fever that altered you so."

Fever, aye? That's a good one, Yarrow.

Hush.

"Surely you must appreciate the import of this affair," the king continued. "My son, your beloved cousin Garith, is to wed into the kingdom of Gaeltheon. Our united realms will be a power unlike this world has seen, and may finally bring peace to our troubled land."

A lofty endeavor. How's he planning to accomplish it, beloved?

For the benefit of his passenger, Yarrow sketched out a crude map in his mind. Selindria and Gaeltheon stood at the east and west ends of their small continent, both roughly triangular in shape. In the north, their apexes leaned together like toppling-over tombstones, while both commanded vast expanses of coastline to the south. Between them, over a dozen small, warring nations occupied a spear-shaped tract of land around the Kanda River. Ruled by warlords, their borders shifted constantly, though none of them stood a chance against either of the larger, wealthy kingdoms surrounding them.

Only the Emiri people, who'd come across the southern seas about a century and a half ago, posed any real threat. They were lithe, androgynous folk with skin the color of wet sand and eyes in hues of crimson, orange, and gold. They possessed nautical skills so superior no nation could begin to compete. Emiri, while not a formal nation, occupied most of the south coast, on both sides of the river. Yarrow knew the word Emiri translated only to "seafarer." Their raiders terrorized Selindria's and Gaeltheon's beaches and ports. They delighted in painting their bodies with permanent swirls and dips to accentuate their musculature. Yarrow found them nearly amphibious: as much at home within the ocean waters as without. They were notoriously dissolute, valuing little more than wealth and pleasure. Yarrow especially enjoyed the company of Emiri boys, and had yet to encounter one who preferred one gender over the other.

He plans to push from both sides, Yarrow's companion noted. *Drive out the smaller nations between Selindria and Gaeltheon. He'll decimate your precious Emiri.*

"That is neither here nor there," Yarrow replied, artfully answering both questions. "The issue is whether or not my talents are necessary to accompany a wedding party. I say, tam, that they are squandered thus."

"Yarroway L'Estrella, you are the greatest magic-wielder of our age!" Agarick protested.

"Of course," Yarrow allowed, mildly pleased. "All the more reason why I shouldn't need to waste my time accompanying the prince to Gaeltheon. You seem to have a fine company established already. I'm certain my cousin will be well protected. Surely, with your vast resources, you can find another mage if you need one."

"You know better than any how few mages exist these days. You are third cousin to this family," Agarick fumed. "You have a duty to the crown and you'll fulfill it. You should be honored to do so."

"I'd really rather not. I hate weddings, Uncle." From the corner of his vision, Yarrow noticed blue velvet curtains cleave open in the window of the carriage second to the end. A dark eye and a sliver of a face appeared for a moment, then disappeared again behind the drapery. Something about the glimpse of that eye intrigued the young mage.

"Tam Yarroway, must I remind you of your past indiscretions?" Agarick bellowed. "I hesitate to use them to compel you, but—"

"Must I remind Your Majesty of indiscretions committed against *my* person?" Yarrow countered, bored, aggravated, and offended. "Many within the walls of this very castle? Shall I name them before everyone here? I will not be forced into this foolish task. It is unworthy of me."

Agarick paled. "No, nephew. I would not discuss them here."

"Good. I'll be going."

The king dared not say another word, and Yarrow had prepared to turn and leave the damp, stinking courtyard when a woman in an emerald gown lined with fox fur rushed around the corner. Breathless, she seized the mage's hands within her soft, suede gloves.

"Dearest Yarrow," she panted. "I beg you to protect my son. I have faith in no one more than you. I have worked years to arrange this marriage. It's more important than you know. There are many who would benefit were this union not to reach fruition. Please. Guide him safely into the arms of his Gaelthonian bride. Do this if you love me."

Who's this strumpet, now? asked the presence within Yarrow's mind. *Why's she making your heart into porridge?*

My Aunt Denna Corina. She's from the island nation of Espero, to the south of Gaeltheon's western peninsula. It's a country of mages. She's always favored me. I think she hoped one of her children might have the gift. She used to show me the loveliest little parlor tricks when I was a boy. She was my first teacher and confidant. I told her... everything, and she accepted it. I can't repay what she did for me as a child.

So what?

"Auntie, I just don't feel I'm needed."

"It would put my mind at ease, knowing you stood by Garith, watched over him. Please, Yarrow, he's my only son."

"You place too much faith in me," Yarrow said, nuzzling the side of his aunt's neck as she continued to clutch his hands. "I will see Garith safely to his nuptials in Gaeltheon."

"Bless you, nephew." She kissed him at the corner of his mouth. "I knew you would not forsake us."

"I do it for you," Yarrow whispered into her hair, "not him." He indicated the king with a subtle cant of his head.

What? Yarrow!

Hush, I said.

"Very well," Agarick said. "Let us see to the details. Back inside, dear wife, lest you catch cold in this rain. Yarroway, come with me." The king motioned the young mage toward the front of the procession. They stopped in front of a long, wooden table strewn with maps, their ink running, turning countries and continents to blobs and making rivers drip from the edges of the parchment. Yarrow helped himself to water from a clay pitcher. His eyes wandered to the large man seated at the foot of the table.

Unlike Agarick's honor guards in their polished armor, this man's heavy plate was dull, dented, and dinged from years of service. While broad-shouldered, the soldier's body still possessed a lanky elegance. Yarrow felt sure he'd be as quick and agile on the battlefield as he would be powerful. Yarrow could see the fine cut of the man's square jaw beneath his close-cropped, dark brown whiskers. Hair the same rich hue was pulled back in a leather loop, the ends just grazing the top of the man's battered armor. A few loose strands dripped rain down his forehead, thick brows, and sharp, high cheekbones. Water pooled in the divot above his mouth. His lips seemed a little too full and shapely to sit on such a stoic face. His eyes were a blend of green and brown, recalling to Yarrow the waters of the Kanda during the spring floods, while he had the deeply tanned complexion of a southerner. He was quite handsome, if a little too stern in countenance for Yarrow's taste.

At the king's approach, the man stood, held an armored hand over his heart, and bowed at the waist. "Your Majesty," he said in a velvety baritone that raised gooseflesh over the mage's arms.

"Tam Duncan Purefroy of the Valenny of Thulemore," Agarick said by way of introduction. "This is my nephew, Yarroway L'Estrella of Lockhaven. He'll be assisting you in your defense of the prince's procession. You may think of him as your second in command. Now, let us sit. We have much to plan and discuss."

This is rotten, Yarrow. Is there a reason we can't consult these maps inside the castle?

I thought you relished all sensation.

The presence made the mental equivalent of a sigh and said, *You know I can't experience it fully unless I take control. Besides, I'm bored of the way your flesh is trembling, and I'm tired of this wet cloth clinging to our skin.*

My *skin.*

As you say, Yarrow. Still, I'd like to feel a fire at my back and some spiced wine warming my throat.

Waiting will only make those things sweeter, Yarrow teased as he sat down on the long bench.

I have been waiting, beloved Yarrow, and I am waiting still.

DUNCAN TRIED to suppress the curl of his lip as the young mage took his place at the table. The queen, the princess, and their ladies-in-waiting spoke often of this Yarroway, and the stories reached Duncan's ears secondhand via servants and guards. The women loved the lad, as he frequently conjured butterflies and bluebirds for their entertainment. He made music play and flowers grow, much to their delight. Duncan supposed the boy had probably been quite a treat for the ladies' eyes before his legendary affliction. He had a pretty, oval face and delicate features, though not at all feminine and still strong. Thick lashes, white as gosling's down now, framed eyes unlike anything Duncan had ever witnessed. While the irises tried for blue, they managed only the faintest hint of pigment, like a frozen lake in moonlight. His large eyes held the knight's attention longer than Duncan liked. Yarrow's lithe body seemed more suited to the dance floor than the battlefield, and why any son of nobility would brazenly mark his face and neck with the paint of pirates, slatterns, and criminal filth of the lowest caliber eluded Duncan completely. Likely it had been some sort of rebellion against his wealthy parents and pampered life. Surprisingly, the sorcerer's skin was nearly as sun-darkened as Duncan's own.

Duncan knew only that his task had just become more difficult. Not only would he need to watch over the fragile little princeling, now he'd be playing nursemaid to this spoiled whelp as well. Still, he had a duty to carry out his king's commands, and nothing would stand in his way. He'd deliver both Garith and this Yarrow-flower safely to Gaeltheon, as befit a servant of the crown. If need be, he'd even feign cooperation with the king's nephew. Nobody would die on his watch, not ever again.

Clearing his throat, Duncan slid the largest of the maps between Agarick and himself. He noticed the mage staring distractedly off into the sky. It was just as well; Duncan doubted Tam Yarroway could contribute much to their conversation.

"Here is the route I propose." Duncan traced his finger along a blurred line that led down the mountains from Agarick's fortress on the highest peak, east across the plains of Everdale, and directly to the banks of the Kanda River. "We can cross into Gaeltheon by way of the Lucasian Bridge, at the port of Meritage."

"That won't do," the mage said dreamily without turning his gaze from the rain clouds.

Balling his fist, Duncan said, "Why is that, tam?"

"Because it would lead us through some very hostile territory. The last time I passed that way, the fighting between the White Feathers of Keth and the Riders of the Dawn was fierce. The territory is unclaimed and completely unstable. Not to mention, the Bridge of Light itself is often besieged by bandits. Meritage is a den of cutthroats, ruled by the criminals who hold the city officials in their pockets. I assure you they won't pass up such a lucrative opportunity. We'd be leading the prince into unnecessary peril."

"What do you propose, Tam Mage?" Duncan asked through gritted teeth, reluctant to admit the wisdom in Yarroway's words.

"Here." The wizard pulled the map in front of him. With his finger, he marked a sparkling trail that continued to flicker brightly despite the damp and gloom. "We head down the mountain and turn toward the north at Everdale. We'll travel inland until we reach Estrella Lake, in my family's valenny. Then we can cross the Starlight Bridge, which is kept secure by my brother's knights. On the other side of the river, we'll only need to pass through a few miles of barbarian land before crossing into Gaeltheon. Afterwards, when we're safe, we can head south again."

"A pretty trick for a lady's salon," Duncan scoffed, watching the prismatic twinkles on the smudged parchment. "But your route adds at least a few weeks to our journey." He couldn't decide if this boy was homesick for his lake, terrified of confrontation, or wise beyond his years. Either way, Duncan couldn't deny the soundness of his proposal, had they the entire world at their feet and time to waste.

"At least the prince will meet his bride with his heart beating," the mage said, his melodic voice dripping condescension like the sky dripped rain.

"Winter is nearly upon us," Duncan argued, more out of pride than practicality. "The Valenny of Lockhaven is treacherous when frozen."

The boy laughed, a bitter edge obvious in his mirth. "Lockhaven is my home. I can lead us safely through. As for the added travel time, I say we send a messenger to Gaeltheon. They're as eager as we are for this union, are they not? I'm sure they'll wait the extra month it will take to ensure it occurs. Let a single courier brave your route, Tam Duncan, whilst we lead our prince safely along mine."

Duncan could formulate no debate. This Yarrow-flower was right. The lad might not be tough, but apparently he was clever. Even so, Duncan would be happy to follow his route without the added burden of protecting him. "Let the king decide," Duncan finally said.

Agarick scratched his whiskers and sat silently for several moments. The rain fell harder, blurring the maps spread before the three men to nonsense. Yarroway pulled his black hood over his contrasting, ash white hair and hugged himself, shivering. Duncan felt a surprising pang of compassion for the young man's discomfort. Unlike Duncan, he hadn't been trained to endure the elements. Such a scrawny thing as the mage would surely feel the cold acutely, and the boy had no servant to throw a cape over his slender shoulders. Duncan couldn't help but wish a maid might fetch the lad a blanket.

Agarick spoke. "I fear my beloved queen would never forgive me were I to place our only son in harm's way. We shall follow the path suggested by my nephew."

"As you will, Your Majesty." Duncan acquiesced with a bow of his head.

The mage, rather than looking triumphant, returned his attention once again to the horizon. "Your Majesty might also send messengers to the many noble households along our route, that they might prepare an appropriate reception for the visiting prince. Lodgings for my cousin and his men. Provisions. A fire to warm his back and spiced wine for his throat." For some reason unknown to Duncan, this suggestion entertained the mage enough to make him chuckle.

"Very good," the king said, standing. "We shall be underway within the hour. I'll send word for my general, Taran Edercrest, to meet you at The Starlight Bridge. He can bolster your ranks before you cross through the barbarian lands on the other side. Tam Duncan, please relay instructions to your men. Be sure their orders are detailed and that each man knows his task. Yarroway, make your way to the stables and select a mount. Our armory is also at your disposal. I see you carry no weapons. Please, nephew, take what you need."

"I have all that I need," the wizard said, holding up his hand and producing a faint, blue glow.

"Great," Duncan muttered under his breath as he turned to inspect the infantry. "His hand sparkles, and he needs no other weapons. This is going to be a long trip."

Chapter Two

AS THE rain continued, a thin layer of ice formed over the rocky trails that wound down the mountain from Agarick's citadel to the plains below. The procession moved slowly as horses picked their way over the slippery stone and carts fishtailed down the steep slopes. In many places their wheels passed precariously close to the edges of the path and the dagger-like rocks far beneath. Duncan, at the front of the group, glanced over his shoulder at the prince's carriage. Spindly icicles decorated the roof like fringe, and the axles creaked as it bobbed from side to side. He'd stationed six mounted men to surround it at all times, men he'd been told were the most loyal and capable. He didn't recognize a single one of these young recruits. The prince faced no danger for quite a while, as they still stood practically on his father's doorstep and would for the next few days, but Duncan saw no harm in his soldiers forming good habits right away.

His gaze turned from time to time to the mage, and Duncan wondered why. The young man rode silently behind the royal carriage, on a small and rather skittish dappled gray mare, a horse more suited to a courier than a knight, though he supposed the lad was no knight. Yarrow had surprised Duncan by not complaining, though a cap of ice had formed on the top of his head and across his shoulders. Duncan had guarded many aristocrats and important people, and he'd expected the little wizard to decry the traveling conditions all the way. So far he'd not said a word, only rode with his hood up and his head down. Duncan saw only his deeply tanned nose, chin, lips, and a whisper of white hair. Why did he feel he needed to look back and check up on the mage, if he wasn't whining or causing trouble? Duncan supposed he didn't trust the boy, didn't really trust anyone who controlled otherworldly forces. He didn't want Yarrow on the expedition, didn't want anything distracting him from protecting the prince. He glanced back at the boy again, and this time Yarrow lifted his face and met Duncan's gaze with his unnerving pale eyes.

His face heating in the cold rain, Duncan looked quickly away, deciding the mage would be nothing but an annoyance. Perhaps he should put him in the cart with his cousin and consolidate the areas he'd need to guard.

They reached the foothills by sunset. The rain had left the ground pitted and marred by frozen ruts. Frost sheathed the high grass as they left the mountains for the plains of Everdale, rattling around the legs of the horses as they cut swathes in the ochre-colored sea. This fertile steppe fed much of Selindria. The failing light turned the grain stalks ruby and gold. As Duncan looked around for a suitable place to camp for the night, Yarroway rode up alongside him.

"Is there something I can do for you, tam?" Duncan asked, not looking at the lad but continuing to scan the flat expanse of grassland, broken only by a shelf of blue rock or a copse of stunted trees here and there.

"You can start by calling me by my name," the boy said lightly.

"As you will, Yarroway."

"Yarrow is even better."

"As you say," Duncan acquiesced. "If there is nothing further, Yarrow, I would prefer for you to stay near the prince's carriage. I've assigned four men to look after your safety, and running back and forth will only make their work more difficult."

"You… assigned men to watch over me?" Yarrow asked, clearly stunned and possibly offended. Duncan didn't care. His duty was to keep the boy alive, not cater to his pride. The two of them rode together a few more moments, neither speaking until the mage said, as if he'd only just realized, "You think I'm worthless."

Duncan looked over and forced himself not to shrink away from Yarrow's disturbing gaze. He found it more difficult than he'd anticipated; unknown but tangible power resided behind those strange eyes. "Tam Yarrow, you are the prince's cousin, and I'm sure your tricks keep the ladies well entertained. But in the face of actual danger, yes, I think you would do us all a favor to stay out of the way and leave the fighting to men trained for it."

Yarrow's nostrils flared and his eyes widened into icy blue orbs surrounded by white. He opened his mouth to speak, lips trembling with fury, but he seemed angry beyond articulation. Tugging his mare's reins, he turned quickly and trotted back to his place beside the prince. This pleased Duncan. Obeying him would keep Yarrow safe, and better safe and affronted than the alternative. Surely the young fellow had never been spoken to in such a way in all of his pampered life, but this was the real world and not a posh library somewhere. Still, he'd impressed Duncan a bit by not defaulting to his noble blood. Forgetting the mage, Duncan turned his attention back to the landscape, locating a small ridge, the leeside of which would afford some protection from the elements. He rode in its direction, and the rest of the procession followed, even the young sorcerer, his eyes burning into the back of Duncan's skull.

The men set up small, efficient tents for themselves and one the size of a country cottage for His Highness. Servants lit fires to prepare supper, while men hoisted casks of wine and ale from the backs of carts. Duncan handed his horse off to a young squire and went to inspect the camp. The men followed his instructions. The six who'd ridden beside the royal carriage now stood guard around the royal tent. Two heavily armed knights escorted Garith, his face obscured by a fur-lined hood, inside. Duncan trusted his men and moved along to check the watch schedule. The movements of the many soldiers and servants soon left muddy tracts in the snow.

Near the outskirts of their makeshift settlement, he spotted Yarrow thoughtfully brushing his mare. It seemed strange that the young aristocrat wouldn't have handed her off to a servant, and even stranger that he sought no attention or accolades for doing the work himself. Instead, he appeared as if he did such things every day and thought nothing of them. Near the lad's feet, Duncan saw a small, simple tent, barely a lean-to, held up at the front with a pair of sticks and scarcely wide enough for the single pillow and old, patched quilt within it. A bluish white fire, redolent of lilies and matching the mage's eyes, burned at the foot of his shelter. The knight wondered at the point of it, as it produced little warmth. Duncan had expected the boy's tent might rival the prince's. Frowning, he realized he'd have to post at least a pair of guards over the lad while he slept.

Yarrow looked over his shoulder as Duncan clanged past in his heavy plate. He scowled at the commander, his face radiating hatred and hurt. The knight looked quickly away, trying to deny he felt any regret over his harsh words. He hurried off to check on the evening meal, and was happy to find it ready. He queued up behind the other soldiers to receive his metal bowl of stew and loaf of coarse bread. After filling his tankard with cold water, he found a seat on an overturned pail. None of the knights or soldiers around him looked familiar, though judging by their banter, quite a few of them had served together before. Duncan half listened to their conversations as he soaked his bread in his broth to soften it. He still preferred to take his meals among his men than alone in his too fancy tent.

"Did you see his face?" said a man with a thick black moustache, an archer judging by his light armor and single leather glove. "How could he be allowed Emiri paint like that? It's a disgrace."

"So go tell him he's not allowed, Malthus. The young mage is camped just over there." The large, ruddy man finished his statement with a chuckle before slurping down his stew in a few gulps. The other men joined him in a laugh, but Malthus looked confused.

"Are you saying he's dangerous?" the archer asked. "He doesn't look it."

"You've not heard the stories," said an older soldier with a grizzled gray beard. "Young Yarroway left home at just fourteen and traveled alone for over five years. He's been over the Lapir Mountains in the east and seen parts of this world not on any map."

"So?" Malthus muttered.

Duncan understood, though. For a whelp of fourteen years to even survive a journey across Selindria on his own spoke of great skill and resourcefulness. No army had crossed the Lapir Mountains in generations, and what lay on the other side belonged to the realms of myth and legend. Except to the young mage, Duncan supposed.

"I heard he used his spells to bring down an entire castle," one man said, and the others grew quiet.

"He must have power, to speak to the king as he does," another agreed.

Duncan joined the conversation, asking, "What is the reason behind the young man's coloring? Have his eyes always been as they are now?" The knight suppressed a shudder as he envisioned them.

"Nay, tam," said the older, bearded soldier. "Tale I heard is that Tam Yarroway got lost in a vast desert in a distant land and nearly died. He crawled into a cave and lay burning with fever for many days. His survival is a miracle."

"I heard it was a snowstorm, and a cave in the mountains at the eastern edge of the world," said the flushed, portly warrior.

"I heard a jungle, full of strange monsters and poisonous beasts," another man argued.

Duncan finished chewing a gristly chunk of meat, swallowed it, and said, "What does that have to do with his hair and eyes?"

"Fever bleached the color right out of him, like a cloth left for a season under a summer sun. Burned it right away. I also heard that he…."

All of them went silent, their eyes fixated on a single point. Duncan looked over his shoulder and saw Yarrow waving away the bowl of stew the cook offered. He took a loaf of bread and filled a large, skin canteen with wine before glaring at them, his eyes almost glowing in the dusk, daring them to say anything more. No man took the risk, and the mage spun on his heel, his black cloak fluttering theatrically as he departed. The topic of conversation changed abruptly.

Duncan watched the young man's back as he hurried toward his secluded campsite. If Yarrow truly possessed the power the others claimed, why hadn't he called Duncan out when he'd accused him of being worthless? Another knight of equal rank would not have hesitated to demand a duel. Though he was certainly no coward, Duncan had never faced a magic-user, and felt secretly relieved that the mage hadn't called him out. Duncan put the idea to the back of his mind as he finished his meal and declined a flask offered by the archer, Malthus. He planned to do another inspection of the camp, check the watch and patrol schedules, look in on the horses, and clean his armor and weapons before retiring. The mage's motivations were hardly his priority.

THE BREAD was awful stuff, rock hard and meant to withstand time and resist spoiling, but Yarrow had had worse. He'd often gone days without a crumb during his travels. At least the wine was passable, if a little too dry. He missed the sweet, golden vintages of Lockhaven, buttery with hints of vanilla and subtle spice. As he sat beneath his tarpaulin, he heard the men talking and the horses whinnying in the distance. He doubted that disagreeable Duncan fellow permitted much drunkenness. At the thought of the man, Yarrow balled his fists. It galled him that the knight found him lacking. Part of him wanted to find Duncan and defend his worth, but he wouldn't give the warrior that satisfaction. What frustrated the mage most was that he cared what Duncan thought. Many years had passed since he'd given a fig for anyone's opinion or appreciation. As a third son, he'd learned early how futile an effort it was to seek his parents' approval. They had an heir and a spare, so their youngest boy mattered little. It hurt as a child, but Yarrow had learned to judge his worth by his own standards, and not on the opinions of others. He'd conditioned himself not to seek accolades or value assessments. Why did he need those cast-off crutches now?

Predictably, the presence in Yarrow's mind emerged to goad him. *I can't believe you let him speak to you like that. The Yarrow I know has killed men for less. Going soft, beloved?*

I am in no mood for your insults, Yarrow said.

Poor little Yarrow. Not afraid of the scary knight, I hope. Let me wear the flesh, and I'll put him in his place. A wave of murderous enthusiasm welled up inside the mage. He felt his control over his mind and body slipping, as if he were falling asleep against his will. His consciousness clawed to the surface as if it towed an anchor, fighting the force that dragged it toward the dark waters of oblivion.

Yarrow grew angry, and with his outrage came a surge of strength. He wrangled the other presence into submission and drove all but the smallest trace of it from his mind. It troubled him to note he'd had more difficulty subduing it than in the past. His appetite gone, Yarrow hurled the brick-like bread into the frozen bracken down the hill from his tent. He took several long pulls from his wineskin before stretching out on the icy ground. He pulled his quilt over his chest and ran his hands over the patches, marveling at how his aunt had created something so warm and beautiful from discarded scraps. The bits of dress fabric, upholstery brocade, and leftover drapery velvet, worthless on their own, transformed into a strong and useful item when pieced together. It had been around the world with Yarrow, the only remnant of home he carried, and it continued to shield him from the cold. Gravel bit his back, but it had been worse. Yes, it had been much worse.

Closing his eyes, Yarrow let the dream come. It came every night, and he thought it best to get it over with. He'd been a boy five years ago, but worldly. Capable, or so he'd thought. He'd crossed Selindria and Gaeltheon, then hired a guide to lead him through the impassable

Lapir Mountains, determined to see the wonders of magic that waited on the other side. If he made it, he'd learn skills unimagined in his homeland. Such power could keep him safe, keep him hidden, if he desired. After a month of fighting daily blizzards, the young man leading him had died despite his heavy furs. Their food and water were gone, and Yarrow found himself hopelessly lost.

Snow and ice pelted his face so hard they drew blood. His lips and skin froze and cracked, and both of his hands had turned black inside his gloves. Though he hadn't felt his feet for almost a week, Yarrow trudged through snow up to his hips. The cold air bit his lungs. He headed east, or at least in the direction where he thought he'd last seen the sun rise. Another heavy storm obscured the sky. Beyond it, Yarrow saw only shelves of rock rising almost vertically, hundreds of feet above him. He no longer felt cold or even hungry, just tired and apathetic. His guide had warned him of these symptoms. They signaled the end. Yarrow wanted only to lie down for a few moments and close his stinging eyes. Only vanity forced him to stay on his feet and search for a way through the imposing mountains.

Day turned to frigid night, and back to day. By the next evening, Yarrow had become completely disoriented as he turned and circled around dozens of times in his attempt to find a way across the rocks. He could no longer tell the snow from the sparkles that swam through his vision. Everything was a fuzzy, white haze. He couldn't go on, couldn't will his foot to lift from the ice that encased it. The world spun around him, swirls of gray and white, and he collapsed on his hands and knees. Refusing to relent, he crawled through snow up to his chin without a scrap of sensation in his flesh. Logic told him he would surely die, but his will said otherwise.

Finally he noticed a cleft in the stone, a small opening just large enough to wedge his body inside. He forced himself within the scant scrap of shelter as the brutal wind howled past. After a while he discerned a tunnel beyond a wall behind him. It was scarcely large enough for him to crawl through, and sharp rocks scraped his knees and back open, but something compelled him to continue. Yarrow had no idea how long he spent descending deeper and deeper into the bowels of the world. It felt like days, weeks even, of dragging himself through darkness heavier and more complete than anything he'd ever imagined. Panic nearly took him many times, and he attempted to scrabble out of the twisting warren backward, as he had no space to turn around. Eventually he heard the faraway drip of water, and he forced himself onward.

The tunnel opened to an underground room decorated with stalactites and stalagmites. They wreathed the greenish pool and dripped from the ceiling, rippling its surface. Yarrow realized he could see by the light that emanated from the water. He hurried to drink, as he hadn't slaked his thirst in days, at least. Then he noticed the presence in the water, calling out to him. He had no energy to resist its attempts to breach his mind.

So someone has come at last.

Who are you? Yarrow asked. *What are you doing down here?* He tried to see it within the oily, brackish water, but perceived only a dark swirl twisting eel-like through the depths.

I am imprisoned here. I have been for a very long time. Somehow it showed him, made him comprehend the eons it had spent in the gloom. Yarrow's mind reeled with the impossible, unfathomable length of years. He hadn't imagined the world so old. *We can help each other.*

How?

I was tricked, it explained. *Robbed of my body, longer ago than you can imagine. I crave the things I've lost, the ability to experience sensation. I wish to smell and taste. To feel the stab of hunger in my belly, the cold wind on my skin. I wish to feel again fingers in my hair, the sun on my shoulders, the softness of a bed. I want to be burned, cut. I need to feel something, anything. A wooden tabletop beneath my fingers, a bruise on my knee. A blade of grass between my fingertips. Dirt in my boot. Everything you take for granted each day. Try to imagine being without it.*

Yarrow tried, but not too hard, lest it drive him mad. *How can I help you?*

Let me inside your body. Share your flesh with me. Let me use your eyes to see, your tongue to taste, and your skin to experience sensation.

What will you do for me in return?

It expressed amusement somehow. *I'll allow you to live. To leave this place.*

Is that all?

Ho ho. I'm truly lucky. Bargaining, even in the face of your certain death. It seems you'll keep me entertained, as well. You're spirited. I like you. Fine. I see you are a magic-user of some talent.

Help me, give me your body, and I'll make you the most powerful wizard that has ever lived. You'll never have to fear being harmed or taken advantage of again. You'll be safe. It allowed Yarrow the briefest of glimpses into its vast wealth of arcane knowledge. Yarrow felt sure any more would have broken his mind. He practically salivated at the idea of it, more power, darker secrets, than he had thought existed. This creature held the power of a god, or more.

What are you?

Something that has been here long before your people. Something as old as the bones of the world. I do not have a word you'd understand.

What would I need to do, to share my body?

Yarrow felt its desperate hunger. Its excitement vibrated through the dank air in the cave, making Yarrow's teeth wiggle and his inner organs tremble. His empty stomach cartwheeled. *So little, beloved. Just open up. Let me in....*

In the days that followed, Yarrow lay in a trembling heap as the presence melded with him. It took root in his consciousness, sending tendrils to every inch of his skin, to every hair, to his every perception. He watched its memories, memories of blood and destruction and things so awful he couldn't name them. Feet of gore covered the ancient ground. He wanted to look away and couldn't. He screamed his throat bloody and convulsed on the wet, rocky floor, praying he'd pass out but unable to. Millennia worth of horrors played out in his mind. Yarrow tasted raw flesh and felt bones crunching in his hands. Armies fell and littered the landscape. Towns burned. People screamed before exploding into red mist. Coagulated blood and bits of innards covered everything he could see. It reeked of feces and rot. What had he done? He felt every disgusting deed as though he did it himself, and he prayed the trauma might kill him. He clawed his palms and thighs raw as it went on and on, an endless massacre, the stuff of a thousand nightmares.

When it finally ended, he was changed, his hair and eyes the least of it. At least another day passed before he could move or even form a cogent thought. Finally, he asked his new companion, *Do you now have my memories as well?*

I do, beloved. My strong Yarrow. I thought you might not make it a few times there. Was I too rough? Let me feel. Let me wear your flesh. I can't wait any longer! Give me the body, and I'll see you out of this place.

Yarrow woke up several weeks later on the other side of the mountains with no memory of how he got there. His frostbite and other wounds had healed, but his hair and eyes remained scorched almost translucent. His mind would never recover. He remembered feeling transformed, broken to bits and pieced back together, stronger, yet somehow diminished.

THE MAGE sat up on his bedroll, sweating and nauseous like always. Through harsh discipline, he'd trained himself not to whimper or cry out during or after the dream. He got shakily to his feet, relieved himself in the bushes, and then made his way toward the barrel to refill his wine. Fires burned low and the camp was quiet, everyone asleep save those on watch. Two men stood not far from Yarrow's camp, and he rolled his eyes at them. The wards he'd placed around his simple tent would deter all but the most dangerous enemies.

On his way back to bed, Yarrow nearly collided with the chest of the knight, Duncan. The two of them regarded one another in the low light for many minutes before Duncan spoke. "I did not mean to hurt your feelings. I wish only to protect those people entrusted to me. I can do that best if those people heed my instructions. Still, I never intended to offend you. I spoke out of line."

Yarrow blew air out his nose and stared into the man's eyes until the knight had to look away. The small victory made Yarrow smile, and he said, "You flatter yourself, tam. In order to offend me, I would have to value your opinion of me. I do not."

Duncan colored and opened his mouth as though to say more, but Yarrow turned away from him and returned to his simple bed. It pleased him how long the knight stood watching before he turned to retire to his own tent.

THE PROCESSION made excellent progress over the next three days. Neither sun nor rain broke through the uniform gray sky. During the day they rode in gloomy half light, which simply petered out to darkness each evening. Relentless wind assailed the tall grass of the plains, though it did little more to impede their progress than make them uncomfortable. Yarrow rode with his hood up. He grew fond of his soot-colored filly. While excitable, she possessed remarkable endurance and a sweet nature. Many animals instinctively feared Yarrow, and the fact she didn't endeared the mare to him. Yarrow took to calling her Syrai, the Emiri word for friend.

Five or six times Yarrow had tried to speak with his cousin, only to receive a halfhearted excuse from his guards: the prince is tired, the prince is at prayer, or the prince wishes to be alone. None of the other soldiers or servants attempted to speak with the mage, least of all their commander, Duncan. Instead, they eyed him suspiciously when he rode past them or came to fetch his food in the evening. What could they be saying about him?

Why do you care what they think, Yarrow? You never have before. This is most unlike you. I'm beginning to wonder why you really agreed to come on this silly excursion.

Shut up.

How dare you speak to me like that?

I'll speak to you however I want. Were it not for me, you'd be back in that filthy pond, devoid of any experience.

And you'd be dead, beloved.

Perhaps. Perhaps not. Either way, I'm in no mood to be mocked. I'll shut you out if you don't stop it.

I wouldn't recommend you do that, Yarrow.

Why is that?

Because there are a great number of lives up ahead. Above us, on those ridges.

Oh? Yarrow asked. He looked at the great cliffs a quarter mile ahead. Their path wound between two veritable walls of stone. While he couldn't see anything atop them, his heightened senses did detect a faint, familiar smell. He'd learned from his companion to sense life energy, and to categorize it. *Men? How many?*

Dozens. Perhaps you should let me take over.

I'm hardly helpless without you. Yarrow broke formation and urged Syrai to the front of the line, where he fell into step next to Duncan.

"So sorry to bother your eminence with my worthless observations," he said. "But it might interest you to know we're walking into a trap."

The knight sighed wearily. When he turned his eyes toward Yarrow, bruise-like circles outlined the appealing olive green, but his patience didn't falter. Yarrow felt a little stab of guilt over his sarcasm.

"Report, tam, if you'd be so kind."

"There are several dozen men waiting on those ridges above the road," Yarrow said simply, abandoning petty meanness. "I can't quite sense their intentions, but I'd wager they're not planning to throw us a banquet."

"I see." Duncan held up a hand and the entire procession skidded to a halt, a few of the carts going askew in their haste to stop. Horses whinnied and pawed at the frosty ground.

Yarrow sat stunned astride his filly. He hadn't expected to be believed.

"Scouts!" the commander called. A regimen of men in light leathers, armed with bows and daggers, surrounded Duncan's huge, bay stallion and looked up at him, awaiting orders. He pointed to the bottleneck between the two stone plateaus, and the soldiers nodded in understanding. Crouching low, they crept toward the vulnerable spot, arrows and knives at the ready. Yarrow watched the scouts taking their time to check for traps and places that could conceal ambushers. They used distance glasses to inspect the top of the rock shelves. Almost an hour later, they returned to their commander with nothing to report.

"Not a thing, tam," said a lad with a shock of sandy blond hair beneath his leather helm. "Nothing at all."

"Are you saying the way ahead is safe?" Duncan demanded.

"Far as we can tell it is, tam."

"Are there not men on those ridges?" Yarrow asked. Straining his own eyes, he perceived only some dead brush and piles of rocks, but he still detected the hum of living things.

The young scout practically wilted under the mage's scrutiny, though Yarrow was only a year or two older. "We can't see a soul, Tam Yarroway. And we can't find any path leading to the tops of those plateaus. We'll have to backtrack half a day to go around them."

"You're sure no one's there?" How could no one be there? Yarrow's companion never made such mistakes. Unless—

"No one's there, tam," the young man repeated.

"Dismissed. Well done, soldier." The knight turned to Yarrow. "I… I do appreciate your concern. Better to be overly cautious than not cautious enough."

As he and the others rode ahead, Yarrow sat astounded. *You... you purposely made a fool of me to punish me for being rude! Son of a dockside whore! You even made me think I sensed men. You will not trifle with me, creature!*

Calm yourself, beloved.

No, you blackguard! This will not be tolerated. You dare to admonish me?

If I did, how would you stop me? But no, Yarrow, I spoke truly. You'd be wise to catch up to your companions. I suspect most of them will perish if you don't. Look there.

Yarrow could just discern hatches opening on top of the ridges. Their wooden tops had been camouflaged with gravel, soil, and grass. Now that the doors stood open, the men who'd been hiding underground spilled out. Archers hurried to the edges of the cliffs but held their fire. Yarrow quickly saw the reason. Other men, larger ones, hauled tree trunks up from their bunkers and began to wedge them beneath the large piles of rock. The boulders would easily crush most of the procession, as it waited entirely within the confines of the narrow pass. The prince's carriage stood at the center, just where it would likely bear the brunt of the assault.

"Ha!" Yarrow yelled, kicking his mare hard in the ribs. She reared and galloped toward the rest of the company. Holding tight to the animal with his thighs, Yarrow reached toward the heavens and drew some arcane symbols in the air. Magical energy swirled around him, and he gathered all that he could hold and hoped it would be enough. Small pebbles rained down on him as he reached the prince. Duncan looked back nervously. "Go!" Yarrow shouted. "Get out of here."

Instead of heeding the warning, the confused men looked up for the source of the gravel. Frustrated, barely holding his concentration and only just clinging to the vast store of magic, Yarrow slapped the haunches of one of the white geldings pulling the prince's carriage. The beast whinnied sharply and trotted away. Larger and larger chunks of rock hailed down into the channel. Finally Duncan, eyes wide, realized their situation. His mouth opened to bark commands, though Yarrow couldn't hear them over the increasing storm of rock and the musical hum of enchantment in his head. Riders and carts hurried to obey the commander, moving as quickly as they could within the clogged, narrow passageway. They weren't fast enough. The first of the large boulders tumbled down. It landed in the back of an open supply cart and smashed it to splinters, snapping the axle in two. Its driver hurried to cut his red pony free.

Another pair of boulders fell from the opposite ridge, each of them twice the size of the first. Yarrow understood the force that drew objects toward the ground, the principle that kept people and things firmly on the world's surface instead of letting them float away. He just needed to reverse it temporarily, to stop those rocks from being pulled toward the ground. Sweating, he aimed for them and caught them, stopping them only four feet above the head of a very shocked infantryman.

"Mage!" he heard one of the bandits shout. "Take him down!" A quartet of arrows flew at Yarrow's head, but he held his hand out and erected a shimmering, blue shield that deflected them easily. Duncan's archers returned fire, though their position left them at a severe disadvantage. A storm of apple-sized rocks pelted the company. Yarrow saw a man fall from his mount, struck unconscious. Horses screamed in fear, trying to stampede toward the open plains at the end of the chute. A sharp stone hit Yarrow's shoulder, almost knocking him off Syrai's back. He yelped in pain but didn't feel any bones break. Another volley of arrows soared past him from the other side of the crevice, and he had no time to move his shield to his opposite shoulder. An arrow caught him, sailing cleanly through his left wrist and out the other side. Yarrow didn't dare let his focus slip enough to remove the bolt or heal himself, and blood cascaded down his arm. He fought to ignore the pain and weakness in his limb and concentrate on his spell.

He had to protect the others until they reached the exit. Sweating, he moved his sparkling screen over his head. Moving his hands frantically, he stretched it thinner and thinner, the way country girls stretched dough for strudel. He had to be just as careful not to tear the magical fabric. Soon it extended over the entire party. Gourd-sized stones struck the shield, and it held. Larger and larger boulders careened down from above, in so great a number it began to grow dark beneath Yarrow's defenses. For a horrible moment, he recalled the underground cavern and thought he might faint.

Arms trembling, Yarrow watched as Duncan directed an orderly withdrawal from the pass. Nearly everyone had made it to safety. As Yarrow watched, feeling like he held the whole of the heavens, the prince passed beneath the edge of his shield with his guards. Yarrow's body shook so hard it caused his mare to fidget. He had to hold the spell. His wounded left arm went numb, though he somehow managed to keep it over his head. A few feet of rock hovered above them now; it would crush to death anyone who hadn't made it to the grassland. Yarrow made a sound between a grunt and scream as he fought to maintain the enchantment.

Need some help? asked a familiar voice.

Yarrow ignored the distraction, though the longer he held the barrier, the more tempting it became to let his companion take over. With its power, it could dispel the rocks easily, maybe even cause them to disintegrate. It would come with a price, though, so Yarrow struggled to keep his arms in the air though his muscles felt like jelly and his bones like powder.

The final cart reached the end of the tunnel. Still holding the mystic aegis over him, Yarrow clicked to his mare and nudged her sides. He let her walk so as not to jar him and disrupt his spell. He had precious little left in him, but he only needed to cross another hundred yards or so. Duncan had dismounted and waited at the edge of the passage.

Almost there. Thick swarms of gray specks swam at the edges of Yarrow's vision, flooding in like an avalanche. He couldn't hold them back nor will them away. His left arm flopped uselessly to his side. In slow motion, he felt himself slip from the back of his horse and land on his right hip and shoulder. A wall of rock crashed down. Yarrow tried feebly to pull himself the last few feet with his undamaged arm, but he'd depleted every ounce of energy he possessed. He couldn't even move, could do nothing to save himself from being buried alive beneath six feet of stone.

Strong arms encased in sharp, angular steel gripped Yarrow around the chest, pulling him back as boulders crushed his legs, trapping him in no time. He heard the clash of swords behind him, saw the blurry lines of arrows flying overhead. A deep, compassionate voice spoke to him, though the words were garbled and unintelligible when they reached his mind. A gauntleted hand touched his face, and he perceived nothing more.

Chapter Three

YARROW WOKE to a gentle rocking and creaking. His broken body shifted from side to side amid heaps of sweet-smelling but scratchy straw. While cold and sore, the mage realized he should be hurt much worse after the events in the pass. He opened his eyes and squinted against the glare of the bright white sky. He detected the scent of horses above the festering odor of decay. With some effort, he pushed himself up on his elbows.

He found himself in the back of a cart, wrapped in the old quilt he traveled with. Someone had removed his boots and splinted and wrapped his legs from the knees down. As a test, he wriggled his chilly toes, relieved when he felt them move. Fresh blood bloomed on the wrappings over his wrist, and though it hurt, he managed to clench his left fist. He looked around and located the source of the foul odor: half a dozen bodies, wrapped in white cloth, rode in the back of a nearby wagon.

"What happened?" Yarrow croaked.

"You don't recall the ambush?" Yarrow looked up to see the commander, Duncan, riding alongside his cart. A cut stretched across the man's neck and dried blood and dirt clung to his plate. His rich brown hair hung loose around his face and fluttered in the cold breeze. His wounds had scabbed over; they were no longer fresh.

Yarrow collapsed back in the straw. "Did I do it?" he asked.

"That you did, Tam Yarroway. Brilliantly."

"Yarrow," he insisted, his mind spinning as he tried to piece together the exact sequence of events. He took the waterskin the commander offered and drank. "The prince?"

"Not even a scratch," Duncan said. "I don't know what would have become of us had you not been quick."

"You'd be dead, obviously. How long have I slept?"

"Almost three days," the knight said.

"What of the bandits?"

"They gave us little trouble once their trap failed. We killed most and a few fled. Still, we lost men both in the avalanche and the battle afterward. Our ambushers were much better trained and equipped than the average brigand. As soon as I can, I'll send a message to His Majesty and ask that a regiment of knights and guards search this area and roust out any stragglers. To have these outlaws operating so near the royal fortress is a disgrace. I fear there may be many more in the area, and they must certainly keep a stronghold somewhere. More importantly, though, I wanted to say—"

"There is no need."

"There is need," the commander demanded, inviting no argument. "I sorely misjudged you, tam. I… I admit I assumed you would be soft, spoiled. I know little of magic, and I never imagined anyone capable of what you did back there. Few of the most loyal knights can fight through such wounds as you suffered. You are honorable and brave. You saved the prince when I could not. I can ask nothing more of the men under my command."

"I'm not under your command," Yarrow protested weakly.

At this, Duncan laughed heartily, a balm to the mage's wounded pride. "I won't speak to your arrogance or abrasive nature, Yarrow, as no man is perfect. I wish only to say, well done."

Those simple words pleased Yarrow, and he smiled even as he felt the presence within him rise up, insults ready. He sought Duncan's eyes and found them regarding him intently, the knight's handsome face mirroring the magician's smile. They regarded one another for long moments, before Duncan finally cleared his throat and returned his attention to the road before them.

"By evening we'll reach the Eyrle of Peregrym's lands. He's a wealthy man with a large household. You'll be able to bathe, eat well, and sleep in a bed this eve."

"Yes, I know the eyrle and his wife," Yarrow said. "We're probably in for quite a feast."

"I can't say it will be unwelcome," Duncan replied. He kicked his charger. "We will speak more later, if you like."

"I would," Yarrow said too quickly. His companion roared with psychic laughter, but the mage ignored it. He situated himself in the straw and let his eyes fall closed, feeling much warmer than he had before. He slept until well after sunset, and woke when the procession arrived outside the Peregrym household.

By the light of the dozens of lanterns lining the drive, Yarrow watched scores of servants hurrying to carry the prince's things inside and take the horses to the stables. Duncan circled his steed around and helped Yarrow down from the cart, unable to mask his amazement when the mage's legs supported him. Yarrow emptied the straw from inside his plain but sturdy black boots and slipped them on. He shook the twigs from his hair. He'd anticipated being fully healed by now, as his companion would see to it once it grew bored of experiencing pain. Duncan dismounted, and he and Yarrow approached the entrance of Peregrym Castle. It was an L-shaped structure with a large, square tower at the corner and surrounded by an outer wall topped with guards. The knight and mage followed the steps into the barbican and found themselves within a vast foyer lit with wall sconces, iron candelabra, and several hanging chandeliers. The smell of smoky tallow was strong. Motes of dust danced in the shafts of yellow light. Otherwise, the dark stone hall felt sparse and utilitarian.

Maidservants waited along the walls with their hands folded in front of them and their eyes on the stone floor. Yarrow and Duncan moved to stand behind the prince. Yarrow couldn't see his cousin's expression as his thick hood cast his face in shadow. They waited, all of them shuffling their feet and some of the soldiers whispering, until a pair of pages flung open the heavy double doors at the end of the hall. A short, elderly man in a long, sleeveless yellow robe lined with fur and embellished with embroidery and beading, moved into the room. He wore a heavy, padded shirt beneath his gown and a simple, golden circlet on his bald head. Behind him, attended by her ladies, his much younger wife wore an elaborate, latticed headdress: two tall cones draped with gauzy, gold filament. The veil covered her face. Only a hint of her dark eyes and lips showed beneath. She wore a bronze shift with wide, bell sleeves and a belt of amber and topaz.

The noble couple hurried forward, and the eyrle dropped to his knees in front of Prince Garith, taking his hand and kissing his many rings. "You honor this household with your presence, Your Highness," he said. Behind him, everyone else prostrated themselves, kneeling until Garith bade them stand. Yarrow stayed upright and waited, absently regarding the doves sleeping in the rafters high above them.

"We cannot thank Peregrym enough for his gracious hospitality," the prince said. "It has been a long journey already, and a night within this goodly house will be most appreciated."

"All of you should rest and refresh yourselves while the feast is prepared," said the eyrle.

Yarrow knew that "all of them" meant Garith, himself, the few courtiers and administrators that accompanied the prince, his priest, and maybe Duncan. The rest of the men would make do with the stable and their leftovers. Such things had always irked the mage. Those who worked hardest saw the least benefit of it. He supposed the world had never been any different. It had been years since he'd felt any connection to their society, anyway. He watched Duncan and Garith split off in different directions and allowed himself to be led through a door and into the western wing by two tittering girls.

Yarrow stood on the outside, and he'd always remain there. Conventions others barely acknowledged seemed wildly absurd to him. An accident of birth hardly made a man worthy of a fine feather mattress and a fire while another bedded down with the beasts. Did no one else find it ludicrous?

The maids showed Yarrow to a simple but comfortable cell with a cheery fire burning and a wooden tub of warm water ready. A change of clothes waited at the foot of the large bed, and a small, dagger-shaped window afforded a view of the kitchen gardens and orchards. Beyond it, the bare branches of fruit trees sparkled with frost as if cast from silver. Swirls of snow flitted across the vegetable patches like spirits fleeing the dawn. Yarrow watched the wind carving patterns reminiscent of Emiri paint in the snow and dropped his small pack in the corner.

"Will you bathe now, tam?" asked one of the maids, her cheeks burning as she looked at anything but the mage.

"Yes, thank you."

"Which of us would you like to assist you, tam?" asked the other girl, a buxom lass with a copper-colored braid down her back. "Or shall we both assist you?"

"I can manage on my own," he told them, sitting on the bench beside the fire.

"Our purpose is to serve you in any way you wish," the redhead dared, taking a step nearer. "Shall I remove your boots? Help you to undress? I will do anything you ask."

"I understand what you propose," Yarrow said, growing irritated, "but I prefer to be alone. Leave me."

They obeyed, perhaps a little too eagerly, and Yarrow undressed. Beneath his bandages, dark bruises covered his legs from the middle of his thighs to his ankles, but anything broken had mended. His wrist had finally scabbed over. Yarrow bathed and cleaned his teeth. He dragged a silver comb through his thick, white hair. His whiskers no longer grew, except for a few downy hairs in front of his ears, so he no longer carried a shaving blade. He looked down at his body in the firelight. He was still too thin. His hipbones and the bottom of his ribcage jutted out from his small waist. Would he ever fill out? His arms and legs were long, slender, and stronger than they appeared. The elaborate, blue Emiri paint wound seductively down his right side, accentuating the dips of muscle along his waist and torso before ending in a flourish just above the patch of sparse, cloud-colored hair between his legs. Running his palm over the ink, Yarrow remembered the boy who'd suggested it with a sharp pang. He felt the presence watching his thoughts, but it didn't dare tease him about this.

Yarrow went to the clothing on the bed. He slipped into the blue-gray shirt, as his own was torn and fouled with blood. It was comfortable, well made with full sleeves and a lace-up front. *No silly collar and no lace on the cuffs, thank the goddesses.* The padded, purple doublet he set aside. Though his loose black pants had been dirtied and ripped by the rockslide, he hated to think of his scrawny legs in the tight, silver leggings his hosts provided, so he washed his trousers and hung them in front of the fire. When they dried he dressed, leaving his leather armor neatly on the bench. He slung his black belt, with his tinder pouch and dagger, over his slim hips and went in search of his cousin.

The four guards posted at the door helped Yarrow find the prince's chamber, as no other soldiers were posted in the quiet halls. He stopped, wondering what to say to them, sorely tempted to enchant them into a deep sleep, or at least an agreeable mood. Instead, he strode confidently toward their leader and said, "I wish to speak with my cousin."

"We have orders that no one sees His Highness," the man said nervously.

"I'm changing those orders," Yarrow said. "I demand to see Garith."

"But Tam Duncan—"

"If I intended the prince any harm, why would I have risked my own life to save him back in that ravine? I know you men mistrust me, and I could care less. You will obey me, however. Now stand aside or I'll make you."

"Do as my cousin asks," the prince said softly from within the chamber.

They hurried to comply, and Yarrow entered Garith's quarters. They were larger and more sumptuous than his own, with upholstered couches, thick rugs, tapestries on the walls, two fireplaces, and a separate washroom. The fires burned low in the hearths, barely more than embers, and a single lantern sputtered on a stand, doing little to drive back the heavy shadows. Yarrow didn't see his cousin in the darkness at first. Then he noticed Garith checking intently behind the decorations and running his fingers over every block in the wall. He wore a pair of tight, black trousers and little else. At the soft sound of Yarrow's boots on the carpet, Garith's spine straightened.

"Yarroway?" he asked, his fists and muscles clenched like a serpent coiled and ready to spring.

"Easy, cousin. It's only me."

Garith turned slowly. When, Yarrow wondered, had the prince developed that body? He was lean but perfectly proportioned. Even the smallest of his muscles was cut and defined. Yarrow stared in awe at his sculpted torso and slender, powerful arms. His gaze traveled up Garith's skin, still damp from the bath and sparkling in the firelight. The prince favored his Esperon mother, but had he always been so dark? Compared to him, Yarrow's sun-kissed complexion seemed pale.

"Cousin Yarroway," the prince said, drawing the mage's attention to his face.

Yarrow squinted, trying to conjure his most recent memory of this man. The prince made it more difficult when he stepped to the side and into a shadow cast by the thick bedpost and its swags. It had been probably five or six years ago, maybe more. They'd been boys, and a lot had happened in between, but Yarrow hardly recognized Garith. Had his lips been so full? Even in the semidarkness, he had the most magnificent eyelashes Yarrow had ever seen on a human face: thick, long, and curled perfectly. Yarrow had never noticed before. Below them, his intense, black eyes smoldered, reflecting firelight. Yarrow didn't recall that powerful gaze. The Garith he'd known had been a decent enough lad, but vapid and effortlessly influenced, an easy boy to order around. He'd never contained such complex passion as radiated from him now. He didn't even blink as he stared into Yarrow's startling eyes. It hardly seemed to the mage as though he regarded the same man.

"You've changed," the prince said evenly, betraying no emotion. "I heard, of course, of your fever. I am a little taken aback by the severity of your transformation. And you wear the paint of the Emiri. Why?"

"I spent time among the Sea People," Yarrow answered. "Learned their ways. What of you, my friend? How have you spent the years since we last chased one another through your father's gardens?"

Garith chuckled melodically and indicated a posh brocade bench strewn with cushions. The cousins sat down. Yarrow pointed at the fire behind Garith's left shoulder, coaxing it to burn a bit brighter. Garith flinched, almost imperceptibly, but composed himself a second later. "The life of a prince is an orderly one. I studied politics, history, and literature. I learned, in theory, to lead an army. I learned to dance and speak well. I practiced with my blade and made my obligatory visits to my father's nobles. Dull, I'm sure, in comparison to your fantastic adventures. I'd love to hear your tales one day." The prince smiled, and it almost felt genuine.

Yarrow didn't remember those pouty, expressive lips. Perhaps he'd just never studied his cousin's mouth as a lad of twelve or thirteen. What other explanation could there be?

"You seem changed as well, Garith." Yarrow was being toyed with, and he didn't like it. He couldn't identify how Garith managed to manipulate him, or why. It was an unusual experience for the mage.

In answer to Yarrow's observation, Garith merely stared at him. Yarrow felt like the prince's eyes delved into his very soul and exposed everything he'd buried there, though they reflected none of Garith's emotions back. Though he wanted to, Yarrow refused to look away from Garith's gaze. He smelled Garith's damp skin, the smoke from the fire, and the soap the prince had used on his long, black hair. Time moved slowly.

"You are not as I remember you," Yarrow said more forcefully. Magic could mask a man's true form temporarily, but Yarrow sensed no enchantment at work. Maybe he was being foolish. It had been a long time, and likely Garith had just grown from an awkward, callow boy into this dark, enigmatic man. "In fact, you're very different than I recall."

"The years can change a man, cousin. You should know that better than anyone." Garith scooted a little closer to Yarrow on the bench. Their knees bumped together. "This fever of yours," the prince continued, pinching a lock of Yarrow's pale hair between his thumb and finger and twisting it around, "I've never heard of an illness changing a man's appearance."

"It was a foreign affliction."

"Tell me how it happened."

Yarrow froze. It almost felt like Garith *knew*.

Go on, beloved. Tell him.

I cannot deal with you right now!

"Cousin Yarroway? Is something wrong?"

"You've not called me by my full name since we were five years old," the mage said. "Why do so now?"

Before Garith could answer, a servant knocked on the door to announce that dinner would soon be served. The prince stood and turned his back to Yarrow. "I must finish dressing. Please send that girl in on your way out to assist me. We can talk later, my friend."

"We certainly will," Yarrow said as he left. He didn't know what possessed him to glare at the lovely maiden with the blonde ringlets as she entered the chamber, but the presence within him howled with wicked mirth.

DUNCAN REMAINED on the wooden bench as the servants picked over the food, gnawing on trenchers, sipping tepid ale, and filling their pockets with bits of dried fruit before clearing the feast away. Hounds followed them eagerly, hoping for scraps. The great fires at either end of the hall burned low and spurted black smoke. It grew cold and chill. Duncan stared into the shadows at his untouched goblet of wine.

It had been a dull dinner, with the nobles engaged in their frivolous, mandatory chatter. Duncan had found himself watching the young mage seated across from him. Yarrow didn't touch the fine, herb-encrusted roasted meats, stuffed fouls, or grilled fish. The knight watched, bewildered, as the lad picked the root vegetables from his stew and rinsed them in his water goblet before eating them. He dropped the savory bits of liver and kidney to the floor for the dogs, and only nibbled at the edges of his trencher that hadn't been touched by the thick brown broth. It was little wonder Yarrow remained so slight, as he seemed to sustain himself on only dehydrated apples, raisins, preserves, and crumbs of bread. If copious amounts of wine could put meat on a boy's bones, the mage might have grown quite sturdy.

Duncan shook his head. He'd planned to continue his earlier conversation with the mage, but the lad had hurried off after the prince as soon as the dinner concluded. He probably needed rest to fully heal his wounds, Duncan thought. Besides, Duncan wanted to check on the prince's guards, the eyrle's guards posted to the walls, and his men residing in the stable. He stood and stretched, feeling almost naked without his trusty plate mail and greatsword. The eyrle's barricades and the soldiers atop would keep out any danger, he supposed. They were still practically on Agarick's lawn.

The halls of the castle were dark and quiet. Random patrols passed servants slumbering against the walls. Most of the candles had burned out, and heavy shadows shrouded alcoves and corners. Outside, a thick, chilly mist covered the grounds. Duncan shivered beneath his functional shirt and tunic. As pleasant as the large meal had been, he looked forward to getting back on the road, into his armor and among his men. He checked on the stables, pleased to find his soldiers feared his wrath too much to risk drunkenness. He knew they hated this rule of his, though he felt sure they respected him in every other aspect. He was a good leader; he did his duty and kept them safe. Carousing could wait until the completion of their task. Once the prince landed safely in Gaeltheon, he'd buy the men a round himself.

Duncan supposed he should retire. Not every day did he receive an invite to sleep on a feather mattress, after all. He felt restless, though, and decided to take a last stroll around the grounds. As he circled the castle a second time, he noticed a slight shadow following him, a dark gash in the fog that moved silently closer and closer. Fists balled and muscles tensed, the knight pretended not to notice, and before long he detected the sound of a boot crunching on the brittle grass. He spun around and aimed his fist at his pursuer's throat, all in a single, fluid motion. The hooded stranger dodged gracefully to the side. Duncan lost his balance and pitched forward. Instead of exploiting his vulnerability, the other grasped Duncan's shoulders and helped him up.

"Peace, friend! I only wish to talk." Yarrow pushed his cowl back and his white tresses stood in sharp contrast to the night sky.

"Forgive me," Duncan mumbled, embarrassed. "What is it you'd like to discuss?"

The mage looked left and right, staring hard into the shadows. He was a pretty young man, the knight thought, even with his odd coloring. Strange, but Duncan found Yarrow's light, almost luminescent hair and eyes more intriguing and exotic than grotesque. Yarrow caught his hand and dragged him behind a stack of hay higher than their heads when a pair of patrolmen passed by. His bright eyes darted nervously from side to side. Once they hid themselves, the mage seized Duncan's elbow and pulled the knight into a crouch beside him.

"Yarrow, what's wrong?"

"How well do you know the prince?" The boy's whisper was hardly discernible from the frigid breeze.

"Not well," Duncan admitted, confused. "I can count on one hand the times we've spoken face to face."

"I've known Garith all my life. As a boy, my mother and I spent many summers at his home. He and I passed almost every day in each other's company, messing about the stables, fighting with sticks, exploring the mountains and valleys around the castle. I can tell you this, Duncan: something is wrong with the prince."

"Wrong?" Duncan asked, worried now. "His Highness seemed well enough at dinner."

"I don't mean that he's hurt or ill," the mage clarified, shaking his head, his frustration plain. "It's—something about his manner isn't right. I hardly recognized him as my childhood companion. It might sound ridiculous, but I'd swear he doesn't even look as he should."

Duncan relaxed back in the frosty hay. He put a hand on Yarrow's shoulder, as the lad seemed genuinely upset. "You haven't seen him in years. Your cousin probably feels the weight of the world on his shoulders. He's still very young to be entrusted with saving the world through this marriage."

"This little spit of land is hardly the world," Yarrow snapped. "The world is stranger and vaster than you can envision."

"Perhaps," Duncan allowed, perplexed by the moody young man. "Even so, over half a decade has gone by since you played in your uncle's courtyard. The prince has become a man since then. Of course he's different from the lad you remember."

The mage shook his head. "There's more to it than that."

"Your concern for him is admirable."

"My concern is not for Garith," Yarrow hissed. "It's for myself. Something's wrong here, and I can't puzzle through it."

"Perhaps a good night's rest will—"

"No. I have something else I need to say. I heard some of your men talking. I don't think they saw me. One of them asked, 'All of them?' Another answered, 'All,' and a third asked, 'The mage as well? I don't like the thought of that.' What do you suppose they meant?"

"They could have meant anything."

"It felt foreboding."

"I'm beginning to worry you're paranoid, Yarrow. If you can point these men out, I'll question them tomorrow, if it will ease your mind."

"I could have done that myself, to far greater effect than you."

"You have a sharp tongue, lad."

He sighed and slumped back in the hay, his shoulder pressed against Duncan's. "I apologize," he said like he swallowed broken glass. "I don't think we should let on that I heard anything. I'll keep my ears open, continue to observe. I have—ways."

Duncan didn't know what to say. The idea that the mage suspected a conspiracy of some sort within his ranks offended him a bit. Perhaps it stemmed from the boy's years on the road by himself, always watching his back, with no one to trust or turn to. The knight couldn't imagine how Yarrow had endured, so young and so completely alone. Duncan felt a swell of pity, but he simply nodded and curled his fingers around Yarrow's collarbone. "If there's nothing else, we should be off to bed."

Yarrow leaned his head back, wrapped his cloak around himself, and sighed. His breath came out in a white plume. "I'd rather sleep right here," he said wistfully. "Perhaps I will. I feel so confined with those stone walls all around me. The servants don't care for me. Neither do your soldiers, or even the eyrle. Not that I give a fig," he hurried to add. "What about you?"

"What about me?"

"Do you find my presence so intolerable?" The young man looked expectant, his eyes wide as he scrutinized the knight.

Duncan chuckled. "Sometimes. But not just now." He felt the mage's eyes burning into his cheek. When he turned, their faces were close, the tips of their noses almost touching. Neither pulled away.

"I never got a chance to thank you," Yarrow said, his warm, wine-scented breath washing over Duncan's lips and chin, making Duncan shiver up his spine. "For pulling me out of that rockslide. You could have left me to die."

"I have a duty to protect you."

"Don't argue, Duncan." The mage's lips moved closer, a hair's width from Duncan's own. They grazed his mouth when Yarrow whispered, "Just accept my thanks. It's not something I offer easily."

The young man seemed ready to offer something quite easily. Duncan's cock bucked in his pants, even as he considered the myriad reasons why this would be wrong. When Yarrow's lips squashed against his, however, he eagerly returned the pressure. Their mouths opened slowly to each other, and the tips of their tongues met just beyond the edges of their teeth. They tested and explored, gingerly at first but with increasing desire. Yarrow's hand closed around a lock of Duncan's hair, drawing his face closer, his kisses growing desperate and needy. Duncan allowed it as he discovered the mage's soft, warm mouth.

A few days ago, he hadn't even liked Yarroway L'Estrella. He still wasn't sure he did, but as the young man submitted to the force of Duncan's tongue, letting the knight dominate their kiss, he couldn't deny an interest, at least. He cradled the back of the mage's slender neck and let his fingers snake into Yarrow's hair. It was chill and damp from the mist, the wet, white strands chunking together in Duncan's hand. Their teeth tapped together as Duncan drove his tongue toward the back of Yarrow's mouth, almost to his throat. The mage moved closer, his nubile body writhing beside the knight, waist arching up into Duncan.

Then Yarrow broke away and wiped his lips with the back of his hand. "I'm sorry."

Though Duncan felt cold in his absence, it was better this way. He had nothing to offer the young man beyond a discreet tumble, and would only wound him if Yarrow sought anything more. While Yarrow seemed practically as free with his body as an Emiri, he also seemed rather lonely. Duncan couldn't, didn't deserve to, be any kind of companion to him. He touched the mage's cheek and admired him a few moments before standing to leave. Yarrow said nothing as he snuggled down in the hay. The knight wouldn't know whether he chose to sleep there or not, but Yarrow turned on his side. Duncan thanked the goddesses. If Yarrow had asked him back, even reached out for him, he doubted he'd have found the strength to refuse.

Chapter Four

AFTER RIDING for a day and a half across the grain fields and grazing lands of the Peregrym estate, the company reached the outskirts of the Forest of Elwyd at the northeastern edge. The men marching beside Yarrow's horse grew agitated and spoke in whispers of the creatures said to dwell within. A few of the higher-ranking soldiers even questioned Duncan's decision to brave it. Yarrow knew they would either need to cross the woods or travel over a week to the bank of the Kanda, territory held by hostile forces. He agreed with the commander's judgment, and he personally feared nothing that might hide among the ancient trees. At the moment, other issues weighed on his mind.

I still don't understand what you were thinking, Yarrow's companion quipped. *The commander is a fine-looking man. If you weren't in the mood to enjoy him, why not let me borrow the body? It seems a waste to pass up pleasure when he was clearly willing.*

No, damn it, Yarrow mentally snapped, watching the back of Duncan's dull plate with frustration. *He doesn't deserve that. He's a good man, much too good for someone like me, and certainly too good for something like you. There can never be anything between us, so let it go.* Yarrow didn't acknowledge to the other the shame he felt at lowering his barriers for the knight, letting Duncan see past the illusion, even the shard he had exposed. Flushing, he recalled practically begging Duncan to like him. It couldn't happen again. The knight needed to be kept at a safe distance.

You're being a child, my beloved. Don't tell me you're being altruistic. Or do I find myself inhabiting the wrong body?

No. I'm just not interested. Contrary to what you believe, I don't strip and bend over for every man with a heartbeat.

Well, what about the prince, then? He was certainly a sight in those tight trousers! Filled them out quite nicely, wouldn't you agree?

He's my cousin, you disgusting creature!

Yet you considered it, Yarrow. I watched that warm little possibility bouncing around your mind while you spoke with him. Do you deny you found him pleasing?

I—no. It only makes me more suspicious of this situation. I never found Garith appealing before, never thought of him in that way in all the years I knew him. I shouldn't feel it now, not even in passing. There's something different about him, something wrong—

Only that the two of you are men now and not little boys!

You make me sick. We're blood relatives.

Ho ho! Has my Yarrow grown a moral code overnight? One that prevents you from enjoying a man even after it's been so long?

There are some deeds even I won't consider.

No matter how you might want to?

I do not *want to,* Yarrow told it, and himself, firmly. *The unfortunate fact is that I can never engage in any kind of intimacy with another. I'm not interested in anything beyond the bed sheets. Not again. Not after—it seems you'll be my only companion.*

An old married couple! The presence howled with sardonic delight before Yarrow pushed it down into its metaphorical box and latched it up tight.

They'd come a fair distance into the dusky wood, and now rode along a path so narrow and winding the carts and carriages barely fit through, and the men on horseback rode single file. Tall, willowy ribbonwoods swayed beside them. Their long, glossy seedpods spiraled down from their branches in plentiful, verdant ringlets like embellishments in a lady's hair. Some were longer than Yarrow was tall. Even mundane trees like arns and filbernuts grew as big around as a barn. The knotted, interlocking trunks of narxiums, with their disturbing, liver-colored leaves and poisonous black sap, appeared here and there. Razor-sharp bloodferns lined the trail and surrounded the trees. Now and then they passed a rounded, moss-encrusted stone: road signs left by an ancient race that had called the forest home.

They passed the day in the perpetual, gray-green gloom, nobody speaking much. The prince remained in his carriage, while Duncan led the party and Yarrow stayed near the back. Evening fell, and not even the mage relished the idea of camping in the forest. Duncan located a clearing free of the carnivorous ferns, but still covered in thorny bracken. The men hacked it down with knives and swords, making space for the tents. It took arduous hours to set up camp, and by the time they'd finished, darkness had fallen. Fires sprung alight as Yarrow stood on the outside of the tightly cramped site, absently stroking Syrai's neck.

Something is coming. The warning repeated over and over again inside his head, and he couldn't tell whether he or his companion voiced it. The men queued up for rations, but Yarrow didn't join them. He perched on a flat rock and sipped the last of Peregrym's good wine from his canteen.

After a while Duncan approached him, holding out a slab of salted meat on a metal plate. Yarrow waved it away.

"You should eat, Yarrow," the knight said, expressing so much genuine concern that Yarrow wanted nothing but to be near him again, to not be alone for a single night, or even a few hours.

Instead, he irritably curled his lip and said, "I dislike meat." He didn't add that ever since he'd bonded with the presence, even the finest victuals tasted of death and decay. Consuming flesh recalled the horrific visions he'd experienced in the cave. He noticed too little difference between the muscle of a beast and the sinew of a man.

Nodding, Duncan took a cloth parcel from the satchel on his hip. Yarrow unwrapped a soft, sweet roll and eagerly bit into it. He made an appreciative noise when he discovered the fig and raisin filling. "I don't need a nursemaid," he retorted.

The lack of gratitude did nothing to wipe the grin from Duncan's lips. "Weak with hunger, Tam Yarroway, you'll be a liability to me and this mission. I can't spare the men to carry you along if you faint."

"You dare imply—"

Duncan's laugh diffused Yarrow's anger. "Peace! I'm only joking. I took some extra sweets from the feast, and I thought you might enjoy one. Now, tell me what troubles you."

Yarrow wanted to say so many things to the knight; he wanted to tell him all the secrets he'd held inside for the past few years. He thought better of it and said only, "I have an ill feeling."

"The men share your intuition, and so do I. I've doubled the guard around the camp and tripled it around your cousin's tent. I actually came to request your aid. Are there any spells you can cast to keep us safe?"

Yarrow looked into the twisted woods. The shadows shifted and changed, morphing from one unsettling suggestion to another. "I can erect wards around the perimeter," he said.

"I'll come along and protect you while you cast."

"I don't require protection!"

"You're valuable to me and my objective, and therefore I shall protect you. Don't argue."

"Is that all?" Yarrow dared.

"Yes. There can be nothing more. I have an obligation."

"I see." Yarrow stalked around the edges of the camp, weaving an enchantment that would immobilize any enemy that crossed it, and alert the mage at the same time. Duncan followed with his sword drawn. When he finished his task, Yarrow returned to his rock and sat down, tired. He took the wineskin from his cloak and swore in Emiri when he found it empty.

"What are the dangers of this forest?" Duncan asked.

"The angry ghosts of those destroyed by our ancestors," Yarrow said. "Those who erected the stone markers we passed earlier. This ground reeks of ancient blood. Bandits, of course. Marlcats frequent this area. Harrow-wolves, said to paralyze men with their howls. Have you heard of sangorms?"

The knight shook his head and touched the hilt of his sword.

"Globule things that ooze out of crevices after dark. While boneless, they can approximate the shape of a man. They creep up on sleeping souls and drape over them like sheets. Then they slowly liquefy them for food. I've heard it's excruciating, being dissolved in that acidic slop. I understand sometimes, the bones of those unfortunate men can be seen suspended in the sangorm's murky jelly."

"Have *you* ever seen this?"

"I've seen many things," Yarrow replied. "I'm even told there may be a wyrm's lair in these woods, though no one has seen a wyrm in two centuries. Possibly the beast has slept for those long years."

Behind them, lights blinked out and tents went dark. Yarrow sat, hugging his knees and watching Duncan's silhouette. With his jaw tense and his shoulders squared, ready to fight, he hardly looked like a man who might crack jokes and hand out pastries. Yarrow wondered how many of his men saw the commander's lighter side. Was he a fool to think himself special?

"Where will you sleep?" the commander finally asked. "You haven't pitched a tent."

"I'll be fine."

"There's an extra cot in my tent," Duncan offered.

"I don't think that would be a good idea."

"As you say. Please try to rest, Yarrow. I plan to push hard for the edge of the woods tomorrow. I don't wish to pass another night here."

Yarrow only nodded and looked away from Duncan as he returned to camp. If he continued watching the commander's powerful but graceful movements any longer, he wouldn't stop himself from accepting that cot, and anything else offered within Duncan's tent.

YARROW AWOKE to pitch black and sat up from the saddlebag he'd used for a pillow. A nightmare about the snow-wraiths in the Lapir Mountains had plagued his rest. Only fire frightened them, and fire had never been a friend to Yarrow. He kicked his old blanket off and stood. In the silence, he heard the faintest shuffling sound. Not a single light burned within the camp. Only the tattered patches of moonlight penetrating the tangled branches illuminated anything. Yarrow winced at the slight sound his soft, old boots made when he leapt down from his rock. Slowly, stepping over thorns that caught and tore his cloak, he crept toward the tents. Someone screamed, and the sound ended with an abrupt gurgle. Yarrow cursed. He'd felt this coming, and should have remained vigilant instead of sleeping. What could have breached his wards? Certainly not marlcats or sangorms. Not bandits, either, unless they employed a skilled mage of their own. That seemed very unlikely, though not impossible. He prayed to the goddesses he'd been misinformed about the wyrm.

Yarrow made for the prince's tent, ducking behind a mushroom-covered stump when he detected movement. Three dark shapes, men or spirits remembering that form, darted past without noticing him. The mage kept his breathing shallow so the condensation in the cold air wouldn't give him away. He dashed from tent to tent, running crouched. Where were the three dozen soldiers paid to prevent something like this? He didn't see or hear a single soul.

Garith's sumptuous blue-and-white-striped tent, emblazoned with the royal arms, waited just ahead. Yarrow tripped over something as he sprinted for it and fell facedown in the briars. He pushed himself up on his hands and knees, over the still warm body of the prince's personal priest. The old man's plump face was frozen in the agony of his last minutes. A black stain bloomed over the chest of his ivory robes, around the ebony hilt of a dagger. The blood Yarrow slipped in steamed in the crisp midnight air. The man hadn't gone to the goddesses long ago.

Goddesses, Garith, he thought, compelled by panic. *Where is Duncan? Where are the men? What in the mother's name got past my wards?*

Another scream cut the silence. Abandoning stealth, Yarrow burst into his cousin's tent through the front flap. A lone figure stood at the center, surrounded by half a dozen bodies. The strong odor of blood and sundered organs assaulted him. Gagging, he lifted a hand wreathed in blue flame and prepared to strike. At the last minute, he recognized the prince's face. He released his spell and hugged his cousin, breathing, "Thank the sisters. What in their names happened here?"

"We must go," Garith said calmly. "We're under attack."

"By whom? Who could have gotten through?"

"You misunderstand, Yarroway. Come with me." Garith seized his hand and dragged Yarrow to the back of the tent, where the two of them slipped below the hem and into the night. The prince moved even more quietly and lightly than the mage, leading Yarrow toward the tree line. They'd almost made it when six men appeared to block their way. They wore mail suits beneath blue-and-white tunics bearing the royal livery.

"What?" Yarrow spat. "Treason?"

Before he could prepare a spell, Garith drove his fingers against the windpipe of the closest man. He brought both of his forearms down on the soldier's collarbones before the unlucky bastard even fell, and they snapped loudly, leaving the traitor's arms crippled. The prince finished him with a quick, clean break to the neck. Yarrow cast an aura around himself and Garith that would sap the strength of any who approached them. Then he dispatched one of the attackers with a bolt of blue energy that burned through the man's chest and out his back. Garith drew his sword just in time to parry a blow from a nasty, spiked flail: a thick metal pole with a vicious, spiked ball attached to the end by a chain. Metal scraped against metal as the two men struggled, and

Garith finally broke free. His next swipe sliced his assailant's stomach, and his innards fell steaming to the ground.

"Get rid of the mage," someone said, and the remaining three men encircled Yarrow. He traced a symbol in front of him, and the frosty ground bubbled up around the soldiers' ankles, holding them in place. Just in case, Yarrow flipped the latch on the box that held his companion, though he didn't open the lid yet. The presence reacted to the carnage with the delight of a child entering a surprise birthday celebration.

Garith cut the throat of an immobilized soldier. The man's head, half-severed, flopped to his chest. A sheet of blood darkened his tunic before he dropped. Yarrow, reaching the end of his endurance, sent a jet of raw energy, destructive magic without direction, at the last two traitors. The crude spell reduced them to ash, but it left its caster weak and wobbly. Yarrow pitched forward and fell to his knees.

Garith wrenched him up by his underarms. "There are more," the prince whispered.

Yarrow nodded and fought through his vertigo. The two men sped into the woods, the ferns slicing their ankles and calves, feeding greedily on the blood dripping down, and low-hanging branches swatted their faces. They reached a small clearing and stopped to catch their breath, Yarrow clutching at the stab in his sides. Before they could manage it, men poured from the shadows, surrounding them on every side. Garith pressed his back against Yarrow's and held one hand out in front of him. His sword waited next to his thigh, still dripping blood. Yarrow tried to concentrate. He'd need a big spell to even slow down the twenty or so soldiers, and it would take time. He considered a blizzard, or a whirling vortex to knock the attackers back, but, sensing the ancient bones beneath his feet, he opted to raise the long dead as allies. It was a dark, complex undertaking he couldn't manage alone. Imbuing old corpses with life and simple intent required vast amounts of energy. Binding them to the caster's will, so they could be commanded, took still more. Yarrow released his companion and felt it throbbing with bloodlust. It tugged hard against Yarrow's control, like a frisky spring colt on the end of a rope. Even the creature would require time for such a grandiose feat. Hopefully Garith could buy them a few moments.

The prince made a valiant effort, his hands moving impossibly quickly in graceful spirals, cutting any man within three feet of him.

Blood splattered him, painting his face and dark clothing. Sheer numbers overwhelmed him before long. An arrow penetrated Yarrow's thigh, breaking his focus. The bones that had begun to hum and stir below him fell still.

Let me have control, beloved! I'll crush these insects!

Not ready to relent just yet, Yarrow kicked a rushing attacker in the stomach and crumpled him. He redoubled his efforts to summon aid. The corpses in the dirt moaned in offense and tried to resist his spell. Yarrow couldn't bend them to his purpose and had to surrender more of his consciousness to the other. The creature laughed with triumph and the delicious experience of raw, firsthand sensation. The world began to look as flat and lifeless as a picture in a book for Yarrow, but he felt the magic strengthening. Bleached bones sprung up like a fence to shield them from their assailants. A big soldier with an axe shattered through most of them. His jagged blade swung for Yarrow's shoulder, and the mage barely managed to drop to the ground and roll clear of it. The axe embedded in the earth, but the burly man quickly dislodged it and raised it over Yarrow's curled body. Before he could deliver the blow, a blade sprouted from his chest and he fell.

Yarrow pushed the heavy, twitching body off him as the other turncoats closed in. There were still so many. The mage's wounded leg throbbed and threatened to buckle. More skeletons rose up behind them and shambled out of the woods. The sight of the walking dead didn't erode the men's morale as Yarrow had hoped it might. Some of the soldiers turned to efficiently dispatch the corpses while the rest continued their attack on the mage and prince. Several of them fell to the quick, powerful man who'd joined the fray.

"Prince Garith?" Duncan called. "Your Highness?" The knight's massive blade carved a man in half as he rushed toward the prince. He hadn't spared the time to dress, and charged bare-chested toward his companions.

Yarrow, though, felt spent. He couldn't even manage a simple burst of energy to knock his attackers back. They surrounded him as Duncan cut a swath to Garith.

Beloved, you must let me.

I—yes. The others must not know. You must restrain yourself. Defend us, and nothing more.

The time for bargaining is done. A flail hit the ground an inch from Yarrow's temple, stirring up a confetti of leaf litter and frozen mud. *You must live, so I can feel.*

A boot heel struck Yarrow's face, and he tasted blood. He kicked a soldier in the groin and made the man double over, but he knew he had no chance on his own. None of them did. Garith and Duncan would die unless—

Do it!

Yarrow relinquished his perceptions and control. The presence took the reins, and Yarrow sank into sweet, soft darkness like a velvet blanket.

HE HAD no idea how much time had passed when he awoke. His jaw hurt, and his tongue swelled inside his mouth. Something hard but consoling cradled his head. *Garith's thighs*, he realized, comforted but agitated by the comfort. He didn't have the strength to protest; the entity's control always sapped him physically. At the edges of his mind, it felt sated, glutted, swollen with sensation and as lazy as a fat nobleman rubbing his gut after a feast.

Garith smoothed Yarrow's hair away from his swollen eyes and sweaty brow. Yarrow forced the tension out of his neck and shoulders and let his body accept the soothing touch. He let his cheeks rest a few moments against those lean, velvet-swathed legs before he willed himself to stir.

"Are we safe?" he croaked. "Duncan?"

"I'm here, Yarrow."

"What?" he rasped. "What happened?"

"We know only that we were betrayed," Garith said. "If not for your magic, fatally so."

"Well done," Duncan agreed.

As Yarrow's eyes focused, he recognized the forest. Watery, white light filtered through the leaves in blurry patches of lemon and green. The brightness stung, but reassured him with its burning clarity. It existed outside his mind, part of the physical world. Garith cupped his chin as Yarrow choked out, "Why? How?"

"It's complex," Garith said, his reserve amazing to the mage after all that had happened.

"Enlighten me," Yarrow said.

"Tam…," Duncan began.

"No. No candied filling, Tam Knight. Tell me what you know."

"Goddesses, Yarroway, your sorcery saved us. I have never witnessed such power. You tore those men apart like paper dolls. The pieces were everywhere! In all my years on the battlefield, I've never seen such a bloodbath. "

"But the traitors! How could they have deceived us? Duncan, how did you not know your own men plotted against you?"

Garith spoke. "My friend, I fear everything you were told about this mission has been a lie. I am not even your cousin, as you've already deduced."

Yarrow leapt out of his lap and backed away from the other two men. Both were covered in blood and marred by small wounds, but otherwise whole. Duncan looked nauseous and angry while Garith, or whoever he was, regarded the mage coolly with his unreadable, black eyes. The prince's lovely face resembled his cousin's, but now Yarrow noticed all the ways it differed: the fullness of his mouth, the arch of his brows, his higher cheekbones and slightly stronger chin. He lacked the small bump on the bridge of his nose, and his eyes slanted subtly.

"You knew in an instant. I saw it on your face," the dark man said. "It was my own fault, I suppose. I was only ever intended to pass as Prince Garith from a distance, which I can do quite adequately. I was told not to speak directly to anyone, and least of all you."

"Told by whom?" Yarrow asked. It all felt so surreal, like an elaborate prank.

"By the king and his advisor. Agarick's plan was for me to pose as the prince and travel with this well-known procession while the real Garith, along with a small band, went to Gaeltheon in secret, disguised as simple merchants. That way, anyone planning to attack the prince or prevent his marriage would come after us. After me. My purpose was to draw the threat away from your cousin."

"Why would you put yourself in that much danger?" Yarrow asked.

"I was paid to do so."

"Duncan, did you know?" Yarrow asked, almost too perplexed to feel betrayed, but not quite.

From the knight's face, Yarrow saw Duncan felt the same way. He hadn't been told, either; Agarick fooled them both. Yarrow supposed he understood his uncle's mistrust of him, but to doubt Duncan, his own vassal?

"Why weren't we told?" Yarrow hissed, balling his fist around the filthy, blood-soaked edges of his cloak.

"No one was to know."

"Wait, who are you really, then?" Duncan joined the conversation. Yarrow noticed his hand moving to his blade. He also observed the other man's quick fingers darting into his trouser pocket. The knight and the stranger stared at one another without blinking.

With a sigh, the dark young man stood and dropped his pants. His small, black undergarment did nothing to hide what it held. Ignoring the others' shocked looks, the man held his genitals out of the way and showed them his inner thigh.

Duncan strangled a scream and hissed, "The red crescent!"

Yarrow was familiar with the Emiri technique of injecting ink into the skin, rendering it permanent. The coin-sized marking on this man, though, wasn't an Emiri design meant to enhance the lines of the body. It was a scarlet outline of a sickle, from which a single droplet fell. Yarrow had never seen such pigment, the brilliant red of fresh blood. It was also the most feared symbol on the continent, even though most didn't believe the Order of the Crimson Scythe actually existed. Yarrow had wondered himself if these idealized, unstoppable killers really stalked the shadows of Selindria and beyond. He'd heard rumors of them during his travels, but the lack of evidence led him to chalk them up to stories meant to inspire terror. He still wasn't sure. Anyone could pay an artisan to inscribe the mark on his skin. The red crescent might have been taboo to Selindrians, but an Emiri painter would gladly take gold for any job. It didn't mean an ancient order really existed.

Duncan scuttled back, paling beneath his tan. Perhaps he held to the superstition that even laying eyes on that symbol meant certain death. It surprised Yarrow to see such a reaction from the seasoned soldier. He considered his words carefully before saying, "You mean for us to believe the Order of the Crimson Scythe is real?"

"It's very real," the man said without a chip in his chilly reserve.

"How many are you?"

The dark man's smile didn't reach his eyes as he pulled up his pants. "Even if I knew, Tam Mage, I wouldn't be allowed to tell you."

"I don't understand," Yarrow persisted. "How did Agarick contact one of you? Why would he want an assassin posing as his son?"

"The king did not contact me directly. The head of my cell selected me for this mission, probably largely based on my youth and looks."

"Looks over skill?" Yarrow wondered.

This question elicited a soft chuckle from the other man. "The only unskilled agents of my order are the dead ones. Think about it, Tam Yarroway. Who better to detect and deter an assassination attempt than an assassin?"

"A fair point."

"I refuse to believe His Majesty would stoop to dealing with… with an organization such as that," Duncan spat. "I find it more likely this massacre was orchestrated by you and your vile associates." He looked at the assassin with disgust, like he'd never witnessed anything more monstrous than the striking young man.

"Feel free to ask your king when you see him again," the assassin said nonchalantly.

"In the meantime, I should take you into custody." The knight drew his sword, but the other man didn't even acknowledge it.

"You're welcome to try," he said in a silky drawl.

Yarrow got to his feet, expecting soreness and glad to notice very little. Even the arrow wound in his leg had healed over, though a rip remained in his trousers. "Stop this. We have larger problems right now. Duncan, do you realize how vast a conspiracy it would take to pull this off? How long would it take for all those men to insinuate themselves into your ranks? Years? Who chose them for this mission? How high up does it go, and who could be behind it? And why?"

"Plenty of the smaller nations wedged between Gaeltheon and Selindria would oppose the unification," Duncan said. "They'll have no chance against such an empire. It's possible they've even banded together to stop it. Maybe the Emiri are to blame."

Yarrow waved the idea away. "The Emiri are too indolent and unorganized to plan something like this. What if Gaeltheon got cold feet?"

"Speculation will get us nowhere," the assassin said. "I am not killed, which says to the traitors that Prince Garith still lives. As you observed, Yarroway, we have no idea how many more people are involved. The conspirators could send others to finish the job. We shouldn't linger here."

"Agreed," Yarrow said.

"Wait," Duncan sputtered. "You aren't suggesting that we travel with, with a… with one of you?"

The assassin shrugged, his black eyes twinkling but his face expressionless.

"He can be of use to us," Yarrow argued. "He fought those traitors beside us!"

"I don't relish the idea of a dagger in my back while I sleep," the knight said.

"You need not worry, Tam Knight," the other man said. "I don't do such things free of charge."

Duncan looked like he might lunge at the assassin, and Yarrow hurried to step between them. "Duncan," he pleaded, "if there's another group that size looking for us, I for one will take any ally I can find. Agarick trusted him, and I think we should too."

"Agarick trusted him to die instead of the prince," Duncan countered. "A mission he failed to complete. We should go back to the king and expose this atrocity."

"We'd only let the conspirators know they had the wrong prince," Yarrow said. "Maybe we should lay low until Garith makes it to Gaeltheon. I don't know. We need to get out of this forest by nightfall, though. You said so yourself. Please, see reason."

"I don't like it, and I hope I won't regret it."

"Thank you," Yarrow said. "I wonder if we'll be safe to go back to the camp and salvage what we can."

"I'll see to it," the assassin said. "If the enemy left any kind of trap behind, I'll find it and disable it. Stay behind me, and you'll be fine."

Yarrow trusted the exotic man's promises, and if Duncan didn't, he followed along anyway.

Chapter
Five

EVEN THOUGH he'd witnessed the battle, the carnage littering the camp still stunned the assassin. He'd been trained by and surrounded with the most efficient killers in the world for as long as he could remember, and still the mage had impressed him. A dozen or so bodies scattered the ground, torn to shreds, limbs and organs flung everywhere. Chunks of meat lay in the streams and pools of blood, and strips of gore even hung from the tree branches. The assassin felt grateful for the cold of the day; he couldn't imagine the stench had it been summer. He did a quick sweep of the site and found it safe, so he motioned for the other two men. Curiously, the mage looked around at the massacre as if he hadn't caused it a few hours before. He went almost as white as his hair before doubling over to vomit. He'd seemed delighted as he'd slain the traitors. The assassin remembered his ringing laughter. Now he sobbed and retched as the knight rubbed his back. It made little sense.

Picking his way around the corpses, if the piles of meat even fitted that description, the assassin made his way to the royal carriage, which lay on its side. He opened the door, dropped lightly inside, and opened the secret compartment in the floor. He quickly collected his various daggers, vials of poisons and antidotes, lengths of sharp wire, powders, scrolls, and the change of clothes he'd kept for just such a situation. He wriggled his arms to the elbows in the black leather gloves with the razor-like spikes over the knuckles and hidden blades below each wrist. He'd change into the rest of his gear as soon as they escaped this cursed forest.

He hoisted himself out of the carriage and went in search of his companions. He'd do his best to protect them until he reached the rest of his order, but not a second longer. If they expected more, they were fools.

The knight stood ready in his breastplate, a small, salvaged tent tucked under his arm and a burlap sack, probably full of provisions, clutched in his opposite hand. Duncan was the kind of iron-fisted authority figure the assassin resented, a judgmental bastard with a sense of moral superiority. Still, the assassin didn't mind a warrior of Duncan's caliber at his back, nor did he object to the treat for his eyes. He raised his hand and approximated a warm smile, because he knew it would annoy the commander. "Where is the mage?" he called.

Glaring, Duncan flicked his chin toward a flat rock where Yarrow sat cross-legged, holding the charred remains of an old blue blanket. This mage intrigued the assassin, and not only because of his arcane prowess. He watched as Yarrow fought to hide his sorrow at the loss of his possessions and put on a blank expression, just as he and the other assassins were taught to do. The assassin nodded with respect. A few moments later, Yarrow leapt from the shelf of stone.

"It looks as though most of my things have been destroyed," he said with a false grin. "Less to carry, I suppose."

"Two of the tents, at least, are in fair condition," Duncan said. "I also managed to acquire some food."

"We should be on our way as quickly as possible," the assassin advised. "They may be expecting us to return here."

"I can't see the last of this place too soon," Yarrow agreed.

The three of them had turned to leave when a racket from the brush made them spin back around. The assassin pulled his dagger with the ruby hilt and beveled, serpentine blade while the knight readied his sword. The magical energy swirling around Yarrow was palpable. All of them tensed, waiting.

The thick bushes parted, and a skittish gray filly emerged. She nickered softly as she trotted toward Yarrow and rubbed her head against his chest. The mage chuckled as he stroked her mane and rubbed her ears to soothe her. "This is great!" he said, beaming. "Syrai can carry our supplies, and we can take turns riding on her back if we grow tired." Yarrow rested his forehead against the mare's flat face, closing his eyes and smiling as he whispered to her in Emiri.

"Where will we go?" Duncan asked.

"If I might make a suggestion," the assassin said, "I propose we continue northeast to the town of Galene. My order maintains safe houses in many locations, and we can find sanctuary there. We might also find information, and possibly assistance. The Crimson Scythe will not look kindly upon being betrayed. My brothers and sisters will make valuable allies."

"That seems solid," Yarrow said, impressing the assassin with his practicality.

"It seems preposterous!" Duncan said, predictably. "Walk willingly into a den of thugs and killers?"

"You will be in no danger."

"How can you even suggest Yarrow and I associate with such filth?" Duncan persisted.

"There's no need to insult the man," Yarrow said. "He's trying to help us."

"I'm insulted he even implies we might sink to his depth," Duncan said. "He knows what he is, and if it offends him that I say it aloud, then I dare him to do something about it."

"Very well," the assassin said, thinking maybe the handsome knight protested too much. "I suppose we'll part ways, then."

"This is foolish," Yarrow said, catching the assassin's arm as he turned to leave. "All of us are in grave danger. We may not even know how grave. We should stay together, fight together."

"We can't trust him, Yarrow!"

"Why, Duncan? Has he given us a reason not to?"

"He's immoral, a sinner!"

"I'm going with him," Yarrow said. "I ask you, Duncan, nay, I *beg* you to come with us. You'll only perish alone, and that would be a bit of a shame."

The assassin watched the knight's resolve weaken beneath the pretty mage's gaze. He wondered if the two of them were lovers. Duncan seemed twisted around Yarrow's little finger. It took a mere moment for the knight to curl his shoulders in resignation and nod.

THANKS TO the fortuitous appearance of the horse, the small band made the edge of the forest by sundown, and the outskirts of Galene a few hours later. The assassin traded the one gold ring he hadn't lost during the battle to stable Syrai in a well-kept barn. Though late, people still filled the streets of the small trading town. The three men made their way cautiously through the slums skirting the more affluent city center with its inns, shops, and merchant booths hawking goods from all across Selindria. Exotic items from as far away as eastern Gaeltheon fetched high prices, and Yarrow saw a small booth offering "authentic" (according to the shingle) magical trinkets from Espero. He rolled his eyes and hurried to fall in step next to the assassin.

"How will you find it?" he asked, excited by the prospect of witnessing this forbidden place. "Have you been here before?"

"I haven't, but there will be signs. Look there." He nodded toward a rickety stall selling archery supplies. A sloppily painted picture of a drawn bow punctuated the craftsman's name. It resembled a crescent, and the point of the arrow indicated a side street. The drip of red paint looked completely accidental. They followed the subtle directions past a line of carts vending fragrant food of all kinds.

"Duncan and I will be welcome?" the mage continued.

"As my guests. Of course, you won't be allowed to see *everything.*"

"You're teasing me on purpose," Yarrow said with a dramatic jut of his lower lip.

The assassin looked over at him, a little mystified. "Tam Yarroway, your companion seems quite appalled by the nature of my work. You seem to have no problem with what I do. Am I wrong?"

"I have less right to judge you than you know, Tam…. What's your real name?"

The assassin chuckled and said, "We don't have permanent names. My name is whatever the mission dictates. It's fluid. I suppose my current name is still Garith, if you need something to call me by."

"I'd rather call you by something else," Yarrow said.

"Why is that, my friend?" The dark man turned and graced Yarrow with the most lascivious smile he'd ever seen. The mage moistened his lips with his tongue and rubbed them together as he stared intently at the sensual curve of the other man's mouth. How had he ever mistaken those lips for his cousin's? The two of them stared at each other, Yarrow no longer aware of the merchants and patrons bustling past.

Something rammed into Yarrow's shoulder hard, and it took him a minute to realize it was Duncan. "Pardon me, Tam Yarroway," the knight said. "I was under the impression we were going somewhere and not just standing in the street."

Yarrow felt a twinge at forgetting Duncan's presence. He'd clearly injured the commander's feelings.

Their nameless companion only continued grinning. "Would either of you like something to eat?"

"I'm sure we're all hungry," Duncan said. He'd managed to salvage little more than hard bread. "Unfortunately, while our attackers were kind enough to leave some of our gear, their compassion ended short of leaving our gold. Tam Yarroway probably blew it halfway to heaven when he dispatched them."

"Why am I Tam Yarroway again all the sudden?"

Before Duncan could answer, the assassin seized his wrist and dropped half a dozen full coin purses in the knight's palm. At first Yarrow worried Duncan might hit the other man, but his fingers closed around the money. "This is really a lot. We haven't even been in town an hour," he said, rather respectfully, it seemed to Yarrow.

Then Duncan cleared his throat and added, "We can't possibly spend these coins. You should return them to their rightful owners." He looked longingly at some birds rotating on a spit. "Although perhaps we could use just enough for a meal. We can donate the rest to a temple."

"That's the spirit," Yarrow agreed, noticing some fancy pastries on a shelf. One spiral roll smelled of cinnamon and dribbled white glaze. Beside it sat a pile of cookies with pink icing.

They spent more than a little of the pilfered coin on food. Yarrow sucked sticky, sweet icing from his fingers as he walked between the knight and the assassin. Though he hadn't encouraged them on purpose, he smiled when he saw them watching him eat. The assassin carefully followed the tiny, subtle markings toward his order's lair. Soon the trio found themselves in a dark alley reeking of garbage, cheap ale, and human waste. Whores groped and propositioned the two attractive men. The assassin ignored them, and Duncan shrugged them off. Yarrow put up his hood, glad of the center position.

Before long the din of taverns died, and the streets emptied out. The houses around them were nothing special, small, shoddy, and tightly packed, but mostly tidy and certainly not the abandoned, cobweb-covered manses Yarrow had envisioned. The assassin stopped and ran his gloved hand over the trunk of an arn tree. Carved there, but looking completely organic, just another whorl in the bark, was a vague suggestion of a scythe. A tiny stone cottage with a straw roof stood just beyond. A solitary candle sputtered in the window. His heart fluttering with excitement, Yarrow followed the assassin to the unassuming wooden door and into the single, dark room.

No one would have suspected this place to be anything other than a simple home, maybe belonging to an artisan or trader. There was a hearth, a table, some dishes on a shelf, and a narrow bed in the corner. A pair of old boots waited by the door, and a couple of cabbages sat on a counter.

Disappointed, beloved?

Where have you been?

Just watching. Waiting. You've realized by now that he's not your cousin. What will you do about that?

Nothing.

You're joking!

I'm not. I'd only hurt him, and I don't want to do that.

He might like it.

Enough. Not even an assassin could abide me, not if he knew the truth. I can't bear for him to be disgusted with me. He'll think I'm a monster.

A dull scraping sound drew Yarrow's attention from his companion. The assassin carefully opened a panel, so well hidden that Yarrow hadn't even noticed a seam. Beyond it, a stair wound down into a soft, red glow. Yarrow hurried toward it. He passed Duncan, but the knight stood frozen with his fists balled. The mage stopped and tentatively touched Duncan's arm at the inside of his elbow, at the gap in his armor. He squeezed the flesh beneath the coarse shirt. "Are you all right?"

"I never imagined I'd set foot in a place like this."

"We never imagined any of this would happen," Yarrow said. "We have no choice but to trust him."

"I can't."

"Then trust me."

Duncan's face softened and he nodded once, touching the apple of Yarrow's cheek with his thumb. "I will," he whispered.

"Follow me please," the assassin said crisply.

At the foot of the stairs, they emerged into a large, circular room supported by stone columns. Candles inside red glass orbs provided the crimson light. Some hung from the vaulted ceiling on chains, while others sat on dark, ornately carved stands. Matching benches with scarlet cushions sat against the walls. Several large paintings of naked or barely clothed men in various erotic poses, often involving suggestively held swords and daggers, adorned the dark paneling. Both Yarrow and Duncan moved to get a closer look at them. The room seemed more a gallery of male beauty, or a specific kind of brothel, than a hideout for criminals. Yarrow felt the assassin come up behind him, though his feet made no noise against the polished stone floor.

"You're wondering if the order values beauty," the assassin guessed. "The answer is yes. It's much easier for attractive people to earn the trust of others. It's easier for them to manipulate people. Beauty opens many doors. But I'm sure you know that firsthand, Yarrow."

The mage gasped at the compliment. Duncan ground his teeth audibly. "So you mean to tell me everyone in the order is as beautiful as—" Yarrow bit back the word when he saw the stricken look on Duncan's face. "As beautiful as the men in these paintings, or that statue?"

The life-sized sculpture of a gorgeous young man, just at the cusp of adolescence, dominated the center of the room. Dozens of red candles surrounded the mountain of skulls on which he stood. Yarrow approached the nude figure. He'd never seen such artistry; this carving looked alive. The twist of his waist was sublime. Yarrow almost felt awareness behind his heavy-lidded eyes. He wore a tattered cloak that covered only his shoulders and the lower half of his face, where it draped over the arm he held horizontally in front of his mouth. His other arm, hanging languidly at his side, culminated in a particularly nasty, jagged long sword.

The assassin knelt down, pushed up his shirtsleeve, drew his dagger and slid the blade across his tricep at the top of his glove. Blood splattered the toes of the beautiful, marble boy. Yarrow noticed rusty stains covering his feet and the carved skulls on which he stood. He also noticed a series of scars near the fresh cut the assassin had made.

"Disgusting," Duncan muttered. "What are you doing?"

Standing and sheathing his knife, the assassin asked, "What do you find so distasteful, Tam Knight? Certainly not the sight of blood? You've seen plenty of death, I'm sure. You spill blood for your king, and I spill it for Thalil." He bowed to the statue. "I don't understand the difference."

Yarrow saw a hundred arguments struggling for dominance behind Duncan's clenched jaw. "What is Thalil?"

"He Who Stands Out of Sight," Yarrow answered, earning a nod of appreciation from the assassin. "The One You See at the Last. The Whisper You Hear Too Late. The Invisible Blade. I could go on. Thalil is one of the Cast-Down, those children disowned by the goddesses. He's a particularly powerful god. The temples of the sisters don't allow his name to be spoken. His worship is punishable by death."

The assassin laughed at that last bit. "Thalil is the patron of my order. Every life we take is dedicated to him."

"You kill people for money," Duncan said. "Don't try to pretend like it's some spiritual mission."

"Why can't it be both?" the assassin wondered.

"It just can't."

Thalil is a vain, self-important little monster, Yarrow's companion said. *Even worse than you, beloved.*

Yarrow ignored it as he followed the assassin beneath an arch and into a shadowy hallway. "Is anyone else here?" he asked his guide.

"It doesn't seem like it," the assassin answered. "Though there are many levels below this one. I can check, if you'd like. You'll have to remain here, though."

"I'm just, just curious about all of this," Yarrow said.

"Intrigued" or "fascinated" might be more appropriate.

"That's all right," the assassin said, turning and showing Yarrow that smile that made the mage's flesh feel like a boiling puddle. "I'm sure this all seems very strange, but I promise you'll be safe here for a night."

"I believe you," Yarrow said. "Duncan believes me."

"Good." The assassin opened a door and lit a candle within the small cubicle. A comfortable bed huddled close to the wall with a chest at its foot. There was room for little else. Duncan entered as if it were a prison cell and scowled at the lewd engraving hanging on the wall. He sat on the edge of the bed and rested his elbows on his knees, not looking at the other two men as they returned to the hall and shut the door. Yarrow stared for a few seconds, remembering the night behind the haystack, before following his host to another chamber.

This room held a much larger, posted bed draped in red velvet. Gold cords held the heavy curtains open, and a dozen cushions of various sizes and shapes practically covered the mattress. A wrought-iron rack cradled several dusty bottles of wine. Upholstered chairs surrounded an elaborately carved table, and fruit sat in a glass bowl on the top. Water waited nearby. An evocative, nude painting of a reclining Thalil holding a skull covered much of the wall. Yarrow stood at the threshold while the assassin lit what seemed like half a hundred candles.

"Is this your room?" the mage asked.

"My room? I hoped we might share it."

"Share?" Yarrow repeated, the sparse hair over his body standing on end and a tremor moving up his spine.

The assassin set down his tinderbox and crossed the room. He peeled the leather gloves slowly from his arms and hands and tossed them on a chair. He took Yarrow's hands and caressed them with his bare thumbs as he moved his face close to the corner of the mage's mouth. "Have I misinterpreted our mutual desire?" He ran the tip of his tongue from the point of Yarrow's chin all the way to his white eyebrow.

Yarrow trembled inside his dark clothing and leather armor, and his eyes fluttered shut. He closed his hands around the assassin's neck, and he pushed the other man back a few inches as he opened his eyes to regard him. The two of them stood panting and flushed, staring hard into each other's faces. Their mouths crashed into one another, teeth scraping as their tongues met forcefully. The assassin released Yarrow's fingers. One of his hands kneaded the mage's ass cheek while his other arm snaked around Yarrow's waist, pulling Yarrow flush against his body. Heat poured from him, like a shard of metal left in the summer sun. Yarrow's fingers wriggled beneath his curtain of shiny, black hair. He let the assassin take control of their kiss, allowing his tongue to pin Yarrow's within his mouth. The mage let his head relax back, and the assassin lifted a hand to catch it. He tugged at Yarrow's hair, inclining his face perpendicular to the rafters, as he broke away from Yarrow's eager mouth to lick and suckle the mage's neck.

Gooseflesh rose over Yarrow's skin as the assassin's lips and tongue traversed his flesh from collarbone to jaw. He panted with delight and ground his erection against the other man's equally swollen cock. His hands skipped down the assassin's back before delving beneath the waistband of his snug trousers. Yarrow clasped the smooth, taut crescents of the other's ass and dug his nails in. Goddesses, the man was delightfully lean and sculpted. His muscle flexed as he shifted, and Yarrow grabbed it harder. The assassin responded with a gasp and a bite to Yarrow's neck, just below the earlobe. The jolt of pain dragged a surprised cry from the mage's throat. Yarrow raked his fingernails up the other man's back, just refraining from breaking skin. He moved them over the assassin's shoulders, across his chest, and down to his rigid little nipples. The pinch he gave them elicited a growl of pleasure from the other man.

Yarrow pulled away, pushing his partner off with a forearm across his chest. He backed against the wall and pulled his cloak around him, hiding his interest and arousal behind its black curtain.

"Something wrong?"

"You don't want to do this with me," Yarrow said, staring at the octagonal stones on the floor, painted with candlelight and shadow. "I'm—not a good man."

"Do you imagine I am?"

"Better than me."

"I doubt it, Yarrow. Besides, what does it matter? You've looked longingly at me from the first moment you saw me. And I admit, I was so enthralled by you that I broke the rules and allowed you into my room at Peregrym Estate. I should have made you leave right away, but I couldn't resist an opportunity to be close to you, to speak with you, touch your hair and look into your eyes up close. I've wanted more ever since that night. If you haven't felt the same, I apologize for my presumption."

"No need. It's true I found you irresistible. But I thought you were my cousin."

"No, you didn't."

"No, I guess not." Yarrow wanted desperately to reach out for the other man, but he stayed his hand. "I don't know if we should be together like this, though."

"Why not?"

"I'm—dangerous."

The assassin chuckled as he took Yarrow's wrists and led him to the center of the brightly lit room. He never broke eye contact with the mage as he picked apart the leather straps of Yarrow's armor. "I know, and I feel all the more drawn to you. The old cliché of the moth and the flame. Besides, I can take care of myself rather well. I'm not a child and neither are you. We're men who know the ways of the world. Men who care little for rules imposed by others. Don't worry; I have no designs on your independence, Yarrow. I'm just proposing we enjoy each other's company. Life is short, is it not? Especially the lives of men such as you and me."

Your life might be exceptionally long, in fact, beloved.

Don't pester me or I won't even let you watch. The intrusion of the presence doused Yarrow's lust a little. Despite everything he'd said, Yarrow doubted the assassin would still want to pursue their tryst if he knew of the uninvited third. Guilt welled inside Yarrow at the deception.

The other man combed his fingers through Yarrow's hair as he pushed Yarrow's pauldrons from his shoulders with his other hand. They fell behind him with a dull thud, and the assassin untied Yarrow's shirt and patiently unlaced the cord. He turned his attention to Yarrow's flesh as he revealed it an inch at a time. He'd reached the mage's belly button when he looked up at Yarrow through his magnificent, black lashes. When he traced his pinky up the trail of white hair between Yarrow's stomach muscles, Yarrow's erection throbbed and leaked, his moisture coating his cockhead. It escaped him how his partner remained so reserved. Even when he gripped the mage's shaft, he merely smiled slowly. "Should I stop, or would you like more?"

"Some pleasure and nothing else?" Yarrow asked, moving close to the assassin again. "No strings later?"

"I wouldn't dream of it," the other man said, grasping Yarrow by the neck, spinning him around and slamming his back against the wall. Their mouths collided again, teeth knocking together as they devoured each other's lips and tongues. Yarrow's lips swelled, and he gasped for breath in the few seconds they spared for air. The assassin's detached demeanor melted away as his skin heated beneath Yarrow's palms. He yanked Yarrow's head back again to nibble along the mage's jaw and nip his earlobe. Yarrow whimpered and the other man chuckled. He stepped back and tore Yarrow's gray shirt from his shoulders, yanking it down until Yarrow's tightly buckled bracers stopped him. It billowed behind him, hanging from his wrists and restricting his range of motion when he reached for his partner's hips.

With another mischievous laugh, the assassin grabbed Yarrow's arms and pinned them to the wall beside his hips. He kissed across Yarrow's chest, circling each nipple with his tongue before pinching it between his teeth. Trapped between his partner and the wall, Yarrow twined his torso in frustration and halfheartedly struggled to free his hands. He just wanted to get them back on the other man's golden skin and the hard, taut cords of sinew beneath. The wet cloth of his trousers clung to his penis. Something occurred to him and he said, "Wait."

The assassin took a step back, allowing an inch of space between his dark shirt and Yarrow's heaving chest. He cupped Yarrow's balls, squeezing and releasing them rhythmically as he asked, "What's wrong now?"

"I want to know your name."

"What does it matter?" The other man's hand moved up to grasp the mage's erection. He leaned in to kiss Yarrow again, but Yarrow seized his shoulder with his free hand and wrenched him off.

"I want to know."

"I don't remember it anymore." With the slightest frown, the assassin looked back at the door.

Yarrow caught his chin and made the assassin face him. His eyes had changed from the fathomless, black mirrors to human eyes unable to mask emotion. Yarrow saw pain behind them, and he stroked the side of the other man's face, kissing softly across his brows. The mage knew only too well how unsettling it felt, finding a breach in one's defenses. Burying his nose in the assassin's silky locks, Yarrow whispered, "Please."

"This isn't—no. We agreed to have some fun, nothing more. I never offered to share my life story with you." He tried to pull away, but Yarrow grabbed his collar and held him.

"I just want to know your name. I didn't think it would upset you. Have I ruined everything?"

His face softened then, and the assassin ceased struggling against Yarrow. "No. Have I?"

Shaking his head, Yarrow said, "I've thought about you often since that night in your room. I want this. You."

"So do I. Yarrow, it's Sasha."

Yarrow grinned and pulled the assassin—Sasha—back into his arms, and they kissed with renewed passion. In no time they forgot the awkward moment. Sasha's lips moved down Yarrow's neck until he reached the Emiri paint below his collarbone. First he traced the intricate loops and flourishes with his fingers and then with his mouth. His tongue and the moist trail it left felt cool on Yarrow's burning flesh. Yarrow buried his hands in Sasha's abundant hair and held it tightly as the other man knelt down. Sasha lavished attention on Yarrow's slim torso, exploring prominent bones and swells of muscle with his fingers and lips. "You're beautiful," he said, his breath washing over Yarrow's flat belly. "I knew you would be."

Sasha untied Yarrow's drawstring and pushed his baggy trousers to his ankles. The mage stepped out of them and toed off his worn boots and wool socks. His erection stood straight out, dark and shining with fluids. The other man licked his lips at the sight of it.

"Very beautiful. More than I expected."

"Are you going to undress?" Yarrow asked, eager to take in Sasha's nude form. "I've had a taste of your body, and I'd like to see the rest."

"I might be persuaded," he teased.

"Do tell."

"Show me something nice while I get out of these clothes. Give me a little incentive." His sparkling onyx eyes darted back to Yarrow's swollen cock.

The mage chuckled as he understood the assassin's request. Yarrow was happy to comply. He was anything but inhibited or shy, and he was proud of his manhood. He didn't consider himself huge, but he was a little bigger than most other men, at least the many he'd seen in an excited state. If it pleased his partner, Yarrow didn't mind showing off a little. He gripped his cock at the base and squeezed. A pearl of semen emerged from his slit, glistening in the candlelight. As Yarrow slid his hand slowly up his length, another rivulet of come dribbled down his crown. Using his thumb, Yarrow swirled the slick liquid over his flesh. He touched himself with slow, teasing strokes as his partner stepped back to disrobe, his eyes never breaking from Yarrow's hand on his shaft.

Sasha pulled his black shirt over his head and flung it to the side. His tight leggings couldn't hide his arousal, and Yarrow wanted to see much, much more. The assassin taunted him, grinning wickedly as he knelt to tug off the fancy boots meant to impersonate a prince, his shiny hair falling in curtains across his face when he bent at the waist. When he stood, he slipped his thumbs into his pants and slowly peeled them from his lean, muscular thighs. Yarrow groaned, his cock bucking in his hand. He struggled to keep his strokes slow and controlled. As aroused as he was, he'd already brought himself close to release, and there was no way he'd let this experience go to waste. He abandoned pleasuring himself long enough to get out of his armor and shirt. He wanted his full range of motion when he got the opportunity to touch

Sasha, so he unbuckled the leather guards encasing his wrists and let them fall. With nothing left to hold it in place, his worn shirt slipped from his wrists and fluttered to the floor behind him.

Sasha stood in nothing but his skimpy undergarment, his arms held out to his sides. "Goddesses, I want to get my hands on you," Yarrow said, his voice husky with need. "Sasha...."

In response, the assassin turned around and bent almost in half. Yarrow choked at the sight. Only a ribbon of black fabric bisected the crescents of his perfect ass. The strip of cloth attached to a gold ring at the top, just above Sasha's cleft. Delicate chains and red gemstones dangled from the metal loop. When the other man finally shed the tiny scrap of silk, his balls dropped into view between his legs, soft and full. Yarrow thumbed his foreskin back and forth and groaned as the other man turned around. The mage had seen plenty of beautiful men, but few had been able to compete with the vision of the lithe assassin. His perfect skin sparkled with sweat, and he'd obviously shaved every inch of his body, so hair obscured absolutely nothing. Yarrow took a step toward him.

"Stay," Sasha said, closing the distance between them and pressing Yarrow's back to the cool stone wall again. His skin felt exquisite against Yarrow's chest, like silk over marble. Yarrow took his face in both hands and kissed him hard, feeling Sasha's jaw work against his palms. He possessed a unique, spicy flavor as exotic as the rest of him. Yarrow didn't stop until Sasha broke away with an extended slurp. He dropped to his knees and buried his nose in Yarrow's triangle of white hair, inhaling deeply of the mage's scent. Yarrow's cock throbbed and skipped next to his face. Sasha grasped it at the root and ran his tongue up the underside, lapping at the sensitive groove beneath the head when he reached it. Yarrow's pelvic muscles clenched, his anus contracting and a fresh fount of come spurting from his dick.

"Mmmm," Sasha purred as he cleaned it away. His lips closed around Yarrow's corona and he sucked hard, the pressure and sensation overwhelming to the mage.

"I'm not going to last," Yarrow warned, "after you teased me for so long. Just looking at you is almost enough. Seeing you do that... your lips on me.... I've dreamed about your lips...." He grasped the back of Sasha's hair and pushed a little deeper into his mouth. The other man relaxed and accepted Yarrow's thrusts, even as they grew rougher and faster. He held Yarrow's hipbone to steady himself as he let Yarrow press into his throat. All the while, his tongue caressed the belly of Yarrow's cock.

Yarrow felt his orgasm building and he couldn't hold it. He threw his head back and smacked it against the wall as the first breaker of pleasure roiled through him. He ignored the smart to his skull and gripped his partner's shoulders with both hands as he trembled with bliss, shooting his seed down Sasha's throat. "Goddesses… Sasha," he panted, his body shaking violently at the intense sensation. He repeated the assassin's name, the sound of it more intimate than everything else they'd shared so far, as after-waves of pleasure washed over him. The other man refused to relinquish his cock until he'd drained it completely, and the mage felt ready to cry after the tremendous experience.

Sasha stood, wiping his full lips with his knuckles. They'd swollen even more since Yarrow had ravaged them. Goddesses, Yarrow wouldn't have thought him able to look more beautiful and seductive than he had before, but he managed it, sparkling with sweat and mopping his amazing mouth with his delicate hand. Dozens of tiny scars crisscrossed his arms, just above and below his elbows, some old and faded, others pink and raised. Yarrow reached for him and licked the last vestiges of his seed from the assassin's mouth as he explored the texture and pattern of his self-inflicted wounds.

"You certainly know what you're doing down there," Yarrow said, stroking his dark hair and thinking many men had likely experienced his arts, but only Yarrow knew his name. The mage smiled at the shred of himself Sasha had relinquished. "Thank you."

Sasha smiled as if he knew how much Yarrow enjoyed seeing it. "Of course, my friend. But now it's my turn."

Yarrow allowed the other man to lead him to the bed and push him playfully down on his back. The mage rose to his elbows and watched Sasha take a small glass vial from his pack. The assassin poured some amber oil into his palm and anointed his cock, reciprocating the show Yarrow had given him, twisting his fist around his deep red tip and pushing his foreskin back and forth. Yarrow spread his legs and slid down the bed until his ass met the edge. He bent his knees and pulled his heels against his cheeks, his legs spread wide in invitation. His partner slathered the remainder of the oil along Yarrow's crevice. It smelled warm and zesty, redolent of Sasha himself. Yarrow groaned as Sasha's slick fingers pressed inside him.

"I don't want to wait," the assassin said, ravishing Yarrow with his eyes. He drove three fingers into Yarrow, twisting and spreading them to prepare Yarrow's body.

Yarrow felt his opening soften and could soon accommodate Sasha's fingers to the knuckles. He was ready and very willing. "I don't want to wait either. Take me."

Sasha lifted Yarrow's ankles to his shoulders and guided his cock to Yarrow's opening. The mage braced for the penetration, but his lover was gentle. Somehow Yarrow hadn't expected consideration from the other man, yet his black eyes, so hollow before but now brimming with want and maybe even tenderness, watched Yarrow's face for any sign of distress. Still, his flesh stretched and stung as Sasha delved slowly deeper.

"Yarrow…," he panted. "You're tight. I'd swear you've never been touched."

"Not untouched," Yarrow grunted. "But it's been some time."

"Lucky me." Sasha circled his hips, thrusting deep into Yarrow and hitting Yarrow's sweet spot. Yarrow's cock swelled instantly, and the other man took it in his oiled fist.

"Could be… I'm the lucky one," Yarrow panted, matching Sasha stroke for stroke, making their skin slap together. He drove against the other man in spite of the sting of his bottom. The pleasure he received was well worth the slight pain. If anything, the smart enhanced his desire.

Sasha picked up speed, biting his lip in an obvious attempt to last longer. Yarrow hoped he would; the internal stimulation almost brought him to climax again. He clenched his inner muscles tight around Sasha's cock, and Sasha groaned with appreciation. Sasha's unoccupied hand toyed with Yarrow's nipple. The mage's head thrashed from side to side. His perspiration wet the sheets. "Give it to me," he said. "I want all of you."

"Oh, Yarrow, yes!" Sasha fell forward, and his body drove Yarrow's knees against his shoulders, letting him push even deeper inside the mage. He jerked Yarrow's cock with short, quick strokes as he pounded relentlessly into him. The friction and heat drove Yarrow closer to release.

Yarrow grabbed his wonderful assassin by the back of the neck. "Kiss me," he demanded.

The other man happily complied, and their tongues dueled as their bodies smacked together. Yarrow's muscles hugged his partner's cock as he approached relief. Above him, the assassin's body quivered. He broke away from Yarrow's mouth and pressed their foreheads together. An artful twist of his hand made Yarrow come between their stomachs, and the rhythmic contractions of the mage's anus drove the other over the edge. He bit into Yarrow between Yarrow's neck and shoulder, tearing the skin and drawing blood. Yarrow, tingling with a second powerful orgasm, noticed the wound but hardly cared. He lay trembling beneath his lover, running his nails up and down Sasha's sweaty back, inhaling his scent and tasting the salt drizzling from his neck.

"You're fantastic," the assassin whispered, plowing Yarrow's damp fringe out of his face, bringing their moist brows to meet again and rubbing their noses together. "By the Cast-Down, Yarrow."

It took a quarter of an hour or so before they caught their breath and stopped shaking. Sasha rose, took a scrap of cloth from his things, and wet it from a clay pitcher on the table. He mopped himself off and returned to the bed, where he wiped the juices from Yarrow's torso. Then he urged Yarrow to roll to his belly so he could clean his backside. Yarrow felt sore and swollen there, but in a pleasant, satisfying way. Sasha's cool rag soothed his ravaged flesh as the assassin held his cheeks apart and dabbed away the fruit of their passion. Afterward, Sasha sat beside the mage's prone body, running a finger up and down Yarrow's spine, pausing to play with Yarrow's stretched opening now and then, making it twitch whenever he touched it. "We'll have to do this again, my friend," he said. "It was wonderful."

"Mmmm," Yarrow noised drowsily in agreement. "Just don't get attached."

"You need not worry. I know better."

As he let sleep claim him, Yarrow waited for the assassin to say something further. Instead, Sasha lay on his back beside Yarrow and pulled the fancy red and gold coverlet over their bodies. Yarrow didn't know what he expected to hear from Sasha, and after a while he abandoned curiosity in favor of needed rest.

Chapter Six

WAKE UP, beloved!

Yarrow bolted up, alone in the bed. By the light of the few candles still burning, he saw the assassin naked at the foot, his muscles tense and a knife in his hand. The consciousness of the mage's companion overlapped his own, allowing him to sense the room through both of their perceptions. Two men, clothed in black from head to foot, stood in the shadowed corners, though the door remained shut. Their hearts beat steadily, loud in Yarrow's head. Yarrow clenched his fists and felt both lust for violence and powerful enchantment singing in his veins. He waited to counter the strangers' attacks when they came, but none of the men in the room so much as twitched.

"Who dares to attack a sanctuary of Thalil?" Sasha said in a soft, threatening voice.

No one answered.

Do you know what's going on? Yarrow asked the presence.

I might.

This is no time to play games! We could be killed.

You know I won't allow you to be killed, beloved.

But Sasha!

He's been betrayed more thoroughly than he realizes.

Yarrow understood. "Sasha," he said, "they're of your order. What are we going to do?"

"If these are my brothers, then they mean us no harm," the assassin said, though his body, taut and ready to fire as a drawn bowstring, didn't relax.

"You're wrong," Yarrow said. "Oh merciful goddesses! What about Duncan?" As soon as he moved an inch toward the edge of the bed, a silver dart sailed toward his face. Sasha knocked it aside with his dagger, but three more followed its path. If Yarrow's companion hadn't protected him with a magical shield, he'd have been blinded in both eyes and struck in the windpipe. He swiped his hand, and the quill-sized projectiles flew to the left and bounced off the wall. Yarrow knew he had to attack, had to save Sasha and himself and find Duncan as quickly as possible. Who knew how many more of the assassins lurked in the labyrinthine hideout?

One of the enemy assassins moved toward Sasha, swinging a sickle-shaped blade on a long chain. He swung for Sasha's head, but the other assassin ducked the blow, stabbing his assailant in the stomach as he rose. The other man doubled over, and Sasha struck him twice in the back. When he dropped to his hands and knees, Sasha flipped neatly over his back and cut his throat from behind. Blood fanned out from the wound and painted the stone floor with a dark crescent. The black-clad assassin fell facedown in the arc of gore, spasmed a few times, and went still.

Yarrow, watching the quick altercation, became so enthralled and impressed with his partner's prowess that he barely noticed the second man creeping toward him on the left. The enemy assassin, his features concealed in the shadows of a heavy hood, raised a reed tube to his lips. The silver dart he fired struck the mage in his bare bicep. Yarrow quickly yanked it out, the barbs tearing his flesh but inflicting little more than discomfort. He tossed it to the floor and ignored the stream of blood, preparing an offensive spell. When he lifted his right hand to attack, he saw three sets of blurry, wavering fingers in front of his face. They became glowing, orange blobs, and black poured in around them. Yarrow tried to swallow but his throat swelled shut. He fought to breathe as he struggled to focus on his magic. Nothing but swirls of light and shadow danced across his vision. He barely perceived his spectral blade recoiling from the ceiling. He was, however, vaguely aware of the black shape approaching with a bright silver line between his hands. *A garrote*, the mage realized. He didn't want that slow, excruciating death. Yarrow aimed magic at him again, but he missed and the beautiful painting of Thalil warped and twisted, the pigment bubbling up and the wooden frame snapping.

Something shiny soared past Yarrow's face, and he managed to focus enough to see a small, simple dagger strike his attacker in the eye. Another pierced his chest, and he spat up blood before collapsing.

Yarrow did the same, falling against the cool, satin sheets, unable to move. He felt his head lifted and his jaw pried open. Bitter liquid flooded his mouth and throat, and he coughed to expel it. A gentle voice scolded him and poured more fluid between his lips. It was garbled, though, and the mage couldn't understand a word it said. This time, a hand clapped over his mouth, preventing him from spitting out the foul brew. Yarrow struggled but couldn't free himself. Someone stroked his throat and blocked his nose, and he finally acquiesced and swallowed. A few minutes later, the world came back into focus. Sasha looked down at Yarrow with concern, holding a tear-shaped blue vial.

"Poison," the mage's companion explained. "I've administered the antidote. Are you feeling all right?"

"Never mind that," Yarrow said, forcing himself to stand on his cramped and weakened legs. He stumbled to the trousers he'd discarded near the wall a few hours before and clumsily stepped into them. "We have to find Duncan and get out of here."

Sasha looked troubled, but he nodded and efficiently dressed himself in blood red leather pants with curving, armored plates over the knees. He fastened the many buckles on the outsides of his legs and pulled on a set of matching, knee-high boots with barbs on the heels and toes. Sasha threw Yarrow's cloak over the mage's shoulders. Then he tossed the rest of his gear and Yarrow's clothing into his pack. The two men hurried down the darkened hall to the room where they'd left the knight.

Yarrow kicked the door open just in time to see a man dressed like the others standing over his companion. He cried out, but too late to stop the man from plunging his serrated blade into Duncan's body. The knight-commander screamed and curled almost in half. Without thinking, Yarrow conjured a large, ethereal hand as an extension of his own. He grasped Duncan's assailant in the translucent, blue fingers and smashed him against one wall of the cell and then the other. He tossed the man's body back and forth, smashing it into red jelly, until Sasha's hand on his shoulder calmed him.

"Duncan," Yarrow gasped, hurrying toward the man he almost thought of as a friend. The commander's mouth moved and scarlet flecked his paling lips. "Don't try to speak. I'll get us out of here," Yarrow said, pressing his palm over Duncan's wound. Blood poured between his fingers. From the corner of his eye, he saw Sasha collecting Duncan's possessions. The assassin strapped the knight's sword to his back, though it was nearly as tall as he was, and attached Duncan's compact crossbow to his belt. "Help me carry him. My magic is used up for the moment," Yarrow said, grasping Duncan around the chest and trying to lift him from the bed.

"Yarrow," Sasha said cautiously, "His wound is fatal. We'll never get out of here if we try to drag him along."

"No!" Yarrow yelled, spinning around to face the assassin. "This is all your fault! I told him we could trust you. I trusted you, and he believed me. You expect me to leave him behind?" The mage shoved the other man's shoulder, and Sasha stumbled back a few steps. He lifted his hand to strike Sasha but the other man didn't flinch.

"I don't know exactly what this knight means to you, Yarrow, but he can't be worth both of our lives. We can't save him."

"Would you want to be left behind like this?" Yarrow demanded.

"No, but I would expect it."

"So you'd leave me?"

"We're wasting time," Sasha said, his calm infuriating Yarrow. "We won't survive if we don't escape. My brethren don't give up easily. They don't give up at all, in fact."

"I won't leave Duncan." Yarrow held the larger man's bleeding torso and dragged him off the bed. An inch at a time, he pulled Duncan from the tiny room and into the hall. He perspired as he struggled to cross the room where Thalil stood enshrined. He'd almost made it to the steps when Sasha lifted the knight's feet and helped Yarrow carry him up the stairs.

"Yarrow," Duncan croaked as the mage and the assassin hauled him through the simple house and out onto the cold street.

"What now?" Sasha asked, his breath freezing around him.

"There," Yarrow said, tipping his head toward an old gray mule attached to a flatbed cart. "You drive while I tend to him."

"Where are we going?" Sasha asked as they hoisted Duncan's body onto the planks.

"Back to the forest," Yarrow suggested. "Maybe your people will be afraid to follow us there."

"No." Sasha leapt up to take the reins. "They won't. We need an open space, where there is nowhere for them to hide."

"Go," Yarrow said. "Go anywhere. Get us out of here. I'm going to start trying to heal him." He knelt beside Duncan on the rough wood, spreading his fingers over the nasty wound and concentrating hard to urge the flesh to mesh together.

The mage, because of his companion's knowledge, understood what lay beneath human flesh and bone. He therefore knew the assassin's blade had pierced the knight's liver and severed his intestines. Duncan had lost too much blood already. His face and lips shone waxy and as pale as Yarrow's hair. Yarrow fought to force Duncan's flesh to mend, and he accomplished it, but the stuff within his organs already swam through the rest of his body, as toxic as the poison the rival assassin had used against the mage. Yarrow tried to dispel it, and then to negate it. He tried to surround it in bubbles of energy and draw it out of Duncan's body. He couldn't quarantine all of it, and Duncan's pulse grew faint. The knight's arms and legs quivered: the dance of death.

An arrow soared over the cart from a rooftop. Dark shapes leapt from building to building in pursuit of the three men. "Sasha, go!" Yarrow yelled, summoning a protective canopy above them even though his energy faltered.

The assassin cracked the reins against the mule's haunches, and the old gray beast picked up speed. A small person, probably a woman, dropped from an awning onto the bench beside Sasha. Yarrow saw them struggling, heard their daggers clashing, but he couldn't spare his attention. His assassin could handle himself, and Duncan was almost gone. Yarrow felt the knight's life force slipping away, and none of his magic could dam the flow.

Yarrow vaguely noticed Sasha throwing his adversary from the wagon as he prepared to employ a dark, obscure enchantment. He reached out to the life forces slumbering in the simple homes they passed. He snatched a bit of vitality, a few days of life, from each being he sensed as they sped by. Distance and distraction worked against Yarrow's efforts. This sinister cantrip was difficult enough with an immobilized victim close to the recipient and quiet to promote concentration. Jostling around in the cart, trying to stabilize Duncan, Yarrow found it close to impossible to harvest any vigor from his prey. He managed to reap a few strong scraps, though. Imbuing Duncan with the stolen energy didn't seem to improve the knight's condition. Yarrow swore with frustration. He didn't know what else to do for Duncan. He'd never been a healer, but with all his power, he couldn't accept that he couldn't save his friend.

They'd left the town and reached the stark Valenny of Merryvale, sister province to Everdale, a similar plain dotted with stone shelves and crisscrossed with frosty hedgerows shimmering beneath the moon. Sasha drove the mule hard, further and further from the dirty light of Galene. Though they'd lost the assassins for the moment, Yarrow had no way to preserve Duncan's life. A tear dropped from his eye to the knight's cheek. "I won't let you die," he whispered through gritted teeth. "I won't let you. I'll do anything."

Anything, beloved?

Can you save him? Get us out of danger?

You have to ask?

What do you want in return?

I ask that, when we reach the next cluster of human lives, you let me wear the flesh for an entire night. You let me do as I will without limitation.

You'll save Duncan?

Aye, beloved. Sasha too.

One condition.

No conditions, Yarrow. Your companion will be dead in minutes.

Still, you must agree to touch neither of these two men, Duncan or Sasha. Have nothing to do with them, and you may use my body for anything else you please. In exchange, you save Duncan and get us out of trouble. Agreed?

Oh yes, dearest Yarrow. Let me have the flesh, and all will be well.

DUNCAN AWOKE to a trivial ache in his belly. He gingerly touched his bare skin and found it sore but unbroken. Slowly, he opened his eyes, giving them time to adjust to the fuzzy white light. He lay on the ground, inside one of the small tents formerly used by the foot soldiers. It was chilly. The sagging peak clarified, and the buzz in Duncan's head faded away. At his right, Yarrow sat on his heels, his eyes closed though he wasn't asleep. Duncan reached out a trembling hand to touch the mage's knee.

Yarrow's lids peeled back slowly, revealing his bloodshot eyes. He smiled weakly, as if it took some effort. "Duncan," he said in a scratchy voice. He reached over and smoothed the hair from Duncan's forehead, letting his hand rest on top of his head afterward. His other hand covered Duncan's on his leg. They looked at each other for a few minutes, Yarrow's smile widening. Something about waking to find the mage watching over him felt very nice to Duncan. He was confused, though. When, and how, had they left the assassin's sanctuary?

"I should apologize to you," Yarrow said. "You were right. It was a bad idea to go to the Order of the Crimson Scythe. You trusted me—another bad idea."

"Bad idea?" Duncan asked, his voice sounding somehow foreign and far away to him. "What do you mean? What happened, Yarrow? I don't remember a thing."

"We were betrayed, and Sasha too."

"Sasha?" Duncan wondered.

"That's our assassin's name. His people turned against him. They attacked us while we slept. One of them ran you through. You nearly died." The mage's fingers curled around Duncan's hair, and his comely face contorted with distress.

Duncan didn't know what to ask him first, so he chose, "Our assassin? We have a pet murderer now?"

His joke didn't earn the smile he'd hoped for. Instead, Yarrow's frown deepened, and a little crease appeared between his white eyebrows. Duncan hurried to change the subject. "I was badly injured," he said. Though he couldn't remember it, he knew it was true. He felt fortunate and knew he'd narrowly escaped tragedy. The eerie sensation made him shiver. Yarrow noticed and pulled the coarse blanket to Duncan's chin. "How have I recovered so quickly?"

"I healed you, of course," Yarrow answered, not imparting his detached arrogance as convincingly as he'd done in the past. Watching his inner struggle play out on his delicate features, Duncan realized what a young man the mage still was, in spite of all his exploits and ability.

"Then I was never in any danger," he said and patted Yarrow's knee.

"This isn't a joke," Yarrow snapped. "You trusted me and it nearly cost you your life. You'd do well to remember that."

"Why do you insist I dislike you?" Duncan asked, moving his hand up the younger man's slender thigh.

"I never said that."

"You expend a great effort to ensure it. I don't blame you for what happened. You may be the greatest magic-user of our age, but that's not the same thing as a clairvoyant." Duncan's hand reached the crease where Yarrow's trousers bunched between his leg and torso. He didn't proceed farther, instead reaching up to hold Yarrow's cheek. "You're not responsible for this. You'll have to find some other way to make me hate you."

"I don't want you to hate me, Duncan. I just need you to understand. I want you to… I want…."

"What? If you're hoping I'll like you, you need not worry."

Yarrow bent at the waist and brought his face an inch from Duncan's. His hair tumbled forward and tickled the knight's cheeks. His locks smelled slightly herbal, with an underlying aroma of campfire smoke and a faint hint of blood. He ran the tip of his nose up the bridge of Duncan's nose, and Duncan let him go, resisting the urge to seize his neck and pull Yarrow closer. Yarrow's lips brushed against his, and Duncan's skin erupted in gooseflesh. He'd barely been able to admit to himself how many moments each evening he lay fantasizing about their first kiss, and with Yarrow so close, Duncan couldn't deny the draw he felt to the young man. The fingers of their left hands braided together on the ground, while their right hands remained in each other's hair. Yarrow's white tresses felt as soft as silk thread. Why had Duncan imagined they'd be coarse and dry? Because they'd been brittle with cold the last time he'd touched them?

All curiosity abandoned Duncan when Yarrow finally kissed him. It was nothing like that first, rushed kiss in the haystack. The young mage took his time, circling Duncan's lips with the tip of his tongue before delving between them and gently licking Duncan's teeth. The knight let his mouth fall open, completely content to allow Yarrow to taste and explore. His tender attention satisfied Duncan even more than his urgency had. Yarrow tilted his head to a better angle and his tongue twined around Duncan's. Neither fought to dominate the other, they just caressed, discovered, and embraced each other's tongues. To Duncan it felt perfect, because he felt sure something existed behind the kiss other than physical desire: curiosity, a longing to know Duncan better, if nothing more profound. It made a fine enough start.

Duncan wriggled his fingers free of Yarrow's grasp and wrapped his arm around the mage's waist. He could no longer resist drawing Yarrow to him. Yarrow let himself be guided, and his chest fell softly against Duncan. The fabric of his shirt felt cool against Duncan's bare torso, but he sensed the mage's heated skin beneath it and enfolded him, squeezing him as hard as he dared. Yarrow felt featherlight, almost insubstantial, on top of Duncan. They kissed a long time before Yarrow pulled away, tugging Duncan's bottom lip with his teeth before relinquishing it.

Moving his face close to Duncan's ear, Yarrow said, "I don't want to lose you. I was so afraid. It would have been all my fault, again."

"Yarrow… please come here."

The mage finally smiled, laughed even, as he swung his leg to straddle Duncan. Their lips met again, still tenderly but with growing yearning. Duncan's hands dove beneath Yarrow's shirt to touch his back. How he'd imagined that warm, soft skin since the night at the Peregrym estate! It felt even warmer and softer than he'd dreamed it could. Pores rose beneath Duncan's fingertips, and the knight smiled at the mage's response to his touch. Above Duncan, Yarrow circled his hips. Duncan felt the mage's erection brushing against his own, felt an enticing heat radiating from Yarrow's bottom. He took hold of his partner's shoulder and urged Yarrow to sit up so he could unlace his blue-gray shirt. When he finished, he brushed the garment from the mage's shoulders, impatient to see his bare body.

An ellipse of punctures surrounded by a nasty bruise commanded Duncan's attention. His cock went soft at the sight of the vicious bite between Yarrow's neck and shoulder. He had no doubt as to who'd left it, and the idea made him sick. He pushed the mage away and turned his head, unable to meet Yarrow's eyes.

"What's wrong?" the young man asked.

"You—you'll give yourself to anyone, won't you? Imagine me being fool enough to think there might be something more."

Yarrow backed away on his knees, clutching his shirt closed over his heart. At first he looked like he might cry, but his features quickly hardened and turned cruel. "If that's what you thought, then you are a fool," he said, sneering. "I'd simply hoped to take some pleasure with you. I don't seek anything else from my partnerships. If you do, look elsewhere, Duncan. I'm not a man you want to be with for more than half an hour." He slapped the tent flap open and departed into the blinding winter light beyond it.

SASHA SAT in the second tent, half a dozen newly sharpened daggers in a semicircle around him. A mortar and pestle, as well as several corked jars, waited beside his bent knee. He used a small funnel to fill emptied eggshells with powdered glass and poisonous concoctions that could paralyze or blind. Afterward he sealed the hole with a dab of wax and covered the eggs with black pitch. If his brothers in Thalil pursued him, he'd need every ruse in his arsenal. These eggs, when thrown in the face of an enemy, would hopefully buy him a few seconds to retaliate and save himself. He'd also prepared a variety of toxic elixirs to apply to his blades. Acrid fumes rose from the small cauldron at the rear of the tent.

It startled Sasha when Yarrow stormed into his tent with his shirt hanging open and his feet bare. The mage's brows pointed inward toward his small nose, and his lips pursed. He carefully stepped over Sasha's gear, casting his top off on the way. It fell over some of the knives. Yarrow squatted above Sasha and grasped his face. He kissed Sasha hard, ravaging Sasha's mouth with his tongue and groping the assassin's crotch. Sasha sat stunned at first, until his body realized the potential for gratification. Then he returned Yarrow's desperate kisses and grabs, cupping Yarrow's lean cheeks and pulling Yarrow into his lap. Their cocks, bellies, and chests pressed together. Yarrow kneaded Sasha's dick and balls desperately through his leather pants as he pummeled Sasha's tongue with his own.

Finally Sasha pushed him away long enough to catch his breath. "What's gotten into you?" he asked Yarrow.

"What do you care? You said you liked my body. Let's do this."

"I do care, Yarrow. I am not a whore. Are you using me as a substitute, a distraction?"

"We agreed to be nothing more than each other's distractions," the mage said, stabbing his hard dick against Sasha's belly. "If you've changed your mind, I can go. It doesn't matter to me."

"No, stay," Sasha breathed, aroused and irritated at the same time. He pushed his gear to the side and tossed Yarrow to his back, almost winding the mage. Then he whisked Yarrow's trousers off in a single, smooth motion. He looked down at Yarrow's purpled cock and the flushed, puckered opening behind his balls. Sasha stood to disrobe.

Though already hard, he pushed his foreskin back and pumped himself. Yarrow raised a brow in expectation, and Sasha dove on him, pushing his legs perpendicular to his body. Sasha spit into his palm and rubbed the warm saliva over his partner's hole. He inserted his thumb and first two fingers into Yarrow's tight hole, easing them apart once they were embedded.

"Sasha, goddesses," Yarrow squealed. Come dripped from his dark, pulsing cockhead and pooled in his belly button.

"Be quiet, Yarrow," Sasha said. "You want it, don't you?" He fumbled in the pack beside him, glad all Order brethren trained in using both hands with equal skill, until he located his thick oil.

"Yes."

Sasha drenched the exposed digits of his hand and Yarrow's cleft with the grease before he let his fingers penetrate Yarrow further. Thalil help him, he almost wanted to hurt the mage. Almost, but not as much as he wanted to see Yarrow trembling with bliss. The way the other man had squirmed and whimpered beneath Sasha's slightest caress the night before had made the assassin feel almost divine. He'd never been with such a responsive partner. Once again Yarrow reveled in Sasha's attention, twining his waist and moaning as Sasha's fingers discovered his interior. His cheeks colored and sweat sparkled above his lip. Sasha pushed his knuckles past Yarrow's snug circle of muscle, and Yarrow shuddered satisfyingly. Sasha's free hand kneaded his neck. "More?" the assassin asked.

"I—anything you want, Sasha." The mage's eyes opened wide, and his icy irises commanded Sasha's attention. By Thalil, he was beautiful. "I just want you."

"Is it really me you want?"

"Of course," Yarrow said, pushing his clenching bottom against Sasha's fingers, begging for more. He seized two fistfuls of Sasha's hair and dragged him down into a kiss. The pulsing of his tongue against Sasha's felt authentic, needy. Sasha couldn't help but return his passion, pushing another finger past his strong ring of muscle. Something about the mage ignited his desire as nothing had in a long time. Was it his lethal power? The way he relinquished that power so freely when he let Sasha use his body? Sasha didn't care, couldn't ponder it, and returned Yarrow's enthusiastic kisses. He put the thought that he was just a convenient, willing body to the back of his mind and delved into Yarrow with his fingers. Yarrow's quickening pulse beat against Sasha's hand. The other man's silken tunnel contracted around his hand, and Yarrow panted Sasha's name.

Yarrow grasped Sasha's wrist and extracted Sasha's hand from his body. He seized both of the assassin's forearms and held them as he rolled over so Sasha lay beneath him. The mage pinned Sasha's wrists to the ground beside his head. His sweltering crevice ground against Sasha's hard dick. Yarrow tried, but couldn't quite manage, to sit down and drive it into himself. Growling with frustration and desire, Yarrow abandoned Sasha's hand to grab the root of his cock and direct it into his expectant opening. Tight heat enveloped Sasha's erection as he penetrated his partner. Yarrow shivered, his eyes screwing shut, as he adjusted to the sensation. Sasha lifted his hips off the ground to thrust deeper into Yarrow.

"You're wonderful," Yarrow said. "Give me more."

Sasha happily complied, driving into the other until his shaved groin pressed against Yarrow's hot, sweating crack. The mage's anus pulsed around his shaft, and Sasha needed little more stimulation. He marveled at Yarrow's ability to bring him to the edge of ecstasy with so little effort as he reached up to fondle the other man's nipples. Yarrow's head inclined at Sasha's touch, his face turning toward the peak of the tent. Sasha enjoyed the graceful stretch of the other man's neck, and scraped his nails from Yarrow's chest to his chin. "You're very beautiful," Sasha said. Yarrow began to move his hips, driving Sasha's erection in and out of his tight, sweet ass.

"You're something, Yarrow," Sasha said as he grasped his partner's protruding hipbones to direct his movement. "I don't know what it is about you—"

"Sasha." The mage dragged out the second syllable of the assassin's first name, hissing it delectably. He lifted his body to ride Sasha's cock as he collapsed forward to kiss him.

Sasha drove his tongue into Yarrow's mouth as his cock plunged into the mage's snug body. Every time he hit Yarrow's gland, his sweet spot, the other man's back arched and his lips parted. The assassin couldn't resist biting into the bronzed globe of Yarrow's shoulder. His teeth left a swollen, bloody oval on the other's tanned skin. Yarrow gasped but didn't protest. He lapped the sweat from Sasha's neck as he plunged down on Sasha with increasing fury. Sasha tasted Yarrow's blood and perspiration, a delightful mix. Their skin smacked together, and the scent of their passion filled the small tent.

Yarrow's muscles began to quiver, and he panted with exertion. He sat up and reached behind himself to grab Sasha's knees, adjusting his body for maximum inner stimulation. The sight of his lithe torso stretched taut, all of his muscles tense and popping, and that nice, big cock sticking straight out brought Sasha to the edge of release. He hurried to stroke his partner, spreading the liberal fluid Yarrow seeped over his erection. They soon established a harmony, Sasha twisting and tugging Yarrow's dick while the mage's balls bounced against Sasha's belly as he rocked on top of Sasha.

"Oh yes, Sasha, that's it!" Yarrow said. His cock jumped in Sasha's hand, and he sprayed white ribbons over the assassin's chest and stomach. His anus clamped down on Sasha's dick, hugging it rhythmically as he whimpered in ecstasy. "Sasha, Sasha, goddesses! You're so good."

At that, Sasha's back arched off the ground as he came hard into Yarrow, filling the other man's twitching ass. He grabbed his partner by the back of the hair and yanked him down, wanting to be as deep within Yarrow as he could. Their passionate climaxes stole both men's eloquence, and they grunted and panted as they caught their breath. Sasha scooped some of Yarrow's seed from beside his nipples and poked his dripping finger between the mage's swollen lips. Yarrow sucked it clean before falling forward to kiss Sasha and share his flavor. To Sasha he tasted like spring rain, or a fresh snowflake caught on the tongue, cold and pure.

Sasha crossed his arms over Yarrow's back. He felt the mage's heart pounding against his own. When Yarrow adjusted his face and snuggled down against Sasha's chest, a melancholy smile touched the assassin's lips. "Yarrow," he said. "I like holding you like this. It's nice just to be with someone."

"I like this too," Yarrow said. "You're a fantastic lover, Sasha."

Sasha sighed and stroked Yarrow's damp hair. He'd hoped to maybe talk with the mage about the betrayal of his order and how he felt like he'd lost the only family, the only sense of belonging he'd ever known. His world had shattered beneath his feet when he'd realized his own had turned against him. He didn't know how to think of himself if not as a brother in the order of Thalil. He considered the many roles he'd played over the years, the masks he'd worn, one on top of the other. If he cast those masks aside down to his bare face, what would he see? He had no idea who he might be beneath those many masks, and thought discussing it with a lover might help him understand himself. But his problems wouldn't interest Yarrow; Yarrow had already gotten the only thing that interested him. It was just as well. He'd been taught not to share his feelings or rely on the sympathies of others, and his training had served him so far.

Still, the mage's warm, light body in his arms banished a bit of the emptiness in Sasha's heart.

Chapter Seven

AFTER MUCH heated debate, the three men agreed to continue north toward Lockhaven and the rendezvous with Agarick's general. They had no way to know if word of the attack had reached the king. Sasha expressed concern that the members of his order might pursue them. The Crimson Scythe never left a job unfinished, he said. He insisted on remaining with Duncan and Yarrow, as he knew the assassins' tricks and felt singularly capable of detecting them. Duncan protested vehemently until Yarrow finally intervened.

The trio made their way across the desolate expanse of Merryvale. They passed little beyond fallow fields covered in snow and the occasional stone hut. Foul weather and the absence of their horses slowed their progress. They ate whatever Duncan killed, usually bushy-tailed erkits or other forest-dwelling rodents, and Yarrow grew even thinner as he consumed the bare minimum required to survive. It grew colder as they approached Lockhaven, and Yarrow often worried over Duncan, alone in his tent, as he lay warm in Sasha's arms.

The knight pushed them hard while the light lasted, worried over his sovereign as the days stretched into weeks. He hoped their contact, the general Tam Taran Edercrest, Bairn of Windwake, might know the whereabouts of the true prince.

"Taran Edercrest?" Sasha asked, his head snapping up. None of them had said a word to each other in hours. "I know that name. He was the only other man present when Agarick explained my mission to me. He may indeed know the route of Garith's procession."

Duncan, a few feet ahead of Sasha and Yarrow, spun around to face them, kicking up a cloud of snow. He stuck his finger in the assassin's face and shouted, "Garith is your prince and Agarick is your king! You'll address them by their proper titles."

"Get your hand out of my face, Duncan." Sasha smacked his wrist with the back of his knuckles. Duncan took a step toward him until their chests almost touched. Though the knight stood half a foot taller than the assassin, Sasha didn't back down. "What right do you have to tell me how to address anyone? My only fealty is to Thalil."

"And look how well that worked out for you. Although I suppose it's hard to stay clean when one lies down in the filth with the hogs." Duncan looked meaningfully at Yarrow. "A wild dog will bite its master eventually, even after years of loyalty."

"Are you finished spouting tired clichés?" Sasha said through gritted teeth. Yarrow saw his hand go to the hilt of the dagger he wore on his left hip.

The mage hurried to pry the two men apart before this spiraled out of control. His companion howled with laughter inside his head, but Yarrow ignored its taunting and focused on his friends. Yarrow couldn't understand why Duncan insisted on being so rude to Sasha. He understood Duncan envied their closeness, but Yarrow had given Duncan his chance. "You go too far, Duncan," Yarrow admonished. He spread his arms to push them farther apart.

"And I suppose you're impartial, Yarrow?"

"That has nothing to do with it." Yarrow had known Duncan would bring this up eventually, but it still irritated him. "Sasha just wanted to share some information, and you started in with the insults again. He's been trying to help us all along."

Duncan made an exasperated noise. "Like he helped us in that hideout?"

"It's completely unprecedented for the order to turn on one of its own," Sasha said.

"I suppose they find you especially expendable, then," Duncan said.

Trying to stay calm, Yarrow said, "Sasha was betrayed too. He's our ally now."

I rather like him too, beloved. His flesh works quite nicely with ours.

With mine, you mean. Duncan's angry voice drew Yarrow's attention back to the physical world.

"I find it more likely he's hoping you'll defend him with your magic, should his former associates return."

"Well, I will," Yarrow said quickly. "I'll defend either of my companions. Isn't that why we're traveling together?"

"Do you suppose it's a coincidence that he hopped into bed with the most powerful person he could find?"

"I can take care of myself," Sasha said, raising his voice, his reserve finally cracking. "Anything between Yarrow and me is none of your affair."

"He deserves better," Duncan said.

"I suppose you think you're better."

"Of course I'm better than you," Duncan said. "I've dedicated my life to serving this country and protecting its people. You're the worst kind of criminal filth."

"Enough," Yarrow demanded. "I won't listen to any more of this. The three of us might be the only people who know of the betrayal. I'm not normally patriotic, but I'm afraid it falls to us to at least inform the king, or this general of his, of the attack. If we perish, the truth might die with us. That could leave the conspirators, the Crimson Scythe possibly included, to continue with their plans. Who knows what those could be? What if they extend to the rest of the royal family? We must pass along what we know. After that, we can part ways if we think it best. But until we reach the meeting place, we must look out for one another."

Sasha smiled and nodded once. Duncan hung his head, shamed by the mage's words. "I will do my duty," he said, "by both of you. Let's move. There's a small wooded valley up ahead that might offer us some shelter should it storm again tonight."

"If I'm not mistaken, there's a town not far from here," Sasha said. "Perhaps we should make our way there. We're desperately in need of supplies."

"No," Yarrow said quickly. "We should camp for the night and visit the town in the morning."

"Why sleep on the ground when we could buy a warm bed at an inn?" Sasha asked, laying his hand on the mage's shoulder.

You're not going to get out of our arrangement, my beloved. I will wear the body tonight, as we agreed.

Can you wait another day or two?

No. Tonight.

"Are you all right, Yarrow?" Sasha asked, moving behind Yarrow, wrapping his arms around Yarrow's waist and resting his chin on Yarrow's shoulder. Duncan glared at them and stomped away toward the copse of trees.

"I'm not going to let Duncan continue to slander you," Yarrow said, resting his temple against Sasha's head.

Ho ho! An excellent deception, Yarrow. But changing the subject won't change my mind.

"Thank you," Sasha whispered against Yarrow's cheek. "For defending me. For promising to defend me. It's not something I'm accustomed to."

"Don't overestimate me," Yarrow said miserably, knowing he wouldn't be able to share his assassin's bed when the sun went down. He wanted to say he'd happily paint the ground with blood for Sasha, but he couldn't say that either.

He felt Sasha shake his head. Yarrow knew the other man well enough to suspect Sasha wanted to argue, but he kept silent. Soon, Yarrow would need to end their association, lest the other suspect his dark secret. If he waited too long, Sasha might even get hurt. It was just sex, but the thought of relinquishing it pained the mage. He'd grown fond of lying with this man, and of waking next to him in the morning. Sasha was delightfully rough and tender at the same time. He didn't pretend to be other than he was. Yarrow would miss the spicy smell of his skin, his hair—

"Move along," Duncan yelled over his shoulder, far ahead of them.

"We'd better hurry, or he might get even more cross," Yarrow said.

"Agreed." Sasha clasped his hand, and the two of them sprinted to catch up with the knight.

"I'm going hunting," Duncan said, brandishing his crossbow. "We're out of meat. Can the two of you manage to set up camp?"

"We'll manage," Sasha said, dropping the heavy pack he carried into the snow.

DUNCAN RETURNED around twilight with a twirl-horn buck slung over his left shoulder. He efficiently skinned and gutted the small beast before skewering it and placing it over the fire to roast. Before long grease dripped and hissed against the coals, and a savory smell roused Sasha's hunger. He took a small paper envelope from a pouch and offered it to Duncan. The knight eyed it suspiciously until Sasha said, "Salt."

"I see," Duncan said. "Thank you."

"I have some herbs as well," Sasha said.

"Let's have them. I need a good meal tonight. You look like you'd benefit from one as well." Duncan took what Sasha gave him and seasoned the meat. It smelled even better than before. The two men stood expectantly, licking their lips and warming their hands above the flames. "I wish I had a few parsnips to toss into the coals," Duncan said wistfully. "Or a loaf of the dark bread they baked back home. They churned the sweetest butter there. I think I miss it most of all."

"You're from Thulemore, correct?" Sasha asked. "Your accent is subdued, but noticeable. I wish we had a keg of your valenny's fine ale."

Duncan laughed. "I haven't tasted it in many years."

"Because you avoid spirits. I've noticed you pass over even the best wine."

"That's none of your business, assassin."

"I apologize. Unlike you, I'm not trying to cause conflict. In fact, I'd hoped we might share a meal as friends."

"I'm not your friend."

"Why? Because of Yarrow? I know you care about him. I'd even wondered if the two of you had been intimate, but as enthusiastic as he is with me, I can't imagine he'd have the energy to please a second man."

"Shut your mouth, you scum!" Duncan drew his sword, and Sasha's hand flitted to his knives. The assassin actually welcomed the confrontation. The time had come and then some to put the arrogant bastard in his place. He was just about ready to crush one of his blinding eggs into the knight's eyes when Yarrow emerged from Sasha's tent, where he'd been resting.

"Something… smells… really good," the mage said, his tone different and his pronunciation awkward, as if he'd forgotten how to use his lips and tongue and needed to relearn how they worked. Yarrow drew his dagger and sliced a hunk of meat from the twirl-horn's haunches. He dropped and sat cross-legged in the snow, gnawing at the undercooked flesh. Blood and grease dripped from his chin. He grunted and belched as he devoured the piece of meat. Duncan and Sasha stood horrified as he yanked the buck's leg and severed it at the hip joint. In mere moments, he'd chewed the raw tissue from the bone of the animal's lower leg. The mage continued feasting, oblivious to the stains down the front of his shirt. Gore covered Yarrow's fingers and saturated his cuffs. To Sasha's amazement, he managed to finish the entire leg. Afterward, he broke the bones and sucked out the marrow. Then Yarrow burped with satisfaction.

"Any… ale?" the mage asked. "Wine?"

Sasha reluctantly passed his companion a skin. Yarrow slurped it down, purple rivulets running from the corners of his mouth.

"Good," the mage growled. "So, Sasha, tell me of the first time you spilled blood."

"You want to hear about that?" Sasha asked, surprised. Yarrow had never been concerned before.

"Yes, very much."

"All right, then." Sasha braced himself. He didn't want the others to know how much the memory disturbed him. He wouldn't show weakness in front of Duncan. "I was fourteen years old, young to receive a solitary mission. It was actually quite an honor. I was assigned to kill a young noblewoman. I learned of a masked ball thrown by her family, and I procured fine clothing and easily gained admission. It didn't take me many dances before I convinced the young woman to join me for a stroll in the gardens. She showed me her flowers; I remember how proud she seemed of each and every bloom: Ix's Necklaces, Heavenscents, Windblossoms, and Fane's Follies. We sat together on a stone bench, and she removed her mask, though I left mine in place. Oh, she was a beauty: big, green eyes and wheat-colored waves of hair. Such a slender, vulnerable neck. Beautiful collarbones, dusted with freckles. She told me her dream of a perfect husband and family, two little girls and a boy, and I pretended to listen. When we kissed, I poked a small, poisoned needle beneath her hair, and I whispered, 'Go to Thalil, and may he be pleased with my offering.'

"She gasped, realizing too late what I was and what I'd done, but it didn't last long. In seconds she fell dead, facedown into my lap. I kissed each of her eyelids and laid her down among her beloved flowers. As proof of my success, I took one of her pearl earrings. I shed a single tear for her as I presented it to my master. He whipped me raw for crying."

"That seems like a harsh reaction," Duncan said. He handed Sasha a few slices of the roast venison.

Sasha shrugged as he took the tin plate. "It was necessary. I never wasted a tear for a mark after that. I eliminated my flaws and became worthy of serving Thalil. I am without weakness now, as he demands."

"Did you ever find out why you were ordered to kill her?" The knight had developed a morbid fascination all of a sudden.

Sasha nodded. "The mother of another young noblewoman hired me. She wanted to eliminate her daughter's competition for the favor of a Bairn's son."

"Disgraceful," Duncan said.

"It happens far more often than you think, Tam Knight. You'd be surprised how much of politics and history are shaped by daggers in the shadows."

"Tell me of... more blood," Yarrow said, licking lips that shimmered with lard.

"Not tonight, my friend," Sasha said. He looked down at the soft, worn leather encasing his chest, feeling if he stripped it away he might find it empty. What was he, beneath that armor? He couldn't think about his lost purpose anymore, let alone speak of it. "Perhaps another time. I think I'll rest for the evening. Will you join me, Yarrow?"

"I'd love to but I can't. I'll sleep off on my... own tonight."

"Without a tent?" Duncan asked.

"I'll be... I'll be fine—" The mage staggered into the bracken as if unused to his legs. He drew his hood over his face and curled in a ball among the ferns and briars.

Sasha opened the flap of his tent and sat just beneath it, watching Yarrow through the slit in the canvas. Duncan cleaned up their dinner and hung the leftover meat in a tree to keep it away from animals. Yarrow's eyes glinted from where he lay in the snow, watching until Duncan entered his tent. Sasha found himself irrationally frightened of Yarrow as he watched the mage huddled in the shadows. Something about Yarrow seemed almost inhuman, like a predatory animal with blood already on his lips, poised to pounce. Even his glowing eyes looked feline and feral. The other man lay still for almost an hour, waiting for the others to retire, before he sat up and looked around, sniffing the air like a wild beast. He sprung to his feet and hurried to the road that led into town. Sasha had neither undressed nor removed his boots, and he got quietly to his feet. Outside of Duncan's tent, he stopped and announced himself.

"What is it you want, Sasha?" Duncan snapped.

"You must come at once, tam. It's Yarrow."

Duncan hurried to the entrance, carrying his heavy breastplate. "What's happened?"

"He's gone. I watched him wait until he thought we were asleep and head for town."

"So what?" Duncan said. "Yarrow is an adult and can go where he likes. Why bother me with this?"

"Don't be a fool," Sasha said, pulling Duncan out of the tent by the wrist. "Leave the armor. There's no time, and it will make noise. Hurry, now, or we'll lose him."

"Why do you think we should follow Yarrow?" Even as he grumbled, Duncan jogged along behind Sasha toward the road and the village beyond it. The mage moved quickly. Already Sasha saw only a tiny sliver of black in the distance.

"I'm worried, Duncan," Sasha confessed. "Yarrow wasn't at all himself at supper. Earlier he wanted to avoid this town, but now he sneaks off to visit it. He's… he's not kept anything from me yet. I can't imagine why he wouldn't tell me his plans." Sasha's quarry crested a hill and disappeared. The assassin ran faster, kicking up snow, and Duncan followed, his heavy boots making more noise than Sasha cared for. Still, Duncan's endurance impressed Sasha as he matched the assassin's pace without tiring.

"I've watched Yarrow practically starve to avoid eating animal flesh," Duncan said. "Tonight, though…."

"Exactly," Sasha said. "As much as I hate to even wonder, do you think Yarrow might betray us?"

Duncan slid to a halt and looked murderously at Sasha. "How dare you?"

"Calm yourself. I'm just being practical. It would hurt me the most if he turned against us, but you were deceived by what you thought were loyal men, and I was tricked and almost murdered by my own brothers. Now our companion sneaks away while we sleep? I'm fond of Yarrow, but we need to be more cautious."

"You're fond of him? I've seen you two together. I think it runs deeper than that, Sasha."

"No, tam, it doesn't."

"You don't love him? Not at all?" Duncan seemed shocked.

"You misunderstand," Sasha said, running with long strides toward the cluster of lights in the distance. "I *can't* love him. I'm unable. From the time I was a child, almost from infancy, I was taught to eliminate those weak feelings. Through training, and occasionally the whip, I did so quite effectively. I can no longer feel love or form an attachment to another person. That part of me is as dead as any of my marks."

"Does Yarrow know that?"

"This isn't important," Sasha said, though for a second he wondered how his mage would react to the knowledge. "All I'm saying is that we should see what Yarrow's up to. If he meets with someone, we should know who he is and what the two of them discuss."

"I dislike admitting it," Duncan said, "but I agree with you. Yarrow was very reluctant to accompany us. We should hurry. Yarrow is almost to the edge of the village."

"We'll need to stay farther back," Sasha advised. "We can't let Yarrow know we're here, or he might abandon whatever he's attempting to do." He pulled the knight behind a small shed just as Yarrow looked over his shoulder.

"I'll defer to your expertise in this matter," Duncan said, though he managed to sound insulting.

"Good." Sasha managed to keep the knight hidden, though he moved clumsily and had no talent for stealth. Eventually they followed Yarrow to a raucous tavern near the opposite edge of the little town. Half a dozen whores mingled with their patrons on the porch, despite the cold of the evening. One man lay drunk across the steps. Sasha and Duncan stepped over him and entered the inn. The number of inebriated guests packed into the single room ensured their ambiguity. Sasha spotted Yarrow in a corner near the bar. He tapped Duncan on the shoulder and pointed.

The young mage stood with a woman of even more dubious morality than a whore. She was older, and the pretty mage's attentions drew peels of artificial laughter from her painted lips. The loose flesh at her neck giggled with her jollity. Sasha grimaced, confused and a little disgusted. He'd seen Yarrow around much more attractive women than this old tart, and the mage had never paid them any mind. He'd barely thought more of the lovely serving maids at the Peregrym estate than he had of the furnishings. Sasha had felt certain Yarrow was not a man who enjoyed either gender, but a man who preferred other men.

The aging strumpet motioned to a friend: a garishly made-up, plump woman in a pink bodice. She touched Yarrow beneath his shirt, and he kissed her deeply. Tawdry magenta lined Yarrow's lips when he came up for a breath. A few of the men and women watching the paramours hooted and clapped. A big man with a bright red beard joined the trio. The man, in his dirty, homespun garments, yanked Yarrow's head back and ravaged his mouth without a hint of romance. When Yarrow pushed against his chest, the man drew back and struck the mage's face with the back of his hand. Blood dribbled from Yarrow's chin even as the other yanked the old whore away to grab Yarrow between the legs. The mage smiled and theatrically licked his lips.

Sasha extended the slim blade beneath his wrist with a soft click and took a step toward his companion. He anticipated killing every person who'd laid a hand on his mage; he looked forward to piercing their flesh in places that would bleed out slowly. They would have been dead within seconds had Duncan not grabbed Sasha's elbow.

"Sasha, I understand why you'd react to this," Duncan said. "But Yarrow isn't protesting. It could be he came to town for this reason. It seems likely, in fact."

As Sasha watched, Yarrow seized a mug of ale from a passing bar wench and drained most of it, spilling the remainder down his chest. The fat slag in pink dropped to her knees. More patrons gathered to watch the show, cheering Yarrow and the old whore on. The bearded man continued to kiss and grope him, smacking Yarrow in the face now and then and laughing at the blood.

"I'll kill them all," Sasha whispered. "Let go of me, Duncan."

"You can't do that," Duncan said, more gently than he'd ever spoken to Sasha. "This is, apparently, what Yarrow wants."

"They're hurting him!"

"He appears to want that too. No matter what you say, this can't be easy for you to watch. I know it isn't for me. Better than him coming here to betray us, though, right?"

"No."

"Sasha, we should probably go." The large man dragged Yarrow toward the stairs that led to rooms above the tavern, wrenching Yarrow's hair if the mage fell behind. The two slovenly women followed eagerly. Some other stragglers, men and women, watched curiously, and a few joined them.

"We must follow as well," Sasha said.

"You really don't want to see this, Sasha, my friend."

"But, but what if this is just a ruse? What if one of these people is a traitor, the one Yarrow is supposed to meet? Don't you think we should make sure?"

"You can't be fool enough to believe that. Don't delude yourself. Don't cause yourself needless pain," Duncan said. "Let's just go back to the camp."

"I… I agree." Sasha looked once at the stairs, trying to stamp down the images his mind conjured, before turning toward the door. He knew he shouldn't be susceptible to the pain, and yet he couldn't deny it. Why would Yarrow subject himself to such treatment? Sasha couldn't imagine his attentions weren't enough. He attended to the mage every night at least, and sometimes twice. Oftentimes they lay together upon waking as well. "It matters little to me how Yarrow spends his time," he said, more to convince himself than Duncan.

The big knight surprised Sasha by patting him on the head and nodding.

They'd almost reached the exit when someone grabbed Sasha's elbow and whispered, "Blood for Thalil, my brother."

Each of Sasha's hands closed around a dagger, and Duncan drew his enormous blade. The auburn-haired, comely young man who'd spoken raised his hands. Sasha recognized him. They'd been on several missions together and occasionally shared a bedroll. "Thalil's favor on you too, my brother," Sasha said.

"I must speak with you," the redhead said, his cheeks nipped pink as though he'd just come in from the cold. His sapphire eyes darted back and forth.

"Speak, then."

"Not here." The young man took Sasha's hand and pulled him into a storage room full of ale kegs, crates of cheese, and shelves of bread. The smell was overwhelming. "My brother," the red-haired man said, "I should not tell you this, but we've been friends in the past. You are betrayed. The Crimson Scythe will reap your life, in Thalil's name. I never knew we could target one of our own, but that's what they've done. The order hunts you now."

"But why?" Sasha asked.

"Coin. They'll be handsomely rewarded if they can pass you off as the dead Prince Garith."

"What of the real prince?" Duncan demanded.

"The order is seeking him," the assassin said. "Seeking him desperately."

"Who is responsible for this?" Duncan roared.

"That I don't know, tam," the young man said. "Whoever he is, he must have deep pockets. I can't believe the order would sacrifice my talented brother otherwise."

"They simply put a price on me," Sasha mused. "My life has a monetary value."

"As do all lives to the Crimson Scythe," the redhead said.

"I was one of them," Sasha said. "I would have sacrificed my life in service to Thalil. Does it mean nothing?"

"I'm sorry, brother."

"I appreciate the information," Sasha said, kissing his former associate on the cheek. "Get away, before you are suspected."

They stood breathing the rancid stench of cheese and stale ale, neither speaking. When Sasha looked at Duncan, he saw concern on the older man's face. "You must believe your life is priceless beyond any gold. All lives are. Are you all right with this?" Duncan finally asked.

Sasha feigned a chuckle. "Of course! My order, to which I belonged since I was a small boy, to which I felt more loyalty to than a family, turned on me for profit. And my lover is in a flea-ridden bed upstairs, spread out for anyone who wants to take a turn. I can't imagine how the day could get better."

To Sasha's shock, Duncan squeezed his shoulder and draped his burly arm across Sasha's back. "I wish I knew what to tell you," the knight said. "I truly wish I could ease your pain."

As much as Sasha wanted to get irritated, to tell the other man he didn't need pity, he found he couldn't be angry. Even though the knight hated him, Duncan truly didn't enjoy seeing Sasha suffer. It was incomprehensible, yet... a little bit comforting. Looking into the knight's eyes, Sasha clearly saw his every emotion: empathy, confusion, and the desire to soothe. He'd never known a man to reveal his heart and its secret contents so freely. Sasha felt unfamiliar with this form of courage, but he stood in awe of the knight's voluntary vulnerability. With his soul laid so bare, Sasha could strike a deathblow. Duncan must've known this and left himself open anyway. Sasha found he'd rather shield the other man, who stood with his roots exposed, like a tree in a barren land wanting soil. He wriggled closer to the larger man, turned his face toward his whiskered chin, and stopped just short of kissing him. "Duncan," Sasha said with a smile, "are you sure I can't kill even two or three of those drunkards?"

"Would it make you feel better?"

"I think it would, yes."

"Ah, friend," the knight said, grinning wide. "If it wouldn't alert your order to our presence here, I'd be sorely tempted to encourage you. In all seriousness, though, Yarrow is a very unusual man."

"Agreed," Sasha said. "Not unusual like this, though. Something else is at work. I just don't know what."

Chapter Eight

YARROW WOKE facedown in the snow. He swallowed air as if he'd been under deep, black water, unable to banish the starved feeling in his lungs. Gradually he became aware of his limbs and extremities, and even more slowly, he remembered how to control his hands and feet. They felt clumsy and heavy, too large for his body. His head felt like a cannonball, but he eventually managed to lift it and spit out the dirt and frozen grass that filled his mouth. The various parts of Yarrow's body scarcely felt connected. Arms shaking, he pushed his chest up next, horrified at what he saw. Blood covered the entire front of his shirt and part of his pant leg. From the way his body felt, Yarrow wondered if the blood was his own. His face felt achy and swollen, like he'd been hit repeatedly. All of his muscles screamed, and his ass and genitals were raw and hot.

Too much blood stained his clothes to have come from his own injuries, Yarrow knew. His stomach flipped, and he vomited bitter ale and questionable meat into the snow. *What did you do?* he screamed at his companion, but it only laughed, mocking him, in response. *Answer me,* Yarrow demanded.

I only enjoyed the vast range of sensory experience available to one who has the flesh to perceive it. I had a lovely time in that beautiful body, beloved. How it pained me to give it back.

Did you hurt anyone? What is this blood?

I... may have overindulged.

Damn it, creature! Give me a straight answer!

No, it said. *I healed the knight, and in exchange I used the flesh as I chose. That is what we agreed, Yarrow.*

What am I going to do now? Yarrow grasped a low hanging branch and pulled himself to his feet. His legs felt like they'd never held him before, and his knees buckled, making him slip and fall. He tried to stand again and fell once more. On his third attempt, his muscles quivered but supported him. Yarrow looked around at the slender, gray trees and snow-covered brush between their trunks. Up the hill, a quarter mile or so in the distance, a wavering column of smoke rose toward the clouds. Yarrow felt frantic. He couldn't possibly go back to camp in his current state.

Instead, he staggered in the opposite direction. His body slowly started to obey him, and before long he didn't need the trees as support. He descended a hill slick with frozen mud and rotted leaves, and was grateful to find a small stream at the bottom.

Yarrow wasted no time, disrobing and laying his surprisingly uncontaminated black cloak and leather armor on a round stone. He peeled off his filthy garments and inspected his body. Other than a few nondescript bruises, nothing but Sasha's love bites marred his skin. That would give him less to explain the next time his partner saw him naked. Bruises could be dismissed as battle injuries or just the result of their recent, rough survival. They also told Yarrow the blood on his shirt undoubtedly came from another.

Shivering hard, though he tried to ignore the bitter cold, Yarrow plunged his shirt and trousers into the stream and scrubbed them as hard as he could. His hands went numb as he dashed his clothes against the rocks of the bank until the water washed away the muddy, red cloud surrounding them. Yarrow wrung the fabric out and left it beside the cloak. Then, though he dreaded it, he stepped into the stream. The water reached his knees at the center. His toes sank into the icy mud of the bed. Yarrow crouched down and splashed some water on his chest and under his arms. The cold stole his breath, but he kept at it until he'd washed every rusty smear from his body. He cupped his hands and washed his mouth out, rinsing and spitting until he no longer tasted bile or rancid meat. Then he hurried to replace his boots and drape the cloak over his shoulders. He shook violently. There was only one other time he could remember being quite so cold.

Yarrow made his way toward the camp, but he stopped a few hundred yards outside it. What would he say to Sasha and Duncan? He didn't know how much of his companion they'd seen the previous night. Perhaps he should avoid them, and the camp, altogether. Eventually everyone noticed something off about Yarrow, and he'd learned to move on before their theories approached the truth. He'd hoped to spend a little more time in the two men's company, but it seemed the day had come. He'd already let them see past the walls he'd erected to protect himself, let them shatter some of the anonymity he nurtured. Yarrow knew only too well he'd cause Sasha and Duncan anguish if he remained. Why did walking out on them, disappearing without a word as he'd done so many times before, cause him such distress?

In the end, Yarrow decided he needed the fireside at least long enough to thaw his frozen flesh and dry his clothes. He needed a place to rest where he would be safe. Yarrow didn't even have the strength to conjure a small, spectral blaze of his own, so he entered the sparse site. Duncan sat cooking the leftover twirl-horn. The smell made Yarrow gag as some hazy memory swam at the edges of his mind. He said nothing as he went to the fire and spread his wet clothes on the ground. He held his cloak tightly shut to cover his nudity.

"Hungry, Tam Yarroway?" the knight asked, not looking up from the small iron pan he held.

Yarrow considered. "I do feel somehow… empty. Is there any bread?"

"Only a little, and it's rock hard. There's plenty of meat left from the tender buck I killed yesterday. Will you have some?"

"You know I dislike it, Duncan."

"Do I now? Perhaps you find it overcooked."

What's going on? Yarrow asked the other. *What's he trying to imply?*

How do I know?

"I… thank you, Tam Knight, but no."

"Suit yourself." Duncan returned his attention to his breakfast.

Sasha emerged from his tent, fully dressed in his skintight dark red leathers with the myriad buckles. His features blank, he asked, "Where have you been already this morning, my friend?"

"I had trouble sleeping. These clothes are so dirty after all this time on the road, so I rose early to wash them in the stream."

"Well, you must be quite worn out," Sasha said.

He knows. Both of them do.

They suspect something, beloved. But they know nothing concrete, so calm yourself.

They're disgusted by me. Why? What did you do? You swore you'd have nothing to do with either of these men.

I kept my word, Yarrow. Maybe they just don't like you as much as you think they do.

I've had enough of you. Leave me in peace for a while.

The presence laughed but complied. Yarrow felt it withdraw entirely from his consciousness. He hadn't been completely free of it since before they'd joined, and it felt bizarrely lonely and frightening to be on his own. He'd had so much faith in his abilities before he'd bonded with the presence, but Yarrow found it difficult to find that confidence again. He needed the damned thing. Sasha's and Duncan's judgmental glares cut Yarrow to the core. They'd never understand.

"I would like to rest," he told them. "If only for a couple of hours. Will I hold us up too much if I lie down?"

They looked at each other, something unsaid passing between them, and Yarrow felt like even more of an outsider. Duncan nodded and said, "As you will, Tam Yarroway."

Yarrow entered Sasha's tent and collapsed on the blankets they'd shared with a dull ache in his chest. The quilts still smelled of a mélange of their scents: new snow and warm spices. He curled on his side and drew the covers to his chin as he inhaled the fragrance and remembered the passion he'd shared with Sasha. No matter how he tried to deny it, the idea that their nights together were over pained Yarrow's heart. He'd been fool enough to think Sasha might understand his situation. Sasha was a killer himself, an interloper who might appreciate the bargain Yarrow had made. He realized now what an absurd fantasy it had been, and he shed a few silent tears. Solitude had always been his destiny, and he'd accepted it until now. He'd continue to accept it. It would be wrong to suck Sasha or Duncan into his catastrophe.

He reminded himself he still lived when he shouldn't and forced that notion to assuage him. Being alone and alive trumped death a hundred times over. Yarrow swallowed his self-pity.

As he lay between wakefulness and sleep, Yarrow watched the oldest dream of the entity that shared his body. It had had flesh, a physical form of its own once, similar to a man's but larger and more muscular, with long, black nails, hair like midnight, and two sets of enormous, curling horns. When it looked at its reflection in the still, mountain pools, a handsome if savage face with solid black eyes looked back. Sometimes it had resplendent azure wings, and other times it chose not to.

It had watched and waited as the other living things of the world evolved. Now and then it destroyed them for fun, like a child squashing insects. They moved from holes in the ground to shelters constructed from wood and animal hides. Their little wars and crude weapons entertained the entity. They soon discovered rudimentary magic. One of them, a young man with skin as brown as a berry, knotted ropes of hair adorned with animal bones, and nothing but a scrap of fur concealing his tender places, ascended the mountain where the presence lived. He was a beauty, and braver than the creature thought his kind capable. He made his way to the entity's cave and sat with his long, lovely legs folded. The two of them spoke, and the presence grew fond of the pretty young human as the weeks and months passed.

The boy was as bright as sunlight on water, sharper than a thorn, and adept at sorcery. The creature schooled him in magic, and he proved an apt pupil. The entity soon found him just as receptive to learning the arts of physical pleasure. It became enamored of the young man, and taught him its every secret. Their nights of exploration and bliss played out before Yarrow. He looked down at the handsome face grimacing with strain as his body accommodated the creature's unusually large member. He watched as the creature taught the primitive shaman every erotic and arcane trick it knew. It detested the simple grunts that comprised the boy's name, and took to calling him "beloved."

After he'd learned everything the presence had to teach, the young man lulled the creature to sleep after an exhaustive bout of lovemaking. He used the very spells he'd learned from the entity to insure it didn't wake for a long time. While it slumbered, the shaman used what he'd discovered to steal the entity's power, bind it, and destroy its physical form since he knew he couldn't kill it. It finally woke, completely immobilized and already fading fast. Yarrow shuddered at the helpless feeling of being unable to move or speak, and the horror of flesh disintegrating, not rotting or burning, just ceasing to be. The being realized its lover's deceit, but by then he could do nothing to stop it. The boy had stolen the creature's magical knowledge and turned it against him. He'd earned the powers of a god and regained his freedom from the presence.

Though he would never dare let the words form in his mind, somewhere deep in his soul, in a hidden place that still belonged to him, Yarrow planned to do the same. He didn't have the knowledge yet, and the longer he stayed bonded to the creature, the more he would learn, the stronger he'd become. Unfortunately, the longer the two remained joined, the more control the being exerted over him. Yarrow already struggled to wrestle it down when it wanted to take over. One day he'd lose the battle, and he shuddered to think what the creature might do if given free rein. He felt it stir, down near the base of his skull, and he banished the embryonic plan from his mind.

Yarrow distracted the creature by conjuring memories of his unions with Sasha, and by imagining how Duncan might be as a lover. The knight would be gentle and attentive, Yarrow knew, and he pictured it in great detail. It added fantasies of its own, more savage and cruel than Yarrow's visions. The images frustrated Yarrow, but he felt too exhausted and far too sore to alleviate his desire with his hand. He lay staring at the bright white peak of the tent until he fell into a fitful sleep.

DUNCAN POLISHED his armor for the third time. Across the camp, Sasha sharpened his knives, checking and double-checking their placement about his person. The assassin stood, stalked around the perimeter of their site, then sat back down on his fallen tree and checked his daggers again. He repeated the routine until Duncan finally spoke.

"Are you quite all right, Sasha?"

"I'm fine. Why wouldn't I be? I'm just impatient to be on our way. Staying in one place will only entice my brethren."

Duncan shook his head. How alike the mage and the assassin seemed at times, using their vitriol as a bulwark to drive others back. Sasha's injured feelings were plain to the knight, but he used surliness as a defense. "Would you like to talk?" Duncan said without much hope of a favorable response.

Sasha ceased his pacing and stood with his back to Duncan. He balled his fists and moved his feet far apart: a fighting stance. The knight braced himself for the other man's ire. Instead, the assassin's head and shoulders drooped, and he shook his head slowly.

"No, it's nothing. I'm just eager to be on the road."

"Are you planning to stay with him?"

"Who?"

"Please, Sasha."

"Fine," the assassin said, spinning around. Duncan had expected everything but the emotionless mask Sasha wore. "I can't stay with him because I'm not with him, not in the way you envision it. You're asking if I'll continue to take physical pleasure with him. The answer to that… I don't know. Does this please you?"

"Nothing about this pleases me. This journey, everything that's happened…. It's been a disaster from the beginning."

"I'm wondering if the end of my association with Yarrow would please you, Tam Knight. Are you thinking to take my place? You need not have waited. I claim no ownership of Yarrow. If he wishes to split his evenings between us, that's his choice."

"That wouldn't trouble you?"

"Why should it?" Sasha said with a shrug. "Ask him into your tent tonight, if you like. I could care less. Or you could join us."

"I can't do that," Duncan said, staring hard at the gauntlet he held.

"Why? Have a wife and some little ones back in Thulemore?"

"No, no wife," Duncan said. "But Yarrow… I don't know if I'd be worthy of his trust. I have responsibilities that must always come first. I fear I might disappoint him."

"Oh, I bet you wouldn't be a disappointment," Sasha purred. His black eyes felt like they peered straight into Duncan's heart, but the knight didn't look away. The stare wasn't a challenge, but something else, something that disturbed and intrigued Duncan. He knew exactly what he felt stirring at the root of his body, but he wouldn't do it the honor of naming it in his mind. His reaction to the assassin confused him. He supposed the Order of the Crimson Scythe trained its agents to manipulate emotion to gain specific responses from others. He'd be more aware of it from now on.

"I'm going to wake him up," Duncan said. "Your assessment is correct. We should be on our way."

Duncan stood and Sasha stepped forward to clasp his hand. "You know, Tam Knight, I think that was the first civilized conversation we've shared. You didn't insult me once. I rather enjoyed it."

A startling thought occurred to Duncan. Had he used disrespect to push Sasha away, the same as Sasha and Yarrow did to him? Why did he need to keep Sasha at a distance? "I still don't approve of you," he said quickly, pulling free from Sasha's hand.

"Perish the thought," Sasha said, smirking as Duncan entered the tent, knelt down, and touched the mage's face to rouse him.

Yarrow flinched at first, but smiled when his eyes opened. "Duncan," Yarrow said, his voice scratchy with sleep. "You're here with me."

"I'm here to wake you," the knight said, ignoring the rush of heat to his cheeks. He didn't remove his fingers from Yarrow's warm skin. "You've slept long enough."

"I…. Using my magic tires me sometimes."

"Understood. Make yourself ready to travel as soon as possible." Duncan rose and left the tent, his mind reeling and a tremor moving through his belly.

Yarrow followed and quickly threw his clothing on. The three men took the same path they had not long ago, none of them speaking. They reached the village they'd visited the night before by midday. Some sort of gathering took place outside the town, and it didn't look like a merry one. Duncan stopped a pimply merchant with a scarf over her hair and a heavy pack on her back. He asked her about the occurrence.

"There was a murder last night, tam. The men who serve as guards are questioning everyone. They're looking for a fair-haired man in a black cape." Her eyes flitted to Yarrow. "I must be on my way," the slim, grubby girl said quickly and hurried off.

"Is there anything we should know, Tam Yarroway?" Duncan asked.

The mage fidgeted with the straps that crossed his chest and secured his shoulder armor. "I don't know what you mean." The confusion on his face seemed sincere.

Duncan had no more time to question his companion before half a dozen burly men with simple weapons, spears and clubs, surrounded them. The knight knew they were probably just local farmers called on to defend the little hamlet on the rare occasions it became necessary. Their leader, a balding man with short gray hair and a fairly good sword, moved to the front of the group. He looked like a shrewd combatant, possibly even a veteran of His Majesty's forces. Duncan hurried to stand between the man and Yarrow and Sasha.

"I am Tam Duncan of Thulemore, here on order of His Majesty Agarick. For what reason do you hinder us?"

The older man crossed an arm over his chest and bowed. "Tam, your presence honors us. These men and I are looking for a man with light blond hair who we suspect brutally killed a tavern wench working in this village. I'm sorry to say so, honorable tam, but your companion closely matches the description of the man seen in the lass's company. Witnesses mentioned Emiri paint. We'd like to speak with him, at least."

"He's been in my camp all night," Duncan said, unsure of why he lied.

"We'll just have a word with him," the other man said, pointing toward Yarrow. Three of his guards surrounded the mage and grabbed him by the elbows, wrenching Yarrow's arms behind his back. So fast Duncan almost missed it, Sasha kicked the third guard in the groin as he drew two daggers. Duncan had no idea how the assassin got behind one of the men restraining Yarrow, but Sasha pressed the edge of his knife against the man's windpipe.

"Get your hands off of him," the assassin hissed. The man opposite Sasha dropped Yarrow's arm and ran. The one with the assassin's blade at his throat sputtered and wet himself. Duncan scowled as the urine pooled between his legs.

"Stand down, Sasha," Duncan said. "Let's hear them out."

"No. No one is taking Yarrow. I pity any man who tries."

A villager near the edge of the crowd called out, and a dozen more men holding sticks and pitchforks hurried from the town to encircle the three of them. Sasha looked right and left, taking them all in and no doubt planning a strategy to obliterate them. Though the men outnumbered the companions, Duncan had never seen a person move as fast as Sasha had, and if Yarrow joined the fight these simple peasants would be annihilated. Duncan didn't know if he could allow that. These men wanted only justice for a slaughtered girl. Goddesses, what if they were right about Yarrow? Duncan didn't know if he could protect the mage if he'd actually butchered an innocent young woman. He hated to believe it, but Yarrow's bizarre behavior the night before caused doubt to worm into Duncan's mind.

"Get back or die," Sasha said, raising his voice but losing none of his deliberate composure. He dropped his knife from the guard's neck and whisked Yarrow a few steps away. The two men stood back to back, a more formidable force than the townspeople had any idea.

"He's a murderer!" a plump, ruddy woman hollered, pointing at the mage.

"Why are you protecting this man, Tam Knight?" the gray-haired soldier asked Duncan.

"I don't want anyone coming to harm," Duncan said, holding up his empty hands. "I think we should discuss this matter without resorting to arms."

"It's too late for that," the other man said, shaking his head. "Your companion threatened and attacked us. These two must be considered dangerous, until proven otherwise."

"The first words of wisdom you've spoken," Sasha said. "Try to take us. I could use a few minutes of entertainment."

"I agree," Yarrow said with a bloodthirsty smile. He raised his left hand above his head and thunder and lightning sundered the sky. Many people cowered or flinched, and the mage laughed at their distress.

"Yarrow, Sasha," Duncan pleaded. "Let us all sit down and discuss this, by the goddesses. Nobody needs to get hurt."

"I don't anticipate getting hurt," Yarrow said.

"Nor do I," Sasha agreed.

"We can't just let them get away with killing one of us," a man said. The villagers inched cautiously forward. The mob had doubled in size by now.

"Who are you, anyway?" another man yelled. "An Emiri slug and some southern serpent think they can get away with killing one of our girls?" His words energized the rabble, and they came forward, pride overcoming fear. Sasha sank into a crouch, raising his knives to his shoulders. A balding fellow in a leather apron ran toward them brandishing an iron hammer, and Yarrow struck him in the chest with an invisible force. The large fellow landed on his back and slid a dozen feet through the snow before colliding against a group of women and toppling two of them. The mage's attack hadn't been lethal, yet.

"I implore you to stand down," Duncan shouted in desperation, both to his companions and the angry throng. "Yarrow, for the love of the goddesses, just go with them and answer their questions."

Sasha turned to glare at the knight. "As much as you want him, you won't lift your sword to defend Yarrow? And you wonder why he chooses me."

"This is not something suited to a public discussion, Sasha," Duncan said, scanning the faces of the aghast villagers. The goddesses forbade physical love between men. If kept quiet, most ignored it, but it couldn't be announced so blatantly. Sasha had added fuel to the fire.

"Disgusting," a woman shouted.

"They're unnatural," another villager added.

"Wait!" Duncan yelled, but too late. The horde rushed them. Yarrow grabbed Duncan's elbow and pulled him close. Then the mage erected a shimmering bubble around the three of them. Those that collided with it bounced off, landing on their asses or knocking themselves unconscious. Duncan saw the sweat above Yarrow's eyebrows and lips and knew the effort strained the mage, who still looked exhausted from the previous night. He wouldn't be able to shield them forever. Outside of the sparkling sphere, people pounded the barrier with crude tools or their bare fists. Its luminescence faltered. Encouraged by the small victory, the multitudes redoubled their efforts. Rocks recoiled from the blockade, and a few of them managed to penetrate it. One struck the assassin on the hip.

"We'll have to face them," Sasha said with his infuriating serenity. "Will you stand with us, Duncan?"

"Goddesses, these are farmers," Duncan said in response.

"You owe him your life," Sasha said mildly. "Back in the Crimson Scythe safe house, you were mortally wounded. I wanted to leave you to die. It was the practical thing. You would have agreed on a battlefield. Yarrow insisted we drag you out. He risked himself and me, and saved you. Yet you won't return the favor. And you say I have no honor."

"Shut your poisonous mouth, Sasha!" Duncan roared. "This is not the time."

"If you won't fight for Yarrow, don't cower in his protection," the assassin said in his velvet drawl. More stones and a shovel and rake breached Yarrow's blockade. Sasha bent his neck to dodge a rolling pin.

"Enough of this nonsense," the mage said, tossing back the villagers toward the front of the throng with a small gesture. "I can handle this on my own." Dark clouds gathered above them. Morning became twilight, and lightning danced between the clouds. Intense thunder shook the ground beneath their boots. Duncan felt like it split his eardrums. A fork of electricity skewered a man, and he fell in a twitching, smoking heap. More flickering power skipped across Yarrow's fingers. "Who wants some?" He giggled with delight as a bolt severed the frozen ground, inches from the shoes of a group of housewives.

To Duncan's repulsion, Sasha laughed in response. "Stop!" he cried. "This isn't right! These people are Selindrians, not our enemies. I implore you to stand down. Yarrow, see reason."

"I won't tolerate these accusations," Yarrow said. "I won't be slandered again."

"Please stop, Yarroway!"

"No."

It would be a fight, then, and Duncan didn't know where to stand. Would he slaughter delusional farmers or turn his back on his companions? Sweat glazed his palms as he reached for his sword. As much as it pained him, he'd battle beside Yarrow. Later, he'd reprimand the lad for being such a self-centered and violent imp. Now, he needed his wits about him. Two dozen or more fanatical villagers surrounded them. Stones rained down. The tines of pitchforks pierced Yarrow's obstacle. Sasha promptly swung at the offender, slicing across his gut and spilling his innards on the ground. It made Duncan ill to see the simple man collapse, holding his belly, in a pool of blood. One woman screamed and another sobbed.

Fueled by vengeance for their fallen friend, the villagers assaulted the magic bubble furiously. A thick tree branch struck Duncan's waist, but his heavy armor prevented it from harming him. He struck his attacker in the diaphragm with his elbow and knocked the wind out of him. Yarrow's enchantment disintegrated, and fists and crude weaponry and tools pummeled the men. Duncan shielded his head with his arms and kicked at the villagers nearest him. Unless absolutely necessary, he didn't plan to kill any of them. Sasha didn't share his philosophy and fought as if possessed, clearly determined to take his anger and confusion out on someone. The assassin's arms moved in blurs, drawing fountains and fans of blood. His blade whizzed past Duncan's cheek and cut the throat of a villager brandishing a shovel. The resulting arc of blood splattered all three of their faces. Duncan gagged but couldn't see a way of ending the fray without more death.

Yarrow screamed as a kitchen knife pierced his shoulder. A clawed hand made of spectral blue seized his assailant around the waist, lifted him a dozen feet into the air, and slammed him against the ground. A young woman howled with anguish as she ran toward the broken body and threw herself across its chest.

The hidden blade below Sasha's wrist plunged into a man's neck below the jaw. The poor fellow clapped a hand over the wound but bled out in minutes. Yarrow raised his arms and turned his palms toward the darkened sky. A burst of energy shot out from the mage and his companions at the epicenter. Everyone around them flew back several feet. Yarrow's eyes mirrored the lightning flashing above them, and his spectral arm reappeared, darting toward its next victim. Duncan seized his shoulder. "Yarrow, stop!" The claw flickered and disappeared. Both Yarrow and Sasha stood panting and covered in gore. The villagers stirred and started to rise. The commotion drew more men and women out of the simple shops and homes.

"What is the meaning of this?" asked a strong voice. Duncan spun around. Though he hadn't heard the approaching hooves over the battle, a man astride a fine golden steed waited a few feet behind them, flanked by eight younger knights. Their commander wore bronze-toned plate and a helmet open to reveal his aged but handsome face.

"Thank the goddesses you're here," said the man with the gray hair. He ran toward the commander and bowed when he reached him. He pointed at Yarrow and said, "That man killed one of our local girls, and his, his *friend* here attacked us when we tried to question him. They've committed unnatural acts on each other; I'm sure of it! Five of us are dead. Please, tam, arrest these whoresons. Er, pardon my language, honorable knight."

"Are you a simpleton?" the knight-commander demanded. "This man is the king's nephew, here on a task for Agarick. All of you will step away from him."

"But tam! Our men! These blackguards have sinned against the goddesses, in more ways than one. What of the poor little wench they killed? Five more of us dead!"

"We were defending ourselves," Sasha retorted.

"Who is this? Wait, I remember you from the meeting with His Majesty. You're the assassin." He tugged his reins to back his horse a little further from Sasha and eyed him warily.

"Assassin?" a villager shouted. "You admit they're killers!"

"And I remember you," Sasha said, ignoring the outcry behind him. "Tam Taran Edercrest. We were to meet you at the Starlight Bridge in Lockhaven. How is it that you're so far south?"

The older man paled but answered. "A group of hunters found what was left of your caravan. We set out in search of survivors. Are there any others? You there, knight."

Duncan bowed and approached the horse. The beast whinnied and tossed its blond mane, probably at the smell of blood. "Tam Taran," Duncan said with a bow. "I am Duncan Purefroy, knight of Thulemore, charged with escorting His Highness Prince Garith to his nuptials in Gaeltheon."

Thunder punctuated Duncan's words, and the knight-commander looked irritably at the sky. "Tam Yarroway, if you would be so kind." He pointed at the clouds.

Yarrow nodded and the thunderheads drifted slowly away. Patches of thin morning light reflected off the knights' and horses' armor. The villagers looked about in confusion. A few women cried softly. Long, tense moments stretched out. When Duncan could bear no more, he spoke just to break the silence. "We were betrayed and attacked in the night," he told Taran. "The prince's entourage and all of my loyal men were slaughtered. Yarrow, Sasha, and I barely survived. We determined it best to make our way toward Lockhaven and meet with you to inform you of the situation."

"A prudent course of action," Tam Taran said, nodding once at Duncan. "However, if you became aware of our ruse, did you think it wise to bring that man along?" He looked beyond Duncan's right shoulder to where the assassin stood.

"Not at first," Duncan admitted. "But Sasha has proved to be a loyal and capable ally. I trust and value him."

The assassin inhaled sharply but said nothing. Duncan continued, saying, "He's given us some very sensitive information. Perhaps we should discuss this matter elsewhere."

"Agreed. Tam Duncan, have you discovered who was to blame for this atrocity?"

"Only partially." Duncan's thoughts turned to the Crimson Scythe. "I assume by your expression you know more."

The older knight nodded gravely. "We believe we have found the ones responsible."

"Who, tam?" Duncan said.

"As you astutely suggested, Tam Duncan, this is not the place to talk of these matters. We are camped a few miles north of here. If you and your companions will join me there, we can speak further."

"Agreed."

"What?" a village woman shouted. "You're going to let them get away with killing one of us?" Others mumbled or yelled their angry assents.

Tam Taran held up a hand to silence them. His powerful, authoritative voice cowed the angry mob into near silence. "These charges against Tam Yarroway L'Estrella, nephew of His Majesty King Agarick, are unfounded fabrications. Return to your homes. I have made my decision as a knight of the realm, and you must abide by it. I have no time for this nonsense. Be thankful I also have no time to see to punishments for peasants attacking a member of the nobility and a knight." He tugged his horse's left rein and the beast turned in a circle.

It seemed to Duncan an added insult to show these poor people his horse's haunches, but he doubted Tam Taran intended it. Sad as it was, nobles like Yarroway got away with indiscretions, even the murders of peasant girls. It had been the same way for as long as anyone could remember. As a younger man, Duncan had dreamt of righting such inequalities, but such struggles felt more futile with each passing year. While Duncan felt relieved at Yarrow's exoneration of a sort, it hurt him that the common people, the very backbone of Selindria, could be denied justice like this. Since nothing he could say or do would make a difference, he followed after the knight-commander, eager to escape the smell of death and the sound of crying.

"My mount is strong, Tam Duncan," Taran said. "You're welcome to ride with me." Duncan smiled and took the commander's hand to get into the saddle. "Your companions, Tam Yarroway and that assassin, may ride with one of my men."

"I'll run beside you," Sasha said. "I'll not slow you down."

Yarrow walked among the knights, assessing them like goods in a market. Finally he settled on a handsome one with black hair and a short beard. He swung his slender leg gracefully over the gray mare's back. The knight started when the mage grasped him around the waist. Duncan just shook his head.

Chapter Nine

"HOW LARGE a company do you have here?" Duncan asked Tam Taran as they walked through the camp. Looking about, Yarrow noticed at least a dozen tents. Soldiers milled around between them, cooking over fires, repairing gear, or just sitting in conversation. They looked up at Yarrow and Sasha and whispered to each other as they passed. Yarrow supposed Duncan, in his well-worn plate, seemed more familiar to them. Blood still covered all three of them, despite their attempts at washing up at the trough outside the camp's makeshift stables. He supposed the men had become accustomed to it too.

"I have a dozen knights and twice as many infantrymen," Taran said.

"A substantial force," Duncan observed.

"Of course. I'd prepared a regiment appropriate to escort Prince Garith to his wedding."

"Yet you knew it wasn't the prince's procession you'd be meeting," Sasha said, folding his arms over his chest and leaning against a tree. "Is that not so?"

"This assassin is bold," Taran said to Duncan, as if Sasha didn't exist. "But his question is legitimate. It is true I knew this man wasn't Garith, but to keep our deception believable I had to behave as though he was. Had I brought a smaller company, my earnest intent to protect His Highness might have been questioned."

"A fair point," Duncan said.

There's more going on here than he's telling us, beloved.

Yes, I know. But what?

We'll know soon enough, won't we? It will be interesting to see.

Tam Taran stopped in front of an elaborate tent guarded by two halberdiers. At his approach, the soldiers uncrossed their weapons. The one on the right lifted the tent flap. "Tam Duncan, Tam Yarroway, please join me," the older man said with a forced smile.

When the knight-commander reached for Yarrow's shoulder, Yarrow flinched and jumped out of the way, his body reacting before his mind knew what he was doing. Tam Taran's hand recoiled as if poisonous daggers covered Yarrow's cloak, but he quickly recovered his smile and repeated his request for the two men to join him inside.

"And Sasha," Yarrow said. The other man's presence made him feel safe, though he couldn't name any immediate danger.

"This is very sensitive information, Tam Yarroway," Taran gently explained. "I'm sure you'll understand if I'd rather keep it privileged."

"I will not. Sasha comes with me, us."

"I must protest, Tam Yarroway. I'm not sure if you know what kind of a man this is, but he's not to be trusted. He'd slit your throat while you slept for a handful of gold. Personally, I'm not at all comfortable in his company." When the older knight looked at Sasha, he tried unsuccessfully to mask his fear.

Coward, Yarrow's passenger muttered, amused.

Or wiser than he looks, Yarrow thought, regarding Sasha. *I think I hate him. I'll make him do as I say. I'm the stronger one.*

Very good, beloved.

"I insist we include Sasha," Yarrow repeated, growing cross.

"Tam, I don't think it wise—"

"Irrelevant," Yarrow said, flicking his fingers as if troubled by a fly. "I am a noble of Selindria, a cousin to the royal family, and I say Sasha joins us. Will you disobey me, Tam Taran?"

"No, my lord," the elder knight said with a scowl. "Come with me, Tam Yarroway, Tam Duncan, *Sasha*...."

Sasha laughed, so close to the back of Yarrow's neck that Yarrow felt his breath ruffling his hair. "You pulled rank," he whispered. "I've never seen you do that before."

Yarrow simply turned and winked at Sasha as the three of them entered the tent. It contained some crates of supplies, a cot covered in furs, and a wooden table. The men sat down around it, Taran and Duncan on one side and Yarrow and Sasha across from them. Yarrow poured water into a clay mug and drank.

Duncan drummed his fingertips against the tabletop impatiently. "You know who orchestrated the attack against us, Tam Taran. Don't leave us in suspense any longer."

"Very well." The older knight rubbed his temples, appearing exhausted. "The man who betrayed you was… Prince Garith."

"Absurd!" Duncan smacked the table with his fist, jarring the cups and pitcher of water.

"It pains me too," Taran said. "If all the evidence we've gathered didn't point to him, I wouldn't believe it either."

"What evidence?" Sasha asked.

The knight-commander ignored him, so Yarrow repeated the query.

"We apprehended some of the assassins who attacked you. You managed to kill most of them, but a few fled. We questioned them. They were hired by the prince and paid for by his mother, the queen. It seems young Garith didn't wish to wed."

"Are you honestly suggesting Garith had all of those men killed because he got cold feet?" Yarrow asked.

"I know it seems a stretch, but everything I and my men found points to Garith and Queen Denna Corina."

"What is everything?" Sasha asked before Yarrow got the chance.

"We found a gemmed bracelet known to belong to the queen, as well as a rare and valuable magical tome from Espero, on one of the assassins. He claimed they were payment for making it seem as though the prince had perished so Garith could escape his marriage."

"That's not right," Sasha said. "The men who attacked us were definitely not of my order. They were clumsy and much too loud. Amateurs. We never would have woken if it had been my former brothers. Furthermore, no member of the Order of the Crimson Scythe would share information about his mission. He would have killed himself if left with no other alternative."

"The Crim—your employers—are not the only assassins in Selindria," Taran said. "Obviously Garith hired others. The point is, he was willing to kill his father's knights and his own cousin to escape his marriage."

"If Garith hired the assassins, why are my brethren hunting him?"

"How could you know that?" Taran asked, his voice a shaky whisper.

"I know many things," Sasha said.

"Provided you're telling the truth."

"What would I have to gain by lying?" Sasha asked.

"I don't claim to understand anything about you or your motives, assassin," Taran said.

"Where is this other assassin now?" Sasha asked. "If you let me speak with him, I can find out a great deal."

"I'm afraid he's dead. They all are."

Convenient, the presence whispered in Yarrow's mind.

Yes, but hardly uncommon. To the living men in the tent, he said, "The word of one assassin, a bracelet, and book. That's hardly damning evidence. The killer could have lied, and the goods could easily have been stolen."

"I'm afraid there's more," Taran said, pouring himself water. "Goddesses, I wish there wasn't. A few nights ago, Eyrle Ambrus Peirs caught his daughter, Ambra, attempting to run away from home. When he questioned the girl, she admitted her plan to meet her secret lover, the prince, and elope. Garith told her no one would ever bother them. A few of the queen's ladies in waiting also divulged that the queen held several clandestine meetings with mysterious men, late at night while Agarick was away, or in the woods beyond the castle. For a queen to see other men at night alone is a punishable offense, and taken with the other evidence, quite suspicious."

"It makes no sense," Yarrow said. "Aunt Den worked for years to arrange this marriage. Why would she sabotage it now?"

"Mothers can act rashly when they see the tears of their children," Duncan said.

"You're not telling me you believe this?" Yarrow asked.

"The arguments are compelling," the knight said, rubbing his forehead. "I just don't know. What are you planning to do next, Tam Taran?"

"The king and queen, their valens, eyrles, and bairns are traveling to Lockhaven."

"For what purpose?" Yarrow asked.

"There will be a trial. The queen's peers will determine her guilt or innocence, and then her fate."

"Why my valenny? Why not hold this trial at the royal estate?" Yarrow wondered. He didn't like the idea of staying at his childhood home. He hadn't spent more than a few hours visiting there in five years. Being around the people who knew him best, his mother and brothers, made him uneasy.

Won't this be an adventure? the presence mocked. *And it will be lovely to see Mother again.*

Be quiet. My head hurts enough already.

"To answer your question, Tam Yarroway, the nobility wanted both a neutral location and a secure one. They expressed fear that more assassins hired by the queen might be hiding in Agarick's castle. Also, you and Tam Duncan are the only living witnesses to the attack. At least the only reputable witnesses. Your testimony will be vital, and we knew if you lived you'd be close to Lockhaven."

"Wait," Sasha said after a long silence. "You knew we'd be here how?"

"This was the route you'd planned. I'm growing weary of you questioning your betters, assassin."

"I can't abide you speaking that way to Sasha," Yarrow said, his voice rising with anger. "I insist you show him the same respect as you'd show me."

"I can't imagine why. I'll honor your wishes, though, Tam Yarroway."

"Good."

"The three of you must be tired," Taran said to end the discussion. "Let me show you to a tent where you can rest for a bit." He stood, and Yarrow, Sasha, and Duncan followed him back out into the cold, bright morning. He led them to a tent near the edge of the camp, a bit removed from the others. "I'll leave you now, and return for you when supper is ready."

Duncan bowed and said a few words of thanks. Yarrow, irritated and partially unsure as to why, slapped the tent flap open with the back of his hand. The senior knight had no business insulting Yarrow's friend, but he'd made amends easily enough. Something else grated on Yarrow, something even beyond his favorite aunt being accused of murder and treason. He searched his heart and mind but couldn't locate the source of his sudden foul mood.

The tent was as cold inside as the forest outside, and it reeked of moldy canvas. At least the oiled cloth kept the worst of the wind at bay. Yarrow collapsed on one of the four cots lining the walls, folded his arms beneath his head, and drew his heels up next to his backside. Duncan sat down across from him and leaned his arms on his knees. Sasha stood near the entrance, his arms crossed.

"There are many things wrong with that man's account," the assassin said calmly. "Are we to believe Garith hired one group of mercenaries to attack us, while someone else hired my order to eliminate him? Who? Why? That second party would have to have known of the prince's plan, unless someone else has a reason for wanting both Garith and the man impersonating him dead. Also, the queen was not present at the meeting between the king and me. How could she have known to send her assassins after us? She wouldn't risk her son's life, and those men showed no signs of sparing me."

"She wouldn't risk me," Yarrow said. "When I was a child, it often seemed she preferred me over her own son. She asked me personally to accompany Garith. She wouldn't have insisted if she'd known it was actually Sasha. Sasha, how much would it cost for the Crimson Scythe to betray one of its own?"

"Since it's never happened before, I really can't say. A high-profile assignment can cost up to a thousand gold sovereigns. I'd guess at least triple, or more. After all, they'd have to compensate for all the profit I'd make them over the course of my life."

Duncan whistled through his teeth. "That's a lot of gold. I don't know if even the queen could acquire so much."

"Agarick keeps records," Yarrow said. "If a sum like that went missing from the royal treasury, it wouldn't go unnoticed."

"Find where that money came from, and we'll solve at least a part of this puzzle," Sasha said.

"How do we do that?" Duncan asked. "If it came from a foreign ruler or barbarian lord, how will we know?"

"You suspect foreigners?" Sasha asked.

"Who else? If the queen is truly not at fault. Goddesses, what are we going to do?"

"We can do little until we reach Lockhaven," Yarrow said. "Then at least I can speak to my Aunt Den. I can't believe she'd do something like this. I don't look forward to going back there, though."

"Bad memories?" Duncan asked.

"Mixed memories," Yarrow answered. "The same as every man holds of the place where he grew up. After all, our first triumphs and tragedies took place at our childhood homes. Sometimes the sweetest recollections are sad in retrospect. Reminders of things lost."

Duncan nodded and offered the mage a knowing smile.

"What of me?" Sasha asked.

Yarrow sat up and extended his arm toward the beautiful man. Sasha's eyes darted to Yarrow's proffered hand and away. He made no effort to approach Yarrow and remained standing with his arms folded over his heart. "Are you thinking of leaving?" Yarrow asked, shocked at the frailty and sorrow in his voice as his hand fell limp beside his thigh.

Not getting attached to this one, are we, beloved?

"I'd rather not leave. My former brethren are hunting me, and I'm far safer surrounded by a regimen of knights than I'd be on my own. In exchange, I can offer the knowledge I hold at this trial. I'm willing to help you search for the culprit behind this convoluted mess. I have unique abilities to assist you."

"A simple business arrangement, then?" Yarrow asked, not looking at the other man and forcing his voice not to crack. "We help to protect you, and you help us with… with whatever we end up doing?"

"Unless I'm not wanted."

"What do you say, Duncan?" Yarrow asked.

The knight's olive eyes locked with Yarrow's, and Duncan frowned and pursed his lips so tightly they went pale. "He seems sincere in his bargain."

"Very well," Yarrow said, flopping down on his cot and rolling to face the moldy wall of the tent. He felt hollow inside, confused and frightened by what lay ahead. He had grown fond of Sasha, physically at least. If ever he'd needed the touch of another, the comfort of just knowing someone was near, it was now. He found he even missed his horse. Neither of his companions moved to fill the void around and within the mage, so he closed his eyes and tried to rest. The superficial cut on his shoulder throbbed and burned, an added aggravation.

Never fear, you'll always have me, my beloved.

I hate you.

Oh, you little whelp, if I thought you really meant that, I might be hurt.

OVER THE next week, Tam Taran pushed hard toward Lockhaven, allowing his men little time for food and rest. Before long, Sasha smelled Estrella Lake, the enormous body of water fed by the northern glaciers and snow. Mythology told that the goddesses had filled it with their tears over the suffering of humanity. Many made religious pilgrimages to the dozens of temples and shrines lining the shores of the lake. It was the heart of the land, with the Kanda River and its many tributaries the arteries that carried life to the soil. Sasha had never seen the lake, and anticipated his first glimpse of its majesty.

They arrived at Yarrow's familial castle in the dead of night, beneath a ruddy crescent moon Sasha would have previously considered a good omen. Now he felt as if the Crimson Scythe had marked the entire square fortress with a celestial sign. The castle looked older than most others the assassin had seen, built before rounded walls became feasible. Huge, thick blocks comprised the single structure, plain but sturdy.

Yarrow beat on the heavy wooden door with the side of his fist. Eventually a stooped, old man in a long nightcap appeared with a lantern. He blinked, and it took a few moments before he opened his arms. "Yarrow, lad! Good to have you home. Please, come inside and wait while I wake your mother. She'll be so happy to see you."

"It's not necessary to wake her, Rendel," Yarrow said. "It's very late. If you can show us to rooms, I can greet my family in the morning."

The old servant wheezed out a laugh. "Mistress Asaria would have my hide!" He limped up the stairs at the opposite end of the hall and disappeared into darkness.

Yarrow fidgeted, shifting his weight from foot to foot until a tall woman descended the steps with three of her ladies. All of them wore lacy nightdresses below heavy wool robes embellished with embroidered flowers. One of the ladies carried the hem of the mistress's robe, which was pale blue and trailed behind her. Her long, golden brown hair stood in a knot at the top of her head. Sasha wondered if Yarrow's hair had once been that color. He'd definitely inherited his mother's delicate features and large, engaging eyes. In the low light, Lady Asaria's irises looked almost as pale as her youngest son's.

The old servant Rendel announced Yarrow's presence. The mage stepped forward, though with reluctance. "Mother," he said.

"Yarrow!" she said with a smile, hurrying forward to embrace her son. "Have you been well? Shall I wake the servants and have them prepare a meal? Are you hungry?"

"No, no, Mother. That isn't necessary."

She held him at arm's length and looked him over. "All three of my boys are back under my roof," she said and shook her head. "If only it were for a happier reason. Still, I'm glad to have you back. It's been far too many years."

"Have most of the others already arrived, then?" Yarrow asked.

"Most. We're only waiting for the valen of Meadow's Edge, far to the south. He's due to arrive by tomorrow afternoon, at the latest."

"Aunt Den is here? Ambra Piers?"

"Why do you ask, Yarrow?"

"I don't know," he said, stepping back from his mother. "This is all so disturbing."

"At least the goddesses have watched over you, my darling boy. You've always garnered their favor."

Yarrow laughed, most inappropriately. "It's very late, Mother. We can talk again tomorrow at breakfast. But where are my manners? Let me introduce my companions. This is Tam Duncan Purefroy of Thulemore, chosen by Agarick to accompany the prince."

"My lady," Duncan said, bowing.

"This is Tam Taran Edercrest, the king's most trusted commander."

"Tam Taran and I have met before," Asaria said. "He served beside your father. Goddesses keep you, Tam Taran."

"You as well, my lady."

"Also, here is Sasha."

Sasha started before stepping forward. He'd expected Yarrow to hide him in shame, not flaunt him. The Crimson Scythe trained its brethren in charm and social graces, however, and he bowed with a flourish to the mage's mother. "It is my honor, my lady."

"Who is this man, Yarrow?" Asaria stiffened so slightly only one trained to observe such things would notice.

"A very valued friend."

"In that case, you are most welcome in this house, Sasha. I'm afraid we have little space to spare with so many guests. Yarrow's room is, of course, exactly as he left it, but the rest of you may have to make do with bedrolls in the dining hall. I'll have servants show you the way."

"There's plenty of room in my chamber for Sasha," Yarrow said, to the assassin's dismay. It wouldn't do for Yarrow's mother to intuit the nature of their association. "Duncan too. We might even squeeze a fourth."

"We are not that desperate yet, my son," Asaria said with a grin. "Rendel will show you and your friends to the room."

"Nonsense, Mother. I remember the way to my own bedchamber." He crossed the hall and started up the stairs, clearly as eager for escape as a rabbit surrounded by hounds. While Yarrow's mother seemed to love him, Sasha also remembered she'd allowed him to leave home, alone, at fourteen. Either she truly trusted her son's abilities, or his fate didn't concern her after all. Not even the most devout trusted the goddesses that far.

Sasha looked at Duncan, and the knight appeared just as perplexed as Sasha felt. Both of them followed their host to the third story of the old fortress, and to a corridor in the northeastern corner. The double doors Yarrow tugged upon opened with a creak. The mage stepped into the room and gestured toward the inglenook. A bright blue blaze sprung alight, illuminating the canopied bed, armoire, upholstered couch, and a table between two chairs but producing almost no heat. The shelves lining the walls sagged beneath the books and trinkets they held.

"Wait," Sasha said. "Let me check the room for traps." He anticipated the others' protests at his implied accusation, but they said nothing, so he crept to the bed and looked beneath it. Next he opened the armoire. Finding it empty except for some dusty tunics and a sleeping gown, he ran his fingers over the walls in search of loose blocks. After that he only needed to check behind the heavy, velvet curtains beyond the table. Sasha cautiously pulled the braided cord. His breath caught in his throat as the drapes opened.

Beyond a small balcony, Estrella Lake spread out before Sasha. He hadn't expected the magnitude; he felt like he looked out over the sea. The far shore of the lake dipped toward the northern horizon and disappeared. Only the tips of the majestic mountains beyond penetrated the thick, distant fog. Sasha heard the waves breaking on the shore and the call of night birds. Mist blurred the lanterns of boats floating miles away. The vivid stars reflected off the surface of the water in rippling, silver pools. It smelled fresh, earthy, and pure. Sasha inhaled the cold air and held it in his lungs. "Beautiful," he exhaled.

"Sasha?" Yarrow whispered behind him. "Is all well?"

"All's well," Sasha answered, moving to rest his palm on the stone railing. Yarrow had woken up to this vista every day. Why had he ever left this place?

The mage joined Sasha on the veranda, breathing the sweet air as Sasha had done. He draped his hand over Sasha's knuckles and gave Sasha's hand a squeeze. Sasha smiled before he had time to think of the appropriate response. He didn't overanalyze his happiness and stood, contented. Even Duncan joined them to enjoy the spectacular view.

"It's easy to forget our troubles in the face of such beauty," the knight said. "'Goddesses, waste not your tears on me, for I am unclean.'" Duncan offered the others a tired smile before dropping his pack and claiming the couch. He began the arduous process of removing his armor. Sasha had understood that most knights required assistance in shedding their heavy plate and usually called for a servant girl or page. Duncan always managed on his own, and Sasha respected his self-sufficiency.

Sasha would be sharing the bed with Yarrow, then. He'd slept far worse places. With a last, long look at the lake, he pulled the curtains closed to preserve the meager heat of the fire. He peeled his own leather garments away, down to his scant black undergarment. Duncan watched him from the couch, but Sasha wasn't modest. In fact, he almost enjoyed the knight's eyes on his body. Just before he slipped beneath the blankets, he shed his final article of clothing.

Yarrow stood so long on the balcony that Sasha wondered if he should check on the mage. He decided to leave Yarrow to his memories, good or ill. Even so, he resisted sleep until Yarrow finally took off his clothes and got into bed. Sasha waited to see if Yarrow might reach for him, or curl his body around him and hold him. Instead, Yarrow lay far off, almost at the opposite edge of the soft mattress. Sasha had thought, earlier, that he'd be relieved if Yarrow left him alone. Memories of the mage in the tavern sickened him. He thought they'd soured Yarrow for him, but it wasn't entirely true. He missed more than the physical gratification Yarrow so willingly provided. He missed the warmth of the mage's body, the comfort of his presence and the steady rhythm of his breath while he slept. Though loath to admit it, Sasha enjoyed being important to someone.

"Have I offended you?" Sasha asked in barely a whisper.

Yarrow rolled to face him, his eyes luminous as stars in the dark. "Never." He reached for Sasha's cheek but hesitated, as if Sasha might recoil.

Sasha grasped Yarrow's wrist and pressed Yarrow's palm against his face. He nuzzled into Yarrow's hand, closing his eyes and breathing the scent of Yarrow's skin, similar in a way to the smell of the cold lake outside. "Don't lay so far off, then."

"I thought… I thought I'd done something to upset you, Sasha."

"You did."

"What?"

"I don't wish to talk about it now. Just come close to me."

"Yes," Yarrow said, sliding over to lay chest to chest and forehead to forehead with Sasha. "I'm happy to. But I won't forget that I made you uneasy, and we *will* talk." He kissed Sasha's brows, and Sasha shuddered with delight.

"Why do you go out of your way to stand up for me?" Sasha asked as he wound his arms around Yarrow's waist, savoring his warmth and solidity.

"Because you deserve respect."

"Do I, Yarrow? You almost treat me as an equal."

"Of course I think of you as an equal! Why not?"

"You're the prince's cousin. The king's nephew, and a noble."

"What of it? It's not a position I earned, and therefore not one I value. I admire wit and skill, not a meaningless title."

"Yet you defend me in front of others, others whose opinions matter little to me. I must say, I can't understand why."

"Sasha," Yarrow said, stroking his dark hair with devotion, "I defend you because you warrant it. I do it because I…. Because you're my friend."

Sasha pressed his mouth to Yarrow's. So what if others had sampled it? Sasha had no right to judge this mage. He'd used his sexuality as a tool innumerable times, and Yarrow had never offered to be exclusively his. He knew he shouldn't feel the pleasure he did in Yarrow's arms; he'd been trained to mistrust such frivolity. But his heart swelled at the other man's words, stirring feelings he'd thought long deceased. "You're my friend too," he told Yarrow. "The first one I've ever had. Thank you."

They fell asleep with their faces close and their limbs entwined. Duncan snored softly a few feet away.

Chapter Ten

THE ASSEMBLED nobles argued the next morning over breakfast. Yarrow knew enough of political intrigue to realize more than the evidence would decide the queen's fate. Many of the aristocrats held lands at her bequest and stood to lose them if she was branded a traitor. Others had daughters ripe to take her place at Agarick's side, should it become vacant. Yarrow hated the covert deals, bribes, and backstabbing that court politics consisted of. He sat quietly between Duncan and Sasha, nibbling pastries as he tried to isolate snippets of conversation amid the cacophony of their petty nattering. The nobles, mostly men, filled the hall to capacity. Harried-looking servants ran back and forth, attempting to meet everyone's demands.

Yarrow's brothers, Valen Rayne and Rowan, sat with their mother and the other valens at a special table near the front of the hall, joined by a blue-robed priestess of Vestrafori, goddess of truth and justice. Yarrow's brothers had greeted him and his companions with stiff formality before the meal. His mother, as she always had, acknowledged his existence, said a few obligatory, kind words, and quickly turned her attention to her elder sons. He couldn't deny it still stung, though he'd swallowed the poison so many times he'd become all but immune. Yarrow knew from past arguments Rayne found him an embarrassment to the family with his Emiri paint and drifting lifestyle. He never tired of telling his brother how much shame Yarrow's so-called reckless, youthful mistakes had brought down on their ancient, noble name. Rowan lacked the courage to say otherwise, if he'd ever had an opinion separate from Rayne. Rayne surrounded himself with people constantly ready to bend their knees and kiss his backside. Even his pregnant wife, whose name Yarrow didn't remember, fawned over his every word and produced artificial laughter when appropriate.

After his companions finished eating, they followed Yarrow to a quiet alcove. Sasha dutifully checked to make sure no one eavesdropped on them. "What's our plan?" he asked the others.

"I need to speak with my aunt," Yarrow said. "She'll be honest with me. One of us should question Ambra Piers. We should try to find out the prince's actual route to Gaeltheon. Sasha, would anyone besides Agarick and Tam Taran have that information?"

He shook his head. "No one else was present. Only those knights who departed with the prince would know which roads to take."

"Goddesses help us if those men weren't loyal. Garith might already be dead," Duncan said.

"We have to find out their course," Yarrow said. "We can't ask Taran or Agarick; they didn't trust us enough to tell the first time."

I can make them talk.

Only as a last resort.

You're no fun, beloved.

"It would also benefit our cause to find the money used to pay the Crimson Scythe," Sasha reminded them.

"How?" Duncan asked. "Every noble house keeps its own records. It would take us weeks to look into every treasury, if they'd even permit us. Only the king can demand such information."

"That's it," Yarrow said. "Duncan, go to the king and tell him of our suspicions. Agarick should be able to obtain the necessary records fairly quickly. His treasurers will discover anything odd. They're very good. Agarick doesn't like his nobles skimping on taxes."

"I'll try, Yarrow, but his nephew might have better luck."

"No, Agarick doesn't trust me at all. I have information that might coerce him, but that would be risky. I'd rather not resort to it. He values you, and surely he wants to help his wife and son."

"I'll do my best. Will we meet in your room before supper?"

"No. On the far shore of the lake is a shrine to Ix, goddess of the wilds. It's rarely visited. Meet me and Sasha there just before sunset. Take a rowboat, not the ferry."

Duncan bowed to them and went on his way.

"I think I can manage to interrogate the young woman," Sasha said with a wink.

To Yarrow's surprise, he felt a ripple of aggression at his assassin's words. "Find out if she's lying, nothing more."

"Relax, Yarrow. I was only joking. I had no idea the thought of me dallying with a young woman might upset you so."

"Of course I'm not upset…."

Liar!

"I just don't want to attract attention or cause any trouble."

"I know what I'm doing." Sasha planted a quick peck at the corner of Yarrow's mouth and hurried off.

Yarrow touched his lips and smiled before moving toward the stairs and his family's finest guest quarters on the second floor. He'd wondered if he'd find Duncan there, though he doubted the king sat idle in his room. Lockhaven boasted fine hunting, fishing, and riding. Yarrow had heard many of the nobles at breakfast making plans to visit the major temples. He found the castle fairly empty as he walked the halls. His home felt familiar and strange at the same time, as if he saw it through new eyes. He'd always felt as a boy that it must be the most beautiful and luxurious palace in the entire world. Looking at it now, after actually seeing a portion of the world, it seemed rustic and rather plain. Birds fluttered in the rough-hewn rafters above, and the stone walls lacked any intricate carving. The blocks comprising them were simple and square, just like the blocks beneath Yarrow's old boots. In the east, beyond the mountains, he'd seen doors of solid gold inlaid with gems unheard of in Selindria. He'd seen them carved from pure crystal. Even Agarick's castle doors bore carvings of hunts and battles. Yarrow passed only plain doors with simple, iron hardware. Nothing gratuitous, like vases of flowers, playful carvings, or painted boards decorated the corridors. The few tapestries were threadbare and the statues of the goddesses worn. Yarrow felt sad at the many things he'd never again be able to consider grand.

What exactly did one do with something broken beyond repair? Hoard the pieces and the memory of the whole, or toss everything aside? Some things, when broken, could never be replaced. Sometimes the pieces would never fit together again.

Yarrow reached the guest quarters located below his own room and blessed with the same view of the lake. It, at least, still impressed the young mage. He'd always wanted to bring Rini here one day, let him swim in the cool, pure water. The Emiri boy had complained about the fabled cold, and both he and Yarrow had been content to bathe in the warm, southern sea, walk the beaches, collect coral and bright shells, spend their days doing nothing and their nights doing everything together. They'd planned to visit one day, someday. And then it was too late.

Yarrow buried the bittersweet memories as he approached the two knights guarding the door. "I wish to speak with my aunt," he told them.

"We can't allow that, tam," said the one on the right, a freckled lad who looked too young for his post. "We have orders not to let the queen leave this room, or let anyone in."

"Nonsense. I'll go where I like in my own home. What do you suppose I'll do, hurl the queen out the window and swim across the lake? Stand aside. I command it."

The two men exchanged worried looks but didn't attempt to impede Yarrow when he reached for the doorknob. The other knight, a man with a thick black beard and an ample belly, said, "We can only give you a few minutes, tam."

"I'll take as long as I like," Yarrow snarled, looking the man dead in the eye until he cowered. "Pester me again and I'll make you regret it."

That's my boy.

Hush.

But, Yarrow, I'm bored! I'm starving for sensation. Can't I borrow the flesh just to eat some roast or swim in the cold water? Burn a fingertip on a candle? Maybe take a tumble with Sasha?

No! Never ask me that again. You'll never lay a finger on him. If you try, I will find a way to make you pay.

Peace, my beloved. Let's visit your pretty aunt.

Just behave yourself.

Yarrow found Denna Corina, Queen of Selindria, sitting in a utilitarian chair beside the balcony with her embroidery. Her long, dark hair hung loose over her shoulders, and she wore a simple marigold shift that flattered her olive skin. Her ladies milled about the large suite, mending her gowns, polishing her shoes, reading, or sitting idly on benches. One girl, maybe twelve, plucked a plaintive melody on a harp. Yarrow didn't see Garith's younger sibling, the Princess Garina. Her absence didn't surprise him as she'd recently married and given birth to a little girl.

At Yarrow's entrance, the queen's head snapped up from her hoop. Happiness quickly replaced her surprise, and she bolted up to embrace her nephew.

"Yarrow, my little flower," she said with her lilting Esperon accent. She kissed both of his cheeks and looked at him through misty eyes. "It mends my broken heart a bit to see you safe."

In response, Yarrow opened his hand. A quartet of vivid purple butterflies flitted from his palm and orbited the queen's head, glitter trailing from their wings. "You taught me that, Aunt Den. Do you remember?"

"Of course, my dearest. You could do it at six. I knew then what a great mage you'd one day become. And look at you! I wasn't wrong. That is why I needed you to go with Garith."

Yarrow broke out of his aunt's embrace and looked around. Every lady-in-waiting stood listening, tasks forgotten and eyes wide. Yarrow ground his teeth with annoyance.

Now, now. It's only human nature to be curious, beloved. Look at that dark-haired lass in the corner. Let me wear the body and have a go at her.

Quiet, filthy beast. "Aunt Den, could we have a few words in private?"

"Of course. The rest of you, go down to the kitchens and tell the staff to give you something sweet, and some fresh cream too." The youngest girl set her harp aside and clapped her hands. All six of the women filed eagerly out the door. Denna Corina took her chair and Yarrow pulled a bench close and sat. "Is it too cold for you, little flower? Shall I close the drapes?"

"You still call me that," he said, grinning and shaking his head.

"Do you mind?"

"No, I like feeling like a boy again, innocent and unaware. And I'm good with the cold. It takes a great deal to bother me now."

She looked out over the lake. "I used to feel it so acutely when I first came to Selindria. Espero is always warm. It's bright with flowers and always smells of the ocean. I'd hoped we might go there together, Yarrow. I'd love to parade you around the university, let you put those self-important scholars to shame. You would love the capital city of Pala Reapaza. There's magic everywhere. You can feel it caress your skin like a warm breeze. Even the ancient colleges and temples were made by enchantment. Ah, sometimes I wish I'd never left. I'd planned to enter the service of Pherara, goddess of magic, before I met Agarick. Now I just wish I could see it one last time." Tears slipped down her dark cheeks.

Yarrow hurried to clasp her hand. "You *will* see your home again, I swear it."

"You're probably too young to look back on the decisions you've made and wonder how your life might be different if you'd taken another path."

"You might be surprised."

"What life would I have had if I'd gone to Pherara's temple instead of coming here? A peaceful one of study and contemplation, I suppose. But I wouldn't have my two beautiful children, or have ever known you, little flower."

"You never would have been a queen."

"Being a queen matters little to me, Yarrow. I suspect you're one of the few who might understand that."

"Yes."

"I married Agarick because I loved him. Now it seems I'll die for it."

"I won't let that happen. I would like to ask you a few things, though. Did you know that the procession I joined contained not your son, but an imposter?"

"No. I've recently learned of it through gossip. The other women think I'm a fool and mock me behind my back."

"This is good. If you didn't know of the ruse, you never could have sent the assassins after us. No one will believe that you intended to harm your own son. This will provide us a strong argument for the trial. I hate to ask, but did you meet with anyone behind the king's back? Men, at night?"

"I've never gone behind Agarick's back. Not in twenty-two years of matrimony."

"Some of your ladies will claim you did. At least one of them has betrayed you. One of them might have even stolen from you. You must weed out the traitors."

She frowned like she tasted something sour and said, "Rest assured, I will."

Yarrow was glad he wasn't one of those treacherous wenches. "A bracelet and a magical tome were found on one of the mercenaries."

"Stolen. Months ago."

"As I suspected. I have one final question, Aunt Den. Did you know anything of a secret relationship between Garith and the lady Ambra Piers?"

"That poor, plain girl? Yarrow, that's laughable."

"Would Garith have confided in you?"

"I have no doubt. We've always been very close. Goddesses, don't you remember how you and I used to talk? How you confided in me?"

"I'll never forget. I'd have taken my own life if not for you. I thought my feelings were so unnatural."

"Oh, my Yarrow. Everyone is different from everyone else. Everyone has different desires. As for my Garith, he's a simple boy, quite different from you. He was perfectly content to marry and carry out a structured life."

"Then Ambra lies. My… my friend Sasha will root out the truth, have no doubt. We'll have plenty of evidence to acquit you at this silly trial. Once Sasha tells the nobles what he knows, they'll have no choice but to proclaim you innocent."

"You have the optimism of youth."

What a laugh!

"No. I have the faith of truth. Sasha, Duncan, and I will speak on your behalf. Hopefully after this farce is concluded, the real culprits can be found."

"But what of Garith, Yarrow? Is he safe?"

Yarrow considered a gentle deception, but this courageous woman deserved better. "No, Aunt Denna. He is hunted by the Crimson Scythe."

"Goddesses, why?" She clapped a hand over her mouth to stifle a sob. "Who would do such a thing? Yarrow, I implore you, go to Garith. Please, go now and save him if you can."

"I wish to represent you at the trial. My companions and I have access to very vital information."

"I don't care. Please, little flower, if you ever loved me, find my son. I'll gladly die if I know Garith is safe."

"I don't even know where to look for him, Aunt Den. Only Agarick and one other knight know the route his caravan took."

She chuckled deep in her belly. "Agarick is still a man. He's as susceptible as any to a woman's charms. I'll find out the prince's course. Come back to me tomorrow morning, and I'll tell you what I've learned. Then will you go after Garith?"

"I will."

"Goddesses bless you, Yarrow." Both of them stood to kiss and embrace again before Yarrow took his leave. "I love you very dearly, nephew."

"Keep your wits, Aunt Den," he said as he approached the door. "You're surrounded by serpents."

"I might offer you the same advice, nephew. I have heard about who you're associating with. You must be very careful, or you'll find a knife in your back."

"I wish you wouldn't think that of him."

"I'm told he's very beautiful. Hard as it is, you must not let that cloud your eyes, dearest Yarrow."

SASHA FOUND a young nobleman about his size, spoke with the man long enough to learn his name and that he held the title of bairn, knocked him out, bound him, and stole his clothing. He made his way to Ambra Peirs's room, a small chamber on the fourth floor. A single sleepy-looking guard stood watch.

"I am Bairn Lugh Solaran, of Grainech in Merryvale. Here to see the lady."

"It's quite unusual to visit a lady in her boudoir, isn't it, tam?"

"You dare question your betters? Stand aside."

The soldier did as commanded, and Sasha entered the tiny room. The lady Ambra sat at the edge of her bed, studying a holy book of some sort. She wasn't a legendary beauty, to be sure. Ambra was too thin, gangly, covered in freckles, and had a pronounced overbite. She started at Sasha's entry.

"May I be of service, tam?" she asked, standing and curtseying.

"Lady Ambra Piers," Sasha said in his best velvet baritone. "How I've awaited speaking with you face to face."

"M-might I know your name, my lord?" she stammered, blushing as red as a summer berry.

"To share anything with such a beautiful woman is a boon from the goddesses," Sasha said with a theatrical bow. He scooped up the lady's hand and kissed each of her knuckles. "I'm Bairn Lugh of Grainech." The young woman tittered; Sasha feared she'd faint.

"My name is Ambra, my lord."

"I know. I noticed you at dinner last night, and again at breakfast this morn. Truth be told, I've noticed little else since my eyes fell upon you. Forgive me for being so bold, but as a young man in search of a wife, I can think of little besides your beauty. Your face torments my waking thoughts and robs me of sleep. When I dream, I envision nothing else. Tell me, lovely Ambra. Do you believe a man and a woman can be destined for each other at first glance?"

"Not until now."

Sasha smiled. He'd begun to worry he'd gone too far, but the young woman ate up his flattery like berries and cream. "I'm so relieved my attentions aren't one-sided. I'd feared I was a fool. Surely such a fine flower as you has many suitors. I didn't know how to stand out among them. That's why I had to come here. Brazen, I know. Yet I couldn't resist the chance to speak to you alone. Now I never want to leave this room. I never want anything to distract me from you."

"My lord." Ambra took Sasha's hand and led him to the bed. They sat down side by side, and Sasha quite effectively pretended to swoon and stare into the maiden's eyes.

"I adore the sound of those words on your lips," he said. "My lady."

"Lord and lady," Ambra said, giggling and blushing.

Sasha pushed a few strands of ginger hair out of her face and trapped them behind her small ear. He lifted her hand to kiss it once again, never breaking eye contact. "I have only one worry. I'm sure the idle hearsay I've noticed is unfounded, but many say you took Prince Garith as a lover. As much as it would pain my heart, I cannot take to wife a woman who's been touched by another man. I care little for the opinions of others. Ambra, if you tell me these rumors are false, that's all I need."

She hung her head. "All of it was a lie. My father beat me and told me I'd never marry a respectable man. He said I was awkward and ugly, that no one wanted me. If I agreed to this deceit, I could join the order of Vestrafori and lead an honorable life."

"Is that the life you want?"

"No. I want a family, a husband and children. No man will have me if he thinks I've been the prince's whore, though."

"Why not tell the truth?" Sasha's fingertips grazed the lady's forearm and raised gooseflesh.

"Because my father says it will ruin our good name, and my hope of finding a husband."

"I don't mind, so long as you tell me the truth. I find you fascinating, Ambra. I'd like to know you better, provided I'm not treading well-traveled roads."

"No, it's not like that! I never even met the prince."

"Will you say so in the trial? I cannot wed a woman with a deceitful tongue." He cupped her chin and kissed her softly. "Your tongue certainly seems sweet, but I must know the truth."

"How do I know you're sincere, tam?"

Sasha pushed the young woman down on the bed, bunched her skirts up around her hips, and dropped down to please her with his mouth. As he moved his tongue in tight circles over her flesh, he imagined how pleased Yarrow would be with his efforts. He closed his eyes and pretended it was Yarrow he pleasured. The young woman writhed beneath him, and Sasha grasped her hips to hold her still. In just a few minutes, he'd satisfied her with his tongue and fingers. He noted the spatter of blood she'd left on the sheets. Luckily he hadn't needed to actually betray Yarrow. He'd never offered exclusivity to the mage, but he'd seen the anguished look on Yarrow's face at the mention of Ambra. The thought of entering this girl's body and breaking his promise to the mage made Sasha almost ill. This little playact was nothing.

"Do you… do you believe me now?" the girl panted.

Sasha looked at the red crescent staining the sheet, and he hurried to pull the quilt over it.

"Is anything wrong?" Ambra asked, touching his hair.

He forced a smile. "I've never been happier," he told the young woman, punctuating his words with a kiss. "You must swear to me that you'll tell the truth at the trial, so we can be together. I don't know how I'll live without you if you don't." He'd have to make sure the girl didn't learn of his ruse until after she'd testified. It wouldn't be difficult to make himself scarce.

"I'll swear to it. I'll do more than that. I'll go to the Temple of Vestrafori this very afternoon and confess my lie to the priestess there. It will do much to unburden my heart."

"A wonderful idea," Sasha said, kissing Ambra's knuckles again and making her color. He stood and bowed.

"Will you visit me later?" she asked, reaching for his wrist. "Tonight?"

"If I can manage it without being discovered."

"I'll say a prayer to the goddess of love."

Sasha left, feeling satisfied he'd ensured the queen's acquittal. Even if the girl lost her nerve to testify at the trial, she'd go the temple in her state of hope and afterglow and tell the priestess everything. The priestess would be bound by her beliefs to speak the truth. Sasha couldn't wait to share his victory with Yarrow and Duncan. He giggled to himself as he skipped down the steps. He hadn't even needed to kill anybody.

DUNCAN'S CHEST and shoulders ached from rowing by the time he reached the far shore of Estrella Lake. His boat sliced through the thick mist until he heard the bottom scrape against the rocky bed. He stepped knee-deep into the frigid water and towed the little vessel ashore. He took the overgrown, winding path to the top of a knoll. Sasha and Yarrow stood by a crude statue of a nude woman with wild hair, sheltered by a simple wooden structure. Moss covered the image of the goddess Ix to her thighs, and completely coated the stone carvings of her sacred animals, the doe and the hare.

The sun dropped quickly behind the majestic peak of Starmont, which marked Selindria's northern border. The bright star that gave the mountain its name burned clearly above the apex. Ix's holy burleberry bushes grew rampant. Pilgrims had tied dozens of colored ribbons around their branches, hoping the goddess might grant their wishes. The last rays of the sunset gilded their shiny evergreen leaves and the strips of silky fabric.

"Duncan." Yarrow ran to take his hands and greet him like a wife whose husband had returned from war. The young man smiled, hesitated a moment, and kissed Duncan on the apple of his cheek. A few feet away, Sasha grinned and shook his head.

"An enthusiastic welcome, friend Yarrow. I assume your afternoon went well?"

"We can't lose," Yarrow said, still grasping both of Duncan's hands in his. "The queen's book and bracelet were stolen, and the stories of her clandestine meetings are lies. Aunt Den plans to find out which of her ladies are disloyal. She's going to use her wiles to make Agarick tell her which way the prince went. I… I promised her I'd go after Garith, save him if I can."

"I'll go with you," Sasha said, putting his hand on Yarrow's shoulder.

"Thank you, *syrai-tama*," Yarrow said.

"That's an Emiri word," Sasha observed. "What does it mean?"

"*Syrai* means 'friend,'" Yarrow said, blushing and fidgeting with Duncan's fingers. "It means… it means an especially good friend."

"A compliment, then," Sasha said, clearly understanding, as Duncan did, what the word really implied: *more than friends*. "I appreciate it."

"Sasha, you must tell Duncan what you managed!"

The three of them moved to some large rocks and sat down. Nearby, crude clay deer and rabbits left by the faithful stood in a heap. Yarrow conjured a bluish white, floral-scented fire between them. It cast stark shadows on the mage and the assassin's faces. Yarrow's eyes either reflected the light or glowed with their own radiance. Duncan had never seen the young man so pleased. For some reason, it pleased him in return to see Yarrow content and happy for once.

"Young Ambra Piers was lying," Sasha said. "I persuaded her to admit it. She's willing to testify. If that should fall through, she's within Vestrafori's temple even now, confessing to the priestesses."

"Ha ha!" Yarrow said, clapping the assassin on the back. "What of you, Duncan? Have you been successful?"

"Partially. Agarick lends no credence to anything Sasha claims, but he has agreed to demand the financial records of every noble house."

"A victory," Yarrow said. "If nothing else, the verdict must be held until those records can be reviewed. By then, goddesses willing, we'll have returned with the prince. We've done it, *syrai*. Any one of the doubts we've raised will be enough to acquit Aunt Den. Together, they're irrefutable. We've saved the queen. All that remains is to pass our information along to someone loyal, since we'll be going after Garith in the morning. Unless you plan to stay, Duncan. I suppose you could be our representative."

"I don't plan to stay, Yarrow. I can serve this kingdom far better in the field than sitting in a stuffy room. I swore from the beginning to protect the prince and see him into the arms of his bride. I plan to fulfill my duty. I'll tell Tam Taran what we've learned and depart with you in the morning. In fact, I'll find him as soon as we cross the lake."

"Are you sure we can trust him?" Yarrow asked.

"Is there a reason we shouldn't?" Duncan answered.

"I… no, I suppose not. I just…."

"Agarick trusts him more than anyone. Even more than either of us. I think we can count on him to relay our testimony at the trial. I know you dislike his treatment of Sasha. I don't like it either, but we mustn't let it color our interpretation of the facts. Besides, I really do want to come with you."

"I'm glad of it," Yarrow said.

"Your sword will serve us well," Sasha agreed. "I must say, we've proved a fine team."

"Those lace-bedecked simpletons never stood a chance," Yarrow said with a mischievous grin, rubbing his palms together over the fire, though it created little heat.

"Which leads me to wonder why your brother rules this land and not you," Sasha said. "You're clearly more powerful and much cleverer."

"Well, Rayne is the firstborn son. Rowan is next in line, and then me, if I'd be allowed the title."

"Why wouldn't you?" Sasha asked.

"The goddesses forbid mages to rule. There's an ancient story about Emperor Fane, who ruled over the Golden Dawn of the world. He was wise and just, and used his magic to make the land prosper. Few people had to labor, so art, architecture, and literature flourished. The legend says he ruled for almost a thousand years before he told his people to worship him instead of the Thirteen Goddesses and their daughters. His subjects gladly agreed, as they loved their emperor, and began erecting temples and statues in his honor. Of course, the goddesses grew angry and demanded they be torn down. Fane refused, and he and his mages battled the goddesses until they'd practically reduced the world to ash. People forgot all they'd learned, and had to start over. Since that time, no mage can be king.

"I wouldn't want it, anyway. Imprisoned in a stuffy castle and bothered with every petty problem. Always acting as people expect. Being proper. It all sounds dull and annoying to me. I'm much happier out exploring, beholden to no one but myself."

Duncan smiled and gazed out across the lake. The castle looked like a structure made of a child's building blocks from here, and stood black against the rich cobalt sky, studded with stars. "I don't suppose we'll make it back in time to sup."

"No, but I don't care," Yarrow said. "I so much prefer the road, the open air, the stars as my only ceiling. This place is wild, unpretentious, and I like it. Let's stay just a bit longer. If the two of you are hungry, I can get you anything you like from the kitchen. I plan to visit the wine cellar, to be sure. We've done well. We deserve to celebrate."

"A fine plan," Sasha said.

"No wine for me," Duncan said. "But a hot meal would be most welcome."

"Why do you avoid wine, Duncan?" Yarrow asked.

The knight looked into the fire. Small shapes, suggesting birds, butterflies, and flowers rose from the flames. He wondered if Yarrow needed much concentration to produce them. He also wondered what to tell his companions. The story begged to be told, and in spite of his rational misgivings, Duncan's heart trusted these men.

"You will think less of me," he warned.

Yarrow chuckled and Sasha said, "Remember who you speak to, Tam Knight."

"Very well. My first mission after being knighted was to escort a young nobleman from Windwake to the port of Meritage. He was a mage and wished to study in Espero. He wasn't like you, Yarrow. He was delicate and scholarly. I never saw him cast a single spell, only read books from dawn until dusk. Still, every mage is valuable with so few born in our time. His name was Aubrey Lancette, a distant relative to the valen. As we traveled, we became friends. Especially good friends, as you might say, Yarrow. Actually, Aubrey was the first friend of that sort I made. Our journey, while long, wasn't terribly dangerous. I… suppose I didn't take it seriously. I was a very young man.

"One night we stopped at an inn. I passed a few hours with Aubrey, and then he fell asleep. I joined the other three knights in the tavern below. We celebrated, I don't know what occasion, long into the night. We held contests to see who could imbibe the most. By the time I staggered to my bed, I was ridiculous with drink. I fell into a deep sleep on the floor and never heard Aubrey cry out when a group of local thugs attacked him. They killed my friend for nothing but the clothes on his back and a few crumbling tomes. He'd trusted me to protect him, and I'd been too drunk. I swore I'd never shirk my duty again. You cannot imagine what that young man's loss did to me. In my youth and naïveté, I thought we'd be together forever." He had no words to express to the others his loss or his profound guilt. He'd gladly have died in young Aubrey's place if given the chance. The idea that the other young man had been robbed of his entire life and all that it might have entailed, because of Duncan's foolishness, hurt more than he could articulate.

"I'm so sorry," Yarrow whispered. "I know what it means to lose a loved one."

"I have mourned him and moved on," Duncan lied. He still saw the pretty mage's soft gray eyes clearly. He saw the trust in Aubrey's face, perfect and absolute. He'd left a hole in Duncan's spirit that would never fill in. "I learned my lesson, though. Duty must come first, long before merriment. Long before anything. That's why I never married or took a permanent companion. That person would always have to be second in my heart to my commitment. It's a lonely life sometimes, but necessary. I can't ask you to understand, but it's what I must do."

"We are much less different than you might imagine," Sasha said. "I, too, have sacrificed much to serve my cause."

"What?" Yarrow asked.

"You must tell him," Duncan said. "Tell him now or risk destroying him later."

"I can't feel love or attachment, Yarrow. I've been conditioned not to. I didn't think such a triviality would matter to you, as we both agreed to keep our relationship physical. But if Duncan wishes it said, there it is. I enjoy spending time with you, but I can never offer more."

"I don't believe you."

"You must. My heart is cold, as Thalil demands. I love only him and Death, his brother."

Yarrow drew his knees up to his chest and frowned as he stared into the fire.

"Well, our victory celebration has certainly taken a sour turn," Duncan said as he stood. "Let's remember the good we've done together. We've saved the life of an innocent woman, our queen. We'll find Garith and save him too. If I may, Yarrow, perhaps I'll indulge in a single glass of your Valenny's fine wine. Come now, let us go."

They boarded one of the rowboats, and Yarrow used his arcane prowess to propel them quickly to the other side of the lake.

Chapter Eleven

IT TOOK a half-dozen kitchen maids to carry all the food Yarrow commissioned. They covered the table in his room with steaming platters overflowing with meat, fish, and fowl. Bowls of root vegetables, sautéed in butter and sprinkled with herbs, sat in earthenware bowls on the couch that served as Duncan's bed. Half a dozen fine cheeses, the pride of Lockhaven, waited beside a loaf of bread and some dried berries. Yet another pot held stew, and a variety of muffins, tarts, pies, and strudels waited on a silver plate at the foot of the bed. Duncan's mouth watered as the savory aromas mingled and filled the room.

"By the goddesses, Yarrow, there's enough here to feed a regiment," Duncan said. "There's scarcely room for us to sit and eat."

The mage whisked a knitted blanket from near his headboard and pillows and spread it on the ground. After positioning some dishes and knives at the center, he sat at the edge with his legs crossed. "We'll eat as though we're on the road. This hearth behind me shall be our campfire." Yarrow reached to his left for Sasha's hand and the lithe, dark man knelt gracefully at his side. To Duncan's surprise, Yarrow took his hand as well and urged him to sit on the stone floor, shoulder to shoulder with Yarrow. "Shall we dine?"

Duncan felt like a boy again, playing at adventuring on a friend's bedroom floor. Not for the first time, he was reminded of Yarrow's youth. The scents wafting from the sumptuous feast quickly distracted him, and he bowed his head. "Thanks be to Berris, goddess of plenty," Duncan said, "and to her many daughters: the rain, the soil, the seed, the sun, and the will to grow."

"None survives but through the demise of another soul," Sasha said. "By Thalil, who stands just out of sight, we are the slayers this day. May he grant us another until we become the slain."

"Morbid," Duncan grumbled.

"You deny the truth of my words?" Sasha asked.

"Not inherently," Duncan said, considering. "It's all a matter of perspective. We can look at this food as a blessing instead of seeing it as slaughter."

"It's both," Sasha said. He swept his hand over the feast. "Everything here has died that we might live a bit longer. One day we'll die so others might live, even if it's just to fertilize the ground as our bodies decay."

"You know, assassin, if I wasn't so hungry you might put me off my food." Since that wasn't the case, Duncan pulled the leg off one of the birds and bit into the crispy, golden skin. Sweet juice burst into his mouth, and he groaned with satisfaction. He finished the drumstick and reached for a slab of venison. Across from him, Sasha delicately pulled flakes of fish from a filet with a long, thin knife. Beside him, so close that the mage's elbow bumped his ribs as he ate, Yarrow picked at fruit, roasted vegetables, and bread.

"I almost forgot to serve the wine," Yarrow said with a grin and a wink. He dusted the bottle on his sleeve, removed the cork, and filled three chalices the size of soup bowls. After passing one to each of his companions, the mage lifted his own goblet. "What shall we drink to?" he asked.

"To victory," Sasha said, touching the rim of his cup to Yarrow's with a chime.

Duncan followed suit and drank, holding Yarrow's wine in his mouth for a moment before letting it slide slowly down his throat. It was crisp and fruity, with undertones of ripe summer berries, meadowsweet, and fresh grass. It warmed Duncan's belly as the fire warmed his back. The breeze off the lake, wafting through the open curtains, felt delightfully bracing in comparison. Duncan cut himself a piece of one of the paler cheeses. It complemented the wine perfectly. The knight lifted his glass. "To the triumph of truth," he said. The others struck their metal chalices against Duncan's and drank again.

Yarrow lowered his cup and stared into the golden liquid it held. Duncan wondered what he pondered for so many moments. Sasha also watched the mage's face. Finally Yarrow lifted his face, a serene smile on his lips. "To friends," he said, lifting his glass.

"Friends," Sasha echoed, mirroring Yarrow's smile. Yarrow touched Sasha's cheek with his free hand.

"Friends," Duncan agreed. When had he become comfortable with their affectionate displays? In some inexplicable way, Duncan felt he belonged here with Yarrow and Sasha, that agreeing to accompany them was the right decision. He shook his head. He shouldn't feel so content with a coldhearted, hired killer and a crazy mage who seemed to have at least two separate personalities, but it felt perfect sitting on the floor with them, feasting and toasting. The three of them joined goblets and drank. Afterward, Yarrow stroked Duncan's folded knee, and Duncan patted the young man's knuckles.

The companions sat together for over an hour, trading stories, picking at the delicious meal, drinking wine, and sitting close against the increasing cold of the night. A waxing crescent moon, ringed with a prismatic halo, hung just beyond the balcony and prevented their closing the drapes. The three men turned to regard it, and Yarrow moved in front of Duncan and leaned back against Duncan's chest. He let the back of his head fall against Duncan's shoulder. The spontaneous gesture of trust and familiarity touched Duncan's heart, and he rested his elbow on the other's shoulder, letting his arm hang across Yarrow's chest. He opened his legs and bent his knees so Yarrow could nestle between them, closer to Duncan's body. Sasha sat flush with Yarrow's shoulder, and their fingers twined together in Sasha's lap. A gust of wind ruffled their hair and made a chime tinkle somewhere along the shore of the lake.

"This has been a good day," Yarrow said, though a nuance of sadness tinged his voice. Duncan pulled him a little closer. Yarrow's soft hair tickled his chin. It felt so natural to hold Yarrow like this.

"It's a lovely evening too," Sasha said. "The stars are so bright here in the north. I can't help but be surprised that everything's worked out so well."

"Yet it has," Duncan said. "This is… this is *nice.*"

Yarrow chuckled and tilted his head so that Duncan could look down into his bright eyes. His shapely lips parted, and he gazed up at the knight expectantly. Duncan recalled the sweet taste of Yarrow's mouth, and the mage's enthusiasm. He couldn't resist dipping in for a quick peck, just to feel the softness and fullness of Yarrow's lips against his own. The small gesture didn't satisfy the mage, though, and he drew Duncan's lower lip between his teeth and held it there, massaging it with the tip of his tongue. When Yarrow's mouth opened, Duncan's did the same, allowing their tongues to meet and pulse against each other. If the wine had tasted delicious from the chalice, it tasted a hundred times sweeter when lapped from Yarrow's palate and sucked from his lips. A tremor moved from their conjoined mouths to the base of Duncan's body. His hand snaked into Yarrow's hair and grabbed his tresses almost of its own volition.

Sasha moved around to face Yarrow and pushed Yarrow's hair aside so he could kiss and nip up and down the mage's neck. Yarrow writhed and groaned in Duncan's arms. His kisses grew forceful, needy and hungry, his tongue thrusting deep into Duncan's mouth. The sounds of Sasha's wet lips against Yarrow's skin and the little noises Yarrow made in response aroused Duncan. When Sasha's hand moved up the knight's forearm, though, Duncan's trance broke and he pulled away from Yarrow's mouth.

"Just… just what's going on here?" he panted as his eyes darted between their faces. Yarrow looked hurt and confused, while Sasha remained unreadable with his black eyes twinkling.

"You're a grown man, Duncan," Sasha said, the gravel in his voice betraying the lust his face managed to mask. "You don't need it explained."

"You mean to suggest that we… that all three of us…."

"Duncan," Yarrow said, reaching up to cup the knight's chin. "What's wrong?"

"Everything. Everything about this is wrong."

"But why?" Yarrow asked. "Twice now you've rejected my affections, though you clearly didn't want to. I've wanted you since I first saw you. Why do you push me away?"

"But you and Sasha!"

To Duncan's shock, Sasha stroked the side of Duncan's hair before resting his hand over Yarrow's. To the knight's even greater shock, he felt no desire to pull away. Quite the opposite.

"I've told you I place no restrictions on Yarrow. We take pleasure together and nothing more. I think the three of us can take a great deal of pleasure with each other. Don't you agree?" Sasha kissed him, much more forcefully than Yarrow had, wrestling against Duncan's tongue until Duncan allowed him to subdue it. His nimble fingers wrapped the back of Duncan's neck, and his nails bit the skin. His tongue filled Duncan's mouth, and Duncan sucked it in even further. Sasha's need spilled from him, and it felt good to be desired so strongly. Sandwiched between them, Yarrow squirmed as his lips moved between Duncan's jaw and the edge of Sasha's ear. Sasha pressed closer, forcing the three of them tighter together. Yarrow's left leg wrapped around the assassin's waist. As he ground against Sasha, Yarrow's back rubbed Duncan's swelling cock.

All of Duncan's internal arguments about why this would be a bad idea evaporated like the mist over the lake would when dawn came. He was only human, and these men were so beautiful. It had been a long time since he'd enjoyed the touch of another, and he couldn't make himself turn away their offer of joy. He'd done his duty for the day; nothing stood between him and what he desperately needed. It had been far too long since he'd felt anything but his own hand on his body. It had been even longer since he'd known how it felt to be wanted like this.

"Oh, Sasha," he breathed. "I… I still don't approve of what you do."

"I don't care, my beautiful knight. It's not approval I want from you just now." Sasha plunged back down on Duncan's mouth. He bit the tip of Duncan's tongue, and Duncan seized him beneath the knees and wrenched his legs around both himself and Yarrow. The flexible assassin easily moved into Yarrow's lap and straddled the other men. "Do you find me desirable?" Sasha asked, his hot breath wafting over Duncan's burning cheek, enveloping him in the aroma of herbs and wine.

"How could I not?" Duncan said. "I'm just a man."

"That's all I need. Don't think too much, Duncan. Just enjoy." Resting on Yarrow's groin, Sasha split his affections between Duncan and Yarrow, kissing one and then the other. Yarrow held onto him for dear life, twining Sasha in his limbs and circling his root furiously against the other man.

Duncan, his breath jagged, his lips swollen, and his cock so hard that it threatened to tear his trousers, reached around to grasp the leather-encased crescents of Sasha's ass. As he kneaded the tantalizing cords of sinew, he suckled along Yarrow's jaw and down his neck, licking away the fresh sweat that broke from the mage's pores. Not a blade of grass would have fit between their bodies. Duncan perspired beneath the quilted shirt he always wore under his armor. Finally, reluctantly, he pulled away from them to strip it off.

As he sat catching his breath, dizzy from his pulse pounding in his head, Duncan watched Yarrow affectionately pick apart the many buckles on Sasha's exotic armor. He peeled it away to reveal golden skin that sparkled with sweat. Sasha looked willowy in his clothes, but out of them his definition was impressive. He stood slowly, with feline grace, to let the mage slide his tight leggings down. Yarrow looked up at Sasha with reverence as he hooked his thumbs beneath the assassin's unusual undergarment. He got it to Sasha's knees before pausing to kiss the gorgeous gully between his stomach muscles. His long, graceful fingers traced the perimeter of Sasha's moon-shaped marking, making Duncan a trace reluctant, reminding him what lay beneath Sasha's beautiful façade. Yet he remembered not just murder hid beneath Sasha's often unreadable exterior. He also held courage, loyalty, and his own peculiar code of honor.

Sasha smiled as he petted Yarrow's hair. No matter what these men said, Duncan saw they cared about each other. At least as much fondness radiated from their flushed faces as base lust. He'd never seen Sasha's face shine with such authentic, unintentional emotion. It magnified his appeal a hundredfold.

Sasha looked like a bronze statue in the firelight, and Duncan yearned to touch him. He wanted to get Yarrow out of the shabby garb he insisted on wearing and finally get his hands on the mage's soft, supple form too. He'd never wanted anything as much. His heart beat so hard it shook his body. Like a drunkard, he stumbled to stand behind Yarrow and put his hand next to Sasha's in Yarrow's hair. Yarrow lavished attention on Sasha's cock, not sucking it yet but pecking around the crown and running his hands up and down the length. Now and then he stopped to peck at the red sickle on Sasha's thigh. Duncan looked away from that spot, ignoring the single, glaring flaw and seeking out the glow of Sasha's unrestricted bliss. The knight's eyes met the assassin's like a flame touching kindling. Duncan seized his neck and kissed him so hard their teeth scraped together. Sasha pushed him playfully away and offered a hand to help Yarrow stand. He began to undo the laces of Yarrow's shirt. It felt like ages since Duncan had done the same, in the small tent after Yarrow had saved his life. He wished he had that opportunity back. While he never would, he had this opportunity, this night, and he wouldn't make the same mistake twice.

Sasha pulled Yarrow's shirt over his head, giving Duncan a fine view of his slender back and pronounced shoulder blades. Duncan ran his fingertip over one ridge of bone and smiled at the gooseflesh that erupted on Yarrow's tan skin. Slowly he moved closer, letting his hands slide down Yarrow's back and around to his flat belly, dusted with sparse, pale hair. Venturing lower, he found Yarrow's erect cock beneath the threadbare, torn cloth of his trousers. It was damp and curled toward the mage's belly button.

"Dear goddesses, Yarrow," Duncan said, surprised at what he found.

"I take it you're impressed," the mage teased.

"Maybe a little afraid," Duncan said, nuzzling into Yarrow's hair and breathing the scent of his arousal as he gripped that big dick through Yarrow's loose pants. "It's been a long time for me. I don't know if I can handle that thing."

Yarrow chuckled and said, "You can give me what you have, then. I don't mind receiving. Not at all!" He inhaled sharply as Sasha pinched his nipple. "It's amazing, being between you two." He grabbed each of their asses with one of his hands and pulled their cocks against him. Duncan's hands squashed between Sasha's and Yarrow's bellies and penises. He could feel their erratic pulses and their two hard shafts, Sasha's slick and bare, rubbing together. "I want to be in the middle," Yarrow said, throwing his head back and moaning.

"How?" Duncan asked. "How will this go?"

"However you like," Yarrow said. "I'm yours. Both of yours. Do anything you want with me."

"First I need to get you two out of those troublesome pants," Sasha said, mopping his upper lip with his tongue.

Duncan had never seen lips like Sasha's, swollen as if with poison. While he didn't agree with Sasha's moral views, the knight couldn't deny his allure. If Sasha and Yarrow could make love just for pleasure, without any commitment, Duncan could as well. In fact, he couldn't wait. The idea of such hedonistic abandon excited him, and he couldn't wish for two more beautiful or eager partners. It felt much different in the privacy of Yarrow's chambers, taking their time, than it had to take a foot soldier against the wall of the barracks. For years Duncan had needed to rush, to finish before being caught. He'd barely been aware of his partners, or they of him, as both valued release over the journey. Duncan decided tonight would be different. He tore his pants off like they were on fire.

Yarrow did the same. When he turned to face the knight, Duncan followed the meandering paths of his paint, finding they led his eyes to all the best places: to the shelf of muscle on his chest, down the side of his waist, over his ribs, diagonally from his sharp hipbone to his glorious erection, and along the divot at the side of his ass.

The mage approached Duncan and scraped his nails from Duncan's knees to his hipbones. "I remember the first time I saw you, Duncan, sitting there dripping wet. I think I was infatuated that very moment, even before you were kind to me. I wondered what you looked like under that armor. You're better than my fantasies, even. Goddesses, I want you, but…." Yarrow nibbled along the muscle that stretched between Duncan's neck and shoulder. He pressed his large erection against Duncan's engorged cock.

"But what, my lovely lad?" Duncan asked. The mage's words had crushed his heart like a fist. Duncan looked down at his own chest, pale where his armor usually sat, and hairy compared to the others. Somehow, neither Yarrow nor Sasha bore lines to indicate where their clothing blocked the sun. He looked at the many scars that served as mementos of his victories and failures. Yarrow touched an old one curving over his kneecap, his eyes unfocused as he smiled languidly.

"Such a perfect man. What is it you want, Duncan?"

Duncan felt Yarrow's wet skin catching against his. He felt the mage's mouth, cool against his flesh, and he felt the white hair on Yarrow's belly brushing against his sensitive flesh. A foot beyond Yarrow's left shoulder, Sasha stood stroking himself, squeezing his balls now and then, letting the two new lovers discover one another. Duncan appreciated his insight, but he wanted to learn the feel of Sasha now, taste the pearl of semen that stood on the tip of the assassin's blood-darkened cock. "I, I want to be inside you, Yarrow," he said. "I've wanted that for so long. Goddesses, I want to do everything with you. With both of you."

"Oh, Duncan." Yarrow threw his arms around Duncan's neck and pushed him back until Duncan's knees struck the edge of the bed. Duncan sat, spread his legs, and drew Yarrow near, between his knees, wanting nothing but to be as close to him as possible. They kissed fervently, barely stopping to breathe. Duncan brushed his fingers from the top of Yarrow's cleft to the base of his balls, and back, pausing to circle his wrinkled opening, impatient to explore it more deeply.

Sasha seized Yarrow's shoulder and spun him around. The two kissed while Sasha guided Yarrow down into Duncan's lap.

So the assassin likes to be in control, Duncan thought as he reached around Yarrow to fondle the rigid flesh of his nipples. His other hand found Sasha's svelte waist and moved up the rungs of his ribs. The mage's slightly spread ass smoldered against Duncan's throbbing erection, begging to be entered. Though Duncan wasn't as large as Yarrow, he was certainly adequate, and he didn't want to damage his partner. He plunged two fingers into his mouth to wet them, and then he pressed them against the snug ring of Yarrow's anus. They breached the circle of muscle, and Yarrow cried out into Sasha's mouth.

"Wait," Sasha said as he broke from Yarrow. He went to his pack and returned with a vial of golden oil.

Understanding, Duncan withdrew his fingers from Yarrow and held his hand out. Sasha dribbled some of the spicy-scented lubricant over the knight's fingers, grasping and rubbing them suggestively as he stared into Duncan's eyes. Yarrow spread his legs wide in provocation, his thighs almost parallel to the edge of the mattress, and this time Duncan's fingers slipped easily within him. His hot, silky tunnel clenched around them as he arched back against the knight's efforts. Duncan found the knot within him, his sweet spot, and massaged it. The mage made a sound almost like weeping.

"Oh, yes, right there," Yarrow whimpered. "Duncan, that's fantastic."

"Let me… let me have you," Duncan panted, aroused beyond reason. "Yarrow, are you ready?"

"Yes!"

Wasting no more time, Duncan positioned his cockhead outside Yarrow's slicked opening and pressed in. Yarrow pushed back to aid his effort, and all resistance broke. The tightness amazed him; he couldn't recall another body ever feeling so good around his, such a perfect fit. As he eased his length into Yarrow, Sasha knelt between Yarrow's legs and lapped at his fat, inflamed corona. Yarrow closed one hand around Sasha's hair while he reached his other hand back to brace himself against Duncan's shoulder.

"Sasha," Yarrow moaned. "Duncan, my goddesses!" He began to move against them, testing the best angles, alternately driving Duncan's cock into his ass and his own erect penis into Sasha's willing mouth. The assassin's dark, incredibly shapely lips gliding over Yarrow's thick shaft made an enticing show. Sasha's eyes clamped shut, and his brows knit with concentration. Duncan couldn't resist reaching down to touch his soft, black hair, and the low groan of pleasure Sasha uttered at his caress surprised and pleased him. Sasha reached up and dug his fingers into the muscle cording over Duncan's forearm. His touch sent sparks of excitement all the way to Duncan's shoulder.

Pushing deep into Yarrow while watching Sasha brought Duncan dangerously close to release. He hadn't been with anyone in a long while, and he'd never been in such a delicious, erotic situation as this. Duncan's brows furrowed as he fought to hold back even as his cock bucked inside the mage. He pressed his palm to the mattress behind him to avoid being pushed to his back and losing the amazing view. The sweet, salty taste of Yarrow's skin, Yarrow's scent, and the enthusiastic noises he made pushed him even closer to the edge, and Duncan lifted his lips from Yarrow's shoulder. Slowing his strokes did little to impede his orgasm. Even when he stilled completely, Yarrow's ass hugged his dick and slid over his shaft as the mage pumped into Sasha's throat.

Sasha withdrew his mouth from Yarrow's cock with a long, slow slurp. A silvery cord of saliva connected them for a moment and then snapped. He stood between Yarrow's splayed legs and kissed him with the deep, enthusiastic sincerity of a lover. Then the assassin broke away, touched Yarrow's face and then Duncan's, and turned his back on the other two men. He raised the bottle of oil, which he'd never relinquished, above his tailbone and let the amber fluid drizzle down. It anointed Sasha's cleft and made his balls beneath it glisten. Golden liquid shimmered down his hamstrings, accentuating their musculature. He lowered himself onto Yarrow, grasping Yarrow's cock and circling the head around his hole.

"Yarrow, have me," Sasha said. "Please."

"Sasha? Let me stretch you, get you ready."

"I want you, Yarrow. I want you right now. I don't want to wait. Don't deny me."

"I won't," the mage said as he pressed forward, a fraction of an inch at a time. With great care and patience, he finally managed to work his cockhead into Sasha. Yarrow drew a shuddering breath and waited, tracing the distended rim of Sasha's hole. Slowly, his length breached the other's snug anus and disappeared within him.

Sasha cried out in a language Duncan didn't understand, but remained on his feet, hands on his knees. Duncan watched Yarrow's penis sink into Sasha's puffy, red hole, pulling the edge taut. Sasha stifled a grunt and pushed back against his partner. Yarrow's arm grasped him, supporting him around the chest. The assassin's black hair swept back and forth as he returned his lover's endeavors. When Sasha pushed back, he also forced Yarrow's ass against Duncan. Before long, they established a tempo, Sasha conducting with the movement of his hips against Yarrow. The mage scratched Duncan's lower back, compelling him forward, even as he wrapped his opposite arm tighter around Sasha to draw him closer.

All of them groaned and grunted, muttering each other's names as they moved faster and more urgently against each other. Duncan reached past Yarrow to grasp Sasha's shoulder and dig his nails into Sasha's golden skin. Next time he'd take Sasha's position, but he'd turn the opposite way so he could watch both of their faces contorting with bliss. He wished he could see them now.

Sasha reached behind himself, seized the back of Yarrow's head, and directed Yarrow's mouth to his shoulder. "Bite," the assassin begged, grabbing Yarrow's hand and sinking his teeth into its web in demonstration. Yarrow squealed and did as requested, which seemed to gratify Sasha. To add to his partner's delight, Duncan let his nails pierce Sasha's skin.

He likes it a little rough, Duncan noted, hopefully for future reference. He scratched down Sasha's tricep.

"Duncan!" Sasha cried out. At that moment, Yarrow reached in front of him and twisted Sasha's penis in his fist. Sasha's words degraded into incomprehensible muttering as he sprayed his seed over the stone floor. "By the Cast-Down! My God! Oh, Yarrow, I—"

"Sasha, yes!" Yarrow's body shook with release. His forehead fell between Sasha's shoulder blades. Duncan grasped him around the waist and kissed the back of his neck as he trembled and went limp for a moment. The mage's anus spasmed around Duncan's cock, finally breaking the knight's resolve. Duncan shot deep into Yarrow, coming harder than he ever had. He slapped his palm against Yarrow's thigh as the intensity of the experience stole his lucidity. The smacks encouraged Yarrow to ride him hard once again. Yarrow braced his feet against the bed frame and drove himself against Duncan, dragging Sasha's languid body along, until Duncan could withstand no further stimulation.

"Stop," Duncan pleaded. "Get off of me. I can't take it!"

Sasha broke away first. He staggered a few steps to support himself against the table. Then Yarrow stood on shaky legs, creamy rivulets running down his inner thighs. Sasha faced him, grasped his white hair in both hands, and held it away from Yarrow's damp face.

Yarrow touched Sasha's lower lip with the pad of his thumb and whispered, "I love you."

"Don't be silly," Sasha chided. "That's not possible between men like you and I. No strings, just as you wanted."

"I… apologize," Yarrow said. To Duncan it sounded unconvincing, pitiful, even. "I didn't mean it. I'm just… that was amazing. I'm not thinking straight."

Despite what he'd said, Sasha kissed Yarrow's brow and rested his face against the mage's cheek for many minutes.

Duncan fell back on the bed, his whole body trembling, weak, and satisfied in a way he never remembered. He also felt sticky and sweaty, and would have dived in Estrella Lake despite the cold. Instead, he contented himself with the washbasin and cloth Yarrow brought until he could bathe in the morning. After they cleaned up, the three men shared Yarrow's childhood bed. Duncan lay in the middle, and Sasha lay curled on his side with his back to the others. The knight ran his fingers up and down the knobs of Sasha's spine while he held Yarrow close with his other arm. The mage dozed on his chest but stirred long enough to kiss Duncan's chin now and then. Every time he giggled, Duncan grinned until his face almost split. Yarrow stretched his arm across Duncan, and he tucked his hand between Sasha's elbow and waist. Nuzzling back against them, Sasha coiled his fingers around Yarrow's wrist and held it tight. When they'd situated themselves, Duncan pulled the blankets over them and folded them in cozily.

Duncan felt a bit sorry for Yarrow after Sasha's harsh rejection of his feelings. Yarrow so rarely dropped the barriers that kept others at bay. He rested his face against the top of Yarrow's head and whispered, "You know I care about you. What we shared was pleasant, but it meant more than that to me."

"I wish what you suggested was possible," Yarrow said, cuddling closer.

"Why isn't it?"

"Because of me, Duncan. I can't."

"I don't care what you've done in the past. I, too, have done things I regret. For a long time I didn't think it would be possible for me to have any kind of companion. I didn't think I could put another person ahead of my duty, nor expect my partner to be second to it in my thoughts. I'm starting to see it may not be so simple. I'm starting to see how empty my life has been. Maybe you can reconsider, as well. Whatever it is that haunts you, Yarrow, it's behind you. Over and done."

"If only it was that simple."

"I don't understand."

"And I can't help you to. I'm sorry. If it means anything, I wish things could be different. Good night, *syrai*."

"Good night, my friend." Duncan lay, contemplating Yarrow's cryptic remarks for a bit while he listened to the other men's breathing growing deep and steady. He was warm between them, and before long the comfort and heat combined with his exertion, and he couldn't fight sleep any longer.

SASHA WOKE first at the scuffling in the hall. He'd been sleeping much deeper than he usually permitted himself. He'd barely stirred when the servants entered the room to clear the food and dishes away. Awake now, he crept out of bed without disturbing the others and slipped into the pants he'd discarded so haphazardly a few hours before. He put his hands into his deadly gloves and strapped his daggers around his body, keeping an especially nasty curved and serrated blade in his hand. An elongated square of dim starlight fell across the bed and part of the floor, shining in from the balcony. Sasha stepped out of the illuminated block and into the shadows, from which he'd be most effective.

Footsteps approached the room in a pathetic attempt at stealth. Yarrow thrashed, sat up, and said, "Yes, damn it. I'm awake now, aren't I?"

Confused, Sasha turned to regard him. The radiant blue of his eyes outlined him, branching out in a vague suggestion of wings. The sight unnerved the assassin. Sasha's hand lifted the dagger before his logic reminded him Yarrow wasn't his enemy. By now Duncan's soft snores had faded, and the knight slowly rose from the bed, twisting his waist, cracking his spine, and moving toward the water pitcher on the table.

The brothers of the Crimson Scythe knew a language consisting only of hand gestures, so they could communicate in absolute silence. Duncan wouldn't know the nuances, but Sasha hoped he'd understand a few simple signals. The assassin held up his hand, palm toward Duncan, and pressed a finger to his lips. He pointed toward the door, and then toward the large sword resting in the corner. Eyes widening in comprehension, Duncan tiptoed toward his blade. Along the way, he scooped up his simple pants and put them on. Sasha inclined his head toward the door, and he and Duncan took their places on either side of it. Unabashedly naked, Yarrow stood between them with his fingers spread in front of his chest.

Predictably, the door burst open, but instead of the mercenaries or thugs Sasha had expected, a dozen guards in Lockhaven livery, the silver lake-wyrm and star against burgundy, filed in. They parted ranks to reveal one of Yarrow's brothers, not the valen, but the other, whose name Sasha didn't recall. Even at this late hour, the elder L'Estrella wore a ceremonial suit of armor and a deep wine-colored cape.

"What's the meaning of this, Rowan?" Yarrow demanded, stepping forward.

"Goddesses, brother, have you no shame?" the older man said, averting his eyes from Yarrow's nudity.

"You ask me that as you break into my chambers in the middle of the night?"

"It's necessary, Yarroway. Stand aside and let my men do their jobs."

"What are you on about, Rowan?"

"Earlier this evening, a few noble ladies discovered a body beside the path to Vestrafori's temple. The young woman's throat had been cut, and she'd also been stabbed in the back. That poor girl was identified as Ambra Piers. Several witnesses reported your... your *companion* visiting Lady Piers not long after breakfast. We're here to take this assassin into custody."

"You'll have to go through me!" Yarrow yelled. "Woe to anyone who lays a finger on Sasha. Come on. Who'll be the first to try?"

The mage moved shoulder to shoulder with the assassin, and Sasha welcomed his skills and his encouraging proximity. Most of the guards cowered, and many stepped back from Yarrow's glowing form. Outside, waves crashed loudly against the shores of the lake. The wind picked up and knocked Yarrow's boyhood trinkets from their shelves.

"Brother, I know what you think this man is to you. Everyone has heard the rumors. But he murdered an innocent girl, and he'll be held accountable. You men, take the assassin."

"No!" Yarrow pointed toward the stone floor and it roiled like boiling liquid, knocking the approaching guards off their feet. Those that didn't fall looked about in terror, as if the ceiling or walls might attack next. Sasha almost chuckled at their paranoia. "Hear me out, brother. Don't make me hurt these men for following your ludicrous orders."

"You mean to tell me you'd kill your own people for this... this.... Goddesses, Yarrow, it makes me sick to my stomach that you associate with this man, let alone...." He grimaced and turned away, unable to finish his tirade or face his younger sibling. "Haven't you embarrassed our family enough? Everything about you is unnatural," Rowan grumbled as he stared at the floor.

"Think what you like, Rowan. Or, rather, keep thinking whatever Rayne spoons into your empty head!"

"You perverse little whelp!" Rowan drew his sword and pointed it at Yarrow's chest.

Yarrow's laughter bounced from the walls of the stone chamber. "Go ahead, if you think you can do it. Won't Rayne be delighted?"

"Enough of this." Duncan hurried forward and forcefully lowered Rowan's arm. He stood between the brothers, keeping them at arm's length. "Tam Rowan, at least hear what Yarrow has to say. I think you'll find it impossible that Sasha could have committed this crime."

"He's been with me since this morning," Yarrow said. "He couldn't have done this."

"Despite your words, my orders are to take him into custody. He never should have been set loose in this house in the first place."

"How dare you," Yarrow hissed, his aura flaring. "Take it back!"

"It's the truth and you know it. He doesn't belong among decent, civilized people, and I will take him."

"See reason, tam," Duncan said. "I, too, can vouch for this man's whereabouts today."

"The valen wants him detained," Rowan said. "Men...."

"I'll warn you one last time," Yarrow said.

"No. Rowan, Yarrow, this is madness. You two are brothers, for the love of the goddesses. Let's talk about this like reasonable men. Don't do something you'll both regret."

"You too, Tam Duncan?" Rowan asked

"What about me?" Duncan asked. "I wish only to serve the truth and avoid unnecessary bloodshed."

"Rayne is doing this just to get at me," Yarrow shouted. "And yet he's too much of a coward to come here himself. I demand he comes here to speak with me."

"You're in no position to demand anything, brother. You're lucky the valen doesn't throw you in the dungeon with your... your *friend* here."

"Try it!"

With a gesture, Rowan directed his men to surround Sasha and Yarrow. More of them appeared from down the hall, and in only a few moments twenty swords pointed at the mage and the assassin. Yarrow brought his back flush with Sasha's. He planned to fight. While Sasha respected his fortitude and appreciated his loyalty, not even the two of them stood much chance against so many. These were trained soldiers with weapons and heavy armor, not a rabble of peasants. They might take quite a few of them, but they'd risk severe injury, maybe even death. His training told Sasha to seek a more favorable approach. The Crimson Scythe didn't fight against the odds; they made the odds fight for them and chose battles they knew they'd win. This was not one of those battles.

More importantly, Sasha didn't want Yarrow to come to harm on his behalf, or Duncan, either. His feelings surprised him. He dropped his jagged dagger to the floor and offered his empty hands.

"Sasha, what are you doing?" Yarrow asked. "We can defeat them! I won't let them take you!"

Fire burned in the mage's eyes, and Sasha knew without a doubt Yarrow would fight for him to his last scrap of energy. Maybe he'd even kill his brother. Sweet, dark god, but Sasha wanted to seize him and kiss him until he couldn't breathe. He also knew he couldn't subject Yarrow to the inevitable pain and guilt. "I'll go with them," he said, "for now."

"Sasha, no!"

"Yarrow, my friend, you've done a great deal for me, and you don't know what it means. I'll go and trust you'll find a way to prove my innocence, just as you did for your aunt. I ask you do what I say." Yarrow still looked conflicted, so Sasha whispered, "Will you deny me?"

"No." Yarrow turned to his brother. "If he's mistreated in any way, if he's even uncomfortable, I will raze this castle and everyone in it to the ground. Am I understood?"

Rowan shuddered and nodded, and Sasha smiled with pride. "Bind him," the elder L'Estrella said.

"Absolutely not," Yarrow said. "He's agreed to go with you. I won't see him molested. Don't even touch him, any of you. Don't lay a fingertip on his skin, or you'll answer to me."

Sasha followed the men. Yarrow's outrage and their fear prevented them from removing Sasha's gloves, which would make it even easier for him to escape from whatever preposterous cell they thought could hold him. He almost laughed out loud, wondering if it might take him a full five minutes. Afterward, he'd hide until Yarrow and Duncan departed in search of the prince, and then he'd join them. It would be much easier that way. He hoped at least Yarrow would intuit his plan. Though it seemed silly, he felt a connection with the mage, and, to a lesser degree, with the knight.

Rowan and his guards led Sasha down to the root cellar, past racks of wine, and to a little barred room next to some ale kegs. Two similar cells stood next to it, but it could hardly be described as a dungeon. Sasha entered his cage and sat down on the cot in the corner. One of the men closed and locked the door. It creaked loudly from disuse. Sasha wondered if the rust in the lock would hinder the picks hidden in his gloves. His escape might take ten minutes, after all.

To Sasha's slight interest, all of the guards departed, leaving him alone. Perhaps they suspected his plan, but he doubted it. Even so, he felt it prudent to wait. His cell contained the bed on which he sat, a wooden stool, and a chamber pot. He drew his legs up and folded them beneath him. By Thalil, Yarrow was really something, and he'd left Sasha sore. He smiled at the memory and let it entertain him for the next quarter of an hour.

Footsteps in the corridor leading to the cells roused Sasha from his reverie. He made no outward sign of noticing the sound, but remained seated with his hands folded in his lap and his eyes on his bare feet. Even when a man (judging by the stature) in a dark cloak stood outside his cell door, Sasha didn't look up.

"May Thalil conceal you always in shadow, one currently called Sasha," said a deep, masculine voice, older and with a note of vicious mirth.

"What can I do for you? Have you come to kill me in spite of my mage's threats? I wouldn't advise it."

"No, no, my friend. Thalil is not finished with you yet."

"According to the rest of my order, he is."

"His ways are often mysterious, friend."

"You call me friend, not brother," Sasha noted. "You're not one of us. Who are you?"

"A simple messenger. Thalil once again calls you to service."

"What service?"

"You're planning to accompany the mage and the knight in search of Prince Garith. My employer asks that you make certain the prince does not make it home. Not only will you be handsomely rewarded, your status within the order will be reinstated."

"Rewarded how handsomely?" Sasha asked. "What you request won't be easy."

"More gold than you've earned in the rest of your calling combined."

"And who offers these riches?"

"What does it matter?"

"I'd like to know for certain that this reward will actually materialize before I take these risks," Sasha said. "Do you realize just how formidable my companions are?"

"I swear it by Thalil's name," the stranger said. "No man takes that oath lightly. Return here, to this cell, when the job is done, and you'll have your payment. Don't forget that this is the only way to stop your brothers and sisters from offering your blood to The Whisper Heard Too Late."

"You know our ways," Sasha conceded. "But this proposal is dubious at best. I don't know if I can agree."

"Don't be a fool," the stranger scolded. "Whose feelings concern you? The mage's? Ridiculous. Do you suppose he loves you? Do you suppose he'll take you off to a country estate where you can live in peace and bliss? A man like you? A killer? Do you mean to become a housewife, Sasha? You can't possibly be that naïve."

"I'm not."

"Then be the man you are. After all, what are you if not a son of Thalil? These men you travel with will never accept your true nature, one called Sasha. Eventually they'll turn away from you in disgust. You'll be left with nothing if you place your future in their hands."

"I know."

"Will you do as the order asks, then?"

"I will, so long as I'm not asked to harm Yarrow or Duncan."

"That is acceptable to my employer, so long as Prince Garith is offered to The Dark and Beautiful One."

"It will be done. I'll expect my payment, or I'll take it in blood, *friend*."

"Good, good. I'll take my leave of you now. Your companions should be along soon to break you out of here. Make yourself ready. The Lockhaven forces won't make it easy for you."

The strange man turned and melted into the shadows, leaving Sasha with nothing but a deep sense of dread. He readied his concealed weapons and waited for whatever might come.

As SOON as Rowan and the guards left the room, Yarrow dressed and started pacing. "Can we go after him now?" he asked Duncan.

You should have let me wear the flesh, beloved. They never would have taken him. Their blood would decorate these walls.

Damn. Maybe I should have. I shouldn't have let him go. I already miss him. I'm worried sick.

You might as well get used to it. He'll be gone soon enough.

Though he knew his companion spoke truly, Yarrow ignored its words for the moment. "Duncan, let's go!"

"I thought you planned to speak to your brother, Rayne, on Sasha's behalf. I'd understood the plan was to prove his innocence as we did for the queen."

Yarrow swore in Emiri. No other language approached the profanity he needed to express his outrage. "The queen sits in the finest guest room the castle has to offer, not a prison cell. She's the damned queen! People like Sasha aren't awarded the same consideration. Do you honestly think they'll give him a trial? This world is not an equitable place. Some people matter and some don't. Do you think any proof we offer will matter to my brother and the other valens?"

"No, I suppose I know better." Duncan lifted his well-used sword and looked intently at the dull metal. "I'll be stripped of my knighthood for this. It won't matter to anyone that my cause was just."

We don't need him, beloved! Come, let's spill some blood.

These are my friends and family. The last thing I want to do is kill them. I hope we won't have to fight. I also don't want to see Duncan lose the duty that means so much to him.

Then leave him behind!

"I don't want to leave him… I don't want to leave you behind, Duncan, but I understand if you can't help me."

"All I ever wanted was to be a knight," the older man said, still staring at his reflection in the polished steel. "As you observed, this world is hardly fair. I wanted to change it. Over the years, I've had less success than I'd hoped. People are still greedy, cruel, and hard-minded. I want to keep trying, though. To champion just causes and defend innocents who need it. In this case, that's Sasha."

Yarrow laughed. "Sasha, innocent. Imagine that." Duncan looked up and met his eyes with a crooked smile on his face. Yarrow knew Duncan remembered the blistering union the assassin instigated. The mage felt his cheeks heat as the same images returned to his mind. "Still, I won't abandon him."

"Neither will I," Duncan said. "I'd started to like the idea of traveling with you two. Goddesses, I must be crazy or a masochist, but I'd like us to stay together a while longer. Besides, even if I'm not reinstated after the truth comes out, I'll always be a knight, whether others recognize me as such or not. If I acted other than honorably, I couldn't call myself by that title."

Yarrow kissed Duncan and Duncan kissed him back. Somehow, it felt like they'd been together a long time, years and not just a few weeks. The nuances of Duncan's kiss felt familiar to Yarrow. Though the presence within him laughed and mocked his sentimentality, Yarrow liked not feeling so alone for once. "Let's go," he said. "Duncan, thank you. It means more than I can tell you that you're standing with us."

"No more talk," Duncan said, coloring a little across his cheekbones and nose. "What do you plan to do?"

Kill every living thing that stands in our way!

No. "I know the castle well, of course. I spent many afternoons exploring the cellars. This fortress is old and has many secrets, including a network of passages below the basement. I think the castle was built on top of them. They're ancient, and I found some very interesting things within them as a boy. More importantly, they led away from the estate and to a small cavern near the southern shore of the lake. Near the river. We'll find a boat."

"And go where? We won't know where to find the prince until morning."

"I don't want to leave Sasha rotting in that cell," Yarrow said, balling his fists. "What if the guards mistreat him against my wishes? What if they kill him?"

Duncan put both his hands on Yarrow's shoulders and massaged away the tension Yarrow hadn't realized he'd stored in them. He couldn't help but relax a little and sigh with a trace of contentment. Duncan kissed his forehead and then said, "Those guards are terrified of you. They won't dare disobey you. And do you honestly think Sasha would be so easy to kill? Dawn is only a few hours off. We need to wait to speak with the queen, and then we'll free him. Come, let's lie down and rest while we can."

"I'll never be able to sleep," Yarrow said. His companion felt restless within Yarrow's consciousness and performed the psychic equivalents of pacing and drumming its fingers. Likely Yarrow's agitation gave it an opening, and it pressed its advantage. Its memories flashed before him, so vivid they overshadowed Duncan's firelit face. Images of carnage replaced the comforting sights of Yarrow's childhood things and Duncan's kind smile. Bile rose in Yarrow's throat and sweat broke from his pores. He clutched Duncan's biceps and fought against the other, struggling to subdue it and failing. It clawed toward the surface, dulling Yarrow's perceptions, taking over. What would it do to Duncan if it succeeded?

Never fear, little Yarrow. I won't hurt him. Much.

No! Yarrow summoned all of his willpower and gave the creature a final, hard push. It relented, though not without Yarrow knowing it let him win.

"I won't sleep either," Duncan said. "But at least we can take the comfort of holding each other."

Though he wanted nothing more than the security of the knight's strong arms, Yarrow broke away. "No, I can't."

"Why under heaven not?"

"I'm sorry, Duncan. I need to be alone."

"What if I don't want to be alone? Does that matter to you?"

"I'm sorry," Yarrow repeated. "It's better if you're not around me just now. That's all I can say."

The knight stiffened when Yarrow kissed his brow. "By some miracle, I'd almost forgotten how selfish you are."

"I'm going out for a walk by the lake." Yarrow turned away, his feet like lead and his chest as heavy as a stone.

Chapter Twelve

YARROW HOPED Duncan might still be asleep when he returned from speaking with the queen. For a long time he stood outside his bedchamber door, his palm and forehead flat against the rough wood.

You're thinking that if it weren't for me you could mate with him, or whatever your people call such unions now. You wish to be rid of me, don't you, beloved?

Goddesses, how he did! The sliver of his mind Yarrow managed to keep from the other presence wanted nothing else. He wanted it so fiercely he worried he'd betray his feelings to the creature. In the years since their blending, though, he'd learned to lie quite effectively, even to deceive himself. *It hardly matters*, he told his companion. *You and I are stuck with one another, and there's nothing we can do about it. I indulged a fantasy for a time, I suppose. That's not so bad. Men may come and go, but you can give me power. Power is forever.*

Smart boy, beloved. Go and fetch him so we can have some fun. I look forward to these battles. It's dull and gray within these walls. I see why you left to wander.

I left for very different reasons.

It hardly matters anymore, except to you. Come now. We should move.

Yarrow nodded and knocked softly. It felt odd to ask permission to enter his own room. He waited many minutes before the knight opened the door. Duncan clearly hadn't slept. His skin looked waxen, and dark splotches underlined his eyes. When he saw Yarrow, he simply stood aside to allow the mage's entrance. Yarrow stepped into the room and looked around at his books and trinkets. They all seemed so trivial. He decided that he'd never return here, never sleep here, especially. Not with the fresh memories he'd recently made within these walls. This wasn't his home, not anymore. He doubted he'd ever find a place to truly call home again. Instead of looking at the knight, who stood fully armed, Yarrow went to the couch and gathered up Sasha's things. Once he had the leather garments, daggers, and pack ready, he turned to the other man.

Neither spoke. They merely nodded once to each other and made their way down the hall, to the stairs, and eventually into the cellar. When they reached Sasha's cell, the assassin rose from the narrow bed where he lay and swung the door open.

Yarrow grinned, not surprised in the least his talented friend had picked the simple lock.

"Finally," Sasha said, stepping out of his cage. "I'd begun to grow achingly bored."

He's not the only one.

"Sasha." Yarrow couldn't help but embrace his friend. Sasha returned his affection, and goddesses, no matter what the other man claimed, to Yarrow, Sasha's relief and gratitude felt genuine. "Did anyone mistreat you? So help me, if they even spoke to you harshly, I'll—"

Lifting a hand to still Yarrow's outrage, Sasha said, "No need, my friend. These men feared your wrath enough to treat me well."

"Then they're not as stupid as they look," Yarrow responded. "We should get out of here."

"Agreed," Sasha said. "We must find Garith as soon as we can. Duncan, are you joining us?"

Both Yarrow and Sasha turned to the knight. Duncan closed his eyes and pinched the bridge of his nose. Afterward he said, "This is what my heart tells me is right."

Yarrow's companion roared. *His heart or his loins, beloved Yarrow?*

Oh, shut up.

You shouldn't be so rude, little mage. You may need me to pass through these tunnels to freedom.

Yes, I may. It occurs to me that you're barely holding up your end of our agreement. You promised to teach me arcane secrets. I can't remember the last time you shared your knowledge. Perhaps I should stop sharing my perceptions.

Demanding brat. What would you like to learn?

I'd like to learn the spell that immobilized you.

Why?

So I can escape my brother's knights and the people of my valenny without killing them, of course.

And that's all?

Of course.

It'll cost you, beloved.

Cost me what?

The body. Let me wear it for a full two days and nights.

Yarrow considered. The knowledge would bring him one step closer to mastering the creature, to being rid of it. Goddesses, maybe then—maybe someday—

Duncan and Sasha are off-limits.

How I enjoy your confusion in regards to them, the creature mocked. *It's like chewing on a piece of unripe apple. It sustains you, though the bitterness bursts out and makes your face curl up and your belly ache. But you take another bite, and then another. Sometimes it bites and you want to spew it out, but you always force it down. Oh, Yarrow… I'll agree. So long as I get the flesh when we reach Meritage.*

Meritage? Why do want control there? What is it about Meritage—

My desires are of no concern to you, beloved. Will you agree or not?

"Yarrow, are you all right?" Duncan asked, snapping Yarrow's attention back to the mundane world.

"Fine." Yarrow said, in answer to both queries. "Meritage."

"What?" Sasha asked.

"We'll find Garith in Meritage, if he hasn't crossed the river to Gaeltheon already. We should make our way there as quickly as we can. I'm… eager to get this over with."

"As am I," Sasha said.

"Let's go," Duncan agreed.

"Give me… just a minute," Yarrow told the two men. To his unseen companion, he said, *Give me the spell.*

Yarrow's creature instructed him as it always had. It showed Yarrow the magic, let him understand the technique, less like teaching and more like whisking a cloth away from a secret treasure. Once Yarrow saw, he understood instantly. He didn't know why he hadn't figured it out on his own, it seemed so simple and intuitive.

"I'm ready. Duncan, Sasha, let's go." He led them past the ale casks to an old, empty shelf. "Help me shift this," he said to Duncan. The two of them moved the dusty wooden stand to reveal a jagged opening in the stone. To enter, Yarrow had to turn sideways. He swatted the thick cobwebs away. The feeling of stone so near both his chest and back conjured horrific recollections, and he swallowed down the panic. To Yarrow, the cavern felt smaller than he knew it was. He only needed to go a few feet before the passageway opened up a little, at least enough that he could walk normally. He wreathed his hand in blue light so he and his companions could pick their way over the uneven ground. Only Duncan had to stoop to avoid his head scraping the ceiling.

The three men said little until they gained a safe distance from the Lockhaven dungeons. After about half an hour of slow progress, Yarrow stopped and handed Sasha his gear. The assassin slipped his arms into the buttery red leather and secured the buckles across his chest. Sasha then replaced the straps that crossed his chest and checked the daggers they held. When he was satisfied, he wriggled his legs into his thigh-high boots.

"What's our plan?" Sasha asked when he'd finished dressing.

"According to my aunt," Yarrow said, "Garith's party planned to cross the Kanda at Meritage. She was able to find out the exact route he took, mostly well-traveled roads. I suggest we retrace my cousin's steps and pray we find him alive."

"What then?" Sasha asked. "Will you escort him to Gaeltheon as planned?"

Yarrow stopped so suddenly a less graceful man might have collided with his back. Even Sasha had to raise his hand and grasp Yarrow's shoulder to catch himself. *Did I hear that right, beloved? What do* you *plan to do? I wonder what your boy toy has in mind? Why not ask him why he won't be there?*

Because it doesn't matter, Yarrow told it, shaking his head as he moved past a tiny stream nurturing a carpet of glowing lichen. *He's never once suggested we had a future together.*

But you hoped. I felt it in you, Yarrow, like a fierce and desperate hunger. It's something I know well. You hoped to remain with both of these men.

Only a deluded child would think such a thing possible.

Yet you thought it. I watched your daydreams of traveling with them. Your mind wanders often to the details of their faces. The knight at least has expressed an interest in something more permanent.

Stop it! Yarrow scolded. *You're only saying these things to hurt me. Why does hurting me like that entertain you so?*

"Yarrow?" Sasha repeated.

"What?" Yarrow snapped, spinning around.

"You didn't answer my question about the prince."

Yarrow sighed, feeling his night of pacing circles around the lake in sudden, acute detail. His muscles trembled with exhaustion, and he wanted nothing more than to stretch out on the cold stone of the passage floor and fall asleep next to the delicate white mushrooms. "I think it more prudent to return Garith to the safety of his father for now. At least until the traitors are caught."

Yarrow braced himself for what needed to be said. "I'll be leaving after that. I'm sick of looking at Selindria, and I'm sick of these foolish politics. I promised to save my cousin if I can, but somebody else will need to sort this mess out. I have an itch to go exploring again."

Neither of Yarrow's companions offered to join him. Foolishly, he'd had arguments ready in case they insisted.

Seems they won't miss you as much as you'd hoped, the presence teased. *At least you'll have me. I'll* never *abandon you.*

Yarrow ignored it and quickened his pace, eager to leave the dank, sulfurous tunnels. About an hour later, the three of them emerged into a small cave. The smell of the lake was clean and strong, and the crash of its waves on the shore a few hundred feet away was thunderous. The mage breathed deeply and squinted against the midmorning light that made the surface of the water sparkle as if drizzled with diamond dust. A light wind ruffled the high, curly rushes, and birds dipped, swirled, and called out. The clarity allowed Yarrow to see practically to the far shore. Since he didn't anticipate enjoying the view again anytime soon, Yarrow walked forward until the cold water lapped against the toes of his boots. Sasha and Duncan stood respectfully back. Even the presence within Yarrow's mind remained silent. The waves soaked Yarrow's stockings and numbed his toes, but he stayed where he was, listening to the chime of the temple bells. When a small shell, ivory ridges on the outside and shimmery, coral pink within, washed up between his feet, Yarrow knelt to retrieve it, glad to have a piece of home to take with him.

After taking a few moments to compose himself, Yarrow turned on his heel and stalked away without looking back.

THEIR FIRST day's travel passed uneventfully. Duncan and his companions encountered only a handful of merchants, some farmers with carts of hay, and the occasional solitary traveler. Yarrow kept his startling appearance hidden beneath his hood, Sasha covered his exotic armor with a coarse cloak, and Duncan carried his plate in a pack with their other supplies. They drew little attention from those they met.

It was with apprehension that Duncan finally stopped to camp for the night, many hours after dark. He simply couldn't ask his companions to continue when he himself felt too weary to take another step. They found no cover to shelter them from the increasing winds of the plains, not even a tree. Hollow stalks of grain rattled like old bones. Duncan dropped his heavy gear and rubbed his sore shoulder. Sasha started to erect a tent while Yarrow lit a healthy blaze so he could see to arrange their cooking equipment. Before long Duncan smelled vegetables roasting. He used his boot to clear away enough snow to sit down. The wet ground still soaked the seat of his trousers.

The bubble of orange light from Yarrow's twig fire surrounded them, smelling of pitch and making Sasha look like a gilded statue, with deep shadows settled in his eye sockets and below his nose. Duncan heard nothing but the high, lonely call of the wind across the empty land, the scrape of desiccated crops bending beneath it, and the occasional pop and hiss of the campfire. Not a single branch creaked, and no dead leaves rustled against the barren branches. The knight felt like the desolation around him echoed the emptiness inside. When he could no longer endure the awkward silence, he spoke. "We made excellent progress today."

"If we keep this pace, we can make Meritage by the end of the week," Sasha agreed. "Within two days, we'll pass beyond the borders of Selindria." He flipped some scorched turnips onto metal plates and passed them around. Duncan scooped some of the thin stew made from flakes of dried meat and melted snow into bowls for Sasha and himself.

"What then?" Yarrow asked. He pulled the cork from a wine bottle with his teeth and spat it into the fire. After taking a long pull, he offered libation to the others.

"Why, then we find Prince Garith and see him safely home." Duncan tried to feign cheerfulness and optimism he couldn't feel. When everything else shattered, at least duty remained, solid and certain.

"That's not what I mean," Yarrow said. "Sasha, you said you don't plan to accompany us. How will you be safe on your own, with the order hunting you? Isn't that the reason you've come with us thus far?"

Duncan swore he saw a tiny crack in the assassin's fascia, a slight tremor passing over his jaw, but the shadows made it hard to be certain. "Perhaps they won't, after the ruse regarding the prince is revealed."

"But that's contrary to everything you've told us of them!" Yarrow's voice rose with distress.

"I would only attract trouble," Sasha said, in his even, emotionless way. "Are you asking me to stay? Do you really want a son of Thalil as a constant companion?"

"I—" Yarrow started to speak, but then his jaw snapped audibly shut. He picked up a frosty twig and prodded the fire, though more than his stoking likely fed the dramatic increase in the flames.

"As I suspected," Sasha answered. "You need feel no shame or guilt over it. Were I you, I wouldn't want me along either. It's the way things are. Mine was always meant to be a solitary life, and I accept it."

"Will you… miss us?" Yarrow asked.

He sounded so young, uncertain, and broken that Duncan fought the urge to go to him and hold him. He braced himself for the words he knew Sasha would say.

"Not in the way you imagine, friend Yarrow. I simply can't. Can you imagine what a misery my life would be, becoming fond of person after person only to lose them?"

"I can, in fact," Yarrow snapped. "Do you suppose you're the only one cursed with this, this isolation?"

"If it means anything, I will remember you. I'll always remember. I just don't have the luxury of pining over everything that's taken. I'd have time for little else."

"I… understand," Yarrow managed.

"You're planning to leave yourself," Duncan reminded him.

"Yes."

The knight knit his fingers together in his lap and looked over at the pretty mage. Only Yarrow's small nose and round chin protruded from the hem of his hood. His skin looked like bridal silk in the low light. Duncan remembered how it felt, hot and smooth beneath his hands and against his body. He recalled every noise of encouragement the mage made at his slightest touch. He didn't love Yarrow. Yarrow was arrogant, irritable, violent, and more than halfway mad. Still, some part of Duncan cared for the young man. There was an innocence and urgency about him that enthralled Duncan. He felt that over time, if he grew to understand Yarrow, if he learned his secrets, then maybe—

Duncan would never know unless he asked. "Would you be agreeable to a traveling companion, friend Yarrow?"

When the mage turned to face him, a bright smile lit his face and his eyes glowed merrily. But in an instant, all the happiness fell from his countenance as if he'd been slapped. "I travel very lightly and very fast," he said, dropping his eyes to stare at his delicate hands.

"I think I could keep up," Duncan said, encouraged by Yarrow's brief but honest look of delight. "I'm not an old man yet."

"I like to be able to go where I will, without consulting another."

"And if I'm amenable to that too?"

"But you have knightly obligations! You can't just follow me around."

"What if I wanted to, Yarrow?"

"No. I'm sorry, Duncan, but it's not possible."

"Why?" Duncan asked, balling his fists. "Why do you rebuke me when you clearly don't want to be alone? Do you find me so wanting?"

"I don't find you wanting at all," Yarrow said. "It's to do with me, not you."

"You're always saying that. What does it mean? I'm willing to overlook your past indiscretions. I'd even overlook Sasha's."

"Would you?" Sasha challenged.

"If you're willing to change. We… don't need to give up what we've found here. We're stronger together than separately. We're not likely to find this again. Any of us."

"And what is it you imagine we've found, Tam Knight?" Sasha asked.

Duncan balked at the formal title. "Companionship, if nothing else. None of us needs to be alone anymore."

"You don't understand," Yarrow said. "Neither of you. How can you know what I—"

"We'll know if you tell us, trust us," Duncan pushed.

"It's not that I don't trust you. I do. I just… I just can't, Duncan. Please respect my wishes."

"Very well," Duncan said. Perhaps he'd been trying to piece together something not meant to interlock, bits of armor that would overlap and grind together, never producing a workable set. Yet... metal could always be reshaped, made to fit together....

"We have tonight," Sasha suggested. "We're together now."

Duncan looked up, right into his assassin's bone-melting smile.

SASHA OPENED the tent flap and lit the lantern that dangled from the wooden supports. For his part, he hoped to enjoy the limited time he had with the other two men. After he dispatched Prince Garith, he knew nothing he could do or say would redeem him in their eyes. But if not Garith, another assignment would sour Sasha for the others. They'd never understand the ways of Thalil, and Sasha didn't expect them to fathom the depths of those shadows. He harbored no delusions, but he did hope they might consent to an evening of pleasure. As he carefully peeled his leather from his limbs, folded it, and placed it neatly at the foot of the coarse blankets, he prepared himself for disappointment. The conversation during their meal didn't bode well for a bout of lovemaking.

Finally Sasha set his undergarment atop the rest and climbed into bed. The ground felt cold and hard beneath his back, and he tossed and turned, trying to get comfortable. Small rocks stabbed his flesh. Posing as the prince had at least afforded him a cot.

Before long Yarrow and Duncan entered the tent and disrobed, Yarrow to nothing and the knight to his shorts, stockings, and padded shirt. At least it would be warmer when they joined Sasha in the makeshift bed. They settled in, Yarrow in the center. Heat radiated from the mage, and by the Cast-Down, he had soft skin. Though he didn't know if he'd be welcome, Sasha cuddled up to Yarrow and turned on his side to drape his arm across Yarrow's chest. Yarrow patted his elbow. While not the reaction Sasha had hoped for, it could have been worse, and he nestled his brow into Yarrow's white hair.

Duncan, too, reached across the mage and stroked Sasha's shoulder. The knight kissed the apple of Yarrow's cheek, and Yarrow smiled. As a test, Sasha kissed his temple and Yarrow's grin widened. A gust of wind struck the side of the tent, and the canvas cracked and the candle sputtered and went out. The three men drew closer as the gale shook the walls of their shelter. Dry snow infiltrated the enclosure at the bottom and powdered their coverings. Sasha's knee bumped

Duncan's when their legs crossed over Yarrow's thighs. They pressed together as tightly as possible for warmth.

Yarrow shivered next to Sasha, and Sasha tried to cover more of his mage's chilled flesh with his body.

"I don't like being cold," Yarrow whimpered. "Especially not at night."

Duncan chuckled, the sound warm and bright in the frigid gloom. "I'll never understand you. You say that, and yet you sleep outside on the ground."

"Don't laugh at me," Yarrow said. "I hate being closed in, but—being in the cold and dark like this brings back bad memories, is all."

"I apologize," Duncan said. "Do you want to talk?"

"No. I don't want to be mocked, either."

Sasha felt the encouraging mood tumble downhill. Yarrow tensed beneath his arm, genuinely affronted.

"I said shut up!" the mage snarled. "Stop laughing at me, damn you."

"No one is laughing at you," Duncan said gently, because no one was. "I never meant any offense."

"Our friend is just cold and uncomfortable, Duncan," Sasha said, using his most sultry drawl in an attempt to salvage the evening. "He'd be much happier if he were warm. I think we could manage to warm Yarrow up. What do you say, Tam Knight?"

For what seemed an eternity, Duncan said nothing. Sasha heard his steady breathing and could almost see his words slowly permeate Duncan's mind.

"Yes," the knight said slowly, "I think we might manage."

Though he couldn't see, Sasha felt like his eyes met Duncan's. Both of them lifted the blanket and dipped their heads beneath. Sasha brushed his fingertips down Yarrow's torso, all the way from his armpit to his prominent hipbone. His mage shuddered delightfully under his ministrations. Sasha loved how responsive Yarrow's body was to his slightest touch. The gooseflesh he felt beneath his hand made him hard, and the way Yarrow's breath already hitched, just from that simple caress, made Sasha leak a little. He dropped his mouth to Yarrow's chest and suckled along his sweet skin until he found his nipple. When the crown of his head touched Duncan's hair, Sasha knew his knight entertained the same idea.

Yarrow twisted, his back arching off the ground, as the two of them nipped and laved his nipples. The mage moaned as if he'd never been touched by a human hand. Sasha's fingers brushed against Duncan's as they explored Yarrow's muscular belly and slender chest. They both understood Yarrow needed this. He needed to feel desired, catered to, if not loved. Though, Sasha thought, if Duncan didn't love Yarrow, then no man had ever loved another. He wondered if such an emotional bond enhanced the physical act. He couldn't imagine joining with others got any better than this.

Like Sasha, Duncan focused all his energy on their mage's pleasure, caressing his waist, kneading his thigh, and tormenting his nipples with his mouth. Sasha knew exactly what he wanted to do, but for the moment he contented himself with exploring Yarrow's body, with pleasing him. He dipped lower, closing his lips over the string of muscle that stretched from Yarrow's rib to his groin. He let his teeth scrape along the sinew, because he knew Yarrow liked it. He'd learned exactly what made his mage tremble and squirm. With a gasp, Yarrow seized Sasha's hair and pressed Sasha's face against his dampening flesh. Sasha smiled against his delectable skin.

Meanwhile, Duncan crept upward to Yarrow's soft throat and tender ears. Duncan's hand found Sasha's hair, and his fingers dug into Sasha's scalp.

"Oh, Sasha," Duncan moaned.

He tried to tug Sasha's head toward him, but the assassin resisted, not ready to relinquish Yarrow's hot, wet, salty skin. The knowledge that he'd soon never taste it again made it all the sweeter, even as he felt it sting his heart. He pushed the weak feeling down to concentrate on the moment. Just before his mouth reached it, Sasha gripped the head of Yarrow's cock and pushed his foreskin back.

"Sasha!" Yarrow echoed Duncan's cry. "Give me your mouth. Just like the first time."

Happy to acquiesce, at least for the moment, Sasha let his tongue dart out to sample the swollen, quivering flesh of his partner's cockhead. He leisurely traced the shelf between the tip and the shaft, the groove on the underside of the corona, and the weeping slit. When he wriggled the tip of his tongue inside the tiny opening, Yarrow seized his hair and found Duncan's fingers ensconced there. The mage took hold of Duncan's wrist and guided his hand lower. The knight's knuckles grazed Sasha's chin on their way down.

"Inside me," Yarrow pleaded.

"Where's your bloody oil, assassin?" Duncan asked, his voice rough with yearning.

Though reluctant to give up the treat he enjoyed, Sasha got to his knees and felt for his pack in the darkness. It seemed to take forever for him to locate the small vial. When he did, he fumbled with the cork and eventually lost it on the ground. Duncan used the brief intermission to finish undressing. Sasha heard the rustle of his clothing slipping from his limbs. Seizing Duncan's wrist, Sasha dribbled the fragrant and expensive concoction over the knight's hand and his own, just in case. Then he tossed it aside. He didn't care if it spilled, no matter how much it cost. All he wanted was to get his lips back around Yarrow's cock, to feel Yarrow melting beneath his attentions. He'd almost achieved it when Duncan's fingers curled around his shoulder.

"Please, let me have a turn at him," he asked.

"Think you're as good as me?" Sasha teased.

"I've never had any complaints."

"Care to let me be the judge of that, Tam Knight? My wonderful Duncan."

"If you like, Sasha," Duncan said slowly.

"What about me?" Yarrow demanded.

Leaning across him, Sasha kissed him hard before moving to nip his earlobe. "How could I forget about you, my beautiful mage? I told you I won't ever forget. Never. Turn on your side."

The covers tangled around Yarrow's waist and legs as he hurried to obey. Sasha pushed the coarse cloth out of his way as he too reclined on his side. He felt out Yarrow's full sac and gave it a tug. Then he found Yarrow's cock, soaked with a fresh coating of fluids, with his mouth. By Thalil, he loved the feel of the hard, thick shaft bucking against the roof of his mouth. Sweet god, he loved Yarrow's taste. Sasha took his pleasure where he found it, but the knowledge that it was Yarrow thrashing beneath his attentions, Yarrow's fingers wrapping the back of his neck....

Snug, wet heat closed around the head of Sasha's dick. Duncan's prowess surprised him a bit; he'd imagined the knight somewhat inexperienced, but was delighted to discover the opposite. The whiskers of Duncan's chin tickled Sasha's balls as the knight's strong tongue massaged the belly of his cock. Duncan sure seemed to be enjoying himself. When Sasha thrust deep into the knight's throat, Duncan accommodated him. The sound of wet, zealous mouths on swollen flesh echoed in the tent. Only Yarrow's lurid declarations interrupted the rhythmic sucking and slurping.

"Stop!" the mage cried out. "Sasha!"

Surprised, Sasha let Yarrow's dick pop out of his mouth. It smacked against the mage's belly. "What's wrong?"

"Nothing's wrong. I just… I don't want to waste this. I want more than this. Please, I need you."

"Tell me what you want, lovely boy," Duncan said, his hand replacing his lips on Sasha's cock.

"I just want us to be together," Yarrow said, clearly senseless with arousal, his voice faltering.

"We're together," Duncan said. "What more? Just ask it."

"I just want you both. I don't know what to say. Please, come kiss me."

Both of them obliged, Sasha at one corner of Yarrow's mouth and Duncan at the other. They sucked Yarrow's lips into their mouths, and their tongues found each other between the mage's teeth. Yarrow's tongue twirled around and encouraged theirs. Soon all three of them thrust their tongues together, forming a messy, moist tangle, a knot connecting them irrevocably to each other. Not once, in his hundreds of encounters, had Sasha felt anything like it. He and Duncan ran their slick hands down Yarrow's belly to his swollen cock, clenched balls, and furnace-hot crevice. When Sasha's finger wriggled into Yarrow, he found Duncan's already embedded in their mage's eager flesh. Yarrow growled and splayed his legs as wide as he could while sandwiched beneath them. He thrust up into the empty air, riding their fingers furiously.

Finally Yarrow broke from their mouths. "Enough. I can't stand it. I need you now! One of you—"

Sasha quickly sprawled across Yarrow. He quite enjoyed Duncan joining in the fun, but *he* would be the one making love to his mage this time. He kissed him, his Yarrow, and it almost felt like he'd never kissed anyone before, not really. The mechanics were all the same, but it felt so new.

"Sasha, I want you so much," Yarrow said.

"Roll over, my… my dear friend." Sasha guided Yarrow to his belly and pulled his hips up. He couldn't resist sinking his teeth into the smooth globe of Yarrow's ass as his fingers traced the perimeter of the other man's puffy hole. Yarrow was open, ready, and so very fervent that Sasha couldn't deny him a moment more. He aligned his flesh to Yarrow's and pushed inside with a deep sigh. "Duncan," he said, reaching out and finding the knight's solid arm. "Time for me to return the favor. On your feet, now."

"Don't order me, assassin," Duncan said even as he hurried to stand.

"I'm not ordering, sweet Duncan, I'm asking." Sasha wrapped one arm around Yarrow's hips as his other hand grasped Duncan's wrist and pulled him close, so close he smelled the arousal oozing from Duncan's pores, earthy and rich. Duncan gripped Sasha's hair roughly and tilted his head up, so that his drawn-up nuts bounced across Sasha's chin. Sasha drew them into his mouth, sucking one and then the other.

"Dear goddesses, Sasha! Your lips are divine!"

With a satisfied chuckle, Sasha drew Duncan's cock into his mouth. To his shock, Duncan pulled away. Instead of breaching Sasha's mouth, he leaned down and kissed him softly, humbly, sending a chill down Sasha's body. Duncan ran the pad of his thumb across Sasha's brow and down his cheek. When he reached Sasha's chin, he pinched it and kissed him again, just a slow, soft peck he held for a long time. For some reason the gesture felt like a blade between Sasha's ribs. His eyes stung and he broke free.

"Let's get on with this." He tried to jest, but the trembling of his voice surprised him, and he defaulted to what he knew best: the physical act. He treated the knight to every shred of his expertise, and within minutes Duncan thrust into Sasha's throat as Sasha thrust into Yarrow. It didn't take long before Duncan's legs trembled with imminent release. Yarrow's broken breathing echoed through the tent, and Sasha considered reaching around him. But he decided he wanted Yarrow to come just from his cock, his lovemaking. He drove into him with all his might, pounding against Yarrow's secret spot. When Yarrow reached his climax, he buried his face in their flat pillows and wept. His release practically shattered his small body. Sasha wrapped an arm around him to hold the pieces together, moaning deep in his throat. Perhaps hearing them drove Duncan to the edge, because he rained a torrent of hot come down Sasha's throat. As his dick softened in Sasha's mouth, he stroked Sasha's face with more gentle reverence than the assassin had ever received from anyone. As Sasha spilled his seed into Yarrow, he almost wanted to cry along with his mage.

Yarrow collapsed, his legs unable to hold him any longer, and Sasha dropped unceremoniously across his back.

Still sobbing softly, and maybe not with joy, Yarrow said, "I know this is all there can be, but I love you. Sasha, Duncan, I do. I'm sorry. I can't help it."

"Oh, sweet Yarrow," Duncan said as he fell against the blankets at Yarrow's side.

Sasha scraped his fingers through Yarrow's hair, kissing Yarrow on the cheek and across the neck and shoulders until his mage calmed. He tried to soothe Yarrow with his mouth and hands, knowing no other way to assuage him, and desperately wanting his friend to be happy. Hearing Yarrow upset caused a strange ache in Sasha's belly he neither recognized nor understood. He could lie like a master when needed, but Sasha couldn't summon his skill at the moment. All he could do was hold Yarrow tight as Duncan caressed his back. The three of them petted each other until they relaxed almost into sleep.

Sasha went and wet a scrap of cloth with a bit of their precious water. After they cleaned themselves, he lay back to back with Yarrow, thinking. He'd wanted to say, "Roll over, my love," and he had only just bitten back the words. Even the thought of them in his mind conjured memories of his master berating him, calling him unworthy of Thalil, and beating him senseless for soft sentimentality. The conditioning nearly erased the warm impression, but not completely. As he lay down, he wondered what would happen if he didn't kill Prince Garith. Could Yarrow and Duncan come to accept him? It didn't matter, though. Abandoning his mission wasn't an option. It could never be an option.

Chapter Thirteen

"IF YOU soak the bread in some warm water, it won't be so coarse," Duncan urged, his hand on Yarrow's shoulder.

"I'm not hungry." Yarrow couldn't bring himself to eat, nor to look Duncan in the eye after his ludicrous display the previous night. He couldn't believe the words he'd let escape, or that he'd cried.

"Please try to eat at least a little. To keep your strength."

"I said I don't want to! Stop treating me like a child!"

"As you wish, Tam Mage." Duncan stood, dropped the small loaf to the ground at Yarrow's feet, and stomped away to pack up the camp.

Yarrow looked at the dirt-covered bread before kicking it into the fire. He drew his cloak tight around himself. The stillness of the morning, absent of any breeze, and the stark brightness that made the edges of everything sharp and hard, intensified the cold. Not a cloud passed in front of the unrelenting sun. The world seemed as frozen as Yarrow's fingers and toes felt.

I don't understand this need you feel, beloved. They aren't food or air. You don't require them to survive, and yet you feel as though you do. It's not like we'll die without them, and there are plenty of cocks in the world.

Leave me alone.

Poor boy. I can make *them love you, if you like. I can make them want nothing in the world but to be with you, to please you. I can make them value you over their next breaths.*

Could you... really?

Heh. With a mere thought.

That boy with the messy hair and the fur around his waist... did you make *him love you?*

He did not love me, Yarrow. He was a deceitful, deplorable wretch, and I won't acknowledge his memory! Never mention him again.

If you didn't love him, you wouldn't be so angry.

I'm angry because he… because he put me in this pathetic state! Now I have to endure your pitiful whining and pining just to get a taste of sensation. You really are such a whimpering babe, beloved. Oh Duncan! Oh Sasha! I love you! I can't help it!

"Stop making fun of me!" Yarrow snarled.

"Yarrow?" Sasha asked, looking at the mage from across the camp.

"I did not address you, Sasha," Yarrow said.

"Oh. Very well." The assassin turned his attention back to the vials of colored liquid he'd been arranging along his belts.

What do you say, beloved? I can make him your eager slave.

Do you think I would ever agree to such an atrocious thing, creature? He wouldn't even be my Sasha anymore.

So? I could also keep him young and beautiful, for your pleasure.

Enough. No more of this talk.

Let me give you something. I grow irritated with this morose state of yours. I'll teach you to bend others to your will, and let you decide whether to use it.

I—

Before Yarrow could protest, the understanding seeped into his mind. As he watched Sasha, he knew just the place inside his skull to nudge, just the suggestions to plant. He saw just where to tether the assassin's will to his own, just where to sow his desires so Sasha would feel them as his own wishes. While he reveled in the power he now commanded, the idea of using it against his friend sickened him to the point where he clutched his empty stomach and gagged.

Both Duncan and Sasha watched Yarrow retch and hug himself, but neither braved his ire to comfort him. Alone, he heaved and spasmed as he waited for the spell to pass.

You can make *them sympathetic, beloved.*

No! I'll never—

We'll see.

"Yarrow, can you travel?" Duncan asked.

"I… am ready," Yarrow choked, struggling to his feet. The others had packed up the camp and waited near the side of the road. Yarrow kept a few hundred yards behind them as they walked south, basically making a circle back toward Agarick's fortress. Duncan and Sasha leaned their heads together, glancing back at the mage now and then.

Yarrow wondered what they discussed, if they discussed him.

Stretch your senses out a bit, beloved. It's not hard.

Yarrow couldn't resist a little eavesdropping. At first their voices sounded muffled and far away, but if he concentrated, he could make out Duncan's words.

"He's always been a bit odd. Why the sudden concern?" the knight asked Sasha.

"He's tearing himself apart," Sasha responded. "What in Thalil's name is wrong with him?"

"Maybe it has to do with the magic."

Yarrow saw Sasha shake his head. "I've known magic-users. I counted some as brothers in the order. I've never seen this. He… talks to himself. He makes no sense sometimes. Look at the things he's done."

"What would you have us do?" Duncan asked.

"I don't know. I have to wonder if we're safe. Yarrow is very powerful."

Yarrow could listen no longer. They feared him, didn't trust him. *It's time to go*, he sadly admitted.

Time and then some, my beloved.

As soon as Garith is safe, we'll be off. What a fool I've been.

I'm happy to hear you say so, little Yarrow.

AT EVERY crossroad a fire burned, and people surrounded the pyres, tossing sticks into the flames.

"This is one of your religious rituals," Sasha said to Duncan. "It marks the beginning of the Dark Year?"

"Yes. Today is the first day of Fayelle's Moon. It is the festival of Fayelle, Goddess of Purity. We inscribe the vices of which we want to be rid onto arn branches and toss them into the fire. With luck, the goddess burns them away, bringing us closer to wholesomeness. Do you want to partake, Sasha? I can help you."

"How ridiculous. I am already free of those things I wish to eliminate: fear and weakness. A child of Thalil is not welcome at such rites. Nor would I want to be."

"The goddess welcomes everyone, Sasha." Duncan touched his dark cheek and caught his eyes. He thought maybe he could see some regret in those black orbs. "It's never too late. You can be forgiven. Lead a virtuous life."

Though he flashed Duncan his disarming smile, Sasha said, "No. I am a creature of vice. I'm a Cast-Down, a shadow-son. I can be nothing else, no matter how badly you want me to be. I'd like to please you, but I can't participate in this farce. Do what you need to do, Duncan. I'll wait with Yarrow."

Duncan watched his assassin move to his mage's side, well behind him. He looked at the two men for many minutes as he wondered how they'd commandeered his every thought. Memories of their faces, their bodies, distracted him constantly. Pretty Yarrow was not only mad, but surly, downright mean at times. He wanted no future association with Duncan. Sasha, dark, alluring, immoral Sasha…. Goddesses, Sasha was sin on legs, and Duncan had fallen for the bait. He walked to the young girl with the bundle of arn twigs, offered her a coin, and took four of them. Then he unsheathed the dagger from his belt.

Into the first branch, Duncan carved "Lust." He tossed it into Fayelle's Fire and closed his eyes, imploring the goddesses to rid him of this sin. The flames quickly consumed the stick, turning it into a column of white, flaking ash. The draft from the pyre whisked it away, and Duncan felt cleansed. Holding the second branch, he wondered what to write. He wanted freedom from silliness, frivolity, impossible fantasies. Eventually he settled on "Distraction" and tossed the wood into the blaze.

Two twigs remained. Into the first, Duncan roughly and quickly chopped "Sasha."

Cutting deep, almost severing the thin branch, Duncan carved "Yarrow" into the other silvery stem. He held the two sticks tight within his fist, his eyes clamped shut and the bark tearing his palms, before he hurled them into the flames.

Fayelle, Goddess, please free me from their pull. Spare me the pain. Don't let them influence me anymore. Purge me of these abominable feelings!

He watched the inscribed sticks burn until they disappeared within the white-hot inferno, and then he turned away, toward the other two men, his temptations and torments.

THE THREE men continued southeast, each, apparently, lost within his own thoughts. Sasha knew they retraced Garith's trail, hoping for some sign of the prince. He felt certain they'd passed beyond the borders of Selindria into the hostile, disputed territory edging the Kanda. Any number of war parties or bandits might have gotten to Garith first. In spite of everything, Sasha hoped the prince was already dead. If Garith had fallen by another hand, maybe Sasha could remain with Yarrow and Duncan a little longer. If he didn't dispatch the prince, maybe—

Sasha shrugged it off. They were making him fragile, undeserving. They wanted to change his immutable nature. He couldn't be rid of Duncan and Yarrow too soon. A prince's blood made a commendable gift to his god. He lapped at his lips in anticipation. He loved Thalil above all else. It was the only love he'd ever been permitted. With this offering, he'd prove it. Before, he'd only ever felt excitement when thinking about a mission. He'd felt joy, the anticipation of blood and victory, not this unusual heaviness filling his lungs and stomach, making him feel half-drowned. For now he could do little but put it to the back of his mind and walk lightly across the thin layer of crispy snow.

Not a word passed between the companions for many hours. Not even the barren landscape changed. Corpse gray clouds hung low and pregnant with snow, but none fell. They passed more of Fayelle's Fires, as Duncan had called them, but the knight didn't pause to offer at any of them. Gradually the sun behind them melted against the flat horizon in a bright, pink puddle. Rose and magenta edged the clouds and bathed the world in a blushing light that softened Sasha's perceptions of the forms he saw. Meritage couldn't be more than a few days southeast. Already the winds felt warmer. Sasha convinced himself he couldn't wait to reach the city. He longed to banish the unfamiliar uncertainty and feel like himself again, a knife in the dark, a shadow, the highest of the elite.

"Stop," Yarrow said. "Something… is coming. Something big."

Their mage didn't sound the way he did before he got really violent, but Sasha found a dagger handle with each hand. Sasha hoped he'd never have to face Yarrow; he doubted he could defeat him.

"What do you mean, Yarroway?" Duncan asked as he freed the large sword from his back.

"I feel it. About a mile ahead of us. We need to be ready. We're in for a fight when we get there."

They were spared the waiting when a huge company of knights and soldiers met them on the road. The galloping horses raised plumes of snow as their riders pulled them to a hasty stop. Sasha counted twenty mounted men, and estimated about triple that amount on foot, armed with halberds and pikes. Many of them wore the royal ursine crest, and a few wore the elaborate lake-wyrm of Lockhaven. Even before the assassin could react, he felt his mage at his back, felt the arcane power warping the air around Yarrow and making Sasha's teeth wiggle.

Duncan, his chin held high, marched in front of them and stretched his sword protectively in front of their chests. "What is the meaning of this?" The knight's strong voice rang out over the stark scene. Nothing but the occasional shuffle of a horse's feet answered him. Sasha smelled the animals, saw the steam of their breath escaping the gaping, pink holes of their nostrils in slow motion. "Announce yourselves!" Duncan demanded again.

"This is it," Sasha breathed, exhilarated. He drew his dagger and kissed the blade. "Sweet Thalil, I beg you claim me when my good service is done."

"Don't talk nonsense, Sasha!" Yarrow hissed. "I won't let you die. I'll burn the world to ash first."

"Ah, Yarrow," Sasha exhaled. "For what it's worth, I believe you would try."

"Watch me." Yarrow seized Sasha's face and kissed him hard, unabashedly, in full view of half a hundred men or more. Then he strode forward, past Duncan, to stand in front of the lead knight.

"I am Yarroway L'Estrella. I'm sure you've heard my name. I insist you tell me under what pretense you dare impede us!" That eerie, blue aura surrounded their mage, branching out into the suggestion of wings and horns. Yarrow seemed several feet taller, and the snow sizzled around his feet. Horses whinnied in fear and backed away, despite their riders' attempts to soothe them. The growing panic fueled Yarrow's power, and somehow Sasha understood how the mage siphoned the psychic energy. He could almost see Yarrow drawing it like iron filings to a magnet. Glowing like a falling star, Yarrow stepped a few feet closer. "Answer me or I'll destroy you." Yarrow didn't threaten, merely stated a fact.

To his credit, the leader of the company urged his skittish mount forward. The man, older than Sasha but younger than Duncan, balanced on his charger as the beast danced beneath him. "Tam Yarroway L'Estrella," he called, "you are a wanted criminal, as are your companions, the Tam Duncan Purefroy of Thulemore, and this scrap of filth assassin."

"Sasha!" Yarrow bellowed. The frozen ground split with the energy he exuded. "You'll show him proper respect or I'll slay your family to the last member!"

Yarrow's passionate defense moved Sasha, but he couldn't help notice how the mage's voice had changed. He'd heard that inflection, and the bloodlust it barely concealed, on a few other occasions. Thalil help these soldiers. For his part, Sasha prepared to dive away from the oncoming carnage. He didn't know if Yarrow could differentiate friend from enemy when he got *that way.*

"I have been ordered to take you into custody!" the young commander shouted. "I have more than enough men to do so. By the goddesses, come quietly back to Lockhaven and stand trial for treason."

"Treason?" Duncan gasped. "What treasonous act have we committed?"

The man pointed his gauntleted finger at Duncan's throat, making Sasha bristle with offense. "You aided in the escape of a known criminal, tam! Do you deny it?"

"You had no right to detain Sasha," Duncan said, his sword like an extension of his arm as he leveled it at the other man. "You have no authority beyond the Selindrian border. Leave us to our business."

"That is not for you to decide, none of it. His Majesty demands you be brought to justice."

"What?" Yarrow's mystic light faltered. "The king ordered this?"

"That is not your affair, Yarroway of Lockhaven. Give us this assassin, and we'll let you be on your way."

"Ha!" Yarrow barked. "You'll take Sasha from me when the Cast-Down fuck the Mother Goddess like a common whore!"

"Filthy degenerate," the commander swore. "Take them all!"

Soldiers encircled them. Yarrow's energy flared and almost knocked Sasha off his feet. Duncan howled with rage and sliced the air before him. To do his part, Sasha readied his poisons and knives. If these men were willing to fight for him, he'd fight to the death by their sides and die happy, just because someone cared that much for him. Of course he'd never expected anyone to value his life; the order taught otherwise. In that moment, Sasha had never been more fulfilled. It surprised him, but he couldn't dwell on it.

Still, for the first time, he hoped he might live a little longer. He wanted a few minutes to say something, he had no idea what, to the men willing to die protecting him.

But three men? *No* three men stood a chance against the fifty now surrounding them, swords, spears, and bows trained on them. The dozen archers alone would undo them. Sasha readied a small vial of narxium sap, astounded when he noticed his hand shaking. In the stillness of the evening, with night descending rapidly, Sasha heard the creak of the bowstrings....

Thalil—

"I'll give you one last chance to save yourselves," the lead knight said. "If you resist, we'll have no choice. We'll bring this assassin back one way or the other."

"Try it!" Yarrow howled. "Duncan, Sasha, get back!"

"Yarrow, what—" Duncan tried to ask.

"Get back!"

The edge to the mage's words compelled Sasha to seize Duncan's elbow and drag the larger man as far from Yarrow as possible. Tugging Duncan along, Sasha ran as fast and as far down the road as he could, his eyes scanning the flat land for a tree, a boulder, even a gentle knoll they might dive behind. There was nothing, so he dropped to his belly, pulled Duncan down beside him, and covered his head with his hands.

Energy pulsed from Yarrow in a heartbeat rhythm. Sasha bit down on his lip until he tasted blood. The archers fired on the mage, but their arrows went askew as soon as they neared his peculiar aura. One of them veered off and struck Sasha in the dense muscle just above his shoulder blade. His leather armor took the worst of it, but the razor-sharp point sank several inches into his flesh, and he choked back a cry at the tearing pain. It wasn't a lethal injury, but the next one, or the next, might be. He and Duncan had no means of shielding themselves, no protection. They might as well have worn targets.

"What is he thinking?" Duncan whispered.

"Do you suppose he thinks at all when he gets like this?" Sasha spoke through teeth gritted against the pain in his back.

"We can't leave him to stand alone," Duncan said.

"At the moment, he's safer than we are. Those arrows can't touch him."

As they watched, power swirled around Yarrow like a shimmering blue cyclone. Eddies of snow and gravel surrounded him. Everything else stood still—the men, the horses, even the red-tinged clouds and pale stars. When Yarrow released that torrent of power, Sasha expected a storm of blood and meat, men reduced to tiny chunks, as they were on the night of the prince's betrayal.

Instead, they froze. The men on their horses stood still as statues, even their breath frozen in clouds around them. Arrows hung in the air. Sasha had never seen anything so bizarre, and he could only stare until Yarrow collapsed facedown in the snow. The energy around him evaporated. Sasha rose, but fell back on his knees, dizzier than he'd anticipated. He turned to Duncan.

"Get this thing out of me," he said, jutting his chin toward his back.

"It needs to be cut out," the knight said. "Just tearing that barbed arrowhead will cause more damage."

"I can take it. We need to get Yarrow."

"Ready yourself," Duncan said simply as he grabbed the wooden shaft and pulled.

Sasha couldn't strangle his scream as the jagged metal rended his flesh as it left him. He fought not to pass out at the agony. In a few seconds it was over, though the hole throbbed and he felt the blood soak his leather and run down his spine. Then he felt a comforting pressure, a slight relief from the torment, as Duncan pressed his palm against Sasha's wound.

"This needs dressing, Sasha."

"Later. We must get Yarrow." He forced himself to stand, willed away the nausea and vertigo, and tried to ignore the pain. He staggered to Yarrow, dropped down, flipped the mage to his back, and slapped his cheek.

Yarrow's eyes fluttered open. His lips had little more color than his pale face. "Sasha."

"How long will your spell last?" Sasha asked.

"My spell? What spell?"

"The one that stopped all these men. Froze them."

"Oh." His faced screwed up as he recalled his cantrip. "I don't know. I've never used it before. We should get out of here. As quickly as possible."

"Agreed," Duncan said from a few feet away. He hurried to take one of Yarrow's elbows and help Sasha get him to his feet.

They ran away from the road, across the scarlet-stained snow, away from the dying light of the west. Yarrow, clearly exhausted, fell several times.

"They'll see our trail," Duncan huffed.

With a deep, weary groan, Yarrow turned around and raised his hands. Wind whipped out from his palms in a serpentine pattern, drifting the snow and obscuring their tracks. When he'd finished, he dropped like a stone and wouldn't rise, no matter how much Sasha and Duncan coerced him.

"Friend Yarrow, please." Sasha grew frantic as he tried to pull the mage to his feet. He seemed so heavy, and Sasha felt so weak. He realized just how much blood he'd lost.

"Leave me," Yarrow said, barely audible.

"You're madder than I thought," Duncan said, "if you think we'd leave you to die."

"I won't die." Yarrow actually chuckled. "It won't let that happen."

"Make sense," Sasha said, stroking Yarrow's cold cheek hard with the back of his hand. "Get up, Yarrow."

"It's just some snow. Sasha, beautiful Sasha, you need to get away from me. Get away from here."

"I won't. Get up. Get up!" He grew angry. Didn't Yarrow care what he was doing to Sasha? How could he be so selfish? Feelings he thought he'd never experience assailed him, and he didn't know how to deal with the new emotions pulling him in a hundred different directions, breaking him to pieces. He grabbed his mage's shoulders and shook them, despite the screaming pain that erupted across his back. Yarrow just flopped around, his head rolling from side to side like a worn cloth doll.

"Peace, Sasha," Duncan said, placing a calming hand on Sasha's shoulder. His touch drained the assassin's anger and growing panic. Then the knight knelt down and draped Yarrow's limp arm across his shoulders like a shawl. He dragged Yarrow's small body along, and Yarrow's feet carved trenches in the snow. "We have to find somewhere. I'm worried about both of you."

"I've had worse," Yarrow croaked.

"We need shelter, a place to hide," Duncan repeated.

Sasha scanned the landscape. It was dark now, the sky bruise purple and the stars and snow bright against it. He saw nowhere they could be safe.

"I can do one last thing," Yarrow said with a voice like an echo of icy wind, brittle and thin. "I can conceal us for a few hours."

"You're too weak," Duncan said.

"I'm not."

"Yarrow, are you sure?" Sasha asked. It seemed like their only option.

He nodded and slipped from Duncan's arms to the ground. The other two men dropped beside him, and the air shimmied and glowed with a mix of colors, like those inside a seashell, for just a few seconds.

"We'll be safe for a while," Yarrow said as his eyes rolled back and he fell unconscious.

Sasha hurried to gather Yarrow into his arms. He pulled Yarrow's face tight to his chest and wrapped his arms around Yarrow to keep him warm. He tucked the mage's black cloak tightly around him. The top of Yarrow's hair nestled beneath his chin, and Duncan wrapped his long arms around both of them, his forehead against Sasha's temple. Though he never thought he'd have allowed himself, Sasha gave his weight to Duncan's strength and let himself be held up. He was so depleted, so weak with physical and emotional strain he couldn't keep his eyes open any longer. Duncan rubbed the back of Sasha's neck, kneading the tense muscles with his fingers and helping the assassin relax a little. Sasha let his head curl into Yarrow's and Duncan's and breathed deeply of their scents as he permitted his body to rest.

He also couldn't sleep, but not because of worry over being discovered or the pain from his injury. One thing gnawed at his mind and soul. Before the battle, for the first time, he'd feared death. He'd actually feared going to the soft, sweet arms of Thalil, where he'd known he'd eventually go since he could comprehend the end of himself. He cursed his disgusting softness and almost wished his master might appear and beat the silly frailty out of him. This weakness, the fact he felt so safe in Duncan's arms, needed to be expunged. But sweet, dark lord, the world contained things he didn't want to leave behind.

Chapter Fourteen

DUNCAN LET Sasha and Yarrow rest until just before dawn. Both of them had whimpered and thrashed as they slept, and Duncan had moved their heads into his lap, one on each thigh. He'd stayed awake to make sure Yarrow's cloak held, to make sure they were safe. Now, as the first, pale pink line of light stretched across the horizon like an old scar, he stroked their hair and looked down at their faces, peaceful at last. He hated to rouse them, but they needed to move.

"Yarrow," he said, his voice rough with fatigue, "Sasha."

The assassin jolted awake, his hand on his dagger before his eyes even opened. Duncan touched his cheek to calm him, and Sasha let out a ragged breath. He winced and groaned, no doubt from his injury, as he sat up. The flush on his cheeks and the sweat sparkling over his lips and brows, despite the brutal cold, made Duncan worry about fever and infection. He needed to get Sasha somewhere he could at least clean his wound, before it festered.

"How are you?" Duncan asked. "Are you feeling all right?"

Sasha looked away, ashamed of something Duncan couldn't fathom. "Of course," he said. "We should be away from here."

"Agreed. Yarrow," he said again, rubbing the mage's shoulder. The small, pale-haired man remained as still as a statue, just like those he'd enchanted.

"Is he—is anything wrong?" Sasha said, betraying more concern than Duncan would have thought him able.

"I think he's just exhausted. I wish I could convince him to eat more." He petted Yarrow's cheek, running his fingers along the intricate, blue swirls.

"He hates that, you know. The way you worry and coddle him."

"I don't think he does, assassin. I think he's young, lonely, lost, and needs someone to care about him. Perhaps you might try showing him some affection yourself."

"Enough of this," Sasha spat. "We should get moving. Yarrow." He shook their mage's shoulder until Yarrow stirred.

Yarrow looked awful. His normally bronzed skin shone waxen and almost as white as the snow drifting around them. Puffy darkness outlined his eyes. His lips were dry and cracked.

"You need water," Duncan said, holding Yarrow still as he wobbled. He reached for his canteen, only to remember he'd lost it, either during the fight or running away afterward. "I need to get you somewhere, both of you, somewhere I can take care of you."

Sasha snorted, and Yarrow stared blankly at the fading stars.

Looking out across the flat, frozen vista, the snow just starting to sparkle with rubicund light, Duncan voiced his confusion. "I don't know where to go. The roads are out of the question. They'll be watched. Somehow, those knights knew where to find us. Where to wait for us."

"Do you realize what you're saying?" Sasha asked, donning his icy mask once more. "If they knew where to find us, which way we'd be going, they learned it from one of the only two men who knew the prince's route and that we'd be following it: Tam Taran or the king."

"Goddesses," Duncan breathed. Sasha's detached logic was dead-on. "It can't be true."

"It can only be true. No one else knew of the ruse, or of our plans."

"The queen knew," Duncan said, feeling sick.

"No," Yarrow said. "No, she would never put me in danger."

"What will we do when we find the prince?" Duncan asked the endless expanse of cloud cover. "How will we know who to trust? Who wants him dead and who doesn't? Tam Taran and his own father! Maybe his own mother! Goddesses, why? How can we keep Garith safe when we find him? How do we even get to him with his own vassals watching the roads to stop us?"

"The river," Yarrow said softly, staring dreamily off to the east. "It isn't far; I can smell it. We can reach the river and take a boat to Meritage."

"What if Garith hasn't reached Meritage?" Duncan asked.

"If he hasn't reached it yet," Sasha said, "he's almost certainly dead alongside the road. Unless you have a better idea, Tam Knight, I say we follow Yarrow's suggestion. There are ports along the river, ports not held by your Selindria, and as you said, we need rest and supplies badly."

"Very well," Duncan acquiesced. "May the goddesses guide and watch over us. Yarrow, do you feel up to walking so far?" He reached out his hand to help the mage up, but Yarrow refused it and stumbled to his feet on his own.

"I'm not a sick girl, Duncan." He wrapped his cloak around himself and stomped off, his face toward the rising sun.

"I told you," Sasha said as he followed.

SELINDRIA WAS vast and varied, but the river towns were all the same. They were cluttered with houses packed tightly together. Docks jutted into the Kanda and boats clotted its surface. People hurried up and down the narrow streets between the land and the water. All manner of goods were transported, displayed, and sold. Likewise, a mélange of people—northerners, southerners, plainsfolk, Gaeltheons, and Esperons, with a few more exotic traders sprinkled on top—mixed and mingled in the markets and along the quayside. Sailors, mostly sun-kissed southern men, worked to secure and unload boats.

Duncan let out a puff of air as he tried to make order of the chaos. He hadn't been so close to the river in a long time, and he'd forgotten the bustle of people fighting for a spot at the Kanda's life-giving teat. He didn't forget they were far from home, with no knights or guards to keep order, in a city as likely as not controlled by criminals. "Where in heaven's name do we go from here? Any of these sailors could be aware of us, ready to betray us to… to our enemies."

"Not those ones," Yarrow said, pointing to a small, streamlined boat with bright sails striped blue and sea green. "That's an Emiri ship."

"And you think we can trust an Emiri? Based on what?"

"Emiri don't care about politics," Yarrow explained. "Not even for money. Intrigue like that is outside their understanding. What's more, neither Tam Taran nor Agarick would consider employing an Emiri against us. You know the opinion most Selindrians hold of the Sea People."

"I'm to understand that opinion is well founded," Duncan dared, aware of their mage's fondness for the foreign seafarers.

"They are not loyal," Yarrow admitted. "Which is to our advantage. We only need transport, and we can pay. I assure you, nothing else will matter to the *mir*, the captain, of that ship."

"I'll trust to your knowledge of these things," Sasha said. "You should speak with this man."

"It may be a woman," Yarrow said. "The Emiri see no difference between the two."

Duncan could scarcely imagine a woman captaining a ship, but he dutifully followed his companions to the river's edge, and the gaily painted, sleek little boat. They walked to the end of the dock.

"*Hai*," Yarrow called. "*Mira tali?*"

Before long a man appeared on the deck, wrapped ridiculously under layers of furs. Wool scarves twined around his head, and the crimson ropes and braids of his hair sprung out beneath them. He was as dark as Sasha, with bright orange eyes, like ripe gourds in autumn. Beautiful, rust-colored paint outlined his face in graceful swirls that culminated at the point of his chin. An intricate red diamond stood between his brows. All of the decoration served to accentuate his fine features, delicate bone structure, and large, expressive eyes. He looked quite young to have a ship under his command.

"*Hai mir?*" he called, smiling brightly, genuine happiness lighting his very appealing, androgynous face.

Yarrow walked up the gangplank and embraced the Emiri sailor. They kissed each other's cheeks like long-lost lovers, and held each other by the waist as they conversed in the exotic tongue.

Duncan didn't understand Emiri customs, so he tried, unsuccessfully, to resist jealousy.

Sasha looked merely bored, and maybe a touch feverish. He dabbed at his sweaty jawline with his leather sleeve, his dark eyes dilated and unfocused. He swayed where he stood, and Duncan worried for him and his wound.

"Come aboard!" Yarrow shouted with a smile.

Reluctantly, Duncan ascended the gangplank, touching Sasha's shoulder as he passed him. The two of them stood facing Yarrow and the Emiri captain, who still held each other around the shoulders, as if they'd been friends for years.

"I'm called Sai," the Emiri said in a languid voice that struck Duncan as slightly amused. He reached out for Sasha, and the assassin allowed himself to be kissed, though he stiffened. Four other Emiri sailors, all of them with bright, long hair arranged in braids and tangled locks and bundled in warm clothing, reclined around the deck. Duncan assumed they were men, but he honestly couldn't be certain.

When his turn came, Duncan withdrew from Sai's reach and extended his hand. "I'm happy to meet you, and grateful for your assistance, tam. I am Duncan Purefroy, knight of Thulemore."

Sai clasped Duncan's hand and stared down at it, obviously perplexed. Finally he lifted Duncan's knuckles to his lips and kissed them. "Welcome. Which of those words is your name?"

"Duncan."

"Duncan," Sai said, his relaxed inflection reminding the knight of a satisfied lover. "Welcome." Before Duncan could resist, the strange, beautiful man grasped the back of his neck and kissed him on the cheek.

"You want food and drink," Sai said, leading them below the deck to a small compartment. It smelled like wet rope. "Have anything you desire." He swept his hand, indicating some bowls of dried fish and seaweed, as well as several ceramic jugs of water and matching cups.

"Do you have any healing supplies, Tam Sai?" Duncan asked, thinking of Sasha's wound.

"I do, of course." The lithe man, smaller even than Yarrow, knelt and pulled a wooden box from beneath a bench. It contained odd items: shells, seaweed, rounded stones, and jars of what looked like water. The Emiri handed Duncan a vial of viscous green sludge. "Put this on your *syrai*'s infected wound after you wash it. I can smell it festering. This will draw out the heat and disease."

"Thank you," Duncan managed, taking the glass container and working the cork loose with his thumb and finger.

"Eat," Sai urged, indicating the rations. "You look hungry. Rest. I'll ferry you to Meritage before you feel a day pass."

Sasha sat down on Sai's padded bench, feverish and exhausted. Duncan hurried to move behind him, unbuckle his leather armor, peel it back, and expose the wound, which was deep, lined in red, and full of pus. Duncan squeezed out as much of the yellow goo as he could before washing the puncture. By the time he finished, dark brown and red splotches covered the rag. Sasha's breath hitched, and he swayed on the bench. Duncan held his shoulder to steady him so he could apply the Emiri poultice to his wound. Sasha sighed with relief as the seaweed ointment did its work. Yarrow followed Sai up the narrow ladder to the deck.

"Thank you, my friend," the assassin whispered as Duncan pressed his hand against Sasha's injury.

"You don't need to thank me, Sasha. I'm happy to do this for you. I… I care about you."

"Don't be a fool."

"I'm no fool, friend. I know what I feel. And I'm not afraid to acknowledge it."

"I fear nothing," Sasha said.

"I don't believe you."

"Yarrow said that too. But you must believe I am a servant of Thalil. Nothing else."

"I see more to you, my Sasha."

"Then you are deluded."

Though he should have been angry, Duncan ached for everything denied to Sasha by his so-called training. The monsters of his order might have been kinder just to kill him. He leaned down and kissed the top of Sasha's head, breathing in the spicy scent of his soft, dark hair. It surprised him when Sasha reached up to touch his cheek and whiskers.

"Duncan, thank you," Sasha repeated, his voice low and maybe a little remorseful.

"Lie down. You should rest." Duncan wiped the ointment and blood from his hand with a scrap of cloth he found on a shelf and balled up some discarded blankets as a pillow for Sasha. Without argument, the assassin lay down on his side. Duncan poured water, which Sasha eagerly drank down. He stood over the other man, stroking the smooth, honey-colored skin of Sasha's bare shoulder until the other man fell asleep. Then Duncan covered him with a multicolored, striped blanket woven from thick but soft wool yarn.

As he turned toward the ladder, he thought of Sasha accepting his care. Despite his words, the assassin had been glad of the comfort, Duncan felt sure. It overjoyed him, being able to offer some balm for Sasha's injured heart. He looked back at the other man, deep in slumber now, grabbed the rung of the ladder, worn glossy from many hands over many years, and soon emerged on the small vessel's deck, blinking in the bright, winter sun.

The other Emiri lounged about, one napping in a hammock, two cross-legged on the smooth planks, playing a game with rocks and shells on the top of a barrel. The fourth sat with his legs dangling over the edge of the boat, fishing in the choppy surf. Yarrow and Sai stood at the opposite end of the ship, near the helm. They had their backs to Duncan, talking excitedly.

Duncan approached them slowly, eager to hear their conversation. When he reached them, he stood behind a stack of crates large enough to almost conceal him.

"Your paint is quite beautiful," Sai said, running his fingertip over Yarrow's face as Duncan had done not so many hours before. "Do you wear it just on your face, or do you have more?"

Yarrow giggled and looked away. "I have plenty more."

"I'd like to see it."

From his hiding place, Duncan felt his cheeks burn as fiery red as Sai's hair.

"I can't tell you how much we appreciate you giving us passage." Yarrow changed the subject. "You're helping us out more than you know."

Sai laughed. "I don't have anything better to do at the moment, so I don't mind. I'm bored of this place anyway. I just came here to sell some items we… we happened upon a while back. I'm finished with that. I have some money. I have *muri-ku* to drink and three very lovely new men to travel with me. It works well enough, in my mind."

"Mine too, *syrai*," Yarrow said, patting Sai on the shoulder.

They turned to face each, and once again Sai touched Yarrow's face, just at the apple of his cheek where his paint tapered off. "Of all of you, I find you the most appealing, Yarrow. You're beautiful and desirable."

"Thank you."

"You're most welcome. Would you like to lie with me? It'll be at least a few hours before the river clears enough for us to embark. We can pass them happily in my quarters."

After Duncan recovered from the shock of Sai's words, he grew angry. He'd heard loose morals afflicted the Emiri, but he'd never dreamed he'd hear something so blatant. He barely breathed as he waited for Yarrow to answer. Duncan gripped the edge of one of the crates until his fingernails shaved curls of wood. What if Yarrow agreed? Duncan realized Yarrow had never made a formal commitment to either him or Sasha. Both of the other men made sure Duncan understood the nature of their association. Even so, Yarrow had said he loved them. Him. He'd said Duncan's name, even if only in the heat of the moment. If Yarrow went to Sai's bed—

As Duncan watched in horror, Yarrow grasped the front of Sai's furs and pulled their faces closer together. The knight expected his mage to ravage the Emiri captain's supple lips, but Yarrow did something even more peculiar.

"You shouldn't do that!" Yarrow hissed at Sai. "You should be more careful who you offer yourself to! How do you know I'm not dangerous? That I won't hurt you?"

"I just thought it might be nice. You seem like a pleasant man, Yarrow, and very beautiful."

Yarrow released him. "I'm sorry. You're also a very appealing man. I didn't mean to get angry. I just don't want to see anything happen to you."

"Perhaps another time," Sai said easily, dismissing any offense he might have felt. "Would you like to play a game? Fish for a while?"

While Yarrow hadn't used his love and fidelity to Duncan to decline Sai's offer, at least they weren't rolling across the Emiri's cushions in the cabin at the center of the deck. Relieved at that much, Duncan stepped out from behind the crates and raised his hand in greeting.

"How is Sasha?" Yarrow asked.

"He's sleeping," Duncan said. "His wound was much more severe than he pretended."

"Will he be all right?"

Duncan nodded. "The Emiri poultice was very effective. My thanks to you, Tam Sai."

"Tam means something friendly among your people, doesn't it, Duncan?"

"I suppose it does, in a way," Duncan said to Sai.

The Emiri laughed. "Well, then, friends it is. We won't be able to sail for a while yet, and until then, my home is yours. Eat and make yourself comfortable. You too, Yarrow. I'll be in my cabin if you want me." He turned and moved gracefully across the deck, despite his cumbersome clothing, and disappeared behind the patterned curtain into his quarters.

Duncan watched Yarrow's eyes follow Sai and wondered if the mage regretted turning him down. "You should rest too, my friend," he said, moving behind Yarrow to massage his neck and shoulders, unsurprised at the knots of tension he felt there. "You wore yourself ragged last night, saving us and keeping us safe. At least lie down for a few hours."

He braced himself for Yarrow's retort and possible insult, but none came. Instead, Yarrow pivoted around and threw his arms over Duncan's shoulders, holding him close and resting his slight weight against Duncan's chest. "I'm so tired it hurts," he confessed, his breath so warm and damp against Duncan's neck the knight's body reacted. "Will you rest with me?"

"I will." Hand in hand, the two of them walked to the tiny hatch that led below deck, to the sleep they both desperately needed.

Chapter Fifteen

THE EMIRI ship was well clear of the port town by the time Sasha, Duncan, and Yarrow woke. Sasha stretched his arms over his head and twisted his waist, feeling much improved, and leaned against the polished wooden railing. Nothing surrounded the small vessel but the wide expanse of the Kanda, gilded red-gold with the late-day sun. Thick mist rose in shimmering sheets from the water, making Sasha wonder if he'd be able to see to Gaeltheon on a clear evening. Calm waves lapped against the hull, and aside from the occasional cry of a bird, and the soothing, rhythmic creak of the boat's wooden planks, nothing interrupted the serenity. Unlike the polluted water around the riverside village, the water here smelled fresh and earthy, like new rain.

As it grew dark, few lights appeared on the water or the shore. Once in a while Sasha noticed a faint twinkle coming from a dock or a bed of reeds, probably a lone fisherman with a single lantern. The moon, almost full, rose and turned the water from gold to silver. The Emiri crew lit a fire in a shallow iron tub. Yarrow called for Sasha to join them on the cushions they'd arranged around the blaze that burned a hole in the chilly mist.

Sasha sat down on a threadbare red pillow, drew his feet against his groin, and wrapped his fingers around his ankles. The colorful sails snapped in the breeze. Some large fish, caught by the sole female Emiri, Lala, roasted on spits. Another sailor, a man with marigold hair and eyes like polished sovereigns, called Toumo, carefully seasoned the meal. It smelled delightful, and Sasha remembered how long it had been since he'd eaten: a simple lunch of dried meat and hard bread before he and the others had encountered the knights. Behind Sasha, a quiet, dark-haired boy called Kin puffed on a long, curved pipe.

As the fish hissed and popped above the fire, the ship's captain, Sai, Sasha thought he remembered, brought out a ceramic jug decorated with leaves and branches pressed into the clay. Yarrow clapped as the Emiri uncorked it. "Ha, you drink *muri-ku, syrai?*"

Yarrow nodded and laughed. "More than I should, sometimes."

Sai took a deep pull, mopped his chin with his sleeve, and passed the jug to Yarrow. After stifling a belch, Sai said, "There's no other way to drink it, is there?"

Yarrow raised the jug, said one of those soft, content, cheerful-sounding words, which the other Emiri repeated, and gulped the liquid inside the clay container. All of the seafarers clapped when he finished. Yarrow shuddered, wiped a watery eye, and grinned.

When Yarrow passed the concoction to him, Sasha took it and sniffed it suspiciously. It felt like it melted the fine stubble beneath his nose and singed his nostrils. Coughing, he turned his head from the noxious fumes. Yarrow and the Emiri laughed heartily, and even Duncan smiled. "What in Tha—" He stopped himself. He'd grown used to invoking his god, a habit he needed to break. "What under heaven is this?"

"The sweet milk of Emir's nurturing teat," Sai said with a wink.

"What?" Sasha repeated.

"Emir is what we call the sea," Toumo said. "We think of her as our mother, since she provides us everything we need."

"It's made from a fermented mix of ocean plants," Yarrow said.

"Seaweed?"

The mage nodded. "And the dried skin of a small eel from the southern waters. Some other things, but those are secret." With that, he smiled at the pretty young captain. "Try some."

Reluctantly, Sasha raised it to his lips and took a small sip. It scorched his throat and burned his belly. He sputtered, fought his gag reflex, and scrubbed at his eyes as the tears flooded out. "That's awful," he said, when he had caught his breath and could speak again.

Everyone laughed, but with camaraderie, not mockery. Soon Sasha joined them. He'd never really been drunk. A few times, when he'd felt safe doing so, usually in a safe house after a successful mission, he allowed himself enough wine to feel relaxed and a little giddy, but never more. He couldn't; he needed to be at his best in case Thalil called. Maybe tonight, on this little boat, surrounded by nothing but the Kanda, he'd indulge himself. His brothers and sisters, while talented, couldn't walk on water.

Duncan took the jug, holding it at arm's length like a twisting serpent. Yarrow and the others cheered him on. Finally, Duncan took a sip so small, Sasha wondered if he faked it. Afterward he coughed and flailed like he'd been poisoned. They all laughed until their sides ached, Sai slapping the planks of his beloved vessel.

"Well done! Well done, *syrai*! Well done, Tam Duncan," Sai said, the Selindrian words harsh and awkward on his tongue.

"Thank you, um, *syrai*," Duncan said, recovering enough to join their merriment.

Sasha felt himself grinning like a fool, the strong, Emiri spirit already soaking into his mind. An Emiri with dark red, almost burgundy hair, called Izu, put the fish on irregular, elliptical plates embossed with shell patterns. The shape of the platters held the long fishes perfectly. Izu garnished them with some wet, green strips. Once again, only the snap of the sails, the crackle of the fire, and the soft caress of the Kanda against the hull broke the silence as everyone devoured his fresh, delicious meal. Famished, Sasha ate the eyes and the brain just as the Emiri did. They finished in no time and tossed the bones overboard. Sai reached behind him for the jug of *muri-ku*. It made three, maybe four rounds before Sasha noticed the others growing blurry.

Everyone grew more cheerful except Yarrow. He stared across the fire at Sai. At first Sasha thought maybe his mage admired the Emiri; he wouldn't blame Yarrow if he did. But as Sasha watched, Yarrow drew his knees tight against his chest and hugged them, rocking back and forth and hiding behind his cloak and hood. His lips pressed into a tight frown, and his eyes sparkled. When he had his turn at the jug, Yarrow gulped the foul, strong brew until it dribbled from the corners of his mouth. The more he drank, the more Yarrow retreated into his grief. Duncan tried to touch his shoulder, but Yarrow swatted the knight's hand away. He said little and continued to drink and watch Sai and the others.

The five Emiri reclined together, shoulder to shoulder, back to chest, or belly to belly. Their arms and legs wrapped around one another, faces close, in easy familiarity as they collapsed into a languid pile, reminding Sasha of the art he saw in the order hideaways, all beauty and innuendo. No wonder these lovely Emiri fascinated Yarrow.

Sasha took his fifth, he thought, maybe sixth, who cared, swig from the jug, dropped to his side, and bent his elbow to rest his face in his hand. The rock of the boat intensified. When Sasha looked at the sky, the stars bled like knife wounds, spilling silvery smears across the wine-colored expanse of heaven. He returned his attention to the Emiri, posed like models for a questionable painting. Their faces looked so innocent despite the suggestive slant of their bodies.

Before he knew he wanted to, Sasha spoke. "All of you live together as friends, do you not?"

"Of course," Lala said. "We're *syrai*."

"And you make love together? Just lie with whoever you will, for pleasure?"

"Tam Sasha—" Duncan cautioned.

"It's all right," Sai said. "Of course we make love. Why not?"

"Are you… are you attached to each other?" Sasha needed an answer to an important question, though his drunken mind couldn't define the query. "Do you care for each other?"

"We're *syrai*," Tomou said, as if it explained everything.

Sasha tried to focus on Tomou's gold eyes, though he saw two of them overlapping in each socket. The red-brown swirls of paint seemed to twine sinuously over his skin as if alive. "Would it hurt you to leave Sai, and Izu, and—" He couldn't remember the names of the others. The mast, the sails, the stars, everything spun around him.

"We are *syrai*," Sai said, slowly, as if speaking to a child.

"What does that mean?" Sasha asked, his voice slurred and rising with frustration. "Can't it just be physical pleasure? Does there have to be more?"

"No," Sai said cautiously, "but there *is* more."

"I envy you," Sasha said. "Everyone you care about always close. Nothing to rip them away—just making love. No other obligations. No, no restrictions. No rules. What does that feel like?"

"It's all we know," Kin said.

"You feel whatever you feel," Sasha mumbled. "You don't have to choose what's allowed."

"Is that even possible, choosing what to feel?" Sai asked. "Who allows some feeling and not another? And how? That's bizarre."

"I envy you," Sasha repeated. "Where is my Yarrow?"

"Your Yarrow?" Sai said. "Aren't you a lucky man? Yarrow is uncommonly beautiful."

"Yes. Where *is* my Yarrow?"

"He's had too much," Izu said, touching Sasha's shoulder and pointing.

Yarrow slumbered in a nest of cushions and worn blankets, his forearm stretched across his eyes. Sasha grasped his shoulder and shook him. "Wake up, Yarroway. I have something I need to tell you."

Yarrow remained unconscious, so Sasha shook him harder. "This is really important, Yarrow!"

Large, strong hands closed around Sasha's shoulders. "Peace, my friend," Duncan said, his face close enough that his breath ruffled Sasha's eyelashes. "He won't wake for at least a few hours. He's drunk, and so are you. Please, Sasha, let me help you to bed."

"I don't need to be at bed, in bed," Sasha slurred. His head hurt. He'd wanted to say something to Duncan, or was it Yarrow? He couldn't remember now. Bed sounded like heaven, now that he thought about it. "Yes, Duncan. All right. Bed, yes."

"Good lad." Duncan's thick arms moved beneath Sasha's armpits and wrapped around his chest. The knight pulled Sasha slowly toward the hatch, and Sasha couldn't, didn't want to, resist. Duncan wouldn't hurt him. Duncan would protect him. Of course he didn't need protection, but Duncan would—

He would. *He cares about me.*

I'm weak! Sweet god, forgive me! Oh Thalil, I can't think about it. I'll worry about it tomorrow. Tonight I just want—

"Here we are, then," Duncan said, lowering Sasha to the bench he'd slept on before. "There you go. Get some rest."

Sasha sank into the thick blankets and let them mold around his body. He reached up to cradle the knight's neck. He felt the soft curls at the base of Duncan's hair, damp against his warm skin. He felt the scintillating sinew that stretched from Duncan's head to the back of his shoulders. He smelled the knight's sweet sweat, his arousal.

"I want you, Duncan," Sasha breathed.

"Rest," Duncan responded.

"I don't want to. I want you to fuck me, Duncan. I know you don't like it said so plainly, but that's what I want."

"Sasha." Duncan kissed his brows and eyelids as he stroked Sasha's cheek. He left his lips pressed against Sasha's forehead as Sasha groped his back and arms clumsily.

"What's wrong? Take me. I never offer, you know. I let Yarrow that once, but… I don't let men take me like that. I give them my mouth but not my body. I'll let you. I want you to. Duncan, fuck me."

"You don't know what you're saying," Duncan argued.

"Course I do. I wouldn't let just anybody—" He rolled over to his belly, hoping his knight would see what he wanted to give.

"You're drunk, Sasha."

"So? Why don't you want me? I know I'm beautiful. I know you care about me, even if I don't understand why. I never let anyone… I'll let you, Duncan. Be inside me. Fuck me. Make me yours."

"I'd rather wait until you really want me."

"I do! I want you until I can't walk. Duncan. Duncan, I want you in me."

"Sleep, love," Duncan said, pushing down the hips Sasha hadn't realized he'd raised. He rubbed taut circles over Sasha's lower back, soothing his muscles.

"No sleep. Take me!"

"Someday, if you're in your right mind and truly want that, Sasha, I'll be honored. But I won't do it until I know you're sure. Sure you really want me."

"I do," Sasha said, his eyes fluttering shut.

"Rest," Duncan said, petting Sasha's hair. "I… I love you. Thank the goddesses you won't remember me saying so. I wish I could say it wasn't true. I wish I could make it go away somehow, but…. Goddesses, I love you."

"I wish I could love you," Sasha whispered, before passing out, "but I can't. I'll hurt you soon, and I… I am sorry."

Sasha fell asleep, dreaming of Duncan's willing body and Prince Garith's blood.

As Yarrow watched the crowded docks of Meritage approach, he felt as though he stood before the gates of the Abode of the Shades, home of the Cast-Down and those sin-darkened souls rejected by the goddesses. He felt the presence within him rearing with excitement and remembered their bargain. He leaned over the side of the boat and vomited into the river.

Duncan came up behind him. "Are you all right?"

"Stay away from me," Yarrow responded. In his heart, he wanted nothing more than to unburden himself to the kind man, the man who loved him in spite of everything. He wanted to be held in those arms that could destroy, yet chose to be gentle.

"Have some water, at least," Duncan urged.

Yarrow turned to face him, his emotions ripping him apart. "I've lived all these years without someone telling me when to eat or drink, Duncan. I think I can manage now."

Duncan's mouth opened as if to argue, but then he pursed his lips, turned away, and went to join Sai and Sasha near the ship's helm.

Yarrow almost reached out for him.

Meritage approaches, sweet beloved. I can't wait to explore it in your lovely skin. So much to see and feel. So many pleasures to be had. Oh so many lives.

Please, Yarrow begged, his mind and soul on their knees. *Can't you wait until we find Garith and I leave Sasha and Duncan? Can't you wait just a little longer, and let them remember me fondly?*

What do I care how they remember us?

Me! Me, me, me! Yarrow! I want them to remember me as a decent man, a man who cared for them, a man worth caring for in return.

Why?

Damn you; it's important to me. Don't you care?

Not really, Yarrow.

Won't you... won't you please, please wait a few more days?

No. I've given you mystic secrets, and now I'll take my payment in sensation through your flesh.

What if I won't let you?

It laughed. *Try to stop me, beloved. How ridiculous.*

You think you're so much more than me? Yarrow raged.

You must be jesting. I am to you what the Kanda is to the smallest pebble along its shore.

We'll see. This body, these organs of perception, are still mine. I am still me!

No, you are us. As much me as you. When we set foot in Meritage, I will wear the flesh. You can do nothing to stop me. No silly mortal being can stop me from anything.

One did, Yarrow ventured in desperation.

How dare you? Do you want to be punished again, beloved? Which one? Sasha or Duncan?

I won't let you!

The creature only laughed in response.

Once again, Yarrow bent over the side of the boat and heaved, but there was nothing left to come up. He would have collapsed, sobbing, if he hadn't seen Duncan, Sasha, and Sai watching him. He stood slowly, wiped his mouth, and smoothed his cloak before walking over to them. The Emiri drink had taken a toll on his companion: Yarrow had never seen Sasha look so pale. Duncan looked well enough, if distraught and exhausted. He'd likely been awake all night, looking out for Yarrow and Sasha.

Martyr. Suffering shows he cares, is that it?

Shut up. He's a noble man.

Aw. Will he keep you safe from me, little Yarrow?

Shut up! "Shut up!"

"Yarrow, are you feeling well?"

"Sasha. I'm fine. Too much muri-ku. I'd forgotten how potent it is."

"It is potent," Sasha agreed, grazing Yarrow's waist.

Please, just wait until I leave them. As soon as we find Garith, I'll go.

I don't want to wait. Your stupid, soft feelings for these fleshy fools don't concern me. You are only a tool, beloved. I'll use you as I will.

I'll stop you. I will.

Again, it only laughed at Yarrow's distress.

SAI EASILY maneuvered his vessel into Meritage's harbor. The Emiri dropped anchor near the center of the Kanda, at the outermost edge of a small bay, so Yarrow, Sasha, and Duncan would need to take the dinghy to the docks.

"Since I have nothing better to do at the moment, I'll wait here until you return," Sai said.

"You don't need to do that," Yarrow said, reluctant to draw this Emiri crew into his tragedy as he had Sasha and Duncan. "Sail to the mouth of the river. Toward warm, welcoming *Emir.*"

"She'll always be waiting for me," Sai said, looking wistfully to the south. "She's not going anywhere. I think the three of you need me now. I'll be here. Sweet blessings on you all, *syrai*. Good luck in your endeavors. I'll be waiting. Maybe soon we can all swim together in the warm waves. I still want to see the rest of your paint, Yarrow."

This Sai is very similar to that other one you liked. What was his name?

Damn you!

Yes, very similar. Young and soft and pretty. Hair like fresh blood. Almost the same eyes. Rini, that was his name, wasn't it?

Yarrow's hands trembled with rage. He wanted to cause the creature inside him pain. He would have smashed his face against the wooden mast until he shattered every bone if he thought he could hurt it. It would only enjoy the new experience, heal Yarrow, and demand his body again. He thrust his hands up under his sleeves and clawed at his forearms in frustration. He felt completely impotent. Nothing he could do would harm the damned thing. He wanted to throw his head back and scream against the sky until he lost his voice, but his companions already thought he was mad. The creature was right. Sai did look a bit like his sweet, lost Rini. Yarrow turned away, unable to face the Emiri or the memories he conjured. When Sai kissed his cheek in farewell, Yarrow couldn't completely swallow a sob.

He hurried down the rope and into the small vessel that bobbed in the frigid, dirty water, where he sat on the bench with his elbows on his knees. He put his hood up to cover his face as Sasha, Duncan, and Toumo joined them. From the corner of his eye, Yarrow watched the approach of the shore, clogged with hundreds of vessels. Buildings with mud walls and thatched roofs occupied every available inch of space. Stinking smoke rose from the houses and shops. The water smelled too, like garbage and human waste. Yarrow felt sicker and sicker as Tomou's oars stirred up refuse, drawing them toward the brown buildings and the thick, gray sky beyond, toward the thousands and thousands of lives, from wealthy merchants to beggars and whores, who called Selindria's largest city home. Agarick held the city, barely, but not the territory surrounding it. As a point of pride, the king kept an estate here. Yarrow had visited it as a boy. Back then, at least in his memories, the water had been as blue as his eyes, the houses like gold in the sun, the boats bouncing brightly on the waves, and the people smiling and friendly.

Now it was filthy, gray and sad, barely a faded ghost of Yarrow's childhood daydreams. Some days Yarrow felt like all the beauty had drained out of the world. It felt alien compared to his recollections from before he'd left home to wander, a distant reflection in a dull mirror. Then he looked at Duncan and Sasha and decided flowers still grew out of the ash.

Tomou guided the dingy to a rickety dock. He tied it to a barnacle-encrusted post. "Well, my friends, I wish you love and luck, and I hope we'll meet again soon." He kissed each of them good-bye, though Yarrow barely felt the pressure against his cheek.

His limbs already felt numb and heavy as he stepped onto the wooden planks, pale and desiccated from decades of being battered by the Kanda. The other was taking control. Yarrow's vision dimmed, and he felt himself slipping toward oblivion, just like when he passed out from too much drink. He fought, fought harder than he ever had to push its tendrils out of his mind as he trudged along behind his companions. Still, the oily tentacles of control snaked into the base of his skull and moved down his spine, spreading out to his limbs and extremities, stealing his sensation as they went.

They'd come ashore in a rough district populated by coarse sailors and the whores who invariably sought them. Though it was early afternoon, noise spilled from raucous taverns. Hundreds of laborers hauled crates from barges, and other men just leaned against the corners of the dilapidated buildings: charlatans, swindlers, cutpurses, and worse. Yarrow was well aware of the stares the three of them attracted. He also saw Sasha's hand on the hilt of his knife.

Black bled in at the corners of his vision. He fought for that last scrap of perception, but it felt like drowning at midnight, being pulled deeper and deeper into nothingness. He'd lost all feeling in his skin, and was no longer aware of drawing breath or lifting his feet. But the fact that he was aware of anything, even the lack of feeling, meant that the other hadn't quite assumed control. It had threatened to punish him. The last time it said that—

No! He had to fight!

Give it up to me, my beloved, it purred, the lover's words repugnant to Yarrow. *Don't fight. Don't make me get rough with my little Yarrow. I'll take it if you give me no other choice. You're mine.*

No, please. He heard Duncan and Sasha talking to him, but their voices sounded garbled and far away. With one last push, the entity took over. Only something unusual happened, and it was different this time. Normally Yarrow blacked out when it assumed control. Not this time. Though Yarrow watched his limbs moving without instructing them, though he had no control over his movements, he wasn't gone. He couldn't control his body, but he could watch and listen, in a way. The world looked gray and blurred, as Agarick's maps had on that rainy afternoon, a lifetime ago. So little contrast existed between the people, the buildings, the ground, and the sky that Yarrow could barely distinguish between them. Everything bled together at the edges. Nothing looked solid. Nothing had any mass, and much of it appeared partially transparent. The sounds came to him as if he'd packed his ears with wool. There were no scents. Their absence unnerved Yarrow as he recalled how they'd always overlapped, hundreds of subtle variations of odors. He'd never really considered them until he lost them. There was no taste in his mouth. He realized, now that it was gone, that he'd always been able to taste something: a hint of his last meal, a vestige of wine, even the flavor of his own tongue and palate.

It was so bleak, so empty and meaningless Yarrow's mind almost broke to escape it. Blacking out would have been a blessing. He tried and couldn't. Did the entity see things this way when Yarrow controlled his body? If it did, was it any wonder it was mad and cruel? Nothing, nobody, could withstand this shadow world, just familiar enough to remind one of the loss of vibrancy and life. Everything around Yarrow felt beyond dead; it felt wiped away, forgotten. Maybe the world as he remembered it had never existed. Maybe—he shuddered at the thought—nothing really existed beyond this realm of shades, ash, and echoes. The thought made him want to scream and cry, but he owned neither his voice nor his tears at that moment.

He could do nothing but observe. Yarrow also felt the creature's enthusiasm and glee at its escape from its forlorn existence. It didn't seem to realize Yarrow watched it. If he tried, really concentrated, Yarrow managed to make the edges of things sharpen. He could at least distinguish Sasha and Duncan walking in front of him, talking about how best to search for the prince. After a while they turned to ask the mage's opinion.

"What do you say, Yarrow? The taverns? You know the prince best." Duncan's voice warbled, the words slow, too deep.

Yarrow tried to answer and couldn't. His guest spoke instead, using Yarrow's voice. How bizarre it sounded, coming out of his throat without his consent or intent. "I don't give a damn about the whelp. Go search for him if you want, but I'm going to have some fun." Yarrow's body turned and started down a side alley, toward a brothel, judging by the scantily clad ladies and young men lounging around the entrance. He tried to stop it, but his legs kept moving, until Duncan seized his arm. He couldn't feel the knight's hand on his bicep, but he saw Duncan's confused face as he spun around.

"What in the name of the goddesses are you saying, Yarrow? Have some fun? Now? We've fought hard to get where we are. We need to find the prince and ensure his safety."

"Get your hands off me," Yarrow's voice said. Though he fought to resist, he saw his arm raise and the back of his hand strike Duncan in the mouth.

Blood ran down the knight's chin, and he drew his sword. "I've suffered enough of your hideous behavior. I put up with it because I thought there might be something between us. I'll suffer no more of your abuse, tam!"

Yarrow heard the echoes of his laughter, bitter and resonant in his ears. "What do you think you can do, you pathetic worm?"

Sasha stood at Duncan's side now, a dagger in each hand. Yarrow saw them almost as charcoal drawings. So beautiful. The men he loved.

"Yarrow, what do you think you're doing?" Sasha asked. "Are you well?"

"Shut up, assassin. I'm so tired of you. Tired of your face always in his head, your body always in his memories. How dull. I should kill you and be done with it."

Sasha looked stunned for half a second, and then angry. "You think you can kill me, Yarrow? Do you care to test your assumption?" His steel flashed in blinding arcs, so fast not even Yarrow's companion could follow the movement. The challenge only made its bloodlust grow. It pressed a palm to Sasha's chest. Though the assassin sliced Yarrow's arm to ribbons, the presence sent a wave of energy into Sasha's body. He fell on his side, seizing against the slimy stones of the street. Yarrow's tongue darted out to lick his lips. He knelt beside Sasha. The creature intended to tether his brain, wipe his identity, and make him a slave. Yarrow fought hard; he'd save Sasha or die. Blood poured from the cuts on his arm. As his body weakened, so did the entity. Yarrow almost perceived the red of the blood spilling from Sasha's mouth.

Stop!

Enjoying the show, beloved? Should I fuck him for you now? I've always wanted to.

Yarrow heard himself groan, saw his fingers tearing at Sasha's snug pants as the other man lay almost unconscious, spitting up blood.

Duncan grabbed the back of Yarrow's neck and hauled him to his feet. The creature's anger spiked. Magic pulsed from Yarrow's body, but Duncan held firm against it, though his pain must've been awful. The knight got his hands around Yarrow's throat. As the sparkles filled his eyes, Yarrow felt his guest draw back.

I'll kill him! I'll kill them both!

It, in Yarrow's skin, broke free from Duncan's hold, grabbed his groin, and sent a shock of magical electricity into the knight's most sensitive places. Duncan's teeth gnashed, and he spasmed, but he held firm to his sword. With a pained look, he drove the point into Yarrow's diaphragm, just below his heart, not enough to cause a lethal wound, but enough to break the skin and tear the muscle beneath. Yarrow watched his hand, wreathed in blue mist, cover Duncan's face. Blood pumped out of Yarrow's chest and soaked his clothing. Duncan howled in agony at the psychic burn of the azure flames. His hair sizzled, stinking.

Wait, Yarrow thought. *I smell it!*

If he really tried, he felt a dull pain in his belly and in his arm where Duncan and Sasha had marked him. He clung to the scrap of sensation, finally aware of why his guest relished hurt. It enjoyed discomfort because it was better than nothing. Yarrow gathered every scrap of energy and will he owned, preparing for the fight of his life. The entity did the same, and it overcame him.

Its attention darted between Sasha, rising from the ground, dagger in hand, and Duncan, doubled over and holding his head. *Choose, beloved.*

No! Yarrow's desperation lent him a fresh surge of strength, but it wasn't enough to reclaim control of his consciousness and body. Still, he kept wrestling with it, hoping at least to distract it from hurting his friends. His efforts earned him a bloody nose as a vein burst with his exertion. He felt sticky wet pouring over his lips. *Felt....*

Goddesses, I can taste it....

He still didn't have the power to stop the thing from moving his limbs. It advanced on Sasha, maybe because, while Yarrow didn't love Sasha more, he'd loved Sasha just a bit longer. It gripped his leather collar and lifted him off the ground. The assassin retaliated, aiming his knife toward Yarrow's throat. With preternatural speed, Yarrow seized his wrist and practically snapped it. Howling in pain, Sasha drove his knee into Yarrow's groin, twice. The agony made the entity withdraw long enough for Yarrow to choke out, "Yes, Sasha! Hurt me!"

"Sick," Sasha snarled. He drove his dagger into the globe of Yarrow's shoulder. Blood fountained out.

Yarrow's guest, enraged, grabbed Sasha's windpipe and squeezed with strength far beyond any man. Though Yarrow struggled, Sasha's face swelled and darkened. His feet twitched, inches above the paving stones.

Something struck Yarrow across the back of the head. He lurched forward and dropped Sasha, who crawled away, retching. The mage's body, still beyond his control, spun to face the knight. His fists balled, and arcane energy wreathed his arms. The energy wasn't the kind that shocked or burned, it was the kind that drained life and vitality, a magic beyond Yarrow's complete comprehension, at least in such strength. Ironically, it was the same enchantment he'd attempted to use healing Duncan, so he knew how fatal it could be. For now, the creature seemed content to strike Duncan with Yarrow's fists. It would torment and toy with him like a marlcat with its prey before finishing him. Yarrow's knee connected with the knight's ribs. Despite his loss of wind, Duncan remained on his feet.

"What… what in the goddesses' names are you… are you doing, friend? Why?"

"Shut up, pig," Yarrow's voice said. He backhanded Duncan in the face again.

"Enough. I don't want to hurt you, but I will defend myself!"

When Yarrow's hand rose for another blow, the edge of Duncan's sword bit his flesh. His foot tried for the knight's knee, but Duncan dodged by stepping to the side. With a howl of rage, the creature warped the air around Yarrow, drawing it in and then sending it out in a gust that knocked Duncan to his back. The thing leapt through the air, pouncing on the knight and straddling him. Just in time, Duncan raised his sword and stopped the hand reaching toward his heart. Another deep gash marred Yarrow's limb. Duncan got hold of his throat and tossed Yarrow off like a ragdoll.

The mage was on his feet before he even landed. Bright, azure wings stretched a dozen feet from each of his shoulders. The street stones melted beneath his boots. "Do you think I can't raze this whole city to ash?" The voice that spoke wasn't entirely his any longer.

"You'll have to go through me," Duncan said, forcing himself to stand.

"And me," Sasha said, moving to stand next to the knight.

It laughed, maniacal and brutal. "That's just an extra treat, fools. I'm done with you. Little Yarrow needs to learn his place, and I plan to teach him." It took a few steps toward the other men, in no hurry, planning to draw it out.

"No, you won't touch them," Yarrow screamed until his throat bled, finally breaking through. He dropped to his knees and clutched his head, tearing clumps of white hair from his scalp. "I don't care what you say, you foul, damnable monster. You'll no longer threaten what I love."

You're strong, beloved. I chose well. But I'm still the one in command.

"No! No more! Not after this!"

And what exactly can you do, little flower?

"You've no right to call me that. Never say it again. Beloved, either. That word makes me cringe."

I'll do what I like, and you can't stop me.

"Can't I? Can't I? I can kill myself! If I'm killed, are you sure you'll die? Will you leave my body, or will your consciousness remain in my rotting shell, covered in earth, eaten by worms, and mired in darkness? After a while, even that will be gone. You know I speak the truth. When my tongue and ears and eyes disintegrate to dust, my taste and sight and hearing will be lost to you. No more sensation. If you don't want to be tethered to my bones, waiting for coincidence to bring another mage to dig them up, stand down."

It retreated, instantly and completely. Before it went, Yarrow felt an exhilarating cloud of emotion waft from it: fear. Exhaustion and injury prevented his enjoyment of the moment. He fell to his side and curled his knees into his chest. The colors returned, so bright they scorched his eyes. He tasted his teeth in his mouth. He smelled the wet stones he lay upon, garbage, human bodies, meat cooking, and the river. It was glorious, but he hurt. He'd never hurt like this, the pain spread across his whole body. As he focused his eyes, he noticed the crimson pool he lay in the center of. He felt his life's blood pumping out of his wounds, but he didn't worry. After his warning, the last thing the creature would do was let him die.

"Get up, Yarrow," an angry voice commanded. "You're attracting attention, and that's the last thing we need. On your feet."

"I can't, Duncan."

Duncan hauled him up with no hint of gentleness, grasping him around the waist and dragging him toward the door of the nearest tavern. "You owe us some explanations. We should have demanded them before now, but this time, you *will* talk."

Yarrow hadn't the strength to argue as he entered the warm, smoky space of a public room. He didn't even have the energy to decide what he'd say to the others, whether he'd try to lie. He had to lie, of course, he just didn't know if he could.

Chapter Sixteen

DUNCAN HAULED Yarrow's delicate body up the stairs to the room he'd rented. Blood covered the mage's clothes, but nothing fresh flowed any longer. It amazed Duncan, after what Sasha had done to Yarrow's arm, but his wounds had closed. Duncan had stabbed him in the gut, by the goddesses, yet Yarrow seemed more tired than anything. When they reached their assigned cell, Duncan unlocked the door and kicked it open with the sole of his boot. It was a large room, but sparsely furnished. Four straw-filled mattresses flanked the empty space, each with a trunk nearby for storage. Other than the hearth and a rickety table, nothing else served to soften the cold, utilitarian room. An old fishing net and a lantern discarded from a boat passed as décor.

Duncan dropped Yarrow unceremoniously on one of the beds. He landed with a grunt, and Duncan could only curl his lip. The knight crossed the room, desiring distance from the mage, and Sasha joined him, arranging the items he'd procured below: a jug of water, bandages, a wheel of hard cheese, wine, and a few loaves of bread. He took a seat beside Duncan and poured water on a scrap of coarse cloth to wipe the drying blood from his chin. His black eyes glowered at the slight, dark-clad form curled across the room.

"Sit up and face us, Yarroway," Duncan said, ignoring his own swollen, split lips, bruised back, and tender pelvis.

With a little whimper, Yarrow pushed himself up and slumped against the rough wooden wall. A line of flaking blood stretched down from one nostril, but Duncan found little pity for him. When he pushed up his sleeve to inspect his arm, Duncan saw, to his astonishment, nothing but some intersecting, raised pink stripes. The cuts Sasha had inflicted had already almost healed, but they would certainly scar.

"Duncan," he croaked, "I'm so sorry."

"That isn't good enough," Duncan said, hitting the floor with the side of his fist. "Not this time. Explain yourself."

"Explain what?" Yarrow said, spreading his fingers and looking down at the offal caked on his palms, most of it from his own injuries. His face twisted, and he retched. "There's nothing to say. Nothing I can tell you will explain any of this."

"Try anyway," Sasha hissed, low and deadly.

"I… I'm just not myself sometimes. I never wanted to hurt either of you. I tried to fight it. I… I thought I could keep it under control until we found Garith. Until I could get away from you two."

"So you're mad after all?" Duncan asked. It seemed a paltry excuse. "Has this something to do with your fever?"

At that, Yarrow clapped a hand over his mouth and sobbed, shaking all over. Eyes screwed tight and fat tears pouring down, he nodded.

"The fever drove you mad?" Sasha repeated, clearly as unimpressed as Duncan with Yarrow's reason for attacking them. "Did it also make you as fast as me, and stronger even than Duncan, this malady? Did it change your voice, the way you pronounce your words, your movements, your facial expressions, and body language? We're taught to read such things in the order. Nothing about you was the same, not down to your most subtle mannerism."

Duncan considered Sasha's words and realized the assassin had the measure of it. "I've never heard of such an affliction."

"It's foreign," Yarrow choked.

"You're lying," Sasha said.

"No. It happened far to the east, halfway across the Lapir Mountains."

"What exactly happened?" Duncan said, softening at the mage's agony. He couldn't help himself.

Yarrow mopped his damp cheeks with the backs of his hands and drew in a halting breath. When he looked at them, his bright, wet eyes were steady and sure. "I don't want you to know what I really am."

"We have a right," Sasha said. "I've told you my secrets, when I thought you would turn from me in disgust. Yet you didn't. You defended me with words and deeds as no one ever has. You saw worth in me. Give me enough credit that I might at least reciprocate that tolerance."

"Trust us," Duncan said. "Don't underestimate us. I've told you many times that I care about you. I still do, even after today. But I must understand. You owe me that much."

The mage nodded, sniffling. "May I please have some wine?"

Sasha slid the jug across to him, and Yarrow started talking. His story began vaguely, and his words halted. As he continued to speak, his voice sped up and his hands moved. He seemed relieved to finally purge himself of the poison he'd held inside for so many years.

He spun an odd tale Duncan didn't completely understand, of a cave in the frozen waste of the mountains. He talked of passageways far below the rock. When he reached the part about an ancient, abandoned pool, home to… to *something,* he spoke with such clarity and infectious terror Duncan broke out in a chilly sweat. Even stoic Sasha reached out for Duncan and twined his fingers around Duncan's knuckles on their scratchy bed. The mage described the entity's atrocities and his own searing agony at bonding with it in such horrific detail Duncan felt sure he'd wake from sleep even years from now at the recollection of it. Yarrow went white and trembled, but he bravely recounted every last, ghastly thing. Afterward he curled in on himself, resting his forearms and shiny, decorated cheek on his tucked-up knees. With his lashes clumped and glistening, he looked as wide-eyed and vulnerable as a newborn foal.

Struck dumb by what he'd heard, Duncan sat and tried to digest it, make sense of it somehow. Sasha clutched his hand, probably just as conflicted.

Yarrow sat for many minutes, awaiting their judgment, before he said, "I'll go." He shifted on his pallet to stand.

"Wait." Sasha spoke the word Duncan wanted to say.

"You'd have me stay? Sasha, I can't. You saw what happens when it gets control of my body. You and Duncan won't be safe around me."

"Let us judge that for ourselves."

"You'd have me?"

"I would," Sasha said.

Duncan just couldn't answer with the same certainty. His head still reeled with the impossible story. The thought of whatever thing inhabited Yarrow's body made his guts twist. He didn't like the idea of the mage's absence, but Yarrow scared him. His power had scared Duncan from the night he'd made mincemeat of Garith's would-be assassins, and his own assault just cemented that fear. He'd stood no chance against Yarrow, or whatever possessed him. If it took over again, he and Sasha would be slaughtered. Much about Yarrow he enjoyed, but he wasn't a fool.

"I'm dangerous," Yarrow argued.

Sasha said, "I know."

"No, you don't!" Yarrow wailed at the top of his voice. "You don't know what it has done!"

"Tell me," Sasha urged. "But be warned, I won't be driven off as easily as you think. Especially not if you can forgive me… as much."

"Fool," Yarrow snarled. "You'll die if you trust me. You'll die just like Rini."

"Rini?" Duncan asked.

Tears spilled from Yarrow's eyes, not in erratic sobs like before, but with old, festering grief that seeped and ached like a wound improperly healed, not fresh, but ever-present. When he spoke, his voice sounded as rough as sand on soft skin. "When I first bonded with it, the other presence, it kept control of my body and senses for a long time. Weeks, maybe months. I don't know. Eventually I awoke on a southern shore, the strong sun scorching my skin. I remember being very thirsty. I was disoriented and wandered the beaches for the better part of a day in search of water. Nobody I approached would help me. They ignored me, shunned me like some diseased beggar. Until I met an Emiri boy with bright red hair and eyes like arn leaves in autumn.

"Rini took care of me. He asked nothing in return. I stayed with him after I was well again. He made me feel calm. He wanted nothing from me, had no expectations. I felt he understood everything about me and accepted it. He was content just to be in my presence. Sometimes, we didn't speak for almost an entire day. We were happy enough to be together that words weren't necessary. Other times, I shared my dreams with him, and he got as excited as if they were his own. Many nights we stayed awake just to talk. He loved me at night with such abandon, so real…. He truly loved every aspect of me, and I of him. Even after everything that happened, I felt so content. We were so happy. There wasn't a single minute we weren't happy. You have no idea how much I loved him. My sweet, sweet boy." Yarrow reached up to touch the paint below his eye.

"What happened?" The frightened whisper that escaped his throat surprised Duncan.

Yarrow hesitated, collecting himself. "I think it was jealous. I made some insult at it, and it threatened to punish me. I didn't think much of that, and I ignored it. Rini and I spent the day swimming and napping on the warm, southern shore. At sunset we went to a secluded lagoon we'd found, and he cooked the fish he'd caught that day. We ate and lay looking at the stars. I… I started to make love to him. The creature took control of my body. I had less influence over it in those early days. I couldn't sense its intentions as easily as I can now. All of my attention was on Rini, and it took over while I was distracted. I don't know what happened exactly, but when I regained my senses Rini lay dead beside me, his throat crushed."

Yarrow cried in earnest then, with deep sobs that shook his small body. "My sweet, beautiful boy. Rini, I loved you. I hope you knew how much I loved you. Sweet boy. I'm so, so sorry." He dropped his brows to his knees and cried for a long time, repeating many of the words he'd spoken. His pain was so raw Duncan felt it as his own, and he thought of Aubrey.

"He deserved better!" Yarrow screamed at the plaster ceiling. "Better than me! He deserved to live a full life, have his own boat. That was all he wanted, a boat of his own. Is that so much to desire? Not riches or power, just a humble boat. He never got it. He'll never have it. Oh my sweet boy!" He dropped his head and cried into his bloody sleeves. Duncan felt like a voyeur, uncomfortable at witnessing such intimate pain. He could do nothing save let his friend exhaust his anguish. It took over half an hour before Yarrow's breathing steadied. Finally he lifted his head. "Should I go?"

"No," Duncan said. "But you must master it."

"And what if I can't?"

"You must." He massaged Sasha's fingers, glad of their warm, solid presence.

The mage stood and nodded. "I'll think on this," he said. "I need to be alone."

Both Duncan and Sasha got to their feet. "This is a very dangerous part of the city," the assassin warned.

Yarrow laughed, though it sounded more broken and pitiable than his cries. "After what I've just told you, what you've seen, do you suppose anybody could trouble me? I need to be on my own."

He turned toward the door, and Duncan sprung to his feet and caught the hem of Yarrow's cloak. Yarrow halted midstep, and spun to face the knight. His sparkling eyes stared, unblinking, into Duncan's.

"Promise me you'll come back."

"Duncan—"

"No. Promise me, on the graves of your ancestors, that you'll come back, or so help me goddesses, I won't let you leave this room."

"I promise. Though I don't know why you'd want me."

Duncan released him. "Neither do I. But I do. Come back by morning."

"I have a request first," Yarrow said.

"Name it."

"I have a request of Sasha."

Duncan stood aside, curious and a little stung, as Sasha faced Yarrow.

"Speak," Sasha said, his posture guarded.

The mage stepped forward and scooped up Sasha's hands. He looked seriously into Sasha's eyes and said, "If I ask you to, will you kill me?"

"Yarrow?"

"Please, my friend. If I feel like I can't control it, if I'm worried it wants to hurt the two of you, can I trust you to do this for me?"

"I don't know. Why ask this of me?"

"Because you can handle it. You can do what needs doing without the guilt of it plaguing your life. Because you said you don't ache for the things you've lost. You can see this as the practical thing. You won't let it destroy you, after. Will you give me your word?"

Sasha looked stricken in a way Duncan wouldn't have thought him able. When he spoke, he couldn't conceal a scrap of his distress. "You think I wouldn't ache?"

"But you said—"

"No, Yarrow. I can't agree to this. I... I need to think about it first."

Yarrow nodded, and then fled like a rabbit through the door and into the darkened hall of the tavern.

AS SOON as the door closed, Sasha hissed out a long, slow breath and dug both hands into his hair, holding it away from his face as he paced the room. Duncan wished he knew what to say to him. He couldn't imagine Yarrow requesting his death at Duncan's hand, or implying that Duncan could carry it out with cruel efficiency and no regret afterward.

"Do you believe his story?" the knight said, hoping to change the subject.

"What?"

"The things Yarrow said. Do you believe them? Do you believe this creature actually lives inside his body?"

"You don't?" Sasha asked, finally halting his agitated movements.

"I… believe he believes it. Sasha, do you think this monster exists? Or is Yarrow truly just insane?"

"Yarrow is most certainly insane," Sasha said, forcing a dry laugh. "But what I said was true. Every aspect of him changes. He moves differently, talks differently. He's not the same person, Duncan. I'd swear it by Thalil. I can't claim to understand half of what he told us, but I can say with absolute certainty that wasn't Yarrow earlier today. Sweet God, it makes sense now. That night in the tavern. He had no memory of it afterward."

"But couldn't that be a madness of some sort?"

"Come, Duncan! You've seen the wings."

"He's a sorcerer."

"Why are you resisting this?"

"Because," Duncan said, though he really didn't know, "how could the goddesses allow such a thing to exist, after everything Yarrow told us it did? That thing he described is even worse than your Thalil."

The assassin stiffened, and Duncan regretted his words. "I'm sorry, Sasha."

"You know, you're going to have to come to accept me. As I am, not as you'd make me."

Duncan stalked over to his mattress and flopped down as he considered Sasha's words. Did he plan to stay? The idea overjoyed Duncan. But could he ever truly accept a man who killed indiscriminately for profit? "You're not a member of the order any longer."

"Only Thalil decides that. Not my brothers or masters. There's only one way to truly leave his service."

"Sasha." Duncan stretched out his arm and was a little surprised when the other man came to him. He wrapped his arm around Sasha's hips and dropped his forehead against his thigh. When he closed his eyes, he felt Sasha's fingers on the back of his neck, in the base of his hair. For a long time he said nothing else, content just to hold Sasha and accept the comfort of his caresses. He smelled of leather, steel, and blood.

"I remember," the assassin whispered.

"Hmm?"

"You didn't think I'd remember what you said, that night on the Emiri boat. But I do."

It took a second or so for Duncan to put together what Sasha meant. When he did, he pulled away, his cheeks hot, and looked up. He found Sasha looking intently down at him, smiling in that way of his that could seduce a cloistered sister. Goddesses, his lips!

But more than his lips, his smoldering eyes, his silky, deep gold skin, his soft dark hair, and beautiful body evoked Duncan's feelings for him. Sasha had proven his bravery. He'd stood by Duncan and Yarrow when he had no reason to do so. Duncan remembered the lengths Sasha had gone to, to protect them, in spite of everything he'd been taught. Everything they'd beaten into him in the damnable order.

"I meant what I said," Duncan managed, his voice thick with confused emotion. He waited for Sasha to respond, but the other man remained silent, his fingers working against Duncan's scalp. Their eyes stayed locked.

"I thought you hated me," Sasha finally said.

"I just didn't understand."

"Now you do?"

"No, Sasha. Not really. But it doesn't change the way I feel."

Sasha knelt down between Duncan's knees and touched his brow, the sides of his face, his lower lip in the center. His eyelids drooped over his ebony irises, his expression a mixture of wantonness and regret. As Yarrow sometimes appeared, Sasha looked so very young to Duncan, young, fragile, and desperate for care. Duncan wanted to give him that feeling of security, of being loved, that he'd never been allowed. He wound his arms around the other man, crossing his elbows over the small of his back. "Sasha… I do love you."

"How? How can you? You despise everything I stand for."

Duncan touched his face. His beauty rendered the knight's heart in two. "I don't despise *you*."

Sasha smiled. "I like it when you touch my cheeks, my lips. Most men don't bother."

"Then they're fools." Since he knew the young man enjoyed it, Duncan took his time exploring Sasha's features. He ran the pad of his thumb over Sasha's slim, dark eyebrows. The assassin's eyes fluttered shut, and Duncan touched his sumptuous lashes. He touched the high, sharp ridges of his cheeks, the straight bridge of his nose, and Sasha trembled. Duncan cupped his chin, feeling the fine bone beneath Sasha's skin. He felt the muscles of his jaw moving in his grasp. Sasha's swollen lips ground together, and Duncan couldn't resist putting his finger on them, and then between them. He wriggled his thumb between those soft, sweet, red-brown mounds. Sasha's tongue flickered out and tasted the tip of Duncan's thumb. "Goddesses," Duncan breathed. "You're the most beautiful thing."

"I meant what I said that night," Sasha said, eyes still closed, fingers digging into Duncan's shoulders.

Duncan kissed his jawline. His sweat and arousal tasted so delicious, his need seeping out of his pores. "You want me?" he asked.

"Yes," Sasha said in a single prolonged breath. He broke away from Duncan's hold and got to his feet. As quickly as he could, he unbuckled his leather armor and tossed it aside. Soon he stood in nothing but his provocative underwear.

"Take off your clothes," the assassin ordered, and Duncan stood in response. Sasha's erection poked past the band of his scant garment, the blood red tip peeking out from his foreskin. Clearish white fluid dripped from his slit. Duncan never took his eyes away from Sasha's weeping cock as he cast off his boots, pants, and shirt. He stood naked, his dick swollen and throbbing, desire overcoming modesty. He wrapped his hand around the base, needing some stimulus. Sasha just watched. Duncan squeezed himself harder, drawing another squirt of precome. He swirled it around his throbbing cock to ease the ministrations of his hand.

Following suit, Sasha took his swollen dick out of his undergarment and stroked it. The two of them stood with a little over a foot of space separating them, touching themselves and looking into each other's eyes.

"Goddesses, please come to me," Duncan said.

In a heartbeat, Sasha stepped out of his garment and was there. He sank down in front of Duncan and kissed him across his belly, his fingers moving up the strip of hair at the center and finally digging into the patch that grew in the middle of Duncan's chest. His light scratches raised gooseflesh down Duncan's arms, and Duncan clutched his lithe shoulders, delighting in the hard muscle he held. Sasha's other hand found the sac that held Duncan's heavy balls, and he squeezed and kneaded them in his fist. His slick lips made their way down the sinew stretching from Duncan's hip to his groin, and he buried his nose in the dark curls that edged the knight's cock. He breathed deeply of Duncan's musk and growled with satisfaction before continuing to explore the terrain of Duncan's torso.

Duncan had known many men over the years, taken temporary lovers where he could, but he'd never felt his body worshipped in this manner. Sasha's mouth and fingers relished every detail of his musculature, neglecting nothing as they moved over his waist, across his chest, down his thighs and calves. It was exquisitely erotic, and Sasha never so much as grazed Duncan's erection. When his tongue circled the edge of Duncan's belly button before plunging in, the knight cried out and pulled Sasha against him, his cock pressed against Sasha's throat. He ground against Sasha's heated flesh, the first rivulets of his seed easing the friction.

Sasha, sensing Duncan's need, sank down to tease Duncan's dripping slit with his tongue.

"No," Duncan gasped, pushing him back. "I don't want what you offer to everyone."

Sasha wiped his mouth on the back of his hand and looked up at Duncan through his thick lashes, a defiant grin tugging at his lips. He didn't like being told what to do, but he allowed it, which intrigued Duncan. He gripped Sasha by his deceptively delicate wrists and guided him to his feet. They kissed for a while, damp bodies pressed close and hard cocks sliding together. The contact hurt Duncan's injured lips, but before long he barely noticed and certainly didn't care. A sudden urge gripped Duncan, and he knelt and picked Sasha up beneath his knees, holding his smaller body in his arms.

True outrage widened the assassin's eyes and curled his lips. "What do you think you're doing?"

"Oh, be quiet," Duncan said with a chuckle. Sasha squirmed against his chest, and Duncan held him tighter and kissed him hard, subduing Sasha's tongue with his own. Finally Sasha consented to be held and relaxed into Duncan's arms. His small surrender pleased Duncan very much, and he held and kissed him a few minutes more before kneeling and laying him softly on his back across the mattress. "It's my turn to show you how beautiful you are, how much I love your body." He pressed his palm against Sasha's chest when the other man tried to rise to his elbows, and again Sasha submitted to it. A smile broke across Duncan's face, and Sasha returned it. He dipped in for a quick taste of those sublime lips before he began his tour of Sasha's flesh, starting at the pulse at his throat. He worked his way down, over muscle much different from his own, lean muscle built for agility and speed. Desire poured from Sasha's skin, and Duncan lapped it from his chest, his arms, his inner thighs, everywhere. Sasha's dick lay throbbing across his belly, his precome like pearls against his dark skin. Duncan harvested one white bead with the tip of his tongue, but just as Sasha had done, he ignored his partner's darkened, dripping penis.

When he reached the small red sickle inscribed beside Sasha's groin, Duncan grasped his knee and pushed his leg aside to have a better view of it. He swiped his thumb across the bright ink as if he could wipe it away, but of course it remained. It would always remain, this part of Sasha Duncan couldn't quite reconcile with the complex, alluring, and surprisingly kind man sprawled out beneath him. He stared hard at the mark, unable to completely quell his unease. When he looked away, he saw Sasha watching him intently, his lips pursed with nerves. With a smile, Duncan pressed his lips to the crimson moon, his fingers grazing the side of Sasha's leg and moving up his waist. He felt Sasha relax back into the mat, felt his muscles release their tension. Sasha touched Duncan's hair, and Duncan continued kissing down his leg.

When he finished kissing the soles of Sasha's feet and sucking his toes, Duncan guided him over to his belly. "I don't think I've ever seen a more beautiful man," he said as he ran his hands up and down the lean muscles of Sasha's back. His wound had healed nicely. "Will it upset you if I say I love you?"

"No," Sasha grunted, circling his pelvis against the coarse-spun cloth. "It means a great deal to me, even if I can't quite understand." His cheeks and lips flushed so dark they looked almost black in the firelit room.

Duncan plowed his hair away and kissed the back of his neck, making his partner whimper and thrash. He explored Sasha's back, but faster than he had his front, his growing need driving him. He reached the taut crescents of Sasha's ass in minutes. Sasha's hips seemed small and fragile in Duncan's large hands as he guided them up as gently as he could. He urged Sasha's legs apart and moved around behind him. After placing a kiss at the base of Sasha's tailbone, he said, "Stay right there."

Sasha laughed, a sensuous sound that made Duncan impatient to hear the noises Sasha would make as he moved inside him. "Be careful digging in my pack. There are things within you'd probably rather not accidentally touch."

Taking his lover's advice, Duncan gingerly sorted through the various vials and powders until he found the one he wanted. Holding it up to the fire light, he saw very little of the amber oil remained, only about an inch worth, but it would be enough. Before they left Meritage, he'd be sure to visit an apothecary and procure more, since it seemed Sasha, at least, planned to stay. That thought, more than anything else, made Duncan's heart hammer and penis buck. It would take compromise and patience for them to come to an understanding, but Duncan had already taken the first step, and he had faith Sasha would try too. Neither would sever the delicate threads binding them together, and they'd gradually forge more. Duncan looked forward to it, even to the difficulties. He hurried back to his partner and knelt down behind him, stroking Sasha's buttocks and the backs of his thighs before easing his cheeks apart.

Duncan wished he had more light to inspect Sasha's most secret places, and thought absently that Yarrow could accomplish it easily. He felt a pang at the mage's absence.

"Duncan," Sasha urged, opening his legs wider in invitation.

He ran a fingertip over Sasha's tiny, puckered entrance, and it twitched at his touch. Sasha groaned and pushed back toward him. "Can't wait, friend?" Duncan teased.

"I've wanted this from you," Sasha said, all his deliberate reserve melting away, his need strong and authentic. Only in these intimate moments did Sasha drop his mask, but Duncan hoped he might feel comfortable at other times, someday. Right now Sasha needed one thing, the same thing Duncan desired so strongly his whole body shook with yearning.

He dropped his face between Sasha's cheeks and inhaled his excited, masculine aroma. He swiped his tongue over the sweltering mound of quivering flesh. He circled it a few times before using his thumbs to spread it open, so he could get his tongue inside and taste Sasha's silky walls.

"Sweet Thalil!" Sasha slapped the dusty old mattress with his palm, raising a small cloud.

Encouraged, Duncan pulled Sasha open a little further so he could trace the rim of his anus with the edges of his tongue. The muscles tried to contract, but he held them apart and drove in, fucking Sasha with his tongue.

Sasha moaned rhythmically, all lucidity gone. Duncan reluctantly pulled away from his hot, damp flesh, leaving one thumb inside him while he felt for the oil. The way Sasha's body hugged his digit made him crazy. He couldn't wait to feel that tight heat around his cock. He uncorked the oil and poured it into his palm. He let it drizzle along Sasha's crack and used the rest on his erection. With the oil easing the way, Duncan replaced his thumb with his two fingers, feeling out the knot of nerves within Sasha. The other man cried out as if in pain, though Duncan knew he felt anything but. He twisted his fingers as he drove them in and out, sure to hit his partner's sweet spot with every stroke. Sasha pushed back against his hand and cried out again and again.

"Duncan," Sasha managed. "Enough. I'm ready."

This time Duncan let himself be ordered, since both of them wanted, needed the same thing. He drew his fingers out, watching Sasha's flesh cling to them as if reluctant to let them go. He positioned himself at Sasha's opening and pushed forward, sliding easily inside after his preparations, the oil, and Sasha's own need. The assassin accommodated Duncan's length with little trouble, and Duncan buried himself to the base. "Goddesses, you're wonderful. My sweet Sasha. Does this feel all right to you?"

"Duncan, yes!" They moved against each other, their thrusts fast, short, rough, and desperate. Skin slapped against skin, and Duncan's balls bounced against Sasha's. Sweat gilded the assassin's limbs, and he trembled all over, breath hitching.

"You're close?"

"Mmm" was the only response the other man could manage.

Wanting to fulfill his lover, Duncan seized the back of Sasha's hair and yanked him up. Sasha straightened his arms and caught himself on his hands, but Duncan pulled him closer, flush against his chest. He wrapped his arms around Sasha's ribs to support him, while his other hand found Sasha's cock. The fluids coating it let Duncan's fist slide easily up the length. Sasha fumbled to brace himself against the wall and return Duncan's enthusiasm. Duncan squeezed him, holding him tighter and halting his movements. "Just let me." Sasha acquiesced, and Duncan drove into him, hard, deep, and savage. It worked, and Sasha's cock bucked in his hand, his balls clenching up. Duncan curled over his back. When he bit the base of Sasha's neck, tasting blood, Sasha came, screaming Duncan's name over and over.

The sound of his name on Sasha's lips, his honest exclamations of passion, pushed Duncan over the edge. Stars erupted behind his eyes as he shot his seed deep inside Sasha's trembling body. He came hard and long, wave after wave of pleasure racking his body, draining him until he almost collapsed with the intensity of it. "Goddess, I love you, Sasha."

He lowered Sasha down until his hands touched the bed and slowly pulled his softening member out of him. After a few deep breaths to ground himself and banish his giddy dizziness, he went to wet a cloth and dropped back down next to Sasha. The mark his teeth left on Sasha's skin oddly gratified Duncan, and he traced the wound with his pinkie. Then he opened Sasha's cheeks to regard the mark he'd left on his body there, skimming the puffed, wide-open rim of his anus. The fruits of his passion streamed out, and he gently washed them away. Afterward, he cleaned Sasha's shrinking penis, loose, relaxed balls, and taut belly. He stretched out, sated and tired, and Sasha spooned up behind him.

Duncan squeezed the hand Sasha buried in his chest hair and whispered, "Thank you."

"For what, my friend? It was at least as enjoyable for me."

"I love you."

Sasha sighed, his breath cooling Duncan's flushed neck and cheek. "You say that so easily. I wonder if you really know me."

"I want to."

"Are you sure? If you delve too deep, you may find things you'd rather not."

"So I should content myself with only what's on the surface?" Duncan asked.

"It would be easier. We can still have fun like this."

"Do you honestly want nothing more, Sasha?"

He kissed Duncan softly on the shoulder. "I don't know. I don't know if I can return your feelings."

"You feel nothing for me, lying close to me right now? Nothing beyond physical satisfaction?"

"I feel… safe. I know you won't hurt me. I can sleep without worrying you'll turn on me while I'm vulnerable."

"That's called trust."

"A weakness we're warned against. I also feel… I'm glad you're here. I'd rather be with you than alone. Even now that I don't want sex any longer."

"That's a start of something, isn't it?" Duncan asked.

"Perhaps. I… it's very disconcerting to allow myself even the possibility of these feelings. It's almost easier to eliminate them. I don't suppose that makes much sense to you."

"I understand how much courage it takes for you to try. You're one of the bravest men I've met, and I admire you, Sasha."

They rested, refreshed themselves, and dozed on and off. During the night, with the fire burning low and the room almost completely dark, Duncan felt Sasha's erection stir against his spine. Sasha guided Duncan's knee up to his chest and used the last of his fragrant oil to make gentle, unhurried love to him. He hadn't been touched that way in many years, and Sasha took great care to make it wonderful.

They'd just finished cleaning up when the door opened. Yarrow grunted at the sad state of the fire, and a second later it, and all the candles and lanterns, burst with such bright flame Duncan had to squint. The mage grinned at Duncan and Sasha, naked together on the single mattress.

"You two seem to have enjoyed a pleasant evening," he teased.

Duncan colored but returned Yarrow's smile. He had no reason to deny it. "And your night, my friend? Are you feeling better?"

He shrugged. "I suppose I am. I found Garith, after all."

Chapter Seventeen

SASHA COULDN'T sleep for the rest of the night. He lay between Yarrow and Duncan, listening to them breathing and shifting in their sleep. Yarrow mumbled and groaned, and out of habit Sasha stroked his arm to soothe him. Over the past several weeks, maybe almost months, he'd honestly lost track, he'd grown used to Yarrow talking in his sleep, used to touching him to drive back the nightmares. He relished the idea his hands could provide comfort and not just death. Now he knew the source of the mage's terrors and found it didn't disturb him as much as it should. The idea that they'd be going to meet with the prince in a few hours troubled him far more.

Sweet God, he'd never been so conflicted. When he'd been with Duncan, he'd nearly made up his mind to abandon his calling. Before that, he'd wanted to get away from the other two men and the weakness they inspired in him. Now, he just didn't know. He'd need to make a decision one way or another. It could be put off no longer. Yarrow made another little whimper, and Sasha kissed the back of his head. The smell of his hair felt familiar, comforting and exciting to Sasha all at once. God, he longed for the days when everything had been black and white, when he'd known exactly what he needed to do and did so without hesitation. He'd never imagined questioning his orders. For the first time in his life, Sasha wished he had someone he could talk with, ask for advice. Yarrow and Duncan were the only friends he'd ever had, and they couldn't understand his position. If he failed to kill the prince, the order would hunt him down. He'd never imagined how much harder it would be to choose his own path than to follow orders.

He lay awake, thinking but reaching no conclusion, until the sun came up and the other men started to stir. It would be a bright, clear day, probably cold, judging by the swirling patterns frost had etched into the glass of the window. Duncan rose and stretched. Sasha smiled as he watched him move toward the pitcher of water, admiring his nude form, noticing the old battle scars carved into his skin. For such a large man, Duncan was surprisingly gentle. Sasha remembered Duncan's hands on his body, their reverence and respect for him. He shook his head and sat up. Something hurt when he twisted to rid his neck of the stiffness, and he recalled Duncan's love bite, made solely for Sasha's benefit, because Duncan showed no personal inclination toward such things.

The knight smiled when Sasha padded over to the water and leftover bread. He pinched Sasha's chin between his thumb and finger, kissed him, and told him good morning. Sasha didn't know how to react. He'd never experienced such an everyday kindness. He could almost imagine beginning each day in such a simple, pleasant fashion, kissing, sitting down to eat…. While it sounded like a wonderful dream, Sasha couldn't hope it could come true, and he turned away to ready himself for reality. He washed himself as well as he could with the basin and cloth, dressed, and checked his weapons.

"Should we wake Yarrow now?" he asked Duncan.

"I hate to," Duncan said, looking down at his curled body. "He seems exhausted. But the sooner I get the prince under my protection, the better I'll feel."

Sasha turned to the window, unable to face either of them, while Yarrow washed and dressed. When he'd finished, he led the two of them through the twisting back alleys of Meritage into worse and worse sections of town. Finally he stopped in front of some crumbling hovels that stood in the perpetual gloom of a large bridge. A few of them didn't even have doors. A muddy little creek carried garbage down the hill toward the Kanda. It reeked of slimy soil, refuse, and rotting fish. Sasha gagged and watched Duncan cover his face.

"What in heaven's name is the prince doing in a place like this?" Duncan asked.

Sasha wondered too. Even whores and the lowest and meanest of dockside thugs avoided this place, because it contained nothing to take. Two mangy dogs fought over the carcass of a rat almost as big as themselves.

"How did you find Prince Garith here?" Duncan asked. "Did you use magic?"

"I'm a mage, Duncan."

"Did you—"

"No. I didn't need to. I have plenty of my own power. So you don't need to ask every time I cast a simple enchantment."

"I didn't mean to offend you," Duncan said. "I'm sorry."

"No, I'm sorry. It's a valid question."

Both Duncan and Sasha stared at Yarrow. In the time they'd known him, they'd never seen him admit a fault. Duncan touched his shoulder, nodded, and asked, "Which way?"

"Here." Yarrow pointed to one of the dilapidated, mud-walled houses, if it even deserved that description, being no larger than a shed with a single, broken window and battered door. Garbage lined the slippery path and edged the walls like a sick parody of a garden. Yarrow knocked on the door, and it surprised Sasha his fist didn't penetrate the rotting gray wood.

A comely young man with fair skin, wild copper curls, and a healthy flush to his cheeks answered the door, sword in hand. Sasha recognized the royal livery on the tabard above his bronze mail. Seeing Yarrow calmed the handsome knight, and he sheathed his blade, though he looked warily to his left and right, and then his eyes settled on Sasha and Duncan. "Who are these men, Tam Yarroway?"

"My friends. I told you of them, tam."

The knight nodded, though his blue-green eyes still held suspicion.

"Sander, who's there?" called a voice from inside.

"Your cousin and his companions, Your Highness."

"See them in, and quickly."

"Yes, Highness." He stood aside and swept his arm toward the interior.

Sasha, Yarrow, and Duncan entered a dank little room with a dirt floor, a heap of dirty blankets in one corner, a broken chair in another, and a grime-encrusted lantern on an overturned barrel. A young man, presumably the prince, hurried to embrace the mage.

"Yarrow. The goddesses themselves must have sent you. What's going on? We were attacked. No one was supposed to know where I was. How has this happened?"

"I don't know," Yarrow said. "Not all of it, at any rate."

Sasha studied the young man as he regained his composure. He didn't seem especially regal in his plain brown trousers and patched green cloak. Garith was handsome enough, not remarkably so, not as dark as Sasha and a few inches taller. Even so, Duncan knelt in the mud before the prince and kissed his hand. "Thank the goddesses you're safe, Your Highness. I am Duncan of Thulemore. Please accept my solemn vow to protect you with my life from this point forth."

"Please rise, Tam Duncan. These last few weeks have dampened my expectations of formality."

Duncan stood, filth on his knees. Sasha hated seeing his friend prostrate himself before this awkward boy—or anyone else, for that matter. He supposed it couldn't be helped in the world Duncan came from. In Sasha's world, all men were equal because they all bled and died the same.

The prince indicated his companion. "Tam Lysander, of the Royal Guard."

"You were sent out with a single guard, Your Highness?" Duncan asked.

"No," Garith said. "I was accompanied by four knights. Sander is the only one left."

"What happened?"

"We were attacked halfway between my father's citadel and this port. Overwhelmed while we camped. Sander barely managed to save me. I'd be dead if not for him." He smiled affectionately at the young knight.

"I live only to serve you, Your Highness."

"Tam Lysander," Sasha said, "did you see the men who ambushed you? Were they dressed like me?"

"Who is this man, Tam Yarroway?" Sander asked.

"My friend," the mage answered.

"Wait," Garith said, his eyes narrowing. "You're the man paid to pose as me, aren't you? You were supposed to distract would-be attackers from us. Why did they come after me and not you?"

"They did," Sasha said. "This is very important. Did the men who attacked you wear armor like mine?"

"Don't answer, Your Highness!" Tam Lysander moved between Sasha and the prince. "How dare you address him directly, assassin? And you two!" He stared daggers at Yarrow and Duncan. "What are you thinking, bringing this… this murdering piece of refuse into the presence of your sovereign?"

Yarrow shouldered past Sasha and struck the knight in the jaw with the back of his hand. Blood flew from the corner of his mouth, and he reached for his blade. "Apologize to him!" Yarrow yelled. Though the mage looked no different, Sasha felt the power pulse around him. His teeth tingled and his hair stood on end. From the look of fear that crossed his face, the young knight sensed it too.

Pride and loyalty surmounted caution, and Tam Lysander spat blood on the floor. "You're out of your mind, Yarroway L'Estrella! I'd heard you were mad, but I had no idea. You'd risk Prince Garith's safety by bringing this scum here? He's likely responsible for everything."

"Shut your mouth, or I'll see you never open it again!"

"Will you, tam?" Sander raised his sword, and Yarrow raised a hand wreathed in blue mist.

At the last minute, Duncan pried them apart. "Cease this nonsense immediately. We're on the same side! Stand down."

"Apologize to Sasha!" Yarrow demanded, reaching for Lysander.

"To a man like that? Never."

"Whoreson! I'll kill you!"

"Yarrow," Duncan said firmly. "Stand down. And you, young knight, will hold your tongue and sheath your blade. Do I make myself perfectly plain?"

"Yes, tam," Sander said, lowering his weapon.

"Yarrow?"

"Duncan, he has no right!"

"Let it go, my friend. Please. We all want to protect the prince and get to the bottom of this mess."

Yarrow sighed with resignation, and Duncan released him. The mage pointed a finger at Sander and said, "Insult my companion again and I'll do things to you that will make you beg for death. That's a solemn promise."

The young knight shuddered, and Sasha smiled. It hardly mattered to him what the man thought of him, but the knight's fear of his mage entertained him immensely. He was wise, wiser than he realized, to fear Yarrow's wrath.

"Let us talk," Duncan said wearily. "Prince Garith, Tam Lysander, Sasha's query is valid. Did your attackers wear armor like his?"

"No," Sander answered. "They wore armor. Nothing uniform, bits and pieces they probably scavenged. Why?"

Duncan looked over his shoulder and met Sasha's eyes. Understanding passed between them, and Sasha felt relief that Duncan wouldn't reveal his affiliations. Lysander knew what kind of work Sasha did; he didn't need to know the details of his very secret order. Sasha had already defended his beliefs more than he'd ever thought he'd bother to.

"Tell us everything you can remember about the ambush," Duncan said.

They relayed what they knew, and then Sasha and his companions described their own experiences. Duncan did most of the talking, describing their betrayal, the plot against Garith and the queen, and the evidence they'd discovered to disprove it. The knight carefully avoided any subject implicating Sasha or Yarrow, careful not to reveal anything he'd learned from his lovers in confidence. Protecting them, Sasha realized. In the past he'd have been offended at such protective treatment, but he appreciated it now. Duncan shielded them not because he found them inept, but because he truly wanted to spare them pain. He did it out of love, not pity.

"What… what in the name of the goddess do we do now?" Lysander asked, clearly overwhelmed by what he'd heard. During the course of their discussion, all of them had opted to sit on the damp dirt floor, exhaustion winning out over pride.

Sasha, who'd been mostly silent until now, spoke. "We would do best to make for Gaeltheon. The prince is not safe in Selindria. We have no idea who can be trusted. We should keep him hidden until we reach the Gaeltheon court."

"No," Garith said. "My mother is on trial for her life! I shall return to Lockhaven and defend her."

"Your Highness, I don't think that wise," Sander said, draping his hand over the prince's wrist. "From what I understand, there are three potential causes of our misfortune: this Tam Taran, the king, and your mother. The last place we should go is the keep where all three of them are gathered. See reason, Garith. I mean, Your Highness."

"There is no need for pretense, Sander. Address me by my name in the presence of these men. I don't mind." They looked at each other and smiled.

Sasha cracked a knowing smile of his own. "Your, um, your knight speaks the truth, Garith."

"You will address him as Prince Garith or Your Highness or—"

"Peace, Sander. It hardly matters," Garith said. "What does matter is my mother is taking the fall for a crime I've been accused of. I will go to Lockhaven, to defend her name and my own."

To Sasha's dismay, Duncan nodded in resignation. "If that is your will, Highness, we'll do everything in our power to see you there safely."

"Thank you, Tam Duncan. I will see your loyalty and courage rewarded."

"Duty is reward enough, Your Highness."

"How will we reach Lockhaven?" Sander said. "By all accounts, the enemy is everywhere. The roads are watched. We can trust no one."

"We can, in fact," Yarrow said with a bright smile. "I have a boat waiting. I can promise we'll be safe onboard."

Chapter Eighteen

"LET ME understand this," Sai said. "You wish for me to sail up river, against the current, and into the frozen waters around Estrella Lake?"

He leaned against the rail of his ship, his back to Yarrow and his eyes on the horizon. It was midday and warmer than it had been lately. The Emiri captain had shed a few layers of his cloaks and furs. Yarrow finally saw the planes of his small, lean body beneath his embroidered leather tunic. "We can pay you well," Yarrow said. "My brother is valen of Lockhaven, and the prince is my cousin."

"This sounds like trouble, *syrai*. Important people always are."

"They also have gold."

"I like you, Yarrow. I do. I just don't know if I can risk my ship and my crew. It'll take forever to sail upstream. My *syrai* will be bored. Our supplies will be low. Emiri ships aren't made for such cold. *We* aren't made for such cold. I just don't think I can agree."

"I don't believe this," Sander spat. "This man is your prince. I order you to transport us to Lockhaven."

Sai turned to face them and clutched his sides as he laughed and pointed at the young knight. "Your friend is delightful, Yarrow!"

"How dare you?"

"Honestly, lad, shut up," Duncan said.

The young man complied but continued to scowl at the Emiri.

Yarrow took Sai's hand. "Please reconsider."

"I've always had a hard time refusing a beautiful man," he responded, touching Yarrow's painted cheek. "I'll ferry you as far as the port of Felgard."

Yarrow breathed out with relief and kissed Sai's forehead. It wasn't the outcome he'd hoped for, but it was better than nothing. If nothing else, they'd be safe in the Kanda's broad embrace for a few days. They could talk and plan. "Thank you, *syrai*. I'll repay you if I ever can."

"Settle in, then. This will be a long journey, especially if we don't have the blessing of the *eru*."

"I can help with the wind," Yarrow said.

Sai arched a shapely brow. "Oh?"

Yarrow made a simple gesture with his hand, and a southerly breeze ruffled Sai's vibrant hair.

A delighted smile broke across Sai's face. "You'd be useful to have on board for many reasons." He winked. "Your skills will be helpful, but we're still in for quite a trek. If you get bored or restless, or if you want to, you can join me in my cabin." He glided across the deck toward his patterned curtain. It parted and Yarrow saw Tomou waiting within.

The others, who'd kept their distance at Yarrow's advice, hurried forward. Strangely, Sasha didn't join the other three men, but instead wandered toward the main mast and climbed a few feet up the rigging. He stood there on the rope, looking west.

Your assassin is troubled. I wonder why that is.

Probably because of you.

It wasn't my idea to tell the poor fools everything.

Yet, they're still here. With me. They didn't run.

Only because they need you. Us. They need our power to get through this fool's errand of theirs.

Do you think that's all?

Beloved, I have known human men since before they were even properly formed men. Closer to animals. They're either using you for your magic, or they're the worst kinds of imbeciles.

"Tam Yarroway, are you listening?" asked Lysander.

"What is it?" Yarrow snapped, irritable after considering his companion's observations.

"This is a poor course of action. How can we trust these Emiri worms? They don't even acknowledge their prince."

"If you have any sense behind that mess of hair, friend, you won't test my temper just now. Emiri have no lord or master. I won't suffer your insults against them. They're good people, and I trust these more than most. Do you have something else you want to say? Consider carefully."

Sander blew air out through his teeth. "Felgard isn't even on Selindrian soil. We'll be taking Garith into very unstable territory. We won't have the protection of our knights."

"Your knights hunted us down and tried to kill us," Yarrow reminded.

"Because, by your own account, that man murdered an innocent girl!" Lysander stabbed a finger toward Sasha, who didn't bother to look down at them.

Let me at him, beloved.

Stop calling me that. "This is the last time I'll warn you not to slander Sasha," Yarrow said.

"You think quite well of yourself and your skills, Tam Mage." The young knight stepped forward until only a few inches separated his chest from Yarrow.

"With good reason. Would you like to see my skills?"

Oh, this will be fun.

"Stop." Garith came forward. "Stand down, Sander. This man is my cousin, and I trust him. I trust this knight of Thulemore, and I trust you to keep me safe. We must endeavor to get along with one another."

"Forgive me, Garith. I care only for your welfare."

"I know, my friend."

Ugh, these two should find a place to be alone.

"Cousin, may I speak with you?" Garith asked.

Yarrow nodded and followed Garith off toward the starboard rail. He'd rather spend his time consulting with Duncan, and he wanted to know what troubled his dear Sasha. They stopped and leaned their elbows on the brightly painted wood, looking out across the calm green water. They listened to the creak of the boards, the lap of the waves, and the cry of the birds. A little way off, Sai and Toumo made soft sounds of bliss within the captain's quarters.

Finally Garith exhaled dramatically. "Is this really happening, Yarrow? It doesn't feel real."

"Would you feel better if I lied to you?"

"No. Goddesses, Yarrow, what do we do?"

"I don't know, Garith. I promised your mother I'd protect you, and I plan to fulfill that oath. I can't begin to imagine what will happen when we reach Lockhaven. We have enemies, powerful enemies, and we must be careful."

"Who would do this to me? My own parents? I've known Tam Taran since I was a small boy. He used to take me hunting. Why are they doing this?"

You have memories of Tam Taran, don't you, beloved? Try to recall them. Taran, the king, the others—

He knew my father. So what?

Interesting, your mind.

What do you mean?

"Yarrow, what do I do?"

"You need to be strong, no matter what happens. You'll soon be a great king, far greater than your father, and you need to act the part."

"I will. I love you and trust you, cousin, but I won't show weakness in front of others. I… I must ask why you keep the company of that assassin."

"His name is Sasha, and I'd appreciate if you used it from now on."

The prince sighed. "Very well. How can you trust this Sasha, cousin? He'll kill anyone he's paid to. What if he's using you to get to me?"

"That's ridiculous. He's fought beside us when he couldn't possibly benefit from doing so."

"Why?"

"He's a good man."

"If you say so, I'll take your word for now. I must speak with Sander. Can you advise me any further, cousin?"

Yarrow softened toward his frightened kinsman. He reached out and rubbed Garith's shoulder. "I advise rest. We're safe for the moment, surrounded by water. Sai is a good man too. He'll take us to Felgard as soon as he can. This boat is swift, and these mariners very capable. We'll reach the next port in short order, he's assured me."

SAI STAYED true to his word, sailing as quickly as possible toward Felgard. Yarrow helped with the winds when he could, but the journey still took time. The three companions spent little of it together. Duncan passed most of the day talking to Tam Lysander, making plans to defend the prince in any situation that might arise. He seemed loath to touch Yarrow or Sasha under the gaze of Garith and his knight. It hurt Yarrow that Duncan was ashamed of them, but he didn't press his friend. Sasha, too, remained distant, keeping to himself and avoiding the other men.

What torments him so, beloved? Don't you wonder? Are you not suspicious?

No. I trust Sasha.

Little fool.

Shut up. He cares about us.

You don't understand what Thalil demands, beloved.

It doesn't matter. He'd never hurt me.

Do you think he feels anything for you? That he can feel anything at all?

Stop it.

Fine. Wait and see, Yarrow.

The peach-colored sun, edges blurred by the river mist, dropped rapidly toward the flat, western horizon, taking the scant heat of the afternoon with it. Yarrow closed his cloak and donned his hood, letting his fingers graze the smooth rail as he paced back and forth. Sai, Toumo, and Lala worked with the riggings and sails, while Izu and Kin sat on the aft deck with their legs folded beneath them. Kin, the dark-haired, quiet boy, played a beautiful, atonal melody on a flutelike instrument made from a conch shell. The music echoed through Yarrow, making him feel even more hollow and alone. He wanted to speak with Sasha, find out what bothered him and ease his discomfort if he could. A few times he even considered visiting Sai in his cabin, just to be with someone. While Sasha might not mind, Duncan certainly would. Yarrow knew that, even if they'd never discussed it, and he didn't want to hurt the knight. He just wanted one of them, or better, both, to spend an hour with him. Looking about, he saw nothing but the strange shadows cast by the masts, sails, and ropes. He could do nothing but lean on the railing and watch the color and light drain out of the world.

Can't we do something for fun, beloved?

Like what?

Care to learn some more magic?

Yarrow's appetite spiked; he couldn't help it. More than a lust for power drove him; it was the compulsion to know how everything functioned and existed, to understand the workings behind the scenes. He'd been thinking about fire lately, true fire and not the blue flames he conjured in camp, which were more akin to lightning, energy that needed no fuel to consume. Working with raw, arcane energy had always come easiest to the mage. He used it to stun and sting, and to conjure spectral extensions of his arms. Since meeting his companion, Yarrow now also showed a talent for manipulating life force, taking from some and imbuing others. Maybe because of his boyhood in cold Lockhaven, or his time in the mountains, he felt an affinity for movement of air and vapor, and effectively wielded wind, weather, and ice. Weather was easy, a simple matter of cooling the air and moving it around the right way. Fire, though, he could only manipulate if already present and with ample fuel, like a blaze in a hearth or a burning candle.

Fire fascinated him, especially lately.

The entity laughed. *Fire is easy, beloved. It wants to feed, to destroy. It's much simpler to coax flame than to milk the rain from the clouds, and this you can do. Your problem is that you don't like things you can't completely control. Fire scares you, because it lives independently of your orders.*

One might call that wisdom.

You're a taker, Yarrow.

What are you on about?

You're selfish; you know how to take. That's why you're good with cold. You can take the heat from the air or the water. It's why you're such an abysmal healer. You can take the magic from all around you to make your pretty little blue sparkles.

I've taken down more than a few men with my little blue sparkles.

It laughed. *Come, hold out your hand. I'll teach you all about fire.* When Yarrow hesitated, it said, *Come, beloved. I won't take over, only guide.* It kept its word, psychically standing behind the mage and draping its hand over Yarrow's wrist, like a man might when teaching a boy to aim and fire a bow. It held his mind in a similar, unobtrusive way, just nudging Yarrow's thoughts toward the proper place. Soon, Yarrow began to understand the volatile element, to feel its need, almost a hunger, similar to—

Yes, just like the lust you feel for the bodies of Sasha and Duncan. Use that. Try.

He furrowed his brow in concentration, trying to conjure fire until his head throbbed. He sensed it, in the lanterns swaying from the ropes, but he couldn't beckon it from himself.

No, no. You must give, beloved. You're interpreting your yearning as something to take. Come now, this shouldn't be so hard. We both know you adore to give your body to those men. Give your heat and energy to the fire.

Yarrow did, smiling with delight as a small flame leapt from his palm. Heat and light sang in his veins. If he concentrated, he could coax it into the form of a bird and send it to fly out across the water. The orange light reflected off the surface until it fizzled out, leaving nothing but a wisp of smoke and a shower of ash.

Easy, isn't it? Try something bigger. I'll help you.

In exchange for what?

Nothing. I'm fond of you at the moment. It's too bad we couldn't have separate bodies for an evening, isn't it? What a time we'd have then. But magic is almost as much fun.

Yarrow shuddered. *It's never that simple with you, is it?*

It never had a chance to answer, because heavy footsteps echoed on the deck and a second later Duncan touched Yarrow's shoulder. That small caress, after so many days of nothing, excited the mage as much as seeing the fire born from his hand. Yarrow didn't turn to face him, only stood enjoying his large, warm presence at his back. After his first quick touch, the knight made no move to put his hands on his lover again. It hurt Yarrow more than it should have.

"You've been avoiding me. Sasha has too. Is it because of what I told you? Because you find me so distasteful now?"

You don't need them, my beloved.

Please, let him answer.

"No, of course not," Duncan said.

"Touch me, then."

"Friend, we can't touch that way in front of the prince. It isn't allowed. I have much more to worry over now that we've found Garith. My first priority must be his protection. That duty must come before everything else. You know and understand this. Right now, I have to focus on Garith."

"I understand what you must do. I don't understand why you can't even touch my hand when we're alone. Why you can't kiss me good night in a private room. You're disgusted by me. Be man enough to admit it."

At that, Duncan took Yarrow's waist and spun him around. He pushed Yarrow's hood back and raked the hair out of his face, fire smoldering behind his eyes. His big hands held Yarrow's cheeks as the knight continued to stare. Their bodies pressed closer, radiating heat. Neither spoke as their breath came harder and faster.

"Duncan—"

"Soon. The prince must come first. After that, I promise." He gave Yarrow a single, lingering peck that almost made Yarrow's knees give out. He'd come to delight in the texture of Duncan's whiskers against his skin. "I love you."

"If I loved you, I'd go. I'm just too selfish to give you up. I'm putting myself ahead of your safety. You understand, don't you?"

"No. I think you're worth the risk, though. Come, let's go below deck and get some rest."

"Is Sasha below?" Yarrow asked.

"I don't know. Why do you ask?"

"He's upset about something, Duncan. I've never seen him this way. I'd like to speak with him."

"He's not a man who easily shares his private thoughts. I've grown to understand him a bit over these past months. Can you believe over three moons have passed since we left Agarick's fortress? We left early in Strella's moon, and now we're well into Fayelle's. It hardly seems possible so much time has gone by. Anyway, I think we should let Sasha come to us."

"I hate to see him suffering alone."

"But you must understand it, Yarrow. Look how long you endured your burdens in silence. He'll talk to us when he feels the time is right. Look at all the horrible things that order did to Sasha's mind. I think he's resisting, but he needs to do it at his own pace."

"I wish we could make love," Yarrow said wistfully.

Duncan laughed. "With the prince and Tam Sander asleep in the next room? It's not like you can keep quiet, friend."

Though he ached for his lovers, Yarrow nodded and smiled. They went below deck, where they found Sasha asleep, or feigning it, on his bench. Duncan spread the cushions and blankets Sai had provided across the floor, and he and Yarrow slept together without touching, like brothers.

SASHA WAITED until the other men's breathing grew slow and steady with deep sleep. He wished he could have initiated sex, really tired them out, but Duncan had been prickly about receiving his slightest touch since they joined the prince and his sharp-tongued vassal. He supposed the knight didn't want to flaunt his association and more with an assassin, or with his liege-lord's own cousin. Sasha wouldn't have cared before. Sexual friendships came and went, but he missed more than spending his seed inside these men, in their mouths, or across their bodies. He longed for those cold nights along the road, as rough as they had been, when it had been just the three of them. He missed sleeping with their limbs twined around him like tangled rope.

He shook off his silly melancholy. He'd known this day would come. Tonight, he had work to do. He sat up and pulled a small dagger from below the mat on his bench. Earlier, he'd sharpened it until it could cut steel. Sasha cautiously stepped over Yarrow and Duncan, careful not to look at their faces in the low light of the oil lantern swinging from the ceiling. Slowly he opened the door that separated their small compartment from the even tinier room that housed the prince and his knight. He'd noticed the door creaked and had oiled the hinges to prevent it. It opened without the smallest sound, and Sasha entered the adjacent cell.

Garith and Lysander slept on the floor. Some crates lined the walls, leaving room for little else. Sasha barely had the space to creep around the prone figures and kneel down next to the prince. He lay on his back, his head rolled to the side, exposing his throat beautifully. Sasha watched the sinew of his neck, the bounce of his pulse below his jaw. He drew his blade and held it an inch from Garith's throat. It would be so easy. If necessary, he could offer Lysander up to Thalil before the young knight ever stirred. Why did he hesitate?

Because he had no escape route. Killing the two men would present no problem, but where would he go from there? He'd have to pass back through the other room, past his sleeping companions, his lovers. Would Yarrow choose Sasha over his cousin? Not likely. Sasha feared facing the mage as he'd never before worried over an enemy. *Enemy.* Sweet Thalil, he didn't want Yarrow to remember him that way. Duncan had vowed to protect the prince with his life, and he'd sworn that duty came before anything.

Even if he made it past them, which he might, he'd have no choice but to dive into the freezing Kanda and swim to the shore. He'd probably survive. Probably. No, he'd wait until they reached Felgard and he could escape into the shadowed streets. Yarrow and Duncan would hate him, curse his name, but he'd be gone by then, back to the order, where he belonged. He'd be a god among assassins for this work. A legend.

Sasha watched the light dance across his blade and twirled it a few times in his fingers before sliding it back into its leather holster over his ribs. Once again, he crept carefully around the two sleeping men and through the door to his own room. He could do little more until they reached the city, so he stepped over Yarrow and Duncan and returned to his bed, feeling sick with doubt and restless to have it all over and done.

He curled on his side on the bench, watching his lovers sleep. Who would calm Yarrow's night terrors after Sasha left? Would Duncan? It gave Sasha small consolation to imagine them together, protecting each other. It also hurt, the idea of that future without Sasha in it. He stamped down the weak feeling, turned away, and tried to sleep.

Garith dies at Felgard. For Thalil. Because I have no choice.

Chapter Nineteen

THEY ARRIVED at the filthy little port of Felgard on the longest night of the year, the twenty-first day of Fayelle's Moon, when the hours of darkness overwhelmed the day. *Thalil's Night*, Sasha thought with a bitter smile. It felt as if his god personally reminded him of his calling. He recalled a tale none outside the order had told for hundreds of years, of Thalil visiting Fayelle, goddess of purity, on this night. The Dark One had used his considerable beauty and craft to seduce even that cold and untouchable sister. To hide her shame, or possibly to prolong her time with her lover, Fayelle extended the hours of darkness, making that night the longest of the year. Of course, the priestesses called the story false, called it blasphemy. No one dared to repeat it or consider it might be truth. Hearing it always made Sasha proud of his service to Thalil. Tonight, he felt very close to his god. Even the waning moon, still a little too swollen to be called a crescent, shone the brown-red of old blood. As he watched Lysander and the prince walk down the gangplank, he swore to his deity he would not fail.

Sasha rolled his eyes at the way Lysander looked left and right, his arm across Garith's back. Could the fool draw any more attention to them if he tried? Duncan followed them closely, his sword concealed on his hip below a cloak, instead of on his back where he normally wore it. The assassin, trying to do his part, scanned the crowd. Many people, the expected sailors and laborers, along with equally predictable gaggles of whores, thugs, and the indolent milled about the docks. More Emiri mingled with the throng than in Meritage. Some of their eyes followed the new arrivals, and Sasha studied the faces and body language of every man who took notice, until he felt content none of them threatened the prince, the knight, or his friends. He kept alert as he followed the others ashore, his hand close to his dagger.

Yarrow took his time bidding the Emiri crew farewell, hugging and kissing each of them, and Sai twice. When he finally departed the boat, he took another few minutes to stare at it with longing.

"We were safe with them," he said, coming up beside Sasha.

Not as safe as you thought, my friend. My love. He said the words in his head that he couldn't voice aloud.

They traversed the grimy streets, where smugglers, cutthroats for hire, and those selling stolen goods didn't even bother to conceal themselves. Lysander glared at each and every one of them, the simpleton. Yarrow knew enough to keep his head down and his hood up, and Duncan seemed to have picked up enough from the assassin and the mage to follow suit. Eventually Sander, who'd somehow become their unofficial leader, chose a tavern and went inside.

It was dark, dirty, and less raucous than the others they'd passed, which piqued Sasha's suspicions. "Wait," he warned, "let me look around first."

Sander started to protest, but Duncan raised a hand and said, "That would be wise. Sasha will see threats the rest of us can't."

The young man nodded and Sasha stepped inside, scanning the small room by only the light of the sputtering candles on the tables. Three or four men sat nursing drinks around rickety tables, clearly thugs but certainly not of the order. They were older, scarred, burly, and anything but beautiful. They looked up from their elbows when the five men entered, but anyone drinking in such an establishment would do the same. They also watched Sasha move around the room's perimeter. He detected no closets, hidden rooms, or even alcoves that might conceal an attacker. A small cell behind the simple wooden bar held ale kegs and crates. A rotund man with an eye patch stood polishing glasses with a rag so filthy Sasha wondered why he bothered with the ruse. He exhaled, deferring to his instincts.

"I don't know if I'd call this place safe," he said to Duncan in a low voice, "but there are no extraordinarily dangerous elements, if you understand my meaning."

"I do. Come, let's have a seat by the fire."

Sasha selected a table at the back of the room, in the corner, from which he could watch the entire space and no one could creep up behind him.

As they sat choking down an oily stew made of unidentifiable sea creatures, Sasha took a small vial from inside his sleeve and dribbled a few drops of the elixir into Lysander's thin wine. "Well, we've made it this far, at least," he said, raising his own glass. All of them nodded and drank.

"I'd like to entertain suggestions as to what we'll do next," Sander said, already more relaxed than he'd probably ever been in his life. "How will we reach Lockhaven without attracting the notice of our enemies? The prince—"

"In god's name, friend, you are truly a sheltered soul," Sasha said, reaching across the table, grasping the young knight by the collar and pulling him close. "You don't broadcast that we're traveling with a prince, fool. To do so only invites a robbery, or worse. You don't speak so freely about our destination, or we'll only arrive there to a regiment of soldiers. Try to think a bit before you open your mouth, or you'll get us all killed, your precious Garith included."

Sasha released him, and his cheeks looked bruised with outrage and humiliation. Garith's eyes darted between his bodyguard and the assassin, but Sasha merely crossed his arms and leaned back in his chair. "To get where we're going, if such a thing is even possible, we must travel completely off the roads. None of them will be safe. We must get supplies here, and not stop again, not even in the smallest settlement, until we reach our destination."

"Why?" Garith asked.

"We can't risk being seen, not by a single milkmaid who might be questioned. We should leave here as soon as possible, and stay to wooded areas. We must be no more than shadows. We need to disappear, and reappear only when we know it will be… appropriate."

"I'm sure you know all about such things, *Sasha*," Sander said

"We owe our lives to this man." It wasn't Yarrow, but Duncan, who defended Sasha. "He is very good at what he does. I'd appreciate you showing him proper respect."

"He deserves no respect from me, Tam Duncan."

"Oh? Do you think the two of you will reach your destination without his particular expertise?"

"Why is he helping us?" Sander ran a hand through his hair, his eyes glazing. "It doesn't make any sense, and I just don't trust this."

Not as big a fool as you look, Lysander, Sasha thought.

"Perhaps he's a good man," Duncan said, with a warm smile for Sasha.

Sasha had to look away. "If you listen to me, I can get you there," he said into the fire. "I cannot make any predictions as to what will happen when I do."

"We should listen to him, Sander," Garith said.

"As you will, Your Hi—I mean, my friend. Sasha, do you think we'll be safe sleeping here tonight? I'm suddenly very tired. I can't keep my eyes open. I don't know what's come over me all of a sudden."

"I'll speak to the owner, and then I'll check upstairs."

"Thank you for helping us, Sasha," Garith said.

Sasha stood, resting his fingers on the tabletop, and looked into the prince's frightened brown eyes. "Know this. Your favor means nothing to me. I don't care who you are. Everything I do is to please my friends."

He smiled as the prince's jaw almost hit the table, and then he went upstairs to do as he promised. He found five rooms, one containing an old sailor who'd be having a rough morning, and another where a couple engaged in enthusiastic sex. The other three stood empty. One had been badly damaged by a leaky roof. Mold covered the plaster walls, and it smelled. In the other two simple cells, Sasha found no hidden panels, no hidden compartments in the ceilings, and not even the loose floorboards where disreputable men and women sometimes hid their coin.

When he returned to tell the others what he'd found, he saw Tam Lysander dozing in his chair, fighting to keep his eyelids up. Sasha knew he'd lose that battle; the sleeping draught he'd administered was quite effective. He could have easily drugged his companions, but he couldn't do that to men who trusted him. He could have poisoned Garith, but of course the others would know. The young knight just stopped his head from hitting the table. "You should probably get your companion into bed," he said to Garith.

The prince touched his knight's cheek, rousing him enough to guide him toward the stairs. As Sander swayed and clutched Garith's elbow, Garith said, "Whatever your reasons for your aid, Sasha, you have our gratitude. Your friendship with my cousin and this honorable knight must be very special. I'll see you in the morning, and we'll follow whatever course you set. Good night, my friends. I thank the goddesses for sending you to me."

"We should retire too," Yarrow said, a hopeful glint in his eye.

"You were quiet at dinner," Duncan observed. "It's… unusual for you."

"I have an ill feeling."

"Goddesses, Yarrow, I remember the last time you said those words. What do you suspect?"

"Nothing in particular. Something just feels off. If Sasha says we're safe, though, I believe him."

"So do I," Duncan agreed.

Sasha fought to stay on his feet. He looked down at his chest, sure he'd see a dagger embedded there. What else could cause such awful pain? He felt the sting of tears as he looked at their trust-filled faces. He'd never see them again after tonight. If he didn't kill Garith, he'd be dead and never see them either. Sweet God, he couldn't bear it. He wanted to confess everything and beg them to understand.

No! I am not weak. I will serve the will of Thalil. "Let's go to bed, and worry over all of this later," he said, his sensual drawl flawless. He moved closer to the other men, stroking Duncan's chest and digging his fingers into the back of Yarrow's hair. "It's been far too long since the three of us enjoyed any privacy."

Both of them reacted, Duncan clasping Sasha's hand and bringing Sasha's knuckles to his lips, and Yarrow whimpering, lips trembling, just from Sasha's hand on the back of his neck. Sasha knew he was probably already hard. He watched Yarrow's hand snake around Duncan's waist and pull the knight closer, drawing them into a tight, crooked triangle.

"Bed, friends," Sasha urged. "We're beginning to attract an audience. Come."

They stumbled up the dark steps, groping each other, unable to keep their hands to themselves after their period of abstinence. Sasha barely managed to unlock the door before they had him on the floor, yanking at the buckles of his armor.

SASHA STOOD and stretched, confident the other men wouldn't wake anytime soon. How could they, after the night they'd enjoyed? The first time had been rough, sloppy, and quick, there on the floor with their clothes barely off, Yarrow screaming and squirming beneath Duncan and Sasha thrusting into the knight's sweet ass. To the assassin's surprise, Duncan had acquired some thick, spicy oil in Meritage. Sasha liked his personal formula better, but Duncan's balm served them well as they fucked with clumsy need, like virgins, messy and hard.

After only about half an hour, all of them felt the time they'd been apart acutely again, Sasha most keenly of all. He knelt on his hands and knees, letting Yarrow fuck him while he sucked Duncan's cock. Then he let them switch so he could take Yarrow in his mouth and feel Duncan inside him, and even after they'd finished he wanted more. He wanted more, because he knew it was the last time. He'd used his own fingers, before Duncan took over while Yarrow's mouth brought Sasha to his third orgasm.

He felt sore as he dressed carefully in his armor and strapped on his packs and pouches, checking his knives and gear with meticulous attention. He hoped his tenderness might last a while, because when it was gone he'd have nothing left of them. Before he stalked out of the room, he spared them one last look as they slept in each other's arms and shed a single tear, as he hadn't done since he'd reaped his first life.

Sasha picked the pitiful excuse for a lock and padded into Garith and Sander's small room. It looked identical to the one he'd shared with his lovers: dirty walls, a cracked window behind fraying curtains, stains on the wooden floor, and two straw-filled mats. Unlike Yarrow, Duncan, and Sasha, the prince and his knight hadn't pushed their cushions close. Sasha didn't know if propriety prevented them or if young Sander had fallen unconscious as soon as he'd hit his mattress. It hardly mattered. Sasha unsheathed his blade, the small, sharp one. He wanted a clean kill, didn't want Garith to suffer. He took lives without remorse, but he'd never delighted in pain the way some of his brothers and sisters enjoyed after a while. Garith slept on his back, naked to the waist, with his arms stretched over his head. Sasha recalled the prince's sincere gratitude. This prince held genuine goodness, and might even have made a fine ruler one day. But that was not for Sasha to decide.

Sasha crouched down. *Just do it*, he told himself. He'd taken dozens of lives, too many to remember. It was his calling. It was an honor.

"For Thalil," Sasha whispered, lifting his blade, positioning the tip just below Garith's ear. One swift cut, and it would be over. One swift cut, and out the window, to disappear among the numerous others hiding among the shadows of Felgard. He thought he might shake, but his hand stayed steady.

"Assassin." Garith spoke without opening his eyes. "I've been expecting you."

Sasha couldn't respond. Why wouldn't his hand move? It wasn't too late. Garith wouldn't be able to scream—

"I may be young, but I'm not a fool, Sasha. If that's really your name. You said it yourself; you care nothing for me or my title. There is only one reason why a man like you might take interest in me. Does my cousin know?"

"No," Sasha managed. "Nor Duncan. They're loyal."

"So you're betraying them too." Garith opened his eyes, but they already looked dead. "Go on. If not you, someone else will get to me. You, you're skilled. Crimson Scythe, are you not? A son of Thalil? I ask you two boons, assassin, if you'll hear me."

"Go on. Your money and power will not stay my hand, however."

"I know. Come to think of it, I need to ask three boons."

"You're pressing your luck, little prince. Make it fast."

"I thank you. I do. Please tell Sander this wasn't his fault. My death is going to destroy him. He can be a good knight, but he's a passionate man. Don't let him be consumed by vengeance."

"I'm afraid I won't speak to him again. What else do you ask of me? Quickly, the time is near."

"No pain."

"There will be very little."

"And… and Sasha, take care of my cousin Yarroway. He seems strong, but he's fragile. He… suffered a great deal as a youth and a young man. Terrible things happened to him before he went away."

"What do you mean? What things?"

"Just take care of him. He has been my friend for as long as I can remember, and I can be at peace if I know Yarrow will be safe and happy. The way he looks at you—please, promise me you'll watch out for him. Promise me, and I'm ready."

"*Thalil, baska retalus!*" Sasha swore in the now dead language of the eastern empire where Thalil's cult originated. Why did Garith have to mention Yarrow? The prince flinched when he plunged his dagger down, into the filthy mattress, inches from Garith's head. A cloud of dust and insects mushroomed out. Sasha stabbed in three times before slicing the coarse burlap to shreds.

"You… missed?"

"Don't be an imbecile." How long ago had he truly decided to spare this prince? Days? Weeks? That first night in the cell below Yarrow's familial home?

"No. Uh, sorry."

Something dark flitted across the window, damping the moonlight for a half a second. Boards creaked in the hallway. The hair on Sasha's neck and arms stood up. "Son of a whore," he hissed. "Get up, little prince. Wake your knight. We need to get out of here if any of us are going to live."

"But Sander! What did you do to him?"

Sasha shook his head, his senses heightening, sharpening. The prince's whispered query sounded like a tempest. "He's been out long enough now that a good slap should rouse him. Stay here. I'll get Yarrow and Duncan. Do you have a weapon?"

"Yes, but—"

"By Thalil, I hope you can use it. Don't leave this room, and don't let anyone in here until I return, if you want to live."

"Sasha, what—"

"Shut your mouth, if you have any sense!" With that, Sasha bounded out the door, back toward his friends' room, scanning the shadows as he went. He didn't see anyone; of course he didn't. His brothers and sisters possessed too much skill for that. The brethren of his order knew what Sasha had been trying to deny—he'd lost his thirst for blood, at least in this case. He'd grown weak. How long had the order been following Sasha? How had he not detected them? Just before he reached the doorknob, an elbow closed over Sasha's throat. The larger man behind Sasha practically lifted him off his feet as he choked him, almost crushing his windpipe.

"You failed Thalil, brother," his deep voice rasped next to Sasha's ear.

Dizziness threatened Sasha, and darkness streamed across his vision. With that small, sharp knife he still held, he stabbed across the man's belly, making contact with flesh just beside his rib. The other assassin's blood poured from his mouth, covering Sasha's cheek, neck and shoulder. Sasha thrust again and again, and still the stranger held tight to his throat. He sputtered and gasped, and finally released Sasha. Banishing vertigo, Sasha spun, crouched, and cut his brother's throat. He kicked the shoddy door, and it popped open.

Yarrow stood within, already dressed, packs ready, outlined in his azure glow. For once, Sasha felt glad to see that manifestation of power. They would need it. Duncan was clothed, but unarmored. "Now!" Sasha shouted. "We're attacked!"

"Your people?" Duncan asked, going white.

Sasha hurried over to clutch his chin and look into his eyes. "They're just men. Flesh and blood, just like me, my love. They'll die the same as anyone else."

The knight broke away. "The prince!" He pushed past Sasha and into the hall, everything else forgotten in the face of his duty.

"Sasha, how many?" Yarrow stumbled across the clothing and gear they'd discarded with so little care a few hours before and grasped Sasha's hands. "Goddesses, you're covered in blood. Are you hurt?"

"No, love. I'm fine."

"How many?"

"Four, at least, inside the building. Others will be waiting on the street. We're in for a fight."

"Bring it."

Sasha laughed in spite of everything and kissed Yarrow. "That's what I love about you. You're always ready to have a good time."

"Let's go."

They raced back down the hall to the prince's room. Along the way, they leapt over a man cleaved practically in half, no doubt by Duncan's large blade. Inside Garith's room, they found two more assassins facing Duncan and Sander, who stood protecting the prince. In one smooth motion, Sasha took a dagger from his belt and threw it, striking one of his brothers between the shoulder blades. The assassin's arms went limp, but the strike wouldn't kill him. Freeing a second blade, Sasha rushed forth to finish the job. He motioned to the second man, and Yarrow nodded, understanding.

From the corner of his eye, Sasha saw Yarrow rush the second assassin in a flash of white hair and dark clothes. A solid projectile shot from Yarrow's palm, shimmering like blue glass. The man fell on his face, and Duncan chopped his head off in one clean blow.

Sasha kicked the legs out from beneath his opponent, and the other assassin landed hard on his chest, winded. With his toe, Sasha flipped him to his back. He was a beautiful, blond young man, even younger than Sasha.

"Curse you, traitor," he choked.

Sasha pounced, driving his blade past the thick bone and into the other man's heart. Blood painted his lips, and he spasmed for a few minutes before he died. Sasha cleaned his blade on the other's leather armor before sheathing it. "Quickly," he said to the others. Garith and Sander looked quite shaken, as if they'd never witnessed death. "The window. Now. I go first, then Lysander and the prince. Yarrow, Duncan, take the flank. Be careful, there may be more of my brothers within the building."

"Your… brothers?" Sander retched. "You did this?"

"Later," Sasha said, inviting no argument. "Out the window. Go!" He shattered the glass with his elbow, balanced on the sill, and then dropped the single story to the street below, landing lightly on the frosty stones. He detected no sign of his brethren, but they were better than that. No one ever saw them until it was too late.

Garith jumped from the window and fell to his knees when he landed. Lysander, still groggy with Sasha's potion, landed even less gracefully. The prince hurried to help his knight to his feet.

"Behind me. Now!" Sasha said, and both of them obeyed. They quickly wedged themselves between his body and the back of the warehouse across the alley. He drew two blades, peering into the foggy shadows surrounding them. Dark shades moved within, he felt certain. He detected them to the left and the right, four on each side, he thought. It made sense for the order to deploy its assassins in groups of four.

Nearby, Yarrow leapt from the window, his black cloak fanning out behind him, and landed almost as lightly as Sasha had. Duncan's heavy boots hit the paving stones hard, but he stayed on his feet. Both of them hurried to their friend and the men he protected. Yarrow skidded to a stop just before he reached them, his eyes going wide.

"What?" Sasha asked.

"Someone is working magic. He's close." Yarrow jerked his gaze to the left, and then he sprinted into the heavy mist.

Duncan called his name and started to follow him, but he never got the chance as the eight assassins crept silently from the shadows, surrounding them on all sides. They backed against the building, Sasha and Duncan in front of Lysander and the prince. Sasha threw both of the knives he held. The first struck a tall man in a red hood neatly between the eyes, dropping him. The other sailed toward the chest of an obviously female assassin with a black scarf wound tightly over her face and hair. Buckled boots similar to Sasha's covered her bare legs to midthigh. At the last second, the woman dodged Sasha's blade, though not completely, and it embedded in her flesh between her chest and shoulder with a dramatic spurt of blood. She wrenched it free and threw it back toward Sasha, all in one fluid movement.

He caught the blade in his gloved hand and held it. His enemies moved closer, too close for ranged combat. They'd effectively trapped Sasha and his companions between themselves and the wall. One man struck at Duncan with a heavy chain and a curved blade attached to each end. He swung the deadly weapon in two wide circles that would shred anything in their path, but the knight parried them and knocked them back again and again with his large blade. Two others attacked Sander and Garith, one with a serrated short sword and the other with a razor-tipped staff. The discordant sound of metal hitting and scraping along metal rang in Sasha's ears. He had no time to follow the battle, though, as the remaining four members of his former order closed in on him: the wounded woman, a man with a sword almost the size of Duncan's, an archer who was possibly another woman, standing at a distance, and a dark-skinned boy carrying a pair of the order's signature, serpentine daggers. His brethren seemed more intent on punishing him as a traitor than eliminating their mark.

Ill at ease being trapped against the wall, Sasha slashed out with his own knife, and the dark boy barely stepped back in time. An arrow whizzed over Sasha's head and stuck in the wood only a few inches above him, as he'd just managed to crouch and avoid a killing blow. He needed to be rid of that archer. As he rose, he kicked hard at the man with the sword, connecting with his diaphragm and winding him. Sasha leapt over his body, sidestepping so he wouldn't expose his back, and sprinted the few hundred feet to the woman. Their eyes met, and the archer readied a barbed arrow before Sasha could close the distance. He raised his dagger to deflect it. While he managed to knock the arrow aside, its nasty, jagged head still grazed the side of his neck, taking skin and flesh, and drawing blood that curtained down Sasha's left arm. It wasn't a fatal wound, so he ignored it and dove for the woman, keenly aware of the other three assassins approaching from behind. In a split second, Sasha straddled the archer, knocking her back, and grasped her head and snapped her neck before her body met the stones. He jumped and spun around, just in time to catch the female assassin's blade with his forearm. His armored gauntlet lessened the injury, but couldn't prevent it, and more blood flowed. Still, better his arm than his eye or neck.

"You disgusting coward," the woman hissed in a voice as cold as the wind across the plains, "you will die for turning your back upon Thalil and your brethren." She stabbed down for Sasha's throat, but he caught her wrist just in time and snapped the small bones. She howled with rage and pain, her knife clattering against the street.

In his peripheral vision, Sasha saw the man with the sword swing off to his left. As he ducked, his arm shot out, striking his assailant in the ribs. He felt his steel find flesh, but the order equipped their assassins well. The wound would be superficial. Over his shoulder, Sasha saw Duncan lift his massive blade above his head and bring it down beside his enemy's head, severing the man's arm and practically cleaving him in two. The chain-blade weapon he'd held clinked to the street. Sasha didn't watch to see if his knight would come to his aid; he knew Duncan was honor-bound to protect the prince first.

He grasped the hilts of his daggers, slippery with blood now, and considered. The three assassins, panting and wounded, regarded their former brother. The woman seemed most dangerous, so Sasha kept her in front of him while he tracked the others from the corners of his eyes. He felt sure he could take out the boy, the weakest of the trio, with one of his black eggs. Blind and poisoned, the youngest assassin would pose little threat. He whisked one from his pouch, prepared to hurl it. The egg seemed heavier than a cannonball and he felt it dragging his arm down. His whole body felt heavy, his legs barely supporting him. He couldn't move; he'd never been so weak.

Not far away, Duncan dropped his sword. Though he clutched the hilt, he lacked the strength to lift it again.

"What in the goddess's name?" Sander screamed, trying desperately to defend his liege with shaking, strained arms. Garith slumped against the wall, holding his forehead in his hands. Only the enemy assassins seemed unaffected by what could only be a spell.

Yarrow had said someone was working magic. Sweet Thalil, Sasha had never been so tired. He'd just sit down for a minute, maybe rest his eyes—

"No," he managed to grunt, jerking his head away just in time to avoid the woman's blade. She nicked his scalp an inch or so beyond his hairline, and a sheet of blood poured into his right eye.

"What's the matter, traitor?" she taunted. "Afraid to meet our god?"

"I… never betrayed… Thalil," Sasha said, the effort exhausting.

"It hardly matters. You stand no chance now. I'm going to cut you to ribbons. Slowly. None of you will survive."

She was right. He could no longer lift his blade. They were dead. Panting, trying to at least die on his feet instead of facedown at this sadistic bitch's boots, Sasha saw a flash of light off in the distance. In his depleted state, he didn't ponder it. A pulse of warm air that smelled, oddly enough, like fresh cream and honey, broke like a wave over the desolate area between the inn and the warehouse. Sasha blinked. What had happened? He still felt drained, but he lifted his dagger with almost his usual speed and managed to slice the woman's throat, taking a piece of her earlobe as he cut across her neck and jaw. She shrieked, pressed the heel of her hand to the gushing wound, and ran off into the mist.

Sasha remembered the egg in his opposite fist. He was just about to launch it when he saw Duncan running toward him, leaving Garith and Lysander to fight quite capably, back to back. The tip of the knight's blade erupted from the other swordsman's chest just as Sasha's glass-dust and venom bloomed before the dark assassin's face. He dropped to his knees, wailing and clawing at his eyes. Sasha approached him slowly, knife in hand.

"Sasha, must you?" Duncan asked. "He's such a young man."

"It is necessary, my friend. If I spare him, I'll have made a blood enemy. An enemy for life. It would be a worse slight than killing him. Turn away if you don't wish to see." Without looking to see if Duncan turned or not, Sasha knelt, grasped the assassin's dark curls, and turned his face toward the sky, stretching and exposing his throat. "Go to Thalil." He sputtered and choked on blood for less than a minute before falling still.

When Sasha rose, he saw that either Garith or Sander had managed to dispatch one of the assassins. The other, attacking with his staff, would not last long, as he managed only to parry blows, attempting no attack of his own. Garith drove his knee into the assassin's groin, and he doubled over. Sasha saw the assassin's elbow draw back, his arm tight to his body and his fist aimed at the prince's belly.

"Damn it," he spat, running past a confused-looking Duncan and diving the last several feet. With all of his might, Sasha plunged his blade deep into his brother's kidneys, one and then the other.

"What? I had him!" Sander whined.

Sasha used his boot to flip the man to his back and kicked his wrist so his arm sprawled out from his body. He pointed to the hidden blade, and Garith's eyes grew wide. "You owe me your life twice over now," he mentioned casually to the prince. Sasha wiped his eye. The drying blood had started to make his lashes clump together.

"What an interesting weapon," Sander said, kneeling and reaching out.

Sasha seized the collar of his tabard just in time. "Idiot," he said. "There's likely enough poison on the blade to kill you with a tiny scratch. On second thought, why in my god's name did I stop you?"

The young knight hissed and pulled away from Sasha, but Duncan and Garith chuckled. The assassin, or the former assassin—what was he now, anyway? Just Sasha, he supposed. He would have to learn exactly what that meant, who he was beneath the order armor and the many masks he'd worn for them. Being so exposed frightened him, but Duncan's hand on his shoulder bolstered his courage. Sasha—however he defined himself now—joined their relieved laughter, which grew giddier and harder, until a scream in the distance startled them back to silence.

"Mother goddess!" Duncan cursed, running in that direction. "Yarrow!"

Chapter Twenty

DUNCAN, INJURED and exhausted, ran hard past the quiet, dockside warehouses toward the flashes of light and clouds of sulfurous smoke. Sasha, covered in blood, bounded along beside him, and the prince and his guard followed a little behind. At the moment, Garith didn't concern Duncan nearly as much as Yarrow. Though they'd had little choice, they'd left the mage to fight alone. Duncan would never forgive himself if something happened to Yarrow, if he failed to protect him.

They rounded the corner and skidded to a halt before the miraculous sight before them. Duncan had never seen magic-users do battle, and in any other situation, he might have been fascinated. The two mages stood hundreds of yards apart, hurling streams of luminous color at one another. As to the function of the dazzling display, Duncan couldn't begin to guess. The enemy sorcerer, his tall, lanky body swathed in armor similar to but simpler than Sasha's, with fewer buckles and no mean, spiked adornments, hurled a sphere of sickly greenish light that reminded Duncan of infection. Yarrow quickly erected his shimmering, bowl-shaped shield and deflected the grotesque stuff. The other enchanter, a stunning young man with long, black hair, and onyx, almond-shaped eyes reminiscent of Sasha but with bone white skin, made some strange hand motions.

A wave of chill air, smelling like an old tomb opened after centuries, rushed toward Yarrow, but he brushed it away like a spider web. It dispersed with a scent that reminded Duncan of the butter churns back home. Yarrow's eyes glowed, trailing light like a falling star when he turned his head. "Is that the best you can do?" he yelled at the other mage. "That same, tired, weakening spell? Against me?"

"Is it him?" Duncan whispered to Sasha.

"What do you mean is it him?" Garith asked, pushing in front of Sander. "Do you recognize that other wizard? Who is he?"

"Your Highness, I must insist you remain behind me, with your faithful bodyguard, for your own safety." When Garith obeyed, Duncan took Sasha's elbow and pulled him out of the range of the other men's ears. "Sasha, is it him?"

The assassin's quick, dark eyes analyzed Yarrow's movements for a few seconds, and he nodded. "The expressions and mannerisms are Yarrow's," he said.

The idea of being observed and evaluated with such skill and scrutiny unnerved Duncan. Surely Sasha had studied him as intently at some point. At the moment, it didn't matter. Yarrow did. "I've never faced a magic-user. Have you?"

"Yes."

The weird bursts of energy volleyed back and forth, Yarrow's blue and silver, scented like snow, summer storms, and burning minerals. The other returned sickly ochre and algae-tinted clouds that reeked of decay. Duncan didn't want to imagine what one of those spells might do if Yarrow didn't repel it.

"You've faced them," he said to Sasha again. "How do we help Yarrow?"

"Spell-casters need to concentrate. Most of them need much more time than Yarrow to prepare an enchantment. If we can distract him, we'll give our mage an opening."

"Should we attack?"

Sasha inclined his head with a barely perceptible nod. "Yes, but from a distance."

Another wave of putrid mist roiled across the muddy tract between the mages.

"Cousin, look out!" Garith yelled.

Yarrow's head snapped in the direction of his voice, and the barrier he'd been erecting faltered. The mucus-green fog engulfed him, and he convulsed, fell to his knees, and clawed at the flesh of his arms. The other wizard laughed like old bones rattling. He reveled in his victory only for a moment, though, before turning and noticing the others, especially Sasha. "Traitor!" he roared, rushing toward the assassin. Though he waved his arms in circles above his head, no power manifested.

"He's used it up," Sasha said. "Go to Yarrow. I have him."

"Tam Lysander, guard the prince," Duncan barked as he hurtled over barrels and crates to reach his mage.

"Tam," Sander said, his fist to his heart. He drew his sword, widened his stance, and moved in front of Garith. The mage-assassin paid them no heed, though; his attention focused on his defector-brother.

Sasha was too quick, diving behind a stack of crates and avoiding the sorcerer's watery flow of power. As soon as Duncan saw Sasha safe, he closed the distance between himself and Yarrow's prostrate form, turned the mage over, and crouched beside him. Yarrow dug at his left arm, and Duncan unlaced his bracer and rolled his sleeve up. The flesh beneath looked grayish green, and it smelled. As Duncan watched, the mysterious infection spread up and down Yarrow's limb.

"Heal yourself!" he told his friend. "Hurry."

His mage whimpered, choked, and managed to gag out Duncan's name. The meat of his arm mortified as Duncan looked on, quickly spreading toward Yarrow's chest and heart.

"Heal!" He slapped Yarrow with his fingers, just enough to sting. Sasha had his hands full with the enemy sorcerer; he needed aid. But Yarrow might rot if he didn't dispel the sinister enchantment. "Heal, Yarrow. You must!"

"It is… hard for me to give," Yarrow breathed, the fingers of his healthy arm moving up and down the putrefying one, drawing glyphs Duncan didn't understand. "Even to myself."

"Do what you must. Can I help you?"

"You're here, Duncan. Keep me safe just a moment." Yarrow's lips moved soundlessly and his hands drew complex symbols in the air before his face. "Yes, yes, I need you. This is insidious. I can't banish it in any of the usual ways. No! Of course I tried that! Get rid of it, but nothing else."

"Who are you talking to, Yarrow?"

"Who do you think?"

"Goddesses." Duncan shivered, but didn't relinquish the mage's small body. Instead he held Yarrow closer, attempting to comfort him as he ousted whatever he needed to be rid of. Seizures racked his slight form, and his head thrashed against Duncan's chest. Duncan tried to still Yarrow's flailing limbs so he wouldn't be struck. After many frightening minutes, he began to calm down, and his tremors subsided. The younger man coughed and retched, depositing a globule of olive-gray mucus on the street. When he'd expelled it, his skin gradually took on its proper, peach-bronze hue, pushing the edges of the fetid patch back until only a small area remained at the inside of his wrist. Then it, too, healed over. His arm returned to a normal pigment, the once gray, shriveled skin growing plump and rosy.

"Nasty spell, that one," he said, already more lucid. He grasped Duncan's hand and Duncan helped him up.

To their left, Sasha darted from crate to barrel and back, drawing the fire of the other mage. *Tiring him out*, Duncan realized with approval. Shards of wood exploded into the sky before clattering to the ground, as the assassin kept one step ahead of the sorcerer. If they'd been in Selindria, the noise, smoke, and bursts of light would have drawn dozens of knights and city guards. In Felgard, though, people kept to their own affairs and avoided things like this. The enemy spellcaster stabbed his arm toward a pile of logs, sending them flying. Sasha didn't completely avoid the attack, just the brunt of it. He fell on his elbows but got to his feet before a second passed. Still, he looked tired. Duncan had never seen anyone with Sasha's speed, but he was human and would slow with fatigue in time. The mage stood with his back to Duncan and Yarrow. Duncan wondered if he could manage to run him through. It would be a cowardly attack, but did this vermin really deserve better?

Yarrow made the decision for him. "Turn around, you son of a whore!" he yelled in a clear, strong voice with no hint of another presence. "I'm not finished with you yet."

"I'd love to play with you some more," the man said over his shoulder in the same artificial, alluring drawl Sasha sometimes used. "Just give me a moment to dispose of the refuse." He turned his attention back to the decimated splinters of wood. "Come out and take what you deserve, you miserable little turncoat!"

"No! Face me!" Yarrow pointed and stung his opponent with a small, blue spark, just enough to draw his attention.

Snarling, the order mage turned on his heel and strode back to where Yarrow stood. Only a few feet separated them. "Fine. If you insist, I'll finish you first. It's a bit of a pity, though. You're quite intriguing. It's not often I meet another mage with as much power as myself."

"You still haven't," Yarrow said, the blue glow sparking up around his silhouette. "I have more power than you could ever dream of."

"Well, we'll see. I do hate to destroy you. Can you imagine all the magical things we might do instead? What's your name, anyway?"

"Shut up." Yarrow's aura flared. The suggestion of wings appeared. Bits of shimmering blue rose toward the smoggy sky and drifted off, like sparks from a campfire. As anyone with a grain of wisdom might, the other magician flinched before regaining his composure. Duncan found it disconcerting how much some of his mannerisms resembled Sasha's. He wore the same emotionless mask, and replaced it just as quickly when some shock made it slip. The order trained its agents well. Even so, the other man took a few steps back.

"What is that power?" he breathed. "I've never felt anything like it."

Instead of answering, Yarrow scooped the man up in the spectral hand he often conjured, slammed him against a warehouse wall, and held him there with his legs dangling a dozen feet above the ground. With a savage grin, Yarrow squeezed the mage until he gasped for air, advancing on him as he tightened his grip. "You dare to compare yourself to me? You try to rot my flesh? To insult and attack a companion of mine?"

Though his face darkened, the other man tried to speak. Yarrow spread the translucent blue fingers and dropped him. He landed hard in a pile of the debris he'd caused. Yarrow jogged to where he huddled, holding his ribs with one arm and cradling his head in his other hand. The hand and arm he'd summoned moved around to his back and arced up from his shoulder blade like a single wing. Sasha and Duncan stood just behind him.

"It doesn't matter if you kill me," the man said, lifting his face out of his hand. Blood seeped from his nostrils. "One of my brothers will finish the job. No one leaves the order." He pointed at Sasha. "Traitor! You betrayed your brethren, turned your back on your calling, and insulted Thalil. The order will see you ended. We'll never stop hunting you. I hoped I'd have the honor of killing you, but it must fall to another. You know you cannot escape us."

"Let Sasha go and I'll let you live."

"That's unwise, Yarrow," Sasha said.

"His life isn't mine to give." The man reached out for Yarrow's exposed arm, and Duncan saw putrid, green energy crawling over his fingers like maggots. In a quick motion worthy of an assassin, he grasped Yarrow's wrist. Duncan would never know what horrible affliction he intended, because upon contact with Yarrow's luminous sheath the wormy power fizzled and disappeared into puffs of sickly yellow smoke. With a scream he pulled his scorched hand back and buried it in his armpit. "They'll never let him go," he repeated, out of breath from the pain.

"We should kill him," Sasha said, a dagger already in his hand. "If you find it distasteful, I'll see to it."

"Wait," Yarrow said.

The order mage used the second of distraction to pull a small, hidden knife from his armor with his burned hand. In an impossibly quick motion, he whipped his arm in Sasha's direction, hissing, "Traitor."

Yarrow was faster. Before the other mage's arm completed its graceful circle, Yarrow's phantasmal arm swung around and intercepted. One of the long, much more solid-looking claws he'd added sliced the other sorcerer's arm just above the elbow. The severed limb flew a few feet to the right and landed in a puddle, still clutching the knife. The pale mage's eyes bulged out and he screamed and screamed, bloody froth flying from his mouth. Duncan noticed the stump didn't bleed, cauterized by Yarrow's power.

The white-haired mage bent down and slapped the black-haired one until he stopped screaming. Then Yarrow grabbed the front of his armor and pulled their faces close. "You wanted to know my name. It's Yarroway L'Estrella. Remember it. Take it back to the masters of your order. Tell them if they come after Sasha again, we're coming after them. I will decimate your order to the last man. I'll hunt them to the corners of the world and kill every last member if another assassin dares to threaten me or my friends. Go. Tell them."

Yarrow released the other mage, and he stumbled to his feet. After retrieving his lost arm, he disappeared down a side street.

"That was a poor decision," Sasha said, putting his hand on Yarrow's shoulder. "He'll seek revenge."

"Let him," Yarrow said, low and deadly.

Garith and Sander, who'd taken shelter behind an overturned wagon, joined the other three men. Both seemed unharmed, if a little shaken.

"Your Highness," Duncan said, a little ashamed. He'd almost forgotten the prince existed. "Thank the goddesses you're safe. Tam Lysander is a very capable guard."

The younger knight smiled and looked bashfully away. "Is that cursed warlock dead?"

"He's gone."

"For now, you mean. I heard what he said. Your friend Sasha will only lure more of his order to the prince. We can't travel with him any longer."

"No, Sander," Garith said. "If not for Sasha I'd already be dead."

"He was hired to kill you!"

Now that the battle rush subsided, the idea of Sasha assassinating the prince percolated down through the layers of Duncan's mind. "He didn't do it," he said, under his breath and more to himself. "He could have. He's been taught all of his life that he must. But… he didn't." Still, he had questions, like who had hired Sasha and when. How long had Sasha been traveling with Duncan and Yarrow only to get close to Garith?

As if reading Duncan's mind, or maybe he'd used his considerable talent for deciphering facial expressions, Sasha said, "I know you have questions, my friend. I'll answer them, but now is not the time. We should get away from here as soon as possible, in case there are more of my former brethren about."

"Where will we go?" the prince asked.

"Away," Sasha said. "Away from where anyone can see us. Out of the city, to begin with. If you follow me, I'll get you out through the dark alleys. The sooner we reach the countryside, the better. Keep alert and stay behind me. Duncan, Yarrow, keep the prince between us."

All of them did as Sasha said, because they knew they wouldn't survive if they didn't.

Chapter
Twenty-One

FOR THE next three days, the small party kept to the woods. They grew suspicious, jumping at any snap of a twig or rustle of a leaf. At night they camped as best as they could, constructing scant shelter from deadfall and huddling together on the ground under the single blanket Yarrow carried to withstand the cold. Sasha's pack contained only things meant to take life, nothing to help sustain it. The others, in their haste to escape the assassins, had left their things in the tavern. Only Duncan knew how to hunt, and he couldn't always find enough game to fill their stomachs. Yarrow felt fortunate he'd learned to create at least a small flame, enabling them to cook their food and providing at least a little warmth. They melted snow for water but couldn't spare enough to wash.

By the fourth day, all five men were cold, hungry, filthy, and exhausted. For the first time, Yarrow saw Sasha's face dusted with black whiskers. Circles almost as dark as his irises lined the assassin's eyes. They'd stopped to rest, as fatigue and poor eating made them all weak. Sasha perched on a snowy stump and took out a whetstone to sharpen a dagger. As usual, Duncan stalked out into the trees in search of small game. Sander and Garith found a fallen tree a few hundred yards off and spoke softly together. Yarrow went to Sasha and gingerly reached for his hair. His fingertips found the soft tresses, and he smiled when Sasha leaned into his touch. He continued dragging his blade across his stone, the rhythmic scraping the only sound in the small clearing, as Yarrow stroked his head and kneaded his scalp.

"I have so much I need to say to you, I don't even know where to begin," he said, watching the winter sun glint off Sasha's dark hair.

"There's no need."

"There is. I understand how much it means. What you did. What you didn't do."

"They called me traitor. Coward." Yarrow heard a slight tremble in Sasha's voice he never imagined he'd find there.

"You're neither. Besides, we killed all of them."

"We did. When I was in the order… Thalil, it still doesn't feel real that I'm not. But when I was, I would have ached for the blood of any member who turned against us. I'd have been just as eager to kill them as they were to kill me."

"They didn't understand the circumstances. Do I even have to say aloud that you did the right thing?"

Sasha looked up, and Yarrow met his beautiful, dark eyes and found pain in them. He wrapped his hand around the back of Sasha's neck, and earned a small, brief smile. "Right and wrong had nothing to do with it, Yarrow. I didn't, don't, care a shred for your cousin. His life has no value to me at all. I just knew that after I did the work, I'd have to leave you and Duncan. It was my own selfishness, and nothing more profound, that saved the prince's life."

"I understand better than you can imagine, Sasha."

"Will Duncan?"

"I don't know.

"Yarrow, is there any chance we can… have something together?"

"I don't know.

Why lie to him, beloved? You don't trust me not to hurt them, but you're just as selfish as your pretty friend. As I see it, you can choose to trust me or you can leave them.

Would you ever let me go?

This is no time to jest, beloved. Especially not about something so absurd. You're far too precious to me to give up. I made a promise to you, and I'll keep it. With my help, you'll be the greatest sorcerer the world has ever known.

What if I don't care anymore?

Beloved, it mocked. *I know you better than that. I know you better than anyone.*

Please leave me alone. Just let me be here with Sasha in peace for a few minutes.

It did, and the two of them stood in silence uninterrupted even by birds. Yarrow moved around behind Sasha and crossed his arms over Sasha's chest. Sasha kissed the back of Yarrow's hand. Neither, Yarrow knew, cared that the prince and his knight might see. Being together for a few minutes meant more than their opinions. Neither of them said another word until Duncan came back from the forest.

"Any luck, my friend?" Sasha asked, his voice unusually thick and coarse.

"No, I'm sorry." He looked away from them. "We should move on. I'll try again this evening. I won't let us go to bed hungry." He left to say a few words to Sander and Garith.

"It hurts him that he can't provide for us," Sasha said, shaking his head. "With everything we're suffering, not being able to take care of us hurts him most."

"He's a good man," Yarrow agreed. "A rare one. We're… we're lucky."

Sasha actually smiled as he followed the knight.

Yarrow fell into step beside him and, as they had for days, they picked their way through the frozen wood. At the head of their sad little procession, Duncan and Sander hacked the thick briars down with their swords to clear a path for the others. Their breath froze in heavy clouds around them with their exertion. When they'd first met, Yarrow had despised Tam Lysander. Watching him now, he thought Sander might be a bit like Duncan as the years passed by. He thought Garith could do much worse.

You're awfully introspective today, beloved.

People are not so far beneath me as I've always thought.

Actually, Yarrow, they are. You're far superior to these insects, and you know it.

I used to think so, but now I'm not so sure.

Think on it later, my mage. Something is coming. You need to be ready.

Yarrow rolled his eyes and almost broke down. *What's coming? Can't we get a moment's rest? It's one thing after the other on this silly errand. I should have listened to you and refused. But if I had—it doesn't matter now. What comes?*

It's far. I'm not sure what it is yet. By evening, I'll know.

Yarrow could do nothing but trudge through the forest, his toes numb inside his boots. The wind picked up, and snow and ice pelted them from the north. Yarrow put his hood up, jammed his hands inside his sleeves, and pushed his shoulders up to his ears. His face tingled with the assault of the frigid air. He bowed his head and just put one foot in front of the other. Afternoon stretched into eternity. His body screamed with cold and exhaustion. He couldn't imagine how his companions bore it. Of any of them, he'd dealt most with such punishment.

The sky finally blushed rose and coral with the coming of evening just as they reached the edge of the forest. Familiar Selindrian farmland stretched as far as the horizon. Sunset painted the fallow fields the soft peach-pink of heated flesh. Yarrow wanted nothing more than to make their rough camp, so at least he could be near his lovers. He'd take their warmth and proximity if he couldn't have their intimate affections. Goddesses, he just wanted to touch them.

It's not to be, beloved. Look there.

At the very limit of his vision, Yarrow perceived a cluster of dark shapes converging on the crest of a hill. He squinted and strained. *Men?* he asked his companion. *Men on horseback? Knights? Can you see the livery?*

You'll know soon enough.

"Duncan," Yarrow yelled. "We should go back into the forest. Men, knights, maybe, are coming. We should hide."

"I don't see anyone," the knight called over his shoulder.

"Please trust me."

"I will. Let's get back beneath the trees."

They all hurried to comply, rushing back into the cover of the wood and crouching behind thick trunks or bracken. Yarrow readied his magic as his companions drew weapons. All of them waited in the lengthening shadows, hoping they hadn't been seen.

Hooves thundered across the fields as a dozen chargers cantered toward the edge of the wood. When they reached it, they spread out, searching. They called back and forth to one another, almost as if they knew what they sought. Then, to the mage's shock, a familiar voice yelled his full name.

"Yarroway L'Estrella, you have nothing to fear from us! We know you're here. I implore you to show yourself and speak with me."

"What do we do?" Sasha hissed, kneeling behind an evergreen shrub. "We're sorely outnumbered by these knights. Should we fight?"

"No," Yarrow said, touching his cheek. "I don't know why he's here, but that's my brother. I'll speak with him. Stay hidden. I swear to the Cast-Down and the goddesses alike, Sasha, I will not let you be harmed."

"I know that. I've always known."

"I love you, Sasha."

"I… Yarrow. I think I feel the same. I've never known love, so I can't be sure. Now is not the time to contemplate these things, though."

"Wait here." Yarrow slowly stepped from behind the tree, his hands held out perpendicular to his waist, fingers spread. He walked to the edge of the forest, where his older brother sat atop a roan stallion. Rowan's dirty-blond hair fluttered in the cold breeze. He looked as serious as a priest at a funeral. "What do you want?" Yarrow asked. "If you've come to take me or one of my friends, you're going to need many more knights."

"Let us talk, brother."

"Are my friends in any danger?"

"No, Yarrow." Rowan swung his leg behind him to dismount and landed lightly on the frozen ground. He took a few tentative steps toward Yarrow. "My men and I have been looking for you."

"Why?" *This could be a trap.*

Anything is possible, beloved.

"You were sent by the queen in search of the prince," Rowan said with growing annoyance. "Did you find him?"

"What if I did?"

"Then we must get him to safety, Yarrow. You've been away a long time. You have no idea what's been going on in your absence."

"Tell me, then," Yarrow insisted, still not fully convinced his companions weren't in danger. Still, Rowan was no master of subterfuge, and he seemed sincere.

"I will, brother. As soon as I get all of you to safety. Our camp is only a few miles from here. We should go quickly."

I don't think he's lying, Yarrow said to the other.

No, I don't either.

Yarrow had to admit that camp, with fresh water, tents, food, blankets, and fires, sounded like paradise. He motioned for his friends to come out of the trees. They emerged and stood behind him.

"Goddesses, Garith!" Rowan said, embracing his cousin. "We'd feared the worst. Thank heaven you still live."

"You should thank your brother," the prince responded, "and his brave and skillful companions. Also, my own guard, Tam Lysander." He broke away from Rowan to present the young knight, who bowed respectfully.

"We'll have time for introductions later, Your Highness. Each of you can ride with one of my knights." As tired as they were after walking for three days, none of them argued, not even Sasha.

TAM ROWAN'S camp stretched for miles across the plain of Everdale, or at least Duncan assumed they'd reached Everdale by now. Thousands of men, from knights to foot soldiers to lowly stable boys moved around hundreds of differently colored tents. Smithies, kitchens complete with bakeries, stables, and armories had been set up, all of them scenting the cold, evening air. Duncan conceived of a million questions, but concern for his companions drove them back. The four younger men had slept little since leaving Felgard and eaten less. All of them looked terrible. They still had injuries from their encounter with the assassins. Thinking of the assassins reminded Duncan how much he craved some conversation with Sasha.

The knights dismounted and handed their animals off to servants. Duncan, unused to riding now, pulled his heels against his ass to stretch his legs before winding through the throng in search of his friends. Several knights spirited Garith and Lysander away before Duncan could protest. He watched them lead the prince and his guard toward a large tent emblazoned with Lockhaven livery. Since Garith would certainly be safe with Yarrow's kinsmen, Duncan made no move to stop them. Sasha found him first, and they made their way over to Yarrow, who stood rubbing the nose of a buckskin gelding.

Rowan joined them after speaking with some of his men. "Come with me," he said. "I'll show you to a tent. You all look like you could use some rest and refreshment." They followed him through the bustling camp to a tent, smaller than many but large enough for Duncan to stand comfortably within. Two mats sat on the floor. Pushed together, they'd be more than big enough for the three of them to sleep comfortably. A table held bread, meat, water, and even a jug of wine. The torches lit and warmed the space, but Duncan's breath still misted when he exhaled. After a few moments, a servant with a pail entered and filled a large, metal basin with hot water. The boy covered it with a towel to hold in the warmth before departing.

"Take some time," Rowan said. "Wash up and eat something. When you're ready, join me in my tent. We have much to discuss."

First, they stripped down to their trousers to wash while the water was still warm. Yarrow dipped his head in the basin to clean his hair. Sasha shaved his face with his dagger and a small mirror taken from his pack. Duncan saw many of Sasha's wounds would certainly scar, the one on the side of his neck worst of all. They'd be constant reminders to the assassin of his betrayal and the decisions he'd made. Duncan wanted to say something to him, but he found himself so overwhelmed by everything that he didn't even know where to begin.

Yarrow tore a loaf of bread in half, took the wine, flopped down on one of the mats, and draped a blanket over his bare shoulders. Before joining him, Duncan ran wet fingers through his hair and tied it back. It, along with his beard, needed trimming as soon as possible.

"How did my brother know we were looking for the prince?" Yarrow wondered aloud. He nestled closer to the heat of Duncan's chest and reached for Sasha, who sat between the mage's open legs and leaned back against him. Yarrow passed him the wine, and Sasha drank deeply.

"We'll have to ask him," Duncan responded.

"Goddesses, I could sleep for days. I never thought I'd be so happy to see the inside of a war tent. This feels like a palace after these last few nights."

"I'm afraid we can't rest yet, Yarrow," Duncan said, stroking his cheek. "I for one am eager to know what's going on. We must speak with Rowan soon."

"Must we?" Sasha asked. "We've delivered the prince to safety. I say we've already done much more than expected. I doubted we'd be able to keep him or ourselves alive as long as we have. Whatever battle they're planning to fight, it isn't necessarily ours."

"It is mine," Duncan said, "as a knight of Selindria."

"Pardon me," Sasha said. "I'd forgotten that not all of us has lost his title and calling to this cause."

"Sasha." Duncan reached across Yarrow to wind his fingers into the assassin's. "I don't have any words to express my gratitude to you. I understand the scale of what you did. I know you feel it as a loss, but maybe you've gained more than you lost. You're free of them now."

"I'm nothing now. Nobody."

"Not to us." Duncan squeezed his hand. "What would you have us do?"

He sighed through his teeth. "I don't know. You feel a duty to these men, but I can hardly reconcile risking my life for people who have treated me worse than trash. I'll never hold a place in their world. Why should I fight for them? Yarrow, what do you say? You don't belong among them either."

"No, that's true. I'd at least like to hear what Rowan has to say. He's my blood, as are Garith and Aunt Den. But you, you and Duncan, you mean even more than blood to me now."

They sat in silence at the magnitude of his words. Duncan wondered if the three of them could really make a place in the world together, if the three broken pieces could form a cogent whole. Could they be what Yarrow suggested, as close as blood kin, a strange sort of family?

"We should get this over with," Yarrow said, kissing each of them on the cheek before standing up to finish dressing. "Will you come, Sasha?"

He carefully finished securing the buckles of his armor. "I'll listen. I can promise no more. I'll wait for the two of you outside. I find I desire some air." He left through the flap.

Yarrow's eyes caught Duncan's gaze. "He's lost everything," the mage whispered. "How can we help him?"

"By being his friends." Duncan didn't know what else to say, so he squeezed Yarrow's delicate wrist and forced a smile.

Yarrow laughed and shook his head. "You know, I didn't think you'd ever count me among your friends when we started this disastrous journey, let alone Sasha. Look at us now."

"I'm glad," Duncan said. "I hope we can hold onto the friendship we've forged. Such friendship as this is uncommon. I don't want to lose it."

He waited for the strangely beautiful young mage to agree, to consent, finally, to be his partner. By now Yarrow could see how precious their love was, couldn't he?

"We should go." Yarrow joined Sasha outside, and Duncan could do little but follow them to the tent in the center of camp, closest to the armory and smithy. It was large enough for thirty horses or more. Lockhaven banners snapped in the breeze, and men in that valenny's livery stood guard at the entrance. They uncrossed their halberds and allowed the three men to enter.

A huge wooden table stood at the center of the tent, strewn with maps and papers. On the benches around it sat Rowan, Garith, Sander, and four other knights from different valennies. Duncan, Yarrow, and Sasha took their places next to the prince and his guard, across from the other knights.

Rowan, at the head of the table, welcomed them. "Thank you for all that you've already done, brother. Tam Duncan, you too have gone beyond what duty dictated. Both of you have my thanks."

"And mine," Garith said. "Now, let's waste no more time. Tam Rowan, please tell me what has happened while I've been in hiding."

"Your Highness, you know already that you and your mother have been falsely accused of orchestrating the attack upon my brother, Duncan, and the assassin paid to pose as you. You have also been accused of an illicit affair with Lady Ambra Piers."

"Ambra?" Garith spat. "I never so much as touched her hand! Why would I? I am engaged to be married. The last thing I need is a bastard child and a scandal."

"I spoke to this woman," Sasha said. "She admitted to me the affair was a lie. Her father coerced her into it. She was even prepared to come forward at the trial."

"Until her untimely death," Rowan said, biting off each word as he glared at Sasha.

"Not by my hand," Sasha said casually.

"How can we believe that?" Rowan said.

"I believe it," Duncan said.

"As do I," Garith added, causing everyone to gasp. "I know this much, if Sasha had wanted poor Ambra dead, he could have made sure she was never found. Or that it looked like an accident, or someone else's work."

"Hardly a compliment, Your Highness," Sander said.

Sasha raised his head and looked every man around that table in the eye. "I have killed many, many people. I don't deny it. I can tell you most of their names, if you'd like. I didn't kill Ambra Piers. I wouldn't be afraid or ashamed if I had, but I didn't."

"Nonetheless, the girl perished before she could refute the allegation of the affair. Since no one could prove otherwise, the accusation was presented at the queen's trial. Also the queen's magical tome and some jewelry used to pay the assassins that attacked the false prince."

"Those items were stolen," Yarrow said, smacking the table.

"No one could prove that, brother. Also, several of the queen's ladies in waiting testified that the queen had been sneaking away to meet with men late at night. It made for damning evidence, all together."

"If only I'd stayed behind," Yarrow lamented. "I could have made those filthy sluts tell the truth."

"Yarrow, I doubt that magically altered testimony would meet with much trust," Rowan said, his distaste for his brother's abilities barely veiled.

With a sharp laugh, Yarrow asked, "Do you think they would have known?"

"I'm the one who should have been there," Garith said. "I should have made these turncoats accuse me to my face. Was, was my mother convicted? What happened?"

Rowan braced himself. "The queen was convicted of treason and sentenced to death. As were you, Garith, should you ever be found."

"No!" Garith shouted, leaping to his feet. Sander joined him. "How did Father let that happen? Goddesses, tell me my mother isn't dead!"

"No, Your Highness," Rowan said. "The king insisted the sentence be held until some financial records could be gathered. That was when it started to go downhill."

"How so?" Duncan asked, shocked almost numb by what he'd heard.

"Most of the valens, bairns, and eyrles didn't look kindly on the king digging around in their treasuries. Some of them insisted the queen be executed and the prince found. His Majesty held his ground, and his loyal nobles stood with him. The others began to rally around Tam Taran. They became more and more vocal, demanding justice be carried out. The priestesses of Vestrafori supported them. It wasn't long before those nobles opposing the king's decision began to gather their forces. King Agarick gathered his own. Then the royal auditors presented their findings, and everything broke in half.

"It didn't take long for the king to see that large sums of gold had gone missing without explanation from several of the noble coffers. You won't be surprised to learn that those nobles who stood against the king and queen were the very same ones with the gold missing from their treasuries. These missing sums go back years. They've been planning this for quite a while. Rayne thinks Garith's impending marriage forced their hands. These traitors knew if they didn't act now, it would be too late. They'd never be able to overthrow the crown once Agarick and Garith had the vast forces of Gaeltheon supporting them. Rayne doesn't think they'd have acted so soon if they didn't have to.

"I doubt you'll be shocked at this point to learn that over four thousand sovereigns have gone missing from the Windwake treasury over the last five years."

"Tam Taran?" Garith gasped. "But why?"

"It hardly matters at this point, Your Highness," Rowan said, rubbing his forehead. "He and the nobles allied with him have been conspiring to frame you and overthrow your father for many years, and now they've gone even further."

"What is the situation, Tam Rowan?" Duncan asked, cold sweat breaking from his pores. Rowan's words implied a coming war: a civil war.

"You're a clever man and a good soldier, Tam Duncan. Your name is well respected. I'm sure you can figure out what happened next. When the king refused to execute the queen, and when he accused Taran and his supporters, they resisted. I'm sorry to say that those nobles standing against the throne outnumber those standing with the true king and queen. They're saying Agarick has no right to rule if he won't bow to justice and the will of his nobles. They've taken up arms."

"Goddesses," Duncan breathed. "We knew from the first attack that this conspiracy ran deep, but I never imagined so many nobles colluded, and to go so far as usurping the throne! It will come to war after all."

"Yes, tam, and maybe a brief one. Taran's forces at Lockhaven outnumber the king's five to one. Rayne is keeping the royal family safe within our citadel's sturdy walls, and has tasked me with gathering as many allies as I can. This is the army I've amassed. I wish it was larger, but many of Agarick's knights are scattered in the wilds around his fortress, rousting out the bandits reportedly terrorizing the area."

"That rotten son of a whore planned that too," Duncan said, recalling their attack in the canyon. "I myself sent word to the king that those bandits needed to be ousted."

"And there is more of the missing gold," Rowan said. "Certainly lining the pockets of those thugs."

"Why is he doing this to my family?" Garith asked again. "We trusted him. My father trusted him above anyone. I… I'll kill this blackguard myself! What puppet is he planning to sit on my father's throne?"

"I don't know, Highness," Rowan said. "These traitors tried very hard to win the support of my elder brother, Valen Rayne, because of our family's ties with your own. They went almost so far as to offer him the crown outright, with many stipulations, of course. Lockhaven will stand with Agarick, though. We are loyal. I'm sorry to say that were we not, this would have already ended with the conspirators' victory. Rayne and our knights are holding the castle, but they won't last forever."

"It is war, then," Duncan said. No matter how many times he repeated it, it didn't seem possible. A war on Selindrian soil, between Selindrians. "Goddesses. War. What is your strategy, Rowan?"

"Beyond gathering our forces and finding the prince, I… I don't know. I must admit I've never led men into battle before. But you have, Tam Duncan, and brilliantly. If you would lend me your wisdom, I'd humbly request that you serve as my second in command. I need a man who has fought before. Please."

"I would be honored, Tam Rowan. We should begin discussing details as soon as we can."

"Agreed. The rest of you are dismissed, though I would like to speak further with my brother. And I have a request of the assassin."

"My name is Sasha. If you wish something of me, you'll use it."

"I would like to speak with you, Sasha. I have a proposition that might interest you."

"I'll listen." Sasha sat back down and waited for the other knights to file out.

Duncan's heart cartwheeled. How could it have come to war in a few short months, and more importantly, was it a war they could win? He longed to study the maps and plan their strategy.

Rowan looked a lot like Yarrow, but he lacked Yarrow's smug self-assurance. The young man stood from his bench, paced across the back of the tent, and then sat back down. He had none of his brother's talent for masking his distress. His head dropped into his hands, and he rubbed his temples.

"Did you have something you wanted to discuss with me, Rowan?" Yarrow asked.

"Yes. I hate to admit it, but I need you. Selindria needs you. As I've said, we're outnumbered. I must ask you to fight with us, with your magic."

"Isn't this rich?" Yarrow said. "All the years you've spent mocking my magic, and now you want me to use it. Are you sure I won't embarrass the family?"

"Yarroway, this is serious!"

"Did Rayne tell you to say that?"

"No! I don't need the valen or the great mage telling me what to do! I'm not so worthless as everyone thinks! Fight for your country or don't, Yarroway, but I'm through being belittled by my brothers."

"I just don't know that I can take the place of a thousand knights," Yarrow said, a little shamed.

"We all know you can, if you're willing to use your power," Rowan said, almost daring his brother. "The choice is yours. Will you stand with your king?"

"I'll use my magic," Yarrow said. "Just don't overestimate my skills. I can't promise to turn the tide."

"Better than nothing," Rowan said. "Assassin—Sasha, I mean. I have a delicate proposal for you. I'd like to speak with you alone."

"Anything you must say can be said in front of my companions," Sasha told him.

"Very well. To be blunt, I'd like you to eliminate Tam Taran. His death won't necessarily win the day for our side, but he is a very charismatic leader and a capable strategist. Without him, his forces will face a severe disadvantage. The blow to the enemy's morale alone will be significant."

"What's the pay?" Sasha asked.

"Five hundred gold sovereigns."

"Not enough. I'll have to sneak behind the enemy's lines. It will be difficult to get past the bairn's guards, and even more difficult to sneak away when I've finished. Double it."

"No! You should be grateful not to be in prison, assassin! You should be honored at such an opportunity to serve Selindria."

"I'm not. Double it, or find someone else. If you think someone else can accomplish this."

"Damn you. Six hundred gold."

"No."

"You should beg to serve your king!"

"What king? I serve Thalil. Give me eight hundred and fifty gold and I'll send this Taran to my god as you request. Offer any less, and I have no more to say to you."

"Fine. Eight hundred and fifty sovereigns. Paid upon completion of your mission."

"Very well," Sasha said. "I don't need to tell you what will happen if you try to exploit or swindle me."

"No. I like sleeping with my eyes closed and my back unmarred. The king has authorized this, and your payment. Fear not. Taran is camped with his army outside our castle. Go there, sneak into his tent, and end him. Bring me his head," Rowan whispered.

"That will cost extra."

"Fine. Just do it, and do it soon. Preferably before he has time to devise his battle strategy and share it with his knights. I can provide you with a swift horse."

"I'll leave for Lockhaven now."

"No, Sasha, wait," Yarrow implored. "Stay the night to rest yourself, at least. Wait until the morning."

Duncan hoped the assassin would agree. He wanted another night with his lovers before they all risked their lives. As much as he hated to think about it, he'd been a soldier too long not to acknowledge that any battle might be a man's last.

"I'll leave for Lockhaven tomorrow at first light, then," Sasha said.

"Good," Duncan said. "We all need rest. We should retire for tonight." He left the tent, his companions following, hopefully as eager for some time alone as Duncan.

Chapter Twenty-Two

THE THREE men hurried into their assigned tent. Stew, water, wine and fresh bread with butter waited on the table, but they ignored it. Yarrow's eyes moved between Sasha and Duncan as they laid their gear and weapons on the dirt floor. They were so different in their musculature, their movements, their expressions and emotions, but both so sublime. Meeting one man who ignited such passion in him was a beautiful bonus on what had otherwise been an ill-fated and miserable errand. But two? Yarrow shucked his cloak off and let it pool on the ground behind him. He worked the worn leather of his armor free and dropped his pauldrons and bracers on top of his hooded cape.

Will we have some fun, beloved?

Oh yes. If I have anything to say about it, we'll have much fun indeed. Just don't be too obtrusive.

Let me experience just a little of it. Can you share with me just a bit, my mage?

You won't try to take over? And you won't numb me to it? I need to feel them.

We can experience it together, beautiful, if you'll allow it. Our sensations can overlap. We'll both feel the sensations to the fullest, and maybe even beyond, as we'll be sharing. You'll experience what I do, and I'll experience your feelings and perceptions. I promise you, beloved, it will be wonderful. It will be wonderful beyond anything you've ever imagined.

I won't put Sasha and Duncan in danger.

Nor will I. I swear it to you. Just let me experience them along with you. You've kept this from me for too long.

"Yarrow, are you all right?" Duncan asked, his massive fists closing protectively over both of Yarrow's hands.

"I am." Yarrow brushed his face against Duncan's whiskers, enjoying the rough texture against his chin and cheek. He angled his face and found Duncan's lips with his own. Their mouths slid against each other's slowly, relishing the sensation. After a moment, Duncan's teeth parted, and his tongue pushed against Yarrow's teeth, begging permission to enter Yarrow's mouth. Yarrow granted it eagerly, spreading his lips and inviting his knight to caress his palate. Sasha stepped behind Yarrow, and then his full, divine lips closed around the muscle of Yarrow's neck.

"Goddesses, yes," Yarrow said to all three presences sharing his experience. "It's been too long. Again." His companion's perceptions sparked along his skin in the wake of his lovers' mouths, deliciously intense. Its need permeated into Yarrow's muscles and skin, intensifying the need he felt. Its craving merged with his own, so strong he couldn't control it. "Take me. Please. I need you."

"What do you need, Yarrow?" Duncan panted against his wet cheek. "Tell me what you want."

"I… I… Duncan. Sasha, please!"

From behind him, Sasha picked at the lacings of Yarrow's shirt, working them open until the garment hung from the mage's slim chest. Duncan's head bowed, and his mouth captured Yarrow's hard nipple. He sucked it into the recesses of his mouth, his teeth teasing the edges of the erect flesh. Yarrow cried out, his hands closing around Duncan's hair. Sasha took full advantage of his exposed flesh, nipping and laving across his shoulders, his wet mouth cooling burning skin.

"Sasha, bite," Yarrow begged, the desperation in his voice surprising him. Maybe the request wasn't completely his own, but he wanted it, wanted it so much. His partner complied, sinking his teeth into the muscle stretching from Yarrow's neck to his shoulder. The pain bloomed in a delicious, compact bud of sensation. "Goddess, yes. More, please," Yarrow whimpered. Sasha sank his teeth deeper, tearing into Yarrow, ripping his skin. It felt so good. "More." Blood dribbled down Yarrow's back, the warm wetness electric against his aroused skin. "Yes." Sasha's teeth withdrew, and he wriggled his tongue into the wounds he'd made.

"More of what, my beautiful mage?" Sasha asked, his breath scraping across Yarrow's skin like sand, gritty yet enticing. He lapped at Yarrow's earlobe before nipping it hard, piercing the skin and drawing blood again.

"You make me so crazy."

Sasha's sensual laugh bounced across Yarrow's cheek, raising gooseflesh. "You were crazy long before you ever met me, my love."

"Say it again," Yarrow moaned, grasping Duncan's hip and grinding their erections together.

"My love," Sasha whispered, his hand moving up Yarrow's belly to scratch lightly over his chest and throat. "I've wanted to call you that for a long time now."

"So have I," Duncan said, capturing Yarrow's mouth again and kissing him until Yarrow feared his legs would give out. As they kissed, Duncan unfastened Yarrow's loose trousers and brushed them from his hips. Cold assailed Yarrow's genitals and legs, and his full balls drew up tight. He shivered and pressed closer to Duncan, still kissing him hard.

He tastes amazing, beloved. And he can really kiss.

Yarrow couldn't answer, because their hands were all over him, tickling his waist, caressing his arms and thighs, teasing his nipples and exploring the terrain of his torso. Duncan broke from his mouth, reached around Yarrow's neck, grasped Sasha by the hair and kissed him, squashing Yarrow between their bodies. His arms were trapped flush against him as both of their arms wound around him. His pants around his ankles fettered his feet, but there was no place he'd have rather been at that moment than tight between them. He never wanted the perfect moment, with all three of them joined, to end. Finally he understood that this was the only way they could be complete. Separately, they were flawed, more so than most men, but together they formed something enduring, something beautiful.

They pecked and nipped eagerly at each other's lips, the naughty sounds right next to Yarrow's ear. Since he could do little else at the moment, Yarrow dove down on the tiny strip of exposed flesh between Duncan's jawline and his collar, sucking the damp flesh between his teeth and savoring the now familiar tang of the knight's arousal.

"You taste like Yarrow," Sasha said, regaining his breath. "And like you underneath. It's alluring."

I want a taste, Yarrow's companion said, and Yarrow repeated it aloud.

Sasha twirled him around, almost making him trip over his tangled pants. Duncan caught him around the ribs as Sasha caught his mouth. The tang of his own blood, Duncan's sweat, and Sasha's sweet lips accosted Yarrow's senses, filling his perception to overflowing.

"Lift your foot," Duncan said. It took a moment for Yarrow to understand the request. "Good lad. Now the other one." After he got Yarrow out of his pants, boots, and stockings, the knight stayed on his knees, kissing his way up the back of Yarrow's leg. The light, reverent touches almost drove Yarrow over the edge. His knees shook, and he growled into Sasha's mouth. When Duncan eased his cheeks apart and ran his tongue up Yarrow's cleft, Yarrow gave up trying to stand, pitched forward against Sasha, and let Sasha hold him up. Duncan lapped up and down, making Yarrow's wrinkled opening convulse every time his tongue passed over it. Yarrow struggled to spread his legs, wanting more and saying so in an incoherent flood of words.

Duncan understood and drilled his tongue inside Yarrow's hole. Yarrow cried out as his muscles clamped down and his eyes screwed shut. He felt Sasha's finger press against his lips, and he tried to draw it into his mouth and suck it. Sasha laughed his mind-numbing laugh and said, "Quiet, my love. We don't need the whole camp knowing what we're about."

Yarrow opened his eyes to Sasha's mischievous grin and sparkling black eyes. *You certainly found yourself a pretty one, beloved.*

A beautiful one, Yarrow agreed, licking Sasha's finger from knuckle to tip. "I love everything about you."

"I know you mean that," Sasha said. "The pretty things and the ugly ones. I love you for that. For accepting me."

They kissed a few minutes more before Sasha sank to his knees. He took Yarrow's balls in one hand and reached for Duncan's hair with the other. He circled the tip of Yarrow's dick with just the point of his tongue, cleaning away the fluids already leaking down. Just as Duncan wiggled a first finger inside Yarrow and felt out his sweet spot, Sasha engulfed his length in the heat of his wonderful mouth.

"Goddesses!" Yarrow shrieked as they both doubled their efforts, pleasuring him from both sides. It felt like they kissed each other through his body; Yarrow had never imagined feeling something so powerfully erotic. It was all he could do not to collapse, and he grabbed Sasha's shoulder, but he couldn't stay on his feet. "I can't… I'm going to fall over…. Please, it's too much."

They pulled away, leaving him cold, and he stumbled to the mat in the corner. Duncan and Sasha, still on their knees, reached for each other, kissed, and even licked each other's cheeks and chins, sharing Yarrow's flavors. "Delicious, isn't he?" Duncan groaned.

"Mmm," Sasha agreed, swiping his tongue across Duncan's lips. "And so are you, my love."

"Don't forget about me," Yarrow said, the thick growl of the other heavy in his voice. Duncan and Sasha looked at each other for a brief, knowing moment. *Can you give me at least the illusion of privacy? Don't ruin this. This could be the last time I get to touch them.*

I'll hold my tongue.

Though surprised, Yarrow didn't question the entity's unexpected gift. It rarely did anything for his pleasure.

Sasha stood and unbuckled his armor, shrugging it off his shoulders. He looked down at Yarrow, his dark eyes burning into the mage. "I told you I'll never forget you, Yarrow. You're the first person ever to defend or value me. Any loyalty I have is to you and Duncan now. You're all that matters to me."

"Show me," Yarrow said, reaching out, desperate to feel Sasha's smooth skin and divine sinew again. He felt like he'd been denied his lovers forever.

Duncan reached up and grasped Sasha's slim thigh, his hand almost completely encircling it. Yarrow knew firsthand how tender the knight's large hands could be, and he wanted them on his body. He stretched his arm and brushed some of the locks that had escaped Duncan's tail from his damp cheek, his touch making Duncan's eyes flutter shut. Duncan shook his head to banish the distraction and looked back up at Sasha. "How can we do this?"

"What do you mean?" Sasha answered. "We can do this any way you like."

"But we finished your oil, and I left my pack back in Felgard."

"It's still not impossible," Yarrow said. As aroused as he felt, he might even like it dry and rough.

But Duncan shook his head. "I'm not willing to hurt you." His eyes met Yarrow's, and Yarrow knew he'd never suffer at Duncan's hands. For the first time in years, he trusted someone completely with his body and his heart. "Neither of you will ever experience pain because of me, not if I can help it." He looked down with disappointment.

Sasha smiled so deviously a tremor moved up Yarrow's back. He thought just looking at that smile might make him come. Sasha reached over to the table and picked up the little clay crock of butter. Yarrow shivered with anticipation as Sasha dug his finger in and scooped up some of the white cream. "I remember you saying how much you liked this," Sasha said, rubbing some of the butter across Duncan's lips, making them glisten.

"Mmm," Duncan said, sucking Sasha's finger into his mouth. His cheeks churned as he cleaned the sweet butter away. Watching them made Yarrow groan and grab his shaft. Finally Sasha drew his finger back. It popped from between Duncan's pursed lips with a slurp.

The assassin crouched down beside Yarrow. "If you thought that was good, my beautiful knight, I bet you'll love this." Sasha put his still damp and greasy hand on the center of Yarrow's chest. "Lie back, my love."

The butter Sasha slathered on his dick and balls felt cold at first, but in no time the heat of Yarrow's flesh and Sasha's palm softened, liquefied, and clarified it. All of the muscles across Yarrow's pelvis contracted at Sasha's ministrations, and when Sasha leaned in to kiss his neck, his cock bucked in Sasha's fist. "Not yet," he told Yarrow. "Duncan."

Yarrow closed his eyes and enjoyed the sweet sensation of Duncan's hands and lips moving up his thighs. Sasha licked and nipped up and down Yarrow's neck, across his clavicle, and down to tease his nipple. Yarrow couldn't even begin to stifle his whimpers and cries as their lips assaulted his body. To the Shade's Abode with the rest of the camp! Yarrow writhed on the mat, but the other men held him gently, Sasha at his shoulder and Duncan at his hip, as they continued their sensual torture. What was Duncan waiting for? Had Sasha spread that butter across his cock and balls for nothing, or would Duncan lick him clean? He couldn't wait much longer. Some broken declarations of love and need spilled from Yarrow's lips. They didn't even make sense to his own ears.

Sasha sat up and pulled his boots and pants off. He stretched out on the mat beside Yarrow, and Duncan moved his hand up Sasha's naked, golden skin as they kissed. Their hands found the assassin's erection at the same time. Some sparse, spiky hair framed it and dusted his balls since he'd neglected shaving. The texture intoxicated Yarrow, and he dragged his fingertips against it. Yarrow swallowed the deep growl Sasha made.

Sasha broke away from Yarrow's mouth. "My love, let me have you. Tell me I can."

"Oh goddesses, Sasha, yes. I love you. I want you to take me." He let Sasha's arm snake beneath his back, let Sasha shift his body onto his chest. Yarrow lay there, feeling his assassin's heart thump between his shoulder blades. He drew his knees up into peaks and put his feet outside Sasha's thighs. The butter was cold again for a second, but melted completely by the time Sasha's finger breached his tight ring of muscle. It jabbed into his knot of nerves, making his cock dribble. "More, Sasha. Duncan…."

Duncan tore his clothes away and tossed them in a pile with Yarrow's, and then just kept nibbling around Yarrow's groin and licking up and down his inner thighs as Sasha added a second, and then a third finger. He drove them in deep, twisting them, preparing Yarrow for him until Yarrow couldn't take anymore. His whole body was one tightly wound ball of his need. He whimpered incoherently, and Sasha understood, positioning himself at Yarrow's opening and pushing in without pretense.

"Duncan, give me your mouth," Yarrow begged. "Please." He felt the knight's warm, attentive lips withdraw from his heated flesh. Sasha thrust up slowly, crossing his arms across Yarrow's chest. When Yarrow's eyes sprung open, he saw Duncan sitting on his heels between their legs, looking down at them intently.

"Yarrow, will you have me?" Duncan asked in a deep, lusty voice, his cheeks burning scarlet.

"Um. What?" Yarrow managed as Sasha drove up into him, stealing his lucidity.

"Will you make love to me? Let me ride you?"

"Are you sure that's what you want?"

He nodded, looking so adorably shy Yarrow's heart melted. He wiggled one arm free from Sasha's grasp and reached out for Duncan's face. "Please come here."

Slowly, Duncan rose to his knees and found the little dish Sasha had forgotten. He climbed into Yarrow's lap, straddling them both. Sasha reached up and fondled Duncan's nipple, making Duncan's whole face and neck blush and perspire. He reached behind himself and spread their makeshift lubricant over his crack. He groaned, entering himself. Yarrow wished he could have watched. As Duncan sank down, letting Yarrow's weeping crown brush against his greased opening, Sasha stilled and nibbled the edge of Yarrow's ear. Duncan braced his hands, one on Sasha's shoulder and the other on Yarrow's, and gradually let Yarrow breach his body. The heat, pressure, and rhythmic contractions felt unreal, amazing, but Duncan's brows knit with pain.

"Take your time, my love," Sasha said. "Don't hurt yourself."

"No. I want this. You. Both of you." Yarrow felt the resistance finally give way, and he sank into Duncan to the hilt. "Yarrow, yes! Goddesses, you really are endowed."

"I… I don't want to hurt you," Yarrow muttered, barely able to form words amid the overwhelming sensations all over and inside his body.

"You're not. I love you." Duncan began to move slowly, circling his hips, his thrusts shallow, pushing himself down on Yarrow's cock and Yarrow's ass against Sasha. They let him set the pace, caressing his arms and chest. "Goddesses, I love looking down at your faces." He touched their cheeks, chins, lips, and brows. "You are both so beautiful." He picked up his pace, and when he'd found his rhythm, Sasha joined him, driving up into Yarrow. The mage could do little but cling to them and enjoy the intense pleasure they provided.

"Goddesses, I love the middle," he managed. "You two are amazing." He recovered the presence of mind to grasp Duncan's cock as their thrusts grew quick, rough, and desperate. They moved against each other in perfect tempo, as if they'd been together forever. To Yarrow, it felt that way. The lonely years before he'd met and loved these men felt like a bad dream. Now, with them all joined as closely as possible, he finally felt whole.

Duncan's muscular thighs shuddered with exertion, but he didn't relent. Instead he fell forward, kissing Yarrow hard, then Sasha, and then Yarrow again. Yarrow, sandwiched between them, could hardly breathe. His hand was squashed between Duncan's hard belly and his own, but he managed to stroke the knight. Duncan's whole body jerked hard, and his muscles locked down on Yarrow's shaft until it almost hurt. Sasha's nails bit Duncan's shoulder, and he bucked up forcefully into Yarrow, making Yarrow squeal.

"Yarrow, Yarrow, my love," the assassin panted, "I love to be inside you, to make love to you like this. You're so tight and sweet and perfect. Oh, Thalil!" He grasped Duncan by the back of the hair and

Yarrow around the throat, right under his jaw. He guided the knight's mouth to the mage's as he spent his passion deep inside Yarrow. "Yes. Love each other," he said as they kissed and he came.

Duncan assailed Yarrow's mouth until Yarrow feared his lips might split, riding Yarrow hard. "I do love you," he grunted, spilling inside Yarrow's fist. "I love you both. Will you come for me, Yarrow? Come inside me?"

"Thank you, Duncan," Yarrow said, grasping Duncan's hips and pulling him down hard as he exploded, blue and silver stars erupting behind his eyes. His entire being shook and everything went black for a second. He clung to his lovers, feeling like he'd be torn apart. He felt the wings flare out of his shoulders, but he managed to stamp them down as the aftershocks of his bliss broke over him again and again and again.

Afterward, Yarrow couldn't even move, he was so depleted. Duncan lifted off him, and then picked him up, cradling him in his arms like a bride before laying him down. He felt content as Sasha cleaned him and wrapped him in a blanket. The other two men kissed Yarrow's face and told him they loved him. He tried to return their sentiments, but nothing he could say would express what he felt.

That night, the three of them lay together over and over, until not even their love could motivate their spent, sore, and exhausted bodies any longer. Then they slept in a pile, clinging to one another like nothing else existed under heaven. Even Yarrow's companion said, *This is something rare, beloved. You don't know how unusual it is for a connection like this to form between even two humans, let alone three.*

Yet you won't let me keep it. Even so, Yarrow felt content and happy down to his bones as he surrendered to unconsciousness, safe and sated between his lovers. *Please, don't let this be the last time.*

But when they woke, late in the morning, Sasha was gone.

YARROW SAT with his legs crossed, one of the blankets from their bed pressed to his cheek. He refused to eat or dress, and his black mood infected Duncan. He didn't know how to ease his mage's pain when he felt Sasha's loss as acutely himself. It no longer felt natural for them to be separate.

Duncan sat beside Yarrow and draped an arm across his slim shoulders. He kissed Yarrow's temple and said, "He'll be back, you know."

"What if he's killed? I should have gone."

"You are not an assassin."

"I could be."

"Yarrow. Sasha is very skilled. He'll be fine, and he'll come back to us. You are needed on the battlefield. Yarrow, do you love me?"

He nodded and made a pathetic attempt at a smile.

Duncan kissed his eye. "Good. I'd like you to do something for me, then."

Yarrow shot him a naughty grin and licked his upper lip.

Duncan chuckled. "No, my beautiful boy. I want you to wash the residue of last night from your skin, brush your hair, get dressed, and eat something. There's porridge with sweet cream, dried apples and cinnamon. Have a few bites, at least. For me. I must meet with your brother and discuss our strategy. Will you do as I ask?"

"I'll try."

"Good lad." He kissed Yarrow again, then filled a bowl and handed it to the mage. After he saw Yarrow take a few spoonfuls, he felt able to make his way to Rowan's tent.

"How is my brother?" Rowan asked as Duncan sat down at the long table. His concern seemed sincere.

"He—Yarrow is an unusual man."

"Yes. But I can feel confident you're protecting him, Tam Duncan?"

Rowan was hardly the empty-headed puppet he'd been painted. "I swear by the goddesses, Tam Rowan, Yarroway will never come to harm if it is within my power to prevent it."

"He's lucky to have a friend such as you. How is your other associate, the assassin?"

"Sasha is gone."

"Well, may the goddesses watch over him, and grant him success in his endeavors."

May his Thalil watch over him, Duncan thought. If the dark god kept his Sasha safe and brought him back soon, it was worth the blasphemy.

"Let's get down to particulars." Rowan spread some maps out and showed Duncan the location of Tam Taran's vast forces. "We have spies watching the enemy and reporting back to us almost constantly. This information should be accurate. What do you think?"

Duncan scratched his overlong whiskers as he studied the maps. He pointed to the Starlight Bridge that breached the Kanda from Lockhaven to Gaeltheon. "Tam Taran's army isn't far from here?" he asked.

"Less than five miles from the bridge," Rowan said.

"Honorable Tam, how would you feel about augmenting our forces?"

"Tam Duncan?"

The knight pointed to an area just beyond the Gaeltheon side of the Starlight Bridge. "This region is controlled by The Thorns of Rosecairn."

"You're… honestly suggesting we hire mercenaries?"

"This group isn't so bad. They do what they do, but without unnecessary cruelty or plunder. They have a reputation for enlisting only skilled and honorable warriors."

"There's nothing honorable about this!"

Duncan sighed and drummed his fingers on the table. As a younger man, he might have been inclined to agree. The wisdom of age just showed him five of Tam Taran's knights to every one of his. No amount of idealism would tip that advantage. He understood a sword held strength with its unyielding rigidity, while the strength of a bow lay in its ability to bend. While different, neither form of power was superior, and a good soldier knew what weapon a challenge demanded. "Rowan, need I remind you that you just employed an assassin to eliminate your enemy? How are paid soldiers any different? We need any help we can get. This force will decimate us. I see no way we can win this battle without an advantage of some kind. There will be no glory in an honorable defeat."

"You think we can trust them?"

"As long as our coin is good, yes."

"I don't like it, Duncan, but I'll bow to your experience in this matter."

"Then we must get word to them as soon as possible. They'll have a ways to travel. Do you have a man you can trust with at least a sizeable down payment, who can ride swiftly and avoid detection?"

Rowan nodded slowly. "Many of the soldiers employed as scouts are as skilled at these things as your assassin friend."

"I doubt that," Duncan said, a little surprised by the pride he felt in Sasha's talents.

"Even so, I can assemble a trustworthy team. Will four men be too many? I don't want a single soldier riding into hostile territory with a target on his back."

"No, tam. Four should be fine. They should disguise themselves and draw as little attention as possible. Time is of the essence. Can you dispatch these couriers right away?"

"I'll send them out this very morning. What instructions would you have them relay to these mercenaries?"

"Assemble as large a force as we can possibly afford. If we're successful, I'm sure His Majesty won't mind the expense. If we're not, it won't matter. Have them cross the Starlight Bridge and assemble here." He pointed to a rocky outcrop near Estrella Lake. "This way we can launch a two-pronged attack, with our men coming from the south while the mercenaries flank them from the northeast. Now, I suggest we position our archers here on this ridge. If possible, you and I should split our infantry and try to surround Taran's forces from behind. Rowan, can Lockhaven hold until we reach it?"

He rubbed his forehead with his palm. "We're well supplied. We have an adequate force, but not an overwhelming one. If they lay siege in earnest... I don't know. Our walls are old and strong, but...."

"We should march, then. As soon as possible. Can these men be ready to move by afternoon?"

"If we break camp now, I think we can."

"Good. I'll lend what assistance I can." Duncan moved to stand.

"Wait. I'm a bit ashamed to admit this, but I don't know my brother as well as I should. He left home at such a young age. Even before, we were never close. You must understand a third son is of little consequence to a noble household, and all of us wanted to distance ourselves from his youthful indiscretions. The things my brother can do... I don't understand them. What is the best way to utilize Yarrow on the battlefield?"

Duncan prickled a little at the way Rowan referred to his mage like a weapon and the way his family had abandoned him as a boy. As he thought about it, he realized he didn't have a much better grasp of Yarrow's abilities than his brother. He remembered the mage tearing their first betrayers to shreds, but Duncan had no idea how he'd done it. His trick of freezing men in place might be useful, but it had tired him out badly. The more Duncan considered it, the more it seemed Yarrow needed his unseen companion to use the large, destructive enchantments. Duncan hated asking him to tap into the creature's power, even if it was their only chance. "I'll have to speak with him," Duncan finally said, "and think on this as we ride."

"Thank you, Tam Duncan." The two men stood and clasped hands. "We can win. The goddesses will certainly stand on the side of the rightful king."

"Send your couriers, Rowan. I'll talk to Yarrow." Though he dreaded it, Duncan knew all of them would perish unless his mage made a deal with his demon. Duncan would have to ask Yarrow to tread those shadows, when he wanted only to keep him from such horrors. His stomach lurched, and he hung his head as he left the command tent.

Chapter Twenty-Three

YARROW'S BROTHER Rowan must be a bit of a romantic, Sasha thought, considering the solid black horse he'd been given. *A dark man on a dark horse—it's a picture right out of a story.* Even so, the little mare was quick and slow to tire, if a bit skittish. Sasha made half the distance to Lockhaven by the time he stopped to camp, well after dark. He ate cold meat and bread, daring no fire. Then he slept with only his saddle as a pillow, and one of the blankets from their tent, which still smelled of Duncan and Yarrow. He missed them, but it felt good to be on a mission again. He'd seen plenty of battle over the past months, but had little enough chance to practice his specialized skills. He hadn't known when he'd left the order that he could continue his career as an assassin. This difficult job made him feel just as he had before: senses heightened, bloodlust singing in his veins, exhilaration at the challenge.

By sundown the next day, Sasha had almost reached L'Estrella Castle. He found a safe place to tie his horse and waited for darkness. Smoke rose from the many fires of Tam Taran's camp, and Sasha heard the bustle of the thousands of men for miles before he saw them. Sasha stayed outside the torchlight until most of the camp retired for the evening. Slowly, staying low, he edged to a cart on the outskirts of the camp, and stayed hidden behind it until he memorized the intervals of the guards' patrols. Tam Taran was being cautious, and while it wouldn't be impossible to sneak past his knights, it would take time. Sasha flitted from the cart to a pile of wood, and then to the darkened side of a tent, staying to the shadows and making sure his boots made no sounds against the hard-packed, frozen ground. He even kept his breathing so shallow as not to cloud and reveal him.

Over an hour later, Tam Taran's large, fancy tent, emblazoned with Windwake livery, a black crag-eagle against rich gold, came into view. Sasha waited across a recently carved footpath, hidden in the shadow of a filbernut tree twice his width. Four well-armed knights surrounded the command tent, and every ten minutes a pair of them circled the back and sides of it, while the others guarded the entrance. Sasha knew he needed to take care of them all before any of them were missed, or could alert others. He could have just dipped beneath the back hem of the tent, but no matter how hard he tried, not every kill could be silent. Sasha reached behind him and took a reed blowgun from his pack. He lifted it to his lips and waited. Early on, he'd learned the most important part of assassination was patience. He'd also need good aim, as the knights' armor left little skin exposed.

The first pair of knights turned the corner, and Sasha struck, planting one dart in a guard's neck and hitting the other in the cheek. They dropped in a heap, and Sasha moved, dragging both heavy bodies behind the tree. Two less men would stand against Duncan and Yarrow's brother. He couldn't take them all out; Tam Taran wouldn't be fool enough to enter an unguarded tent. Hurrying back around the corner, Sasha replaced his lethal darts with some made to induce grogginess and delirium. It would allow the remaining knights to stay at their posts, but they'd be too inebriated to notice or care what went on inside the tent. Anything they might hear, they'd never remember by morning. Crouching low, he hit a man guarding the door in the ear. The knight reached up and brushed his face, probably knocking the needle-sized projectile from his flesh. Sasha skirted the tent again and hit the knight on the other side of the entrance. As soon as he noticed his elixir taking effect, he returned to the back of the tent and snuck inside. After inspecting the space and placing everything just as he wanted it, he found a place to hide behind a large crate piled with leather gear, scrolls, weapons, and tools.

Tam Taran entered with a younger knight who helped him out of his gold-colored plate before departing. He took off his boots, ran his fingers through his hair, and washed his face and hands in a basin. Then he sat down at his table, looking exhausted as he carved a slab of meat into thin strips and ate them. He pulled the cork from a half-full bottle of wine, poured most of it into a metal goblet, and drank deeply. After a few minutes, he finished and poured out the rest of the bottle.

Sasha waited.

Taran studied some maps and letters, but soon lost interest in them and set them aside. He swayed on his stool and caught his forehead in his palm. He lifted his head and tried to shake it off, but when he stood, his legs gave out and he fell to his knees. Using the edge of the table, he managed to pull himself back up and stumble to his cot. He sat on the edge, taking deep, slow breaths and holding his head.

Sasha rose slowly, soundlessly, and put out the lantern. Taran gasped and scanned the darkness, but he still couldn't locate Sasha. Only a single candle in a glass jar illuminated the tent. Anyone watching from outside would assume Taran had gone to bed for the night. The older man's eyes widened and darted side to side. He tried again to stand but couldn't even rise an inch.

Sasha drew his dagger, deliberately letting the swish and hum of the unsheathed blade echo in the small space. He slowly stepped from the shadows, knowing to Tam Taran it looked as though he materialized from them. Clinging to the legends and superstitious fear the Crimson Scythe inspired pleased Sasha. The older man tried to scuttle away, but by now he could hardly move, thanks to the poison in his wine. Sasha moved into the bubble of golden light, where Taran could see his face and the long, sharp dagger, and Sasha could see the sweat beading above Taran's lip and across his forehead.

"You…," Taran panted, his immobilized arms jerking as he tried to lift them.

"There's no point in trying to move," Sasha purred, moving closer. "I come on behalf of Thalil."

"No, please. Please, I'm sorry."

"One can learn a great deal from a man in the minutes before his death, Tam Taran. I must admit, I didn't imagine you'd beg."

He hung his head. "I suppose I deserve this. It happened so long ago, I'd almost forgotten. Tell him I'm sorry."

"Who?"

"Your mage. Isn't that why you're here? Because of what we did?"

"Tell me exactly what happened," Sasha said, dropping his hand to his side. It was a risky move, but he couldn't leave without knowing what had happened to Yarrow. He saw a glint of hope in Taran's eyes, and Sasha knew he'd talk, though it wouldn't save his life.

"You… you don't know?"

"I want to hear it from you," Sasha said, revealing nothing.

"We never forced him."

Sasha's stomach twisted up, but he made sure none of it showed on his face. "Go on. The time is short."

"Agarick said the lad was curious. He'd had him before, and he told us Yarrow wanted it, that he was enthusiastic and as sweet as a fresh flower. That he couldn't get his fill of the male body. The king, some of the knights, and I gave him wine. At first he really did seem to like it, but then… then he changed his mind. He was so weak at that point, he really couldn't protest or fight. It was easy to pretend his cries were pleasure. I—we never meant to hurt him or make him bleed as he did."

Sasha's angry pulse in his head almost drowned the knight's words, and his hand on his dagger shook with rage and anticipation. "How old was he?"

"Maybe twelve? Or thirteen? Still slender and lovely. But isn't that the time in a boy's life when he begins to crave such experiences? In the beginning, he seemed quite intrigued."

"And this happened just the once?"

"No. He must have enjoyed something about it, or he wouldn't have kept visiting the king's fortress, would he?"

"*Baska*! It's no wonder he craved power, that he did what he did to get it!" Sasha pressed the edge of his knife to the other man's throat. "You can't honestly believe that a drunken twelve-year-old had any ability to deny half a dozen grown men? He wasn't even old enough to choose such things."

"Please. The king assured us he was quite eager."

Sasha struck him in the mouth, and blood and teeth flew. It made sense now, what Yarrow had said about having information against King Agarick. But he'd never mentioned Tam Taran and spoke with him as though he'd never met him. Perhaps his poor young mind had shielded him from the pain of the memory. Sasha had seen such things before. It made him sick, the way these nobles did as they pleased, even to one of their own. He'd right the wrong against Yarrow. "I'm finished with you. Go to Thalil, though you aren't worthy to lick the filth from his feet." He aimed the point of his knife at Taran's windpipe, just above his collarbone.

"Wait! You don't know what you're doing! You don't know what those witches are trying to do!"

"I don't care. I thank my god that he sent me to you. You've spent far too much time in the light of this world already."

"No. See reason, assassin. They must be stopped. I'll pay you anything you ask."

"Die." Sasha drove his blade home, avoiding any spot that pumped life's blood and watching with grim satisfaction as his lover's rapist sucked air through the gap in his throat. He died slowly, and in agony. When the last spasms shook his body and he went still, Sasha bent over him and began to saw his head free. He'd never taken a head, and it took longer than he'd have thought to sever the spine. Finally he managed it, and wrapped the foul thing in one of Tam Taran's bed sheets before stuffing it into his pack. Blood covered his leather armor, and he did his best to wash it away at the basin before slipping under the hem of the tent.

It took him only half as long to sneak out of the camp as it had to sneak in. In half an hour, he stood safely away from the few lanterns and torches still burning, shrouded in blessed darkness. Safe. He'd done it. He could easily make his way to his horse and be back in Rowan's company within a day and a half. They'd be marching by now. Sasha knew he should go, but he stood looking at the black silhouette of L'Estrella Castle, a few miles away. He thought of King Agarick sleeping safely within its walls, and made a decision.

Since he had no chance of scaling the high and heavily guarded walls of L'Estrella Castle, Sasha made his way to the lakeside cave Yarrow had used to lead him to freedom. He needed to hurry; the moon hung low in the sky, marking dawn as only four or five hours away. Darkness was Sasha's ally and he needed it, especially to accomplish what he planned.

He hurried through the stone corridors and into the wine and root cellars beneath Yarrow's family home. The old shelf hadn't even been replaced. Sasha found no one among the ale casks and drying vegetables. It took a few moments for him to remember the way to the stairs and floors above. A few times he hid from servants, but no guards patrolled the corridors of the old citadel. It seemed the royal family and the nobles of Lockhaven felt safe enough within these walls. Most of the soldiers likely waited in the stables, or in tents outside the castle.

Sasha ascended the stairs to the second floor. He remembered Yarrow's room on the third story; it had been witness to his first tryst with his mage and his knight. The best guest room lay directly beneath, with a fine view of that beautiful lake. Sasha knew he'd find the king within.

The door was locked, of course, but Sasha picked his way in easily enough. The fire in the room burned low, but the curtains to the balcony stood open, giving the assassin more than enough light. Agarick lay alone in the large bed. Sasha looked down at his broad, furry chest, tangled hair, and thick beard. His mouth hung open in sleep, and his arms folded above his head, just as his son's had when Sasha had contemplated wetting his steel with Garith's blood. Sasha pictured an adolescent Yarrow pinned beneath that large body, crying, begging, and bleeding, and he drew his blade.

"Sweet Thalil, this is justice. I give him to you. A king." He plunged his dagger into the king's heart and clapped his hand over Agarick's mouth so he couldn't scream. Horrible images of what had been done to Yarrow flashed before Sasha's eyes, and he stabbed down again and again, breaking the king's sternum and tearing his heart to shreds. It was an ugly death, just as he deserved. When it ended, Sasha looked for something to take as proof of the deed, and his eyes found Agarick's ring with his royal seal. He pulled his dagger from the king's chest and severed his finger at the knuckle. Then, still imagining what his lover had endured, he drove his blade deep into Agarick's chest one final time and left it embedded there.

Sasha planned to escape from the window. He could easily jump two stories and make his way around the enemy camp and to his horse. He balanced on the ledge and prepared to drop down.

"Sasha, wait." He turned, and saw an attractive woman step from the shadowy corner of the room. Had she been there all along? How had she escaped his detection? Then Sasha remembered: the queen of Selindria, Yarrow's aunt, was a mage. Wishing he'd retained his dagger, he prepared to defend himself. He had other knives, but facing a magic-user always proved a test.

"Stay where you are, woman," he warned, a poison dart between his fingers. "I've faced greater mages than you."

"No doubt," she said wearily. "My dear nephew thinks you are the very sun and stars. I know what happened to him, Sasha. He told me." She moved along the foot of the bed and touched her king's cooling cheek. "I loved my husband once. He was a beautiful man, burning to make this world better, sure he could do it with just his sword. That was many years ago, though. It takes something much more calculated and subtle to shape the future than a simple man with a sword."

"Something like a man in the dark, with a dagger?"

"Perhaps. Though this went wrong long ago. I think Agarick resented the love I showed Yarrow. It's true; I hoped to produce a mage. But I still loved my children and my king." She held a hand to her mouth to stifle a sob. "Why are you still here?"

"My lady?"

"You should go," she said. "Get back to Yarrow. Goddesses, they'll certainly blame this on me too."

Sasha leapt lightly from the railing, drawing a knife. He advanced until he stood chest to chest with the queen of Selindria. "Why didn't you stop him?" he whispered.

"I wish I'd done more," she said, holding his gaze. "I didn't know what to do. Of course I put a stop to it when I could, but far later than I'd have liked. I loved Yarrow."

"You did nothing to show it," Sasha said, holding his knife to her belly. "You let it go on for years! I should kill you."

"It wasn't until years later that Yarrow told me. I wish he'd trusted me sooner."

"A pathetic excuse, wench. I cannot believe you didn't know what awful things went on under your own roof. You deserve to die." His fingers caressed the hilt of his knife, only inches from the queen's heart. By Thalil, he wanted her blood, too, but he couldn't let greed sway his hand.

"Why bother? Once my husband is found murdered, even our staunchest allies will turn against me. I'll be beheaded, and our cause will be lost. Is that what you want, Sasha? Is that what Yarrow would want?"

"Bitch." He pushed her away and returned his attention to the deceased king. "I do this for Yarrow, not for you. Remember that." He drew his blade. Upon Agarick's still chest, he carved the symbol of his order: the red crescent and its single drop of blood. No one, not even a queen, would dare usurp that signature. "You are in my debt, Your Majesty. I won't forget it."

"Get out of here Sasha," she said, pointing at the window. "The night will abandon you soon. Go." She sat down in the blood and gore and held the king's hand in her lap. Sasha heard her crying softly and speaking to her husband under her breath.

Sasha swung his legs over the balcony wall and dropped into the retreating shadows. As soon as his boots hit the ground, he ran. He still almost expected the queen to scream and call her guards once her initial shock at the murder waned. Even if she did, their petty standoff would work in Sasha's favor. Lockhaven wouldn't spare men to search the countryside for him when their enemies camped on their doorstep. He sprinted around the side of the castle and swore. The crown of the sun broke the horizon behind him, washing the dirty snow in purplish light. He ran harder, desperate to cross the few miles of empty countryside before the men in the castle and the camps started to stir. Now and then a copse of bedraggled trees or a mound of stone offered scant shelter, but he knew if anyone bothered to watch, they'd certainly see the dark shape flitting from shadow to shadow. As yet, not even a winter bird called out at his passing.

Sasha thought about what he'd done. His dagger rested in the heart of a king, marking him among the greatest of assassins, but he could never tell anyone. He wondered how his companions might react. Duncan, while loyal to the throne, would surely understand. Wouldn't he? What of Yarrow? Certainly he must hate his uncle, who'd probably broken the mage's mind apart long before Yarrow encountered the creature in the mountains. The king's actions had probably made Yarrow easy prey. Pieces clicked together in Sasha's mind. Yarrow had left Selindria because of a scandal. Thalil, they'd probably painted Yarrow as a wanton boy who'd seduced and possibly enchanted the king and his men. They'd put the blame on him and sent him away. Had they thought it was funny, fulfilling what they saw as Yarrow's unnatural urges in the cruelest way? Had they justified what they'd done by imagining the young mage's sin greater than their own? Sasha remembered the blood on Agarick's lips, in his beard. Had he known, all those years ago, fate would one day ask a price?

At whose feet would they lay the blame for the king's murder, Sasha wondered as he found his horse, asleep on her feet where he'd left her. The reek of blood on him made her nicker, paw the ground, and back away. He held the reins firmly until she calmed, and then he mounted up, digging his heels into her ribs. Since his mount had rested, Sasha drove her hard, eager to get well away from L'Estrella Castle before morning. If they caught him, with Tam Taran's head in his pack and the king's ring finger in his pocket, he knew his death would take weeks. Suddenly he wished he'd said good-bye to Duncan and Yarrow instead of sneaking off while they slept, trying to spare them the anguish of an awkward farewell. He smiled, remembering how much trouble he'd had disengaging from their limbs, and renewed his determination to return to them.

When full light fell on the world, Sasha abandoned the road and kept to wooded gullies and weeded tracts between fields. Rowan's army would march from the southeast, so he moved in that direction, confident he wouldn't miss the large force. He tried not to think about what would happen when he joined them. Before, he'd have taken his payment and left. He'd never had an interest in battlefield combat, and he still didn't, but Duncan and Yarrow were there, and he ached to be with them again. It was weak to feel such need, such dependence, but he accepted it. It hadn't prevented him from reaping the lives of both the true king and the pretender, and altering the course of everything yet to come. Now, he could only wait and see what was to be.

Chapter
Twenty-four

MERE MILES separated Rowan and Duncan's army from Tam Taran's forces. Yarrow sat on his horse, regarding the hundreds of gray tendrils rising from the enemy fires. A clear, cold day had only just dawned, but no one slept. Men hurried about, making their final preparations for the inevitable battle. Far in the distance, looking no larger than his little finger, stood Yarrow's childhood home.

There are so many of them.

Yes, beloved. Almost ten thousand men to your brother's three and a half.

What chance do we stand? We can't win this fight.

The sound of approaching hooves snapped Yarrow from his bleak ruminations. He looked over his shoulder and saw Duncan approaching at a trot, some papers tucked beneath his elbow.

"Yarrow. We must prepare."

"Has Sasha come back yet?"

The knight, his cheeks nipped crimson with cold and his hair and beard freshly trimmed, shook his head, unable to meet Yarrow's eyes.

"He should have been back by now. It's been almost four days." He wanted Duncan to say something, offer some reason for their assassin's absence, comfort Yarrow's troubled mind. The knight just lifted his chin and stared north. "Do you think he's…? Do you think he was unsuccessful?"

"How can I know any better than you? Should I lie to you and tell you everything will be fine, that this will all be over and we'll be singing and drinking wine together by sundown?"

"I'm sorry."

"I am." Duncan rode up alongside Yarrow and took his hand. Red ringed his green eyes, and Yarrow wondered if he'd been crying. The thought of Duncan scared or wounded enough to cry terrified him. "I didn't mean to sound so harsh, Yarrow. I have a great many things on my mind."

"This is madness," Yarrow whispered. "We can't possibly prevail."

"We have some advantage. Tam Taran, if he still lives, will be fighting on two fronts, trying to take the castle while fighting our forces at his flank. Goddesses willing, we can surround them and press them between our men and your valenny's archers. Goddesses willing, the men I've hired will reach us in time and spread their attentions even thinner."

"Have there been any signs of these men?"

"No."

"Duncan, three thousand men against almost ten?"

"My dear, dear Yarrow. I want you to know how glad I am to have met you. Your companionship, your love, has meant more to me than probably anything in my life. These past months with you and Sasha have been like a beautiful dream, even in spite of everything we've been through."

"Stop talking like you're going to die!" Yarrow wanted to slap him in the face. "You sound as though it's already over."

"As you noted, we're woefully outnumbered, my love."

"Stop it!" *Is there, goddesses, is there anything you can do?*

Don't be a little fool. Were I wearing the flesh, my mouth might water at the thought of everything I can do to these insects. Yarrow shuddered at the surge of hunger and bloodlust that burned through his veins. The sparks of blue energy crackled and danced over his skin, evoking a pleasant tremble of his muscles.

"I must ask something of you, Yarrow. If… if it looks as though we can't win, if all seems lost, will you draw upon your power?"

"I've planned to fight all along," the mage said. He felt his companion scrutinizing his thoughts and emotions, the psychic equivalent of a toothy grin on it.

"You don't understand my meaning. Goddesses, it pains me to ask you this. If we run out of options, will you draw on the power of the thing inside you?"

You'll owe me, beloved.

I know. He stared down at his hand, so small enveloped in Duncan's fist. He remembered the carnage the creature had wrought at their forest camp, the threat it had posed to Duncan and Sasha in Meritage. He remembered the world of shades, ash, and echoes it inhabited, that he'd inhabit if he gave it control. *Rini*.... Finally, he remembered the horrific scenes of violence and senseless destruction he'd gained when they'd first bonded. Even now, after viewing them hundreds of times in his nightmares, those images made him gag and fight not to fall into unconsciousness to escape.

"Yarrow?"

He drew a deep, faltering breath. "I will do this on two terms. First, if it comes to that, you must get our men back. I… may not be able to discriminate. Have a plan in place. The retreat must be fast and complete."

"Very well. I'll inform your brother."

"Duncan, this next part is the most important." He found the knight's gaze and held it, watching Duncan's eyes for any sign of misunderstanding. There could be no trace of hesitance. "If I do this, I may need to go away for a while, after. If I tell you I must go, you must swear you'll make no move to stop me. You must swear you won't follow me or try to find me. I need your absolute oath that you'll let me go."

"How can I swear that oath?"

"Those are my terms. Agree to them unconditionally, or I will not fight."

"You'd let your king and queen fall, over, what? Some petty mind game or egotistical whim?"

"I'm sorry you see it that way, but yes. I won't fight unless you swear, unconditionally, that after our victory you'll let me go. Alone."

"After Garith is wed. Allow me to be the selfish one, just this once."

"Very well. After the wedding."

"Then… then I swear. I will let you do as you think you must."

"I hope we'll see Sasha again."

At that, the knight pressed his fist against his lips and turned away. He took a few moments to compose himself and then said, "The goddesses must have plans for us. The three of us meeting, everything that's happened, can't be blind chance. Why would they bring us together like this, if not for a reason?"

"Do you really believe such things, Duncan?"

"I don't know. I try to believe them." He looked up at the clear, ice blue sky and then at the men toiling around them. "I must go. I must make sure these men are as prepared as they can be. No matter what I do, many of them won't make it home. I hope we'll all be together again. But we might not, and I can't even kiss you good-bye. Yet this is the world I fight for. Sometimes I have to wonder why." He turned his horse hard, hurrying away before he broke apart.

Yarrow's eyes stung, and he wiped his wet cheeks with his knuckles, sniffling like a pathetic child. Then, from nowhere, anger replaced his melancholy: anger at fate, at the goddesses, at a ridiculous world where Duncan couldn't kiss him good-bye and Sasha could be used like a tool but not allowed to sit at the table with his employers afterward. *I will raze this world to ash before I lose them. I'd rather destroy it than let it keep us apart.* He let his rage bubble up inside him, burning his lungs and heart until it boiled over into a hungry, ringing laugh his companion eagerly echoed. Clutching his sides, he cackled unabashedly at the sky, mentally daring The Thirteen Goddesses or anyone else to stand in his way. He found he couldn't wait for the battle to begin, couldn't wait to show them all how weak they were. *Ants under my boots! I'll make them pay!* By now, Yarrow and his guest's minds overlapped so much he couldn't be sure which of them spoke, and he didn't care. His whole body sprang alight with the hunger for blood and combat. He felt like he'd fly away if he leapt from his horse. Instead, holding tight to a shred of reality, he made his way toward the cliff where he would join the archers.

"THEY COME," Rowan said, pointing at the cloud of dust and snow raised by the thousands of men running toward them. He turned his horse to face his men. Prince Garith, Lysander, and Duncan also turned. Duncan looked out across the sea of fearful, hopeless faces, the faces of men thinking about wives and children they wouldn't see again. He looked over at Rowan's pale face, so similar to Yarrow's it almost summoned tears. It would take a miracle for him to be reunited with his own, odd little family.

Rowan cleared his throat. "My countrymen and kinsmen, we find ourselves on this field today because we have no choice but to fight. We have no choice but to stand against Selindria's enemies, no matter what the odds. We fight for the true king and queen, against the lowest of traitors. We fight because to do otherwise would be cowardice. Selindria has never bred cowards, and looking at you now, ready to spill blood for her true sovereign, I see her ancient strength and bravery in every one of your faces. We may be fewer than our enemy, but know the goddesses stand with us, because our cause is just. We will prevail; we must prevail, because we are the true Selindrians! As such, we cannot allow our beloved homeland to fall under the yoke of usurpers. We must spill their blood as a warning to any who would turn their backs on this kingdom!"

A halfhearted holler of assent rose from the men. Some of them beat their swords against their shields or stamped their boots. If their morale didn't lift quickly, they'd lose the battle even faster than they feared. The men soon fell silent again as the red-robed men, the priests of Myint, goddess of battle, moved among them, fanning the smoke from the censers over the soldiers to impart their deity's blessing.

Prince Garith raised his hand. "I am Garith, son of Agarick, your true king. Even when I was betrayed by my own people, I never doubted my loyal subjects would see justice done. I knew that even if I lost my life, my good people, my nobles, knights, and brave soldiers, would put things right. That is why I don't fear riding into this battle. For no matter what befalls me, so long as one loyal Selindrian draws breath, treason and greed will never darken this kingdom. For Agarick!" he shouted, sword raised above his head.

"For Agarick!" the men yelled back.

"For justice! For Selindria!" The soldiers repeated the prince's oaths, but they still knew they marched to their deaths, and no speech could raise their battle-lust in the face of that cold fact.

"Highness, a rider approaches," Sander said, touching Garith's elbow and pointing. Rowan, Duncan, and several other knights closed around the prince and drew their swords. Duncan squinted to the west, seeing only a dark dot moving toward their forces. He wondered how a single rider had made it through Taran's men, unless he'd gone well around. Maybe the rider delivered some message of compromise, some hope of avoiding the bloodshed to come. Slowly he came into focus: a black-clad man on a black horse, his dark cloak fluttering out behind him. Duncan's pulse quickened, and it felt like forever before his hope was confirmed.

Sasha!

When the assassin reined in his horse, Duncan fought the urge to go to him, to hold him, kiss him and assure himself Sasha really existed outside his desperate hope. Instead he smiled, raised his hand, and let it fall. Sasha's black eyes captured his gaze, and his smile said more than words could ever express. He reached around to his pack and pulled out a bloody wad of cloth, which he handed to Rowan.

Rowan looked like he might be sick, but he gingerly took what Sasha offered and peeled back the fabric. His eyes grew wide, and a look of triumph quickly replaced his look of disgust. He jerked his mount back around and held the severed, graying head of Tam Taran Edercrest aloft by its hair. "The goddesses have smiled on us, my friends!" Sasha rolled his eyes as Rowan spoke. "The serpent who led these traitors is no more! Taran Edercrest is dead! Let's do the same to the rest of them!"

The men went wild, crying out bloody oaths and clanging their weapons. Duncan hoped for a few seconds to speak with Sasha, so he might tell him to avoid the worst of the combat, but he never got them. Rowan impaled Taran's head on a pike and drove it into the ground just as the enemy army came into range.

"Archers!" Duncan yelled and pointed. A rain of arrows showered the advancing men, stopping many near the front, men and horses alike. "Again!" This time, tongues of lightning descended with the arrows, each of them striking a target, sometimes killing them but always knocking them down. *Good. Yarrow is pacing himself.* The mage and the archers managed to fire twice more before the enemy reached Duncan's front lines.

"We need to surround them," he reminded Rowan, turning his steed and galloping left, followed by about a quarter of their number. "Lysander, get His Highness out of danger! We can't afford to lose the prince. Sasha—" Duncan looked all around but couldn't locate the dark man amid the growing chaos. "Sasha!"

He had no time to look for the assassin before the battle exploded around him. He lifted his sword just in time to parry a blow from another knight's mace. He pushed his attacker back and punched him in the side of the head, knocking him from his horse. Duncan tugged his own steed around and thrust his blade into the chest of a knight to his left. The man's horse screamed and tried to flee the fray. A soldier on the ground rushed toward Duncan, halberd raised. An archer took him before he reached Duncan, but Duncan caught the attention of another pair of knights. By the time he'd fought them back, blood and sweat, some of it his own, smeared his armor.

Duncan steered his charger to a relative quiet spot, where he could assess the battle. Already it went poorly. Instead of surrounding their enemy, his men had only managed to break off into two, smaller, more vulnerable groups. The traitors, with their superior numbers, had engulfed each of these groups. If something didn't change soon, they'd be wiped out before an hour passed. Duncan hurried toward his men, cracking the skull of a foot soldier as he rode toward them. He plunged his sword into the back of one knight, piercing his armor, and then the thigh of another. He swung his arm at a horseman attacking a man in a burgundy Lockhaven tabard, and caught him between his helmet and breastplate. Blood poured down the enemy's armor in sheets. Duncan didn't know how long he'd fought or how many dozen men he vanquished before he reached his own. Goddesses, they were completely surrounded. With a hoarse cry, Duncan chopped down into a scout approaching him, severing the man's arm. His muscles screamed already, and he knew he'd been wounded, though nothing life-threatening.

Desperately Duncan looked around, trying to get some bearing while fending off attackers. Already dead and dying men littered the ground. Blood soaked the snow and soldiers slipped in it. The ring of metal meeting metal echoed in Duncan's skull. Smoke obscured his vision, and all the men, in their fouled armor and filthy tabards, looked alike. Finally he managed to locate Rowan, though hundreds of enemy soldiers separated his group from Duncan and his men. Growling with determination, the knight began cutting his way through. "After me," he called.

Amazingly, they gained ground, though inches at a time and at great cost of life. Their archers, aiming carefully instead of quickly, aided their efforts. They'd almost reached Rowan, but the enemy forces closed at their flank, boxing them in, completely sealing them off. All the loyal soldiers stood surrounded at the center of thousands of men. Though they fought their way out desperately, the attackers just closed in tighter, until they swung their weapons almost back to back. There was nothing they could do. The enemy's superior numbers simply overwhelmed them. The archers picked off adversaries along the edges of the vast force, but Duncan knew it was over.

A huge fork of lightning struck the ground off to the right. The men nearest it burned to a crisp, and dozens more went flying back. Duncan blinked away the afterimage burned into his eyes and coughed at the smoke. The hole Yarrow's spell opened quickly closed, though, before any of Duncan's people escaped. The mage struck again and again, cutting a path out of the sea of soldiers. Dozens of destructive forks of power soon widened a gap. Pointing, Duncan hollered, "There!" He kicked his mount hard and the animal jumped the fallen bodies, galloping toward open space.

Though he still fought stragglers, Duncan managed to locate Rowan, following his brother's path of destruction toward freedom. If all hope wasn't already lost, they needed to regroup. The sky darkened and rumbled as Yarrow blasted men out of the way whenever they tried to cut Rowan off.

"Get rid of that goddess-damned mage," a knight in dark plate called to another in silver mail, who stood a few hundred yards away. The silver knight motioned to the men he commanded, and they broke from the rest of the battle, heading for the smooth slope that led to cliff where Yarrow stood with the archers.

"No!" Duncan yelled, charging after them, hoping his men would follow. "Protect the archers!" With renewed energy born from outrage and the need to protect the mage, Duncan tore through the few dozen men between himself and the silver knight and pursued him up the hill. Other enemies chased after him, and one sank a blade deep into his horse's haunches. The animal screamed and went down. Duncan just managed to dismount before the steed's fall broke his legs. He landed hard on his side and rolled away from another horse's pounding hooves. Fighting his way back to his feet, Duncan continued up the knoll, his sword swinging wildly, knocking men out of his way.

A large knight, his helmet obscuring his face and a Morningstar in each hand, blocked Duncan's path. He wore the traitorous yellow-and-black livery of Windwake. Advancing slowly, he swung his gruesome chains and the spiked balls at their ends in figure eights. Duncan lifted his sword and managed to meet the first blow, though the force of it sent him staggering back. The second connected with his shoulder, and he sprawled on his back. Horses and men ran past him. The other knight wasted no time, and stood over Duncan, his arm raised to crush Duncan's skull. Before he could, he fell across Duncan's chest, a dagger jutting from the back of his neck. Duncan freed himself from the other man's dead weight and grasped the delicate, gloved hand reaching down for him. He caught his wind, steadied himself, and swung into the saddle behind Sasha.

They reached the archers, who, while better at a distance, weren't helpless at close range. They'd already whittled down the enemy. Sasha controlled his horse while Duncan fought, cracking skulls, severing limbs and heads, and piercing backs and chests. From this vantage point, he saw just how badly the enemies below outnumbered his men. He also noticed a fresh batch of knights and soldiers heading their way, though they had quite a space to cross. Still, they didn't have much chance. For the first time in his life, and only for a second, Duncan considered collecting Yarrow and fleeing the massacre.

A horn sounded from the east. Duncan dared a glance in that direction. Men, several hundred of them, ran and rode toward the fray, flanking many of the enemy. From his distance, Duncan barely made out the details, but he knew these new fighters were fresh and uninjured. They could only be the mercenaries he'd hired. At their appearance, the enemy soldiers who'd been advancing on the cliff turned their attention away, rushing instead toward the new and more imminent threat. Duncan kept slaying the knights around him, and the archers helped. Sasha's quick hand and sharp blade made blood bloom all around him. After a hard fight, they'd eliminated their adversaries on the hill, though more would certainly replace them.

The well-trained and seasoned archers quickly fell into formation and aimed for the enemies below. Where under heaven was Yarrow? Even amid such pandemonium, the mage was hard to miss. "Sasha," Duncan said, pointing to the rim of the ledge. Sasha guided his mount past the bodies, and Duncan looked down on the battle. Arrows whizzed over their heads. Even with the addition of the mercenary fighters, he didn't see much chance of victory. The tiny group of men in mismatched armor had quickly been pushed to the eastern edge of the fray, and their numbers dwindled. Those soldiers Rowan commanded, the remnants of Duncan's forces, had been swallowed up again by the enemy.

Looking back at Duncan over his shoulder, Sasha said, "The enemy is too many, my love. This battle cannot be won. We should find Yarrow as soon as we can and get away from here."

"Are you suggesting we run?"

"Yes! Alive, we can keep working against these traitors, if that's what you want. What good can we do by dying here today?"

"We can't just give up."

Sasha's face twisted with anger. "Look," he shouted, shaking his fist at the horrific scene below them. "This cause is lost! I won't lose you to this nonsense."

Duncan's eyes moved down Sasha's slim arm. The small, desperate group of men fighting for Agarick grew smaller by the minute. Rowan and the rest were completely overcome. Not even a group of the world's best warriors could defeat the enemy's greater numbers. Maybe Sasha was right, but—

"I can't run away while the men fighting for me are slaughtered. I can't run away and let them die!"

"Damn it, Duncan! I'll make you if I must!"

"Oh, will you?" Duncan asked, getting frustrated, watching his men perish and wanting to fight beside them.

"Yes! As soon as we find Yarrow."

"Find me? I'm just here."

Both of them turned toward the mage's oddly amused voice, only a few feet away. Despite the long battle, not so much as a speck of dirt marred Yarrow's skin or clothing. Blue light spilled from his eyes, streaming out at the corners. Duncan flinched at the sight of him, irrationally afraid, and moved closer to Sasha. The azure glow spread over Yarrow's skin and beyond, into the shape of wings so solid and detailed Duncan swore he saw individual feathers. The arm that wielded his sword jerked in the mage's direction, even as Sasha's horse reared and tried to run. Sasha barely managed to calm her and keep them from being thrown.

"Duncan, it's time to get your men out of the way, as we discussed. And don't forget his other condition."

"His? Who am I speaking with?" the knight asked, his voice high and trembling as a frightened child's.

"Oh, I think you know. But I'm here too, Duncan." The second statement sounded slightly different, more familiar. "Hurry. Get your people as far from here as you can."

"Sasha, dismount," Duncan said. "I must reach Rowan!"

"No!" Yarrow shrieked. "Don't leave Sasha alone with me!"

So, even though it strained the poor pony, Duncan and Sasha rode together into the bedlam of smoke, clashing swords, shouts, and blood. Duncan knew the worst was yet to come.

NOW, BELOVED, now! I can't wait any longer! Do you know how many centuries I've longed for this?

Just a little longer, Yarrow said, trying to counter his companion's insatiable bloodlust with calm. He felt like he was trying to hold a starving man, a man much stronger than himself, back from a banquet table. On the field, Duncan, Rowan, and Sasha tried to get their people out of the battle. The mercenaries had already retreated, but Tam Taran's forces kept Agarick's surrounded, preventing their escape. When they finally broke through and fled, many of the traitor's men pursued.

Beloved if we don't act soon, we won't have any left!

And? The battle will still be over.

Oh no, little mage. That will not do. I'll have blood today, and plenty. If I can't take it from your enemies—

Enough. What must we do?

That depends on you, beloved. I can just take over, or we can do this together. You have vast stores of energy for a human, and I can teach you much. Our combined powers will make this quicker.

All right. Let's get it over with.

The other presence snapped into place in Yarrow's mind, and he saw the world through both of their eyes. Their essences mingled together. *This isn't something to rush, my sweet beloved. This is something to savor.*

Yes.... It was right. Yarrow felt power burning through his veins, searing through his flesh and spilling out of his pores. He was on fire, but it didn't hurt. It felt delicious, his body lighter than air, caught up in the warm torrents of arcane energy that seemed to caress him. He felt like he'd finished several bottles of good wine, but his head was clear, more than clear. He could hear every soldier's heart on that field, hear them breathing, smell their sweat. The tang of their fear and confusion was strong in his mouth.

Isn't it delicious, beloved? This is how it feels to truly live.

Yarrow spread his shimmering wings and drifted off the cliff, landing in the center of the battle. Men dropped their weapons and trampled each other as they tried to run. Their screams were like music. With a thought, Yarrow stole their essence and slowed them to a crawl. "You have nowhere to run, insects!" both their voices yelled. The ground shook and split beneath them. Some of the men fell into the fissures. Yarrow couldn't feel his skin or bones anymore. He felt only the intoxicating burn and hum of the power. "I will have this world. You will all crawl at my feet!"

"Enough! They're running away! It's over!"

"No, beloved! We will show them our power! I know you want to. I feel you aching for release."

I... I—

Show them what we can do, beloved!

How? What do you want? The energy was too much; he'd black out and surrender complete control to the other.

Beloved, I want you to... give.

He did, in a sudden, complete, orgasmic rush, and the sky ripped open. A column of flame as wide as a tower descended from the heavens, scorching the earth and reducing the men within half a mile of it to cinders. Yarrow heard maniacal laughter, but he wasn't sure if it came from him or not. He moved his hands and the inferno shifted, contorting into a tornado of fire. The flames swirled around the mage, spinning out from him, faster and farther, gathering up those enemy soldiers who tried to run, crawl, or drag themselves away on their elbows.

We will have this world. We'll be a mage king and rule it for eternity. It's our right.

Yes....

And for all of that, you didn't even need me, beloved. Look what you can do with nothing but your own energy.

What?

Oh, my sweet mage. My sweet, perfect, powerful beloved. You did all of this yourself.

No....

Oh yes. We'll talk later about what you can trade me for the lesson.

No. Yarrow's feet hit the ground. He hadn't realized he'd been hovering above it. The flames dissipated into the ether. The compacted soil around him, probably for a mile or more, was black and barren. Smoke hung thick in the air, but other than that there was nothing.

Nothing, not even a corpse, a skeleton, a weapon or a scrap of armor. He'd obliterated it all, all on his own. The murderous delight had been all his. Now he stood in a field of nothing but swirling ash and the echoes of screams.

He felt his knees strike the ground. He was dizzy, and his limbs felt like lead. The last thing Yarrow perceived were familiar voices calling his name, and two shadows moving toward him through the acrid fumes, coughing and shielding their eyes. He wanted to reach out for them, speak to them, but he couldn't. He'd given all he had.

It was over. Yarrow's face smacked the scorched ground, and he knew nothing else.

Chapter Twenty-Five

WHILE HE wasn't ready to open his eyes yet, Yarrow wondered how he'd spend the day. Maybe he'd go down to the shore of the lake and coax the waves into the shapes of wyrms and unicorns. Or maybe he'd go out on the plains and beguile some cows so he could watch the milkmaids chase them. Maybe he'd ride east to the river and drop stones off the Starlight Bridge. First, he'd go down to the kitchen for some sweet cream, muffins, and honey. Lockhaven provided endless entertainments for a young boy.

Then the memory of burning bodies slammed against Yarrow's drowsy mind, and he bolted up in bed, screaming. Red-gold evening light poured in from the balcony and painted the blankets. A healthy fire burned in the hearth. Duncan sat nearby on the bench, and Sasha dozed with his cheek on the knight's shoulder. He started and sat up at Yarrow's cry, his eyes puffy and dark. It took Yarrow a minute to notice their unusual clothing. Duncan wore new brown pants and a green velvet doublet with gold detail. It complemented his coloring. Sasha wore black: snug leggings, a shirt with billowing sleeves, and a tight vest embossed with a diamond pattern.

"What's going on?" Yarrow asked in a voice rough from disuse.

"You've been sleeping," Sasha said, "for almost three days."

Rubbing his forehead, Yarrow tried to piece together the events of the battle, and the weeks and months that led up to it. He decided to delay his analysis of his own actions and motivations until he felt more alert. He just wasn't ready to deal with what he'd done, the enormity of it, not yet.

Feeling better, beloved? I allowed you pleasant dreams. Your spirit should be strong.

I don't feel any pain.

You were never wounded.

"We were victorious," Yarrow said, mostly to convince himself. "What now?"

"The king would very much like to see you," Duncan said. "Your mother and aunt will also be delighted to find you awake. Do you feel well enough to bathe?"

With a nod, Yarrow got out of bed. He still wore his faded black clothes, though they weren't as dirty as they should have been. He looked at Duncan and Sasha and knew they'd been sitting with him the entire time. The thought brought a smile to his face, and the other men returned it.

"Do you need any assistance?" Sasha said, the tip of his tongue parting his lips for a second.

Yarrow laughed. "My dear friend, I think I need a meal and a bit more rest before I can handle any assistance."

All of them chuckled, and Yarrow went down the hall to wash. While he relaxed in the water, a servant brought fresh clothes and set them on the bench: gray trousers and a gauzy shirt, new boots, and a sleeveless doublet of lightning blue silk with silver embroidery around the edges. As he put them on, Yarrow already missed his well-worn traveling clothes. These were court clothes, but not as frilly as some, and they suited him. He probably had his aunt to thank for that.

Sasha and Duncan approved of his attire, and they ravished him with their eyes as they made their way to the dining hall. The knight even reached over and stroked the silk over the swell of Yarrow's butt, a bold move for Duncan in public. It pleased the mage.

The servants had just brought out the first course when the three of them entered the room. Conversation died on the lips of those seated there, and every eye turned to Yarrow. He felt nervous and shifted his weight from foot to foot. Surely they all knew what he'd done and felt horrified by his unnatural presence. Garith, in spectacular crimson velvet, rose from the head of the table and stared at his cousin for many minutes before he started clapping. One by one, the other knights and nobles rose and clapped as well. Their reaction caught Yarrow off guard at first, but after a moment he basked in it. He deserved it, after all. They'd be dead if not for his concession.

Soon everyone sat back down, and Yarrow took his place beside the prince, who wore a braided gold circlet over his hair. Sasha sat beside him, and Duncan across the table. Aunt Den was there, as were

Asaria, Rayne, Rowan, their wives, and some knights and officials Yarrow didn't recognize. More importantly, "Where is the king?"

All of them bowed their heads. Sasha, leaning close, whispered, "He was killed."

"In the battle?" Yarrow asked aloud.

Garith shook his head. "My father fell victim to the conspirators' treachery. He was murdered. We couldn't wait on the coronation with the instability in our land. I was crowned two days ago. I wish you could have been there, cousin."

"Agarick is dead?" Yarrow mused, relieved in an odd way he didn't comprehend. "You are king now, Garith?"

"Thanks largely to you. I'd very much like you to stay on and advise me, Yarrow."

"I'm not terribly fond of staying in one place."

"Can you give me any wisdom now, then? What should I do next?"

Yarrow considered. Then he looked up and met his cousin's gaze. "You must be merciless, Garith. You must hunt down and kill every man and woman who took even a small part in this treason. If you let them live, they may try again. You won't be safe or secure in your rule until you're rid of them."

"It will be difficult. Many of them fled after Tam Taran's defeat."

"They might yet be found," Sasha said, his voice low and devoid of emotion. The others at the table fidgeted and found things on their plates and in their goblets that needed attention. Chairs scraped stone as a few of them edged away. "If you send the right person looking. It will be difficult, as you said, and… expensive."

"You should consider his words," Yarrow said.

"Yes, I will. But for now, on to lighter matters," Garith said, watching Sasha warily from the corner of his eye. "Tam Duncan. Windwake, it seems, finds herself in need of a Bairn."

"Your Majesty?" The knight, for all his size and power, blushed like a spring bride. Yarrow found it absolutely endearing.

"It's the least I can do to reward your courage and loyalty, tam, rather, Bairn Duncan. Take these lands, with my blessing."

"I'm honored, Your Majesty."

"Rowan L'Estrella, you commanded my troops at the Battle of the Starlight Bridge with skill, fortitude, and dedication—"

"Battle of the Starlight Bridge?" Yarrow interrupted. "That's completely inaccurate."

"I suppose the historians find it more succinct than 'The Battle on a Patch of Ground with No Distinguishing Features A Couple of Miles from the Starlight Bridge,'" Rowan said, annoyed at the disruption to his praise.

Garith grinned and continued. "Tam Rowan, for your services to the crown, I'd like you to have Greyrclif, on the eastern coast."

"Thank you, Your Majesty."

"It's my honor, Eyrle Rowan. Rule it well. And as for my dear cousin Yarroway, without whom we'd all have perished, you shall name your reward. Ask, and I will grant you any land, title, or treasure within my power to give."

"I would ask that, when you are lord of both Selindria and Gaeltheon, you don't destroy or drive out the Emiri people."

Garith shook his head. "You know I can't make that promise."

"Then I humbly ask Bairn Duncan of Windwake if I might build a modest fortress in a secluded corner of his land, where I might rest between my travels. In return I'll use my power to protect his subjects."

"Yarrow, you even need to ask?" Duncan responded, smiling broadly at the implications. "I grant it, of course."

"What from me, cousin?" Garith persisted.

"Give me the lands on the south coast, then, when you reclaim them."

"That may take many years."

"I'll wait," Yarrow said. "Those are the lands I desire, to the south and along the Kanda. Give me a valenny there."

"You will have it."

Clever, beloved. Sanctuary for your Emiri and a valenny ruled by a mage. Well done.

Thank you.

After they dined, the men retired to the library and left the women to plan what would be the wedding of the ages.

A WEEK later, they marched for Meritage, accompanied by fifty royal knights, as none of them desired a repeat of recent events. The weather, while cold, impeded them with no storm, and they made good progress along well-traveled roads. When they passed villages and farmholds, many of the new king's subjects came out to cheer and offer winter flowers. Garith indulged them, waving and kissing their babies. His patience never wore thin. He would be well loved.

A few days later, they settled into Agarick's—now Garith's—grand estate in the bustling port city. Yarrow, Duncan, and Sasha were given separate rooms, though close enough to one another that they found it easy to spend time together in the evenings. Wedding preparations commenced. Cartloads of food, wine, and ale arrived daily. Guests arrived from both nations, filling the many spare chambers. Barges carried thousands of flowers up the river from the south. Servants used them, along with silk and velvet ribbons and strands of beads, to decorate the entire house. Bright blooms covered every column, shelf, windowpane, and archway. Though it was still winter, the inside of the manor looked and smelled like a summer afternoon.

They'd just finished their preparation of the great hall, where the ceremony would be held, when a harried-looking maidservant with disheveled black hair burst in, looking for Yarrow. The mage had promised to conjure birds and butterflies during the service, and was trying to decide upon the best time and place for the enchantments.

"Tam Yarroway," the serving girl said, catching her breath. "You must come to the front entrance at once."

"What for? I'm busy here."

She flinched like he'd hit her. "The princess has arrived, tam. Everyone has come out to greet her, and Prince Garith, his sister Garina, and Denna Corina request your presence at once."

"Oh, very well." He followed her to the courtyard, where the entire household and all the guests stood assembled. The girl escorted Yarrow to the front of the throng, and he took his place beside his aunt and cousin while the maid scurried away. A beautiful ivory carriage drawn by two palomino horses and embellished with carved roses and gold leaf stopped at the end of the lane. The driver leapt down, opened the door, and helped a young woman to the damp paving stones. She had fair skin, round, pink cheeks, soft brown eyes, and honey-colored hair streaked with gold. If he'd been interested in such things, Yarrow supposed he'd probably find her beautiful. She wore a mint green dress beneath a darker green cloak lined in tawny fur. Her smile was warm and sincere.

A little too pure and innocent for my tastes. What do you think, beloved?

What does it matter? I'm not marrying her.

Garith took his betrothed's hand and held it up between them, to much applause. Yarrow thought his cousin looked happy. "Her Highness Cothryn, of the Royal House of Gaeltheon, and our beautiful future queen." More cheers rose from the audience, almost surpassing what was appropriate for a polite gathering. "We welcome you to our fair Selindria, my Lady. We are honored and delighted. May I present my mother, Denna Corina of Espero?"

"By all means." The two women clasped hands and kissed one another's cheeks. "How good to see you in person after our many letters, Your Highness." There was something calculating in the way they smiled at one another, but Yarrow couldn't name it. "Thank you for your efforts to unite our two great kingdoms. In Gaeltheon, they're already saying this marriage will mark the beginning of a Blessed Epoch of peace and plenty."

"Thank you, dear lady," Aunt Den said. "I am happier than you can imagine to welcome you to my family. Please, let me present some of the brave men who protected your betrothed, my dear Garith, and defeated the conspiracy against us. First, here is Bairn Duncan, of Windwake."

Duncan knelt and kissed the princess's knuckles. "I have heard great tales of your courage and dedication, honorable knight. Please rise."

"I am honored to have served, my lady."

The former queen presented Rayne, Rowan, Lysander, and several other knights and nobles in a similar fashion.

Beloved, I'm getting bored. Can't we slip away?

We shouldn't. I don't want to embarrass my mother or my aunt.

You and these women.

Hush. Besides, something is afoot. I sense the faintest echo of enchantment, and not from Aunt Den.

Heh. Yes, I do feel something subtle....

Finally the former queen said, "Lady Cothryn, let me present my dear nephew, Yarroway L'Estrella of Lockhaven, soon to be Valen of the South Coast. I have told you of him."

"Yes," she said, casting Denna Corina a knowing glance. "I have heard of everything you did in service to my future husband. I am eternally grateful to you."

Then he heard the future queen's voice inside his head, saying: *And I'm always pleased to meet another possessing the gift. I understand it is strong in you, Yarroway. We'll have to speak privately someday.*

"Thank you," Yarrow managed as he inclined his head slightly and backed away from her. *She's a mage,* he said to his companion. *Can she hear us talking to each other?*

Of course not, beloved.

Goddesses, I understand it all now!

Hmm?

Don't you see what they've done? Mages are forbidden to rule. Directly, at least. Women can only ever stand second to the king. Without being married to a king, Aunt Den can no longer hold the title of queen. Garith is a good man and intelligent, but he's easy to influence. He'll value the counsel of his mother and his wife more than most men might. This great, united realm, this Blessed Epoch, as they're calling it, is effectively ruled by two female mages. I wonder how much of this they planned? How much of it they knew of and just let unfold?

I doubt we'll ever know.

Only women would have the patience to see such a thing to completion. Men are too rash. No matter how it came about, this may be good for our world. I've often wondered how things might change if women made important decisions. They're kinder than men for the most part. Aunt Den is very wise.

I suppose it will be interesting, if it lasts.

Yarrow stood thinking for a long time, at first about the two women, the two mages, and then about the impending wedding. He knew what he had to do, but it saddened him. Tomorrow evening, after the festivities, he needed to leave.

Where will we go, beloved?

I don't know yet. I need to understand some things. I need to understand what happened with you and me, and what we are to one another. I've taken it for granted too long. I want to know what you truly are, and where you came from. I can't get any answers from you, so I'll find someone who can teach me. Somewhere. More than that, though, I need to understand myself, my power, and why I enjoyed massacring those men as I did. In those moments, standing in that cone of fire, I thought I could rule the world

You could.

I'm afraid I'd be cruel, a tyrant. I've never suffered insult, but I didn't know I could be so murderous.

For those answers, you must examine the depths of your own mind.

I know. Until I do, Duncan and Sasha may be in more danger from me than you. I can't subject them to it.

Why not make it their choice?

No. They'll choose me over themselves.

Is it not their right?

No. For the first time in my life, I must be unselfish. I must put them before my own needs.

That is *a first. Have you noticed yet that everyone has gone? You're staring off into the street like a simpleton.*

I don't care. I could use a bottle of wine, though. Perhaps it will water down some of this despair.

Chapter
Twenty-Six

YARROW RETURNED to the house, disrobed to his trousers, and sat alone in his small but comfortable room. As he sipped his wine, he played with the flames in his hearth, shaping them into birds, porpoises, and horses that trotted across the mantle before disappearing with a wisp of smoke. *Impermanent*, he thought. *Fleeting….*

Like everything, beloved.

Yes. He took a deep drink from his bottle. The rest of the room was dark, and eerie shadows danced on the walls. *Shades, ash, and echoes are all that remain.*

A few minutes later a soft knock startled Yarrow out of his bleak thoughts. He ignored it, but the knocker persisted. "Leave me in peace," Yarrow snapped.

Instead, the door creaked open and Duncan stepped cautiously inside. He walked to the bed where Yarrow sat cross-legged, smiled gently, and held out a selection of breads and desserts on a cloth napkin. "You missed dinner."

Yarrow recalled the knight's first offering of a sweet roll, so long ago in that cold forest. Tears stung his eyes and he turned away. "I'm not a pet for you to feed, or a child who can't look after himself."

Duncan chuckled, and it raised gooseflesh on Yarrow's bare arms. "I know you enjoy it when I do such things, so be as rude as you like." The mattress sagged and groaned when Duncan sat next to Yarrow and laid the treats on his thigh. He pinched Yarrow's chin between his finger and thumb to make Yarrow face him. When he saw the mage's tears, he kissed the corners of his eyes, then let his forehead rest against Yarrow's temple. "Aren't we past this, my love? Go ahead and eat them. We both know you want to."

Yarrow laughed. "Am I so obvious?"

"To me."

As he ate, Duncan sat silently raking his fingers through Yarrow's white hair. When he finished, they sat together without speaking until Yarrow finally whispered, "Tomorrow is the twentieth day of Sarmine's Moon. Garith and Cothryn will be wed in the morning."

"I can't even begin to understand why you want to leave us."

"I know."

"We love you."

"I know. I need to figure some things out."

"Can't Sasha and I help with that?"

"Where is Sasha?"

"Out on another of his errands for your cousin. He believes one of the traitors is hiding here in Meritage. I swear, he'll soon be richer than the crown."

"At one time you'd have been offended by that. You seem to accept it now."

"I'm trying. I love Sasha, and I love you. Can't either of us, or both of us, help you work through your problems?"

"No."

"You know you'll break my heart?"

"I'm sorry." He couldn't help crying then, and Duncan held his face and wouldn't let him look away. He kissed warm, salty wetness from Yarrow's cheeks, and when their lips brushed together, Yarrow tasted his own sorrow. He pressed his mouth flush with Duncan's, never more in need of love, never more desperate to be held and cherished for a time.

Duncan carefully set the leftover desserts on the floor and took Yarrow's face in both of his big hands. They kissed softly, slowly savoring the feel of each other as if it were the first time and not the last. Duncan moved his fingertips down Yarrow's neck, just grazing his skin and sending tremors of longing through Yarrow's body. The light touch against his chest made him tremble and whimper into Duncan's mouth.

Pulling a hair's width away, Duncan said, "It takes so little to please you. I love that. The way you react to my slightest touch."

"I love you."

Wrapping his fingers around Yarrow's shoulders, Duncan gently guided him to his back. He slipped his shirt over his head and lay chest to chest with Yarrow kissing him deeply but slowly, twirling his tongue around Yarrow's again and again. His heart thumped against Yarrow's heart, and his chest hair tickled Yarrow's skin. Yarrow caressed Duncan's muscular shoulders and broad back, relishing the softness of his skin over his hard muscle. Duncan pushed Yarrow's loose pants down and stroked his naked hip. Then he stood, took a small vial from his pocket, and shed his own pants and boots before whisking Yarrow's trousers away.

For a long time they lay against each other, kissing and stroking each other like neither had touched a man before. Finally Duncan eased Yarrow's knees up to his armpits, slicked himself, and pressed carefully inside. Yarrow shuddered and tossed his head back at the penetration. Duncan let him adjust to the feeling, kissing across his brows and down his face as Yarrow panted. When Yarrow felt comfortable, he began circling his hips against Duncan, and Duncan thrust back, his strokes leisurely and shallow.

Yarrow's ankles crossed behind Duncan's back, pulling him closer as he found Duncan's hair and guided their mouths back together. They pushed against each other, making love slowly, relishing every breath, every kiss, caress, thrust and wiggle. Soon, too soon, Yarrow felt his muscles clenching, hugging Duncan's rigid flesh, holding him inside. He moaned and sucked Duncan's lip into his mouth, tasting it with his tongue as he grasped the head of his dick. The knight quickly pried Yarrow's fingers away and took over, his large fist engulfing the mage's quivering flesh. Yarrow choked back a sob as he came, and Duncan followed him seconds later.

After they spent their passion, they lay in each other's arms, bodies still joined. Duncan's hot breath warmed Yarrow's neck and jaw until the mage wondered if he'd fallen asleep. He would have been content with Duncan inside him all night. After a while Duncan stirred, rolling off and out of Yarrow and kissing his eyes and cheeks again. "I love you so much. And tomorrow you'll turn your back and walk away from me."

"I'll come back if I can."

"Small comfort." Duncan stood and pulled his pants on, balling the rest of his clothes under his elbow.

Yarrow sat up and draped his legs over the edge of the bed. "Damn it, Duncan! You swore to me."

He turned and looked so deep into Yarrow's eyes it hurt Yarrow's head, the ache spreading down his chest and settling in his stomach. "I'll keep my oath to you, even if it destroys me. Forgive me, I need to be alone." He took his things and slammed Yarrow's door on his way out.

Yarrow curled on his side and hugged his knees, too broken even to cry. He closed his eyes and reviewed every memory he owned of Duncan or Sasha: their time on the road, the nights they'd spent talking over a campfire, the times they'd risked their lives defending one another, the moments they'd simply sat together, needing nothing more.

I have to leave tonight. Now.

Very wise, beloved. They'll cause quite a scene after the wedding.

Sneak away, then? Disappear without explanation as we always have?

It's worked well so far.

I must at least write to Sasha.

Be quick. It's time and then some that we were on the road. The world is wide and wonderful, and it calls to me. I know it calls you too, beloved.

Yarrow found a scrap of parchment, his inkwell, and quill. *I don't know what to say to him. I love him. Can you understand?*

Not really.

Yarrow scrolled something down about love and hope for the future, but it felt so hollow he balled it up and tossed it on the floor. He'd have to hope Sasha would know how he felt, understand his reasons. Words on a paper would never convey the complexity of it all.

He knows how you felt or he doesn't, beloved.

How I feel.

As you say. Gather your things and get dressed. It's time to go.

I know. Yarrow donned the new traveling clothes he'd procured: thick, dark trousers, a plain but sturdy shirt, and a doublet made of hardened leather. He placed his old, trustworthy armor on top and looked at his pack. He decided he didn't need it. What could it provide that his magic couldn't?

Let's go.

Yarrow left his room and hurried down the corridor toward the front entrance. He'd go to the waterfront and hopefully find a ship he could board. An Emiri ship would be ideal. As he sneaked past the dining hall, he heard the nobles engaged in optimistic jollity. They thought Garith and Cothryn's marriage would bring them unimaginable prosperity. Maybe they were right, though Yarrow doubted things would be so simple.

When Yarrow reached the central stairwell, the one leading to the front entrance, he noticed a dark shape at the edge of his vision. Before he could open the door, it blocked his path.

"Where are you going?" Sasha demanded.

"Away. I need to be on my own."

"You're leaving us?"

"For a time."

"No," Sasha said, brandishing a knife with a serpentine blade. "I won't let you."

"I was promised that if I swayed the battle in Lockhaven, I would be permitted to leave without interference."

"I promised no such thing," Sasha said. "I love you, and I won't let you slip away."

"Sasha, I must. I have things I must do."

"No. You're mine. I'm not letting you go off alone, putting yourself in danger. We're in this together, from here on."

"I need to be alone for a while."

"No, Yarrow! You're not leaving me. Don't make me stop you, because I will."

"Get out of my way." Yarrow hated threatening Sasha, but he couldn't risk losing his resolve, so he embraced the irritation he felt at being commanded. "I don't want the last words we share to be in anger."

Sasha grasped Yarrow's shoulder and pushed his back against the wall. His other hand closed around Yarrow's throat. "You selfish bastard! I gave up everything I had and everything I was for you. You're not walking away from me now."

"Going to kill me, Sasha?" Yarrow hissed, swatting the assassin's hand away from his neck.

In response Sasha slammed him against the wall again, making Yarrow bite his tongue. Hurt and angry now, the hint of blood in his mouth, Yarrow struck him in the stomach, just hard enough to make Sasha let go. Sasha wrapped his arm around his belly and staggered back a few steps. Yarrow wondered for how many people the cold determination on his lover's beautiful face had been the final sight they'd seen in this world. "I won't let you go." He grabbed Yarrow and threw him, so fast Yarrow barely saw Sasha move before his back hit the stone steps. Sasha stood over him with his legs spread and his dagger ready.

"Go ahead," Yarrow yelled, presenting his empty hands. "You wouldn't kill me when I asked, but you'll kill me now? I won't stop you."

Sasha screamed and threw his knife. It pinged off the stone across the hall and slid across the floor. He covered his face with both hands.

Yarrow was torn between comforting Sasha, tackling him to the floor and pummeling him, and just fleeing the painful situation. Slowly he lifted his bruised body from the staircase and rubbed his back. As much as he wanted to run, he went to Sasha instead and hugged him around the shoulders. Sasha resisted his embrace at first and swatted him away. Yarrow persisted, and the assassin consented to be held. They wound their arms around each other, both heaving dry sobs. "I need you to tell me it's all right," Yarrow pleaded, stroking Sasha's hair and hoping he'd never forget the feel of it. "I need to do this. I *will* come back if I can. Please, if you can't forgive me, at least try to understand."

"You made me weak. Thalil, look at what I've become. I've never had nor needed so much as a friend, let alone—"

"You have me." Duncan stood on the landing, his face in shadow as he looked down at them.

"Go to him," Yarrow whispered. "He's a good man, and he cares about us."

Sasha shook his head against Yarrow's neck and squeezed him tighter.

"Sasha, let me go." Yarrow lifted his face by the chin, swept the damp, dark hair out of his face, and gave him a long, last kiss. "This is how I want to remember you."

Nodding with resignation, Sasha pulled away. Yarrow fought not to reach for him, instead plunging his hands inside his sleeves and digging his nails into his arms. Bile stung the back of his throat, and he choked it back. Looking up the stairs into the shadows, he saw his lovers holding each other, Duncan's arm wrapped around the back of Sasha's head. He took some small comfort in knowing they'd look out for each other, die for each other if they had to. Though he wanted nothing more than to take his place beside them, where he belonged, he turned away, forcing his feet to move him toward the door. With his hand on the handle, he looked over his shoulder at them one final time and said, "Good-bye. I love you." Before he could change his mind, he hurried out into the night, sprinting down the narrow lanes toward the water.

Soon the river and the ships came into view. Yarrow knew a wild, beautiful world, full of untold knowledge and unlimited power, waited beyond. It called to him, the prospect of setting foot on lands none had visited. Maybe some adventure would fill the hole in his heart, or at least staunch the bleeding. He wondered if he'd ever feel complete again.

He looked back toward the manor house and tried to locate which of the lit windows Duncan and Sasha might be peering out. "I will be back," he swore out loud, ignoring the perplexed gazes of those around him. "As long as I live, as soon as I can, I'll be back." The possibility of future happiness, as remote as it might have been, made him feel a little better.

Yarrow spotted the bright sails of an Emiri ship, and he hurried toward it, putting his hood up and slipping into anonymity. He melted into the crowd, letting the shadows soak him up and carry him toward whatever future might come.

Don't miss this
excerpt of

Ice and Embers

Blessed Epoch: Book Two

By August Li

Despite their disparate natures, Yarrow, Duncan, and Sasha united against overwhelming odds to save Prince Garith's life. Now Garith is king and the three friends may be facing their undoing.

Distraught over Yarrow's departure to find the cure to his magical affliction, Duncan struggles with his new role as Bairn of Windwake, a realm left bankrupt and in turmoil by his predecessor. Many of Duncan's vassals conspire against him, and Sasha's unorthodox solutions to Duncan's problem have earned them the contempt of Garith's nobles.

When word reaches Duncan and Sasha that Yarrow is in danger, they want nothing more than to rush to his aid. But Duncan's absence could tip Windwake into the hands of his enemies. In addition, a near-mythic order of assassins wants Sasha dead. Without Yarrow, Duncan and Sasha can't take the fight to the assassins. They are stuck, entangled in a political world they don't understand. But finding Yarrow may cause more problems, and with his court divided, King Garith must strike a balance between supporting his friends and assuaging the nobles who want Duncan punished—and Sasha executed.

Coming soon to DSP Publications
http://www.dsppublications.com

Chapter One

THE BAIRN of Windwake cast off his golden ceremonial cloak emblazoned with the crag eagle livery and let it fall heavily to the stone floor of his chambers. Duncan collapsed into an upholstered chair by the inglenook and rubbed his forehead. The fire had long ago diminished to embers, leaving the expansive suite dark and chill on this early spring night. Ruling Windwake had turned out nothing like he'd imagined, and the stresses of yet another day of listening to the demands of squabbling nobles wore on him. When Duncan had been granted his lands and title, he'd anticipated protecting and providing for his people, much as he'd done when he'd been a knight. The reality clashed hard against his expectations. He'd rather face an entire field of soldiers than those nattering, duplicitous aristocrats any day. At least men with swords were honest about wanting to destroy him, and he knew how to counter them.

Duncan had no sooner let his eyes fall shut and his head rest against the padded velvet of the chair when he heard a sound, even softer than the flutter of a night bird's wings, on the balcony opposite his hearth. He tensed, his exhaustion replaced by alertness. Many of his vassals couldn't be trusted; he found them avaricious, their only loyalty to their own treasuries. Some of them still owed fealty to Taran Edercrest, the traitor whose mantle Duncan had assumed after the man's death in a failed attempt to overthrow Selindria's true king. Duncan knew at least a few of the backstabbing nobles might stoop to murder if they could profit from it. He crept as quietly as he could to the weapons stand and picked up his greatsword. He held it in both hands as he approached the balcony, ready to defend himself.

With the sole of his boot, Duncan nudged the wooden double doors, and they swung open with a rasp and a groan. The red-tinged crescent moon provided little light as he glanced from one end of the parapet to the other. Nothing moved except a few leaves tumbling across the stone in the light breeze. Duncan blinked hard as sweat dripped into his eyes. He knew he'd heard something, but now he wondered if the combination of his weariness and the ever-present threat of treachery toyed with his mind. He'd never been a paranoid man, but as he stood looking out from the western side of Windust Castle, over the deep, round Barrier Bay, sheltered on three sides by high cliffs, he heard nothing but the gentle lap of the waves against the strong, gray ironstone that made up so much of Windwake. On a clear day, Duncan could see almost to the southern shore of Lockhaven from this balcony, but the gloom of the night and the chill mist rising from the water restricted his vision to the dozens of ships huddled close to the shore, bobbing gently on the calm tide.

"You should be more careful."

Duncan started and turned toward the low, velvety voice. He scanned the shadows but couldn't locate the speaker. Then, at the opposite end of the terrace, a sliver of shade separated from the wall, and a lithe silhouette tiptoed along the thin, stone railing before leaping down in front of Duncan without even disturbing the leaves. His boots met the stone silently, and the leather armor he wore didn't even creak or rustle.

Duncan blew out an extended breath and lowered his weapon. "Goddesses, Sasha. Why must you sneak around like that? I could have cut you in two before I recognized you."

Sasha answered with a sensuous laugh devoid of any genuine amusement. "I don't think you could have."

"Perhaps not," Duncan conceded, his happiness at his lover's return trumping his slight annoyance. Besides, he knew Sasha spoke not out of arrogance but simply stated the truth. Sasha had been trained by a cult of assassins so legendary and feared most doubted they even existed. The Order of the Crimson Scythe held mythical status throughout Selindria and Gaeltheon, and Duncan had witnessed Sasha's lethal skill on more than one occasion. If he'd been inclined, Sasha could have cut Duncan's throat while Duncan stood watching the boats like a dull-witted child.

Sasha's training was also responsible for what Duncan saw when he stepped closer to his partner: a face that, while exotically beautiful, betrayed no hint of emotion. Shrewd, black eyes offered no clue of the intentions behind them. Though they hadn't seen each other in weeks, Duncan looked into the cold face of a killer, not the warm smile of a lover. He tried, unsuccessfully, to staunch the hurt by reminding himself Sasha had been taught almost since birth not to feel love or attachment, let alone show evidence of what he'd been told was weakness.

Duncan reached up and stroked the soft, black hair that fell to Sasha's slender shoulders. Sasha batted his long, thick lashes and smiled mischievously. He had the most amazing, full, dark lips Duncan had ever seen, and the sight of them curling up and parting slightly sent a tremor of desire down Duncan's spine. He hoped Sasha showed sincere pleasure at his touch, as much pleasure as he experienced feeling the smooth skin of Sasha's cheek again after what seemed like forever. Sasha had no reason to perform with Duncan, but Duncan knew old habits held on tenaciously sometimes, like a cough that lingered after the fever had passed.

"I missed you," he said, pressing a kiss to Sasha's forehead. "But you could try using the front gate like a normal man. Or are you trying to impress me?"

Sasha curled his body against Duncan and brushed their bellies together. He rubbed his face against Duncan's whiskers and whispered close to his ear. "Did it work?"

Duncan glanced over the railing at the sheer, four-story drop to the sharp rocks surrounding the fortress. A wide gravel road wound out around those cliffs from the docks to the gate at the southern wall, on the opposite side of the fortress. Aside from that entrance, Windust was virtually impenetrable. "I suppose it did. Did your—" Duncan still felt uncomfortable discussing Sasha's work. "Were you successful?"

Sasha snorted as if insulted and crossed his arms over his slim chest. His devastating smile widened. "Pym Goodsal and his associates will cause no more trouble for your friend Garith."

"His Majesty will be pleased," Duncan said, taking Sasha's gloved hand, careful of the thin blades hidden at his wrists and the razor-like spikes over his knuckles, and leading him inside.

Sasha shrugged. "So long as he produces the agreed-upon gold."

Duncan almost asked what Sasha would do if Garith, High King of Selindria and Gaeltheon, the largest and most powerful kingdom in the known world, withheld the payment. He thought better of it, though, and went instead to add logs to the fire and stir up the coals. By now, Duncan knew Sasha regarded a prince and a beggar alike only as men who bled and died for his Cast-Down god.

Sasha removed his gloves, loosening the buckles and then tugging them off one finger at a time, while Duncan poked at the ashes in the hearth. Sasha unbuckled the belts over his hips that held daggers and pouches likely full of poisons, and then he unfastened the strap crossing his chest, along with the weapons it held, and let it drop onto a wooden bench. Sasha effortlessly disarmed himself in absolute silence. Duncan admired Sasha's grace and fluidity of movement from the corner of his eye as he tended the fire. The room soon glowed warm and bright as the flames flickered and grew. Orange light reflected off the snug, deep red leather wrapping Sasha's slender limbs and made shadows dance across his face. The fire couldn't melt the icy mask the assassin wore, but Duncan knew what might. He replaced the iron poker and crossed the room to Sasha, who stood only a few feet from the balcony door, as if waiting to be invited inside, seemingly unsure of his welcome.

Duncan curled his big hands around Sasha's waist, almost encircling it. He drew Sasha's chest against his, rubbed his palm up Sasha's back to his neck, and guided Sasha's head to his shoulder. Burying his face in the top of Sasha's hair, he inhaled the spicy fragrance that almost masked the scents of leather, steel, and blood. "Sasha, this is your home as much as mine. I wouldn't have any of it if it hadn't been for you. You don't have to enter it in secret."

Sasha laughed icily, but his lips and nose felt warm as he nuzzled against Duncan's neck. The tickle of his breath against Duncan's dampening skin when he spoke made Duncan shudder. "So, you'd parade me before your nobles and officials? Claim me as part of your household, as your friend?"

Holding Sasha's cheeks in both hands, Duncan tilted his face upward and made Sasha meet his eyes. He searched for some trace of emotion in those glittering, black orbs but saw only his own conflicted face reflected back at him in distorted miniature. "I would. Why do you make it sound so absurd? I'll tell them anything you like, anything that will make you happy. Sasha, you know I love you."

"I know." The assassin tried to look away as he furrowed his brow and turned down his lips, but Duncan held him, not letting him hide what he felt.

A fake smile replaced Sasha's concerned expression. "You'd lose your bairny if anyone discovered the nature of our association," he said with false cheer. "I understand better than most the need for secrecy. It's of little consequence how I enter the castle, anyway. I'm used to standing in the shadows."

Duncan hated it when his partner walled himself off, but he didn't know how to breach barriers that had been in place so long. Battering them down would not do, he'd learned. If he pushed too hard, Sasha would instinctively close him out, so he slid his hands down Sasha's lithe arms, clasped his hands, and led him to the massive bed canopied in gold and black velvet. They sat facing each other on the edge. Sasha pulled his heel to his crotch.

"Are you hungry?" Duncan asked, stroking up and down Sasha's thigh, savoring the feel of taut muscles beneath buttery leather. "Shall I have something sent up from the kitchens? My servants, at least, still respect my wishes."

Sasha edged closer and draped his hand over Duncan's knee. "Thank you, my friend. But not just now. Is there nothing on your mind besides food?" He moved his hand to Duncan's groin and cupped his balls as he leaned in and brushed his lips against Duncan's. When Duncan tried to return the kiss, Sasha pulled away with a grin. He wrapped Duncan's ponytail around his hand and tugged Duncan's head back so he could nibble up and down the side of Duncan's neck. As he dragged his magnificent lips over Duncan's rapidly heating skin, Sasha squeezed and fondled his balls through his cloth trousers. Duncan caught himself on his palms as Sasha pulled lightly on his hair, urging him to move farther onto the bed. Sasha swung his leg across Duncan and straddled him with his knees on the mattress and his thighs tensed and straight. When he looked down at Duncan with his lips even more swollen from Duncan's coarse whiskers and a beautiful, red flush across his high cheekbones and the straight, slender bridge of his nose, Duncan sensed a minute crack in the icy sheath Sasha wore like armor. Sasha never looked more desirable to Duncan than when he gave Duncan a glimpse at everything he hid from the rest of the world.

Duncan fell lightly on his back and grasped Sasha's hips just where the buckles of his armor crossed over the prominent curves of bone. He tried to pull Sasha into his lap so he could feel the contact between them he craved so much, feel Sasha's heat against him, but Sasha resisted, instead grabbing Duncan's wrist and bringing it to his mouth, where he ran his tongue over the sensitive skin and bit softly at the mound of flesh below Duncan's thumb. When Duncan reached for the tantalizing erection obvious beneath Sasha's skintight armor, Sasha again caught his hand, wove their fingers together, and let them fall next to his hip.

Sasha pressed Duncan's hand to his heart and just looked down at Duncan, his need and devotion radiating from him like a physical force. He smiled, and Duncan had no doubt he felt everything he showed in his expression, and it was Duncan's alone.

"I neglected to say I missed you too." Sasha released Duncan's wrist and scraped the back of his hand down Duncan's bearded cheek. "I'm not used to noticing the absence of another, and I was surprised how much it hurt to be without you. Truly, Duncan, I almost didn't enjoy my work."

"I'd hate to be the one who put you off murder." Duncan ran his free hand up Sasha's leg and over his chest until he could cup his shoulder. "Goddesses, you're beautiful." He worked the buckle over Sasha's throat free, then moved to the one across his collarbones, peeled the leather armor open, and bunched up the snug, hooded tunic beneath it. Duncan touched Sasha's warm, deep gold skin as he revealed it an inch at a time and watched Sasha's frozen blockade melt away with his arousal. Finally he pulled the armor open up the center and ran his hand over Sasha's lean, defined stomach, shaved, as always, and like silk beneath Duncan's palm. Duncan reached inside the leather to push it off Sasha's shoulder. "You could give it all up, you know. Never have to leave me."

Sasha shrugged out of his protective clothing and let it fall across Duncan's legs behind him. He pulled a small knife in a leather sheath from the waistband of his trousers and tossed it to the floor. "What, never leave your bed? Just be here naked and ready whenever you might want me?"

"All right." Duncan tugged at the buckle below Sasha's belly button, all his earlier worries forgotten. Nothing mattered to him but pleasing Sasha, feeling Sasha shiver with bliss and drop all the veneers he wore. Only in these intimate moments did Sasha completely bare himself for Duncan, and it drove Duncan crazy. He also knew Sasha liked to be in control, so when Sasha caught his hands, he allowed it. For the moment.

"So you'd turn me into a whore?" Sasha dropped a few inches, just grazing Duncan's swollen cock with his leather-encased bottom.

"No whore," Duncan panted, done with Sasha's teasing. He seized Sasha's waist and pulled him down, thrusting against the seam of his leather leggings, precome coating his cockhead and wetting the cloth of his trousers. "No sharing. You're mine, Sasha. Mine. Come here." He caught Sasha's shoulders and neck, bringing their faces and lips together. He nibbled Sasha's lips before thrusting his tongue between them, past Sasha's teeth and into the silken heat of his mouth. Sasha resisted, sparring with Duncan's tongue before submitting to it. Duncan growled and dug his fingers into Sasha's flesh. He wrapped his thick arms around Sasha's ribs and rolled so Sasha lay beneath him, and then he kissed him until his tongue ached and his lips felt ready to split, and he still wanted more.

"Tell me you're mine," Duncan panted. He stripped his linen tunic off and flung it beside the bed.

"You know I am." Sasha ruffled the hair on Duncan's chest and brushed his thumbs over Duncan's nipples, making them tighten to little pink beads. "I kill to protect you. I ask nothing in return."

"My love, you don't have to kill to show me you love me. I have guards—I—"

"I want to," Sasha said, yanking Duncan's fancy trousers to his thighs, making his erection smack him in the belly. "I want to show them what happens to anyone who threatens what's mine. In the order, I spilled blood for Thalil. Now I spill it for you, because I love you. Show me you love me even though I kill, Duncan. Take those silly clothes off."

Lifting one leg from the bed at a time, never taking his eyes off his beautiful partner, Duncan shed his trousers, boots, and stockings. Though a powerful, muscular man, he still felt a little self-conscious beneath Sasha's scrutiny. Where Sasha was lithe and graceful with uniform, bronzed skin, Duncan's body was pale from the neck down and covered in a dusting of dark brown hair and a network of battle scars. They had that in common now, he supposed, as he touched the pallid, raised, satiny strip on the side of Sasha's neck. He'd earned it when he'd chosen Duncan and their erstwhile companion Yarroway L'Estrella over his brothers in the order. A series of crisscrossing gashes, healed now, marked the inside of Sasha's forearm, and Duncan closed his eyes as he explored their texture. The scars felt like blades of grass scattered across Sasha's warm skin. Much about Sasha had horrified Duncan initially, and in those early days, he'd never thought he'd reconcile his code of honor with his love for this assassin and his beautiful, deadly, mad, broken Yarrow….

"You're thinking about him," Sasha said in a scratchy voice.

"No. I'm thinking about you, Sasha. About everything you've done for me. All you've given up. I'm thinking about how much I love it when I get you so aroused you'll submit to me, relinquish control to me. I love that the most." Duncan kept working on the buckles of Sasha's trousers, and Sasha lay contented beneath him, resting his arms on the pillow above his head. He even lifted his hips so Duncan could peel the leather away and remove the two hidden daggers crossed above his tailbone.

"Why?" Sasha asked as Duncan stood to pull his boots off, shaking his head and smiling when he found yet another knife at Sasha's left calf.

"Because I can see you," Duncan said, easing Sasha's legs open and sitting on his heels between them. "You don't hide from me. When you give yourself to me like that, I know you trust me. Goddesses, Sasha. You don't know how much that means. I know what your trust is worth."

Sasha spread his legs farther and arched his back off the bed. "You talk too much, Duncan. Show me."

"Don't order me, assassin," Duncan mumbled even as he found the vial of oil he kept under the bed and drizzled it over his hand and his cock. Funny how the title he'd once used to insult Sasha had evolved into an intimate endearment. Life could be strange, but Duncan didn't ponder it. Sasha lay looking up at him with trusting eyes, sprawled over the fancy, embroidered bedclothes in absolute complacency.

"Duncan, I'm yours."

Duncan bent to suckle Sasha's dark red nipple as he rubbed his slicked fingers over Sasha's cleft. His opening clenched every time Duncan caressed it, and Sasha pressed against Duncan's hand, practically begging to be entered. He tossed his head from side to side on Duncan's pillows as he opened and then closed his mouth without saying anything coherent. Duncan slipped his finger inside Sasha's open and very eager hole, easily sliding the entire length of it into his slick heat and feeling out the sweet spot within him. As soon as he grazed that clump of nerves, Sasha cried out in a language Duncan couldn't recognize.

"More," Sasha groaned.

"What is that language?" Duncan asked as he withdrew his finger and replaced it with his thumb, driving it home and watching Sasha twist his waist with pleasure. "I want to know what you're saying."

"I'm—Fuck." Sasha quivered as Duncan added another finger. "I'm calling out to Thalil. In… oh, that's good. In a dead language spoken by those who first worshipped him. Does it bother you?"

"No." It should have; Thalil was a disease: god of murder, seduction, and deceit. Even speaking his name was forbidden to the righteous. But as he pressed a third finger into Sasha's willing flesh and felt it squeeze him rhythmically, Duncan couldn't care. He loved this man, assassin or not, disciple of Thalil or not. This was his Sasha writhing beneath him, spreading his legs to accept Duncan's hand into him and flushing with delight at Duncan's touch. Duncan knew what it meant for Sasha to leave himself so vulnerable. It went against everything he'd ever been taught. "I love you for trusting me, for sharing your secrets."

"Duncan—"

"Tell me."

"Thalil, I need you. Need you now." Sasha rested one calf on Duncan's shoulder and wrapped his other leg around Duncan's waist, urging Duncan closer, clear in what he wanted.

Duncan slipped his fingers out of Sasha's body though Sasha's flesh clung to them as if unwilling to let them go. The desperation on his face as he looked up at Duncan spoke as loudly as his words, and it vanquished Duncan.

"I'll do anything for you, Sasha. I love you."

Sasha rolled his eyes. "Then stop talking."

Before entering Sasha, Duncan touched the small mark on the inside of Sasha's thigh: the crescent dripping blood, the sign of his order. That accursed symbol still unnerved Duncan, but it was a part of Sasha, and he'd accept it. "I love everything about you. Goddesses, tell me I can have you."

"Yes," Sasha breathed, spread his willowy limbs over the bed, and fluttered his eyelids. "Yes, yours."

Duncan gripped himself at the base of his erection and thrust into Sasha, burying himself to the hilt in Sasha's hot, clenching body. He looked down at Sasha's face, slack with ecstasy, and he couldn't hold back. Sasha curled his pelvis against Duncan, and Duncan thrust in, hard and deep, with no pretense of gentleness. Neither of them wanted that; they both wanted it hard, urgent, and raw, as if to reclaim each other after their time apart. Sasha dug his nails into Duncan's lower back to encourage him, and Duncan gave Sasha all he had.

"Bite," Sasha said, bowing his back and stretching his neck. "Duncan—"

Duncan knew of this peculiarity of Sasha's, and while he didn't share it, he enjoyed anything that brought his beautiful assassin pleasure. He pushed deep into Sasha as he sunk his teeth into the muscle between Sasha's neck and shoulder, tearing the skin with his teeth because he knew Sasha liked it. The coppery tang of blood filled Duncan's mouth as he came into Sasha, his whole body convulsing and sprays of light erupting behind his eyes. His flesh melted after his release, and he fell across his partner's body as he rode wave after wave of pleasure.

Sasha made a small, dissatisfied sound that roused Duncan from his torpor. He lifted his forehead from Sasha's sweaty chest and kissed him before pulling out and flipping him to his belly. He lifted Sasha to his knees, guided his legs apart, and lapped at Sasha's open hole, tasting his own seed leaking out and mingling with the spicy flavor of Sasha's heated flesh. Duncan ran his finger along the rim of Sasha's distended opening before venturing deeper, his fluids easing the way. He gripped Sasha with his other hand and pushed his hood back to expose his moist cockhead. As he worked his hand into him, Duncan stroked Sasha in time with his thrusts.

Sasha's breath hitched and grew irregular; Duncan knew he was close. "Goddesses, I want to see you come. I want you to come for me." He curled forward and bit Sasha's ass cheek, sinking his teeth deep into the dense crescent of muscle until he tasted blood again.

Sasha loosed a raspy scream, dropped his head to the pillows, and came into Duncan's fist. His whole body seized, and his inner muscles clamped down on Duncan's hand. Duncan licked the blood from his lips and wrapped his arms around Sasha's chest, kissing gently across his shoulders as he whimpered and moaned. He'd given Sasha what he needed, so now Duncan could take his pleasure in the soft, slow kisses and caresses he relished.

When Sasha collapsed, Duncan pulled away, gently rolled Sasha to his side and lay down beside him, pressing their foreheads together. He held Sasha close, and Sasha wrapped his arms around Duncan's head. Neither of them said anything for probably a quarter of an hour as they drifted slowly down from the pinnacles of their bliss.

Finally, Sasha spoke in a low, contented tone tainted with melancholy. "You think of Yarrow too."

"There is no point in this," Duncan said, though his heart felt suddenly chilled, pierced by a cold, forgotten dagger.

"No. I'm tired of this unspoken agreement not to talk about him. I miss him. I long for him, and I know you do too. We should look for him. It's been over a year. He said he'd come back, and he hasn't. We should find him. Bring him back."

Duncan drew Sasha closer, enfolding him in his arms. It was true; their bed felt incomplete without their white-haired mage sharing it. "But I swore to him I'd let him go. He has much to work through, Sasha."

"It hurts," Sasha admitted in a small voice, like a boy who skinned his knee for the first time.

"I know. But right now, I have to try to bring some sort of order to Windwake."

Sasha rose to his elbow and propped his face on his hand, looking down at Duncan with those black eyes that cut to the core of him like the sharpest blades. "Windwake is yours. You are bairn. What more?"

Duncan rolled to his back and folded his arms beneath his head. "Bairn. High King Garith says so, but what are words worth?" He waved his hand at his finely furnished chamber, full of elaborate tapestries, posh benches, ornate weapons, statuary and paintings. "This is like a masquerade, Sasha. I wear the trappings of the bairn of Windwake, but it's a joke. The nobles are still loyal to Taran Edercrest, because he promised them money and lands. They care only about their own treasuries, not Windwake as a whole. Few of my vassals will even acknowledge me."

"I'll kill the disloyal ones," Sasha said, as if it were just that easy.

"No, love," Duncan said, burrowing his face into Sasha's neck, tired to his core of thinking about the greedy aristocrats. "It's not so simple."

"Why not?" Sasha asked and then yawned.

"Because it isn't. I'm too worn out to put it into words. I just want to hold you tonight. It's been too long."

"It has. Good night, my love." Sasha nestled against Duncan and fell asleep without another word.

Duncan drew Sasha so close their bones pressed together. He relished Sasha's slight weight against his chest, the way Sasha's breath moistened his skin, Sasha's come drying on his hand. In the world of deceit and illusion he found himself inhabiting, at least Duncan had one real thing, one thing he could trust amidst all the greed and deception. He touched the bite mark he'd left on Sasha's shoulder and kissed his forehead. Then Duncan let his head sink into the pillows. Tomorrow he'd have to face his vassals again, and he needed rest if he hoped to gain any ground. As he lay listening to his lover's slow breathing, the distant crash of saltwater against stone, and the evening breeze rattling the shutters of the ancient fortress he now called home, Duncan's mind conjured images of ice blue eyes, hair like fresh snow, and a handsome face painted with blue ink. He wondered where Yarrow could be and if Yarrow thought of him and Sasha like this sometimes, just before falling asleep. The recollections ached like an old wound reopened, but Duncan didn't banish them, and his memories carried over into his dreams.

August (Gus) Li is a creator of fantasy worlds. When not writing, he enjoys drawing, illustration, costuming and cosplay, and making things in general. He lives near Philadelphia with two cats and too many ball-jointed dolls. He loves to travel and is trying to see as much of the world as possible. Other hobbies include reading (of course), tattoos, and playing video games.

For more info, visit Books by Eon and Gus:

http://www.booksbyeonandgus.com

DSP PUBLICATIONS

visit us online.
WWW.DSPPUBLICATIONS.COM